P9-CNH-237

Larry McMurtry

AND

Diana Ossana

PRETTY BOY FLOYD

A Novel

SIMON & SCHUSTER

NEW YORK   LONDON   TORONTO   SYDNEY   TOKYO   SINGAPORE

SIMON & SCHUSTER
Rockefeller Center
1230 Avenue of the Americas
New York, New York 10020

This book is a work of fiction. Names, characters, places and incidents are either products of the author's imagination or are used fictitiously. Any resemblance to actual events or locales or persons, living or dead, is entirely coincidental.

Copyright © 1994 by Larry McMurtry and Diana Ossana

All rights reserved,
including the right of reproduction
in whole or in part in any form whatsoever.

SIMON & SCHUSTER and colophon are registered trademarks
of Simon & Schuster Inc.

Designed by Levavi & Levavi
Manufactured in the United States of America

10 9 8 7 6 5 4 3 2 1

Library of Congress Cataloging-in-Publication Data
McMurtry, Larry.
   Pretty Boy Floyd : a novel / Larry McMurtry and Diana Ossana.
      p.   cm.
   1. Floyd, Pretty Boy, 1904–1934—Fiction.   2. Criminals—United States
—Fiction.   I. Ossana, Diana.   II. Title.
PS3563.A319P74   1994
813′.54—dc20   94-18863
                                                                CIP

ISBN: 0-671-89165-0

"The Ballad of Pretty Boy Floyd" by Woody Guthrie © Copyright 1958
(renewed) by FALL RIVER MUSIC INC. All rights reserved. Used by
permission.

For
Livio Albert Aldo Ossana, Sr.
1924–1993

Collaborators' Note

In 1993 we wrote, for Warner Bros., a screenplay about Charles Arthur "Pretty Boy" Floyd. The screenplay is an austere form; it welcomes no *longeurs*. So while we were writing our screenplay, we both decided that we would like to write at more length about the life (as we imagined it) of Charley Floyd.

We began by talking out, and then writing down, an extensive, detailed outline of the book as we envisioned it. Each day, L.M. wrote a skeletal five pages; then D.O., putting flesh onto bone, made them ten.

The book before you is the result.

LARRY MCMURTRY
DIANA OSSANA

"I knowed Purty Boy Floyd. I knowed his ma. They was good folks. He was full a hell, sure, like a good boy oughta be . . . He done a little bad thing an' they hurt 'im, caught 'im an' hurt him . . . They shot at him like a varmint, then they run him like a coyote, an' him a-snappin', an' a-snarlin', mean as a lobo. An' he was mad. He wasn't no boy or no man no more, he was jus' a walkin' chunk a mean-mad. But the folks that knowed him didn' hurt 'im. He wasn' mad at them. Finally they run him down an' killed 'im. No matter how they say it in the paper how he was bad —that's how it was."

MA JOAD.
John Steinbeck,
The Grapes of Wrath

If you'll gather round me, children,
A story I will tell,
About Pretty Boy Floyd, the outlaw,
Oklahoma knew him well. . . .

WOODY GUTHRIE,
"The Ballad of Pretty Boy Floyd"

He would be thirty years old forever.

MICHAEL WALLIS, biographer,
*Pretty Boy: The Life and Times
of Charles Arthur Floyd*

Book One

1925-1929

1

Bill "the Killer" Miller rubbed his pistol—rubbing it reassured him—as they waited for the armored car to pull up. Charley blew on his hands to warm them. An hour before, he had been at work on the second floor of the Kroger Bakery, catching hot bread trays as they came whirling down the bread chute, twenty-four loaves to the tray. If he had blown on his hands then, it would have been to cool them. Even wearing thick gloves, it was all Charley could do to handle the hot trays.

"Stop rubbin' that gun, you're makin' me nervous," he said to Billy. "That gun's ready to shoot. You don't need to rub it."

"I guess I know how to treat guns," Billy said, annoyed that a big hick like Charley Floyd, a country boy with no polish, would have the gall to tell him how to pull off a robbery.

"It's my gun, remember?" Charley said. "The only reason I'm lettin' you handle the firearms is because I figure I'm better at tyin' knots. You keep the guards covered while I hogtie 'em. Then we'll grab the money, and scram."

Billy Miller felt a little rueful. Only the week before, he had been the proud owner of a nickel-plated Colt .38, but he had lost it in a poker game at Mother Ash's boarding house, where he and Charley stayed.

"Wally Ash cheated, the rat-faced little turd," Billy said. "Otherwise, I'd be carryin' my own weapon. I should plug the son-of-a-bitch."

"I wouldn't do that if I was you," Charley said. "If you shoot Wally, Ma Ash'll throw us out, and the grub's good."

"Who cares? We'll have to leave anyway, once we pull this job," Billy replied.

"Speak for yourself," Charley said. "I might leave, or I might not."

"If you don't, it won't be the grub that's keepin' you," Billy said.

Billy was rubbing the handle of the pistol again. He was too nervous to sit still while they waited for the armored car with the Kroger payroll in it. The Mississippi was only a few miles east, but it was so foggy that morning, Billy couldn't have seen the water if he'd been standing on the Eads Bridge.

"I might leave, and I might not," Charley said again, wondering if he ought to put the headlights on. Ahead, across Chouteau Avenue, were the train yards. Now and then, he could hear a train whistle, but he couldn't see the yards, much less downtown St. Louis a mile away to the north. In fact, he couldn't see past the front of the car—it occurred to him that if the armored car happened to stop behind them instead of in front of them, the guards would be inside with the payroll before he and Billy even knew they were there.

"You think you're gonna get in Beulah Baird's britches, that's why you don't want to vamoose," Billy said, smugly. "Don't give me that bull about the grub."

"Aw, applesauce," Charley said. "I'm a married man. It's Beulah's hard luck that Ruby saw me first."

He grinned when he said it, to show Billy that he was mostly joshing. Bragging about girls while waiting to pull a robbery might be bad luck, for all Charley knew. He was new to city life, and wanted to do things the way they were supposed to be done —particularly serious things, like robbing the Kroger payroll.

Beulah Baird wasn't any more serious than jelly on a biscuit; not that Charley was anyone to turn up his nose at jelly on a biscuit. The minute he saw Beulah coming in from the kitchen of the boarding house with a plate of pork chops in one hand and a bowl of spuds in the other, he liked her—and the feeling seemed to be mutual.

"Hey, pretty boy, where'd you come from?" Beulah asked immediately, to the great annoyance of her fiancé, the same rat-faced Wally Ash who had won Billy's pistol from him in the poker game.

"Oklahoma," Charley said. He didn't care to name the town, which happened to be Akins, a wide place in the road just east of Sallisaw.

"You don't say—I didn't know they growed 'em as good-lookin' as you, down in Oklahoma," Beulah said. She then proceeded to wave her tail in his face two or three times while she was serving the spuds and pork chops. Charley noticed that her sister Rose was no mud fence, either. Rose kept the beer coming, but she couldn't match her sister when it came to gab.

"Being married may stop you, but it won't stop Beulah," Billy Miller said, remembering that he had felt a little sour when he saw Beulah take an immediate shine to such a hick. Billy would have given a pretty penny to squire Beulah Baird around himself, but the one time he had worked up his nerve to ask her out, she had turned him down flat.

"Forget it, you're too short," Beulah had told him, coolly. "Ask Rose, she likes shrimpy little guys."

"Shut up, I think I hear the armored car coming," Charley said. Now that they were about to be partners in crime, he thought it behooved Billy to keep his mind on the business at hand.

"That ain't no armored car, that's a milk truck, the Pevely Dairy's just around the corner," Billy said.

No sooner were the words out of his mouth than the armored car from Tower Grove Bank drove up to the curb, and stopped.

15

2

As soon as he saw the driver come around to the back of the armored car to unlock it, Charley hopped out of the flivver and walked up to the man.

"Hold it right there, sir, this is a stickup," Charley said. The moment he said it, he realized he wasn't armed: Billy had the gun. All he himself was armed with was some twine for tying up the guards.

"What? It's so foggy I can't hear you, son," the guard said. He was an elderly man, a little stooped.

"A stickup—a robbery," Charley repeated. Then he realized he couldn't see Billy anywhere. He didn't know whether Billy was in the car or out of the car, pointing the gun or not pointing the gun. For all Charley knew, Billy might have skedaddled back in the general direction of Ma Ash's boarding house, leaving him to rob an armored car with nothing but a pocketful of #3 twine.

"Say, are you available to cover this man?" Charley asked, over his shoulder.

"He's covered," Billy replied, from somewhere behind him.

"How many of you are there, boys?" the guard asked. "I couldn't see six feet if my life depended on it."

"Your life depends on openin' the door of this car," Charley said, trying to sound stern. He had no idea exactly where Billy Miller was. From the sound of his voice, he was somewhere behind the flivver, whereas the old, stooped guard and the armored car were directly in front of it. If Billy was fool enough to shoot, it would be anybody's guess who he'd hit—the guard, Charley, or nobody.

"Don't get nervous, son," the old guard said. "There's a right way and a wrong way to do everything, and the right way to do this here would be for me to knock on the door a few times, so's Cecil will know there's a commotion. He's likely asleep, and if we wake him up sudden, he's apt to be cranky."

16

He proceeded to rap on the door a few times with his knuckles.

"You wasn't supposed to let him knock on the door," Billy Miller said. He had just bruised his shin on the rear bumper of the flivver, and realized he was slightly out of position.

Charley found the remark irritating, coming as it did from somewhere in the fog, well behind him.

"Get around here and help, if you know so much about it," Charley told him.

To the guard, he said, "Sir, I'll take your keys."

"Okay," the guard said, handing him a hefty set of keys.

"You're supposed to take his gun before you tie him up," Billy cautioned. He was feeling his way around the flivver as best he could.

"That was your job," Charley said, getting more and more irritated. He hadn't so much as glimpsed his partner since the robbery started.

"I forgot it," said the guard.

"Forgot what?" Charley asked.

"Forgot my gun," the guard said. "Left it in the office. I was meaning to go back and get it right after this drop."

"He's not armed, hurry up," Charley said. Just then, he saw a hand with a pistol in it poke out of the fog. The pistol—his pistol—was cocked, and it was pointed at *him*, not at the guard.

"Tie him up, I'll shoot him if he moves," Billy Miller said.

"Not unless you aim to the right about six feet," Charley said. "Right now, you've got me dead in your sights."

"I want to be on target if he tries to get the jump on you," Billy said.

"Uncock that pistol and help me figure out which key fits that lock," Charley said.

"It's the brass key that's round on top," the guard said, dryly. "I never interfere with professionals, but I can't vouch for Cecil —he might be cranky."

3

Cecil, the guard inside the armored car, was studying the sports page of the *St. Louis Post-Dispatch* when Charley swung the rear door open. Cecil wore glasses, but he had taken them off for a moment in order to squint closely at a picture of Babe Ruth, who had just been fined five thousand dollars by the baseball commissioner for misconduct. Why should they care what else the Babe did, so long as he kept hitting home runs? Cecil was certainly no athlete himself—he was pudgy, and had a fair case of acne. Charley would have guessed him to be around eighteen years old, though when questioned about the robbery by a *Post-Dispatch* reporter later, he claimed to be twenty-three.

There was a shotgun propped against some money bags right in front of Cecil, but Charley reached in and grabbed the shotgun while Cecil was fumbling with his glasses.

"Hands off, that's company property," Cecil said. "Who are you?"

"Don't expect him to give his name, he's robbing us," the elderly guard said.

"Jump on down here, sir," Charley said politely. "I guarantee you won't be hurt."

Cecil was piqued at being captured so easily—in his view, it was entirely the fault of Wayne, the elderly guard. Wayne was far too lazy and easygoing to be trusted with an armored car full of valuable money.

"Why'd you give 'em the keys?" Cecil asked, as Charley was tying Wayne's hands behind his back with what looked like baling twine.

"You could've run," he added, when Wayne made no reply. "It's so foggy, they couldn't have hit you if they'd been shooting a cannon."

"The short fellow with the hogleg might have got off a lucky

18

shot, that's why," Wayne replied. "I'll be retiring in about six months—I don't want no .38 slug to retire me six months early."

While Wayne was waiting for Charley to finish tying him up, he imagined how Gertie, his shrewish wife of forty years, might take the news that he had been shot and killed by a couple of bold young robbers. If Wayne's pension was lost because two hooligans chose to rob the Kroger Bakery payroll on this particular morning, these boys would have more to worry about than cops. Contemplating Gertie on a rampage made Wayne shiver.

"You cold, sir?" Charley inquired.

"Just thinkin' about my wife," Wayne admitted.

"You married, son?" he added.

Charley thought it best not to answer the old man.

He soon had Wayne secured. Billy Miller kept cocking and uncocking the pistol, another nervous habit of Billy's which soon got on Charley's nerves.

"Hop in there and grab the money," he instructed, reaching out his hand for the gun.

At that point, Cecil made a mad dash into the fog. Billy had just uncocked the gun, and Cecil was out of sight before he could recock it, much less fire it.

Before Charley could even grab the pistol, he heard a heavy thud. A second later, Cecil reappeared, blood pouring down his face. He staggered right into Billy Miller, knocking Billy back against the radiator of the flivver.

"Kill him, he's ruint my suit," Billy said, noticing to his horror that the front of his suit was covered with Cecil's blood—he had just got the suit out of the cleaners that morning.

Cecil collapsed on the pavement, and rolled around, groaning. Charley held the pistol, but he had no intention of killing the young man, who was semiconscious at best.

"Who slugged him?" Charley asked, peering into the fog. What if somebody was lurking on the sidewalk, waiting to rob them once they finished pilfering the truck?

"He forgot about that lamppost," Wayne said. "I done the same thing once, and it wasn't even foggy."

"How'd you happen to run into a lamppost if it wasn't foggy?" Charley asked.

19

"By being drunk," Wayne admitted.

Billy Miller tried to wipe off his coat, but only succeeded in getting blood on the front of his shirt.

"I thought you were going to get the money," Charley said to Billy. "I better tie up Cecil."

He knelt and tied Cecil's legs, though Cecil had stopped being semiconscious. Now he was out cold, his forehead split wide open.

Billy jumped up in the armored car. The first money bag he grabbed was so heavy he had to use both hands to lift it.

"What's in this sucker, horseshoes?" he asked.

"Just get the paper money," Charley said. "That was the plan —that sack is probably filled with pennies."

"Nope, two-bit pieces," Wayne corrected. "There's plenty of paper money, though. It's in them sacks to the front, on the right side."

Charley rolled Cecil over. Looking at the boy's bloody forehead was making him kind of sick to his stomach. He tied Cecil's hands behind his back as Billy Miller was crawling around inside the armored car, looking for a not-so-heavy sack with paper money in it.

Charley had become suspicious of Wayne, the old guard who was planning to retire in six months. The basis of his suspicion was that Wayne was being too helpful. Cecil had at least tried to hightail it into the fog; he'd just had the bad luck to run smack into a lamppost. But Wayne had been as pleasant as could be, which didn't make sense. After all, his job was to protect the money. Charley decided to tie his feet as well as his hands, in case he had some trick up his sleeve.

"Sir, would you mind sittin' down—I need to tie your feet," Charley said.

"I don't mind myself, but my rheumatism won't be too happy about it," Wayne said, easing himself down on the pavement.

"Ask him if there's any gold in this truck, I'd like to steal some gold," Billy said. He pitched three sacks full of paper money down by Charley, who was busy looping twine around Wayne's ankles.

"What'd you boys do before you took up robbery?" Wayne asked.

20

"Not much," Charley said. "Farmed a little."

"You should of stuck with it, son," Wayne informed him. "Farming's hard, but the outlaw life's harder."

"You must've been plowin' softer ground than I plowed, if you think that," Charley said. "All I've had to do today is tie you up. I just tied Cecil up for practice, he was knocked out anyway."

"Oh, the robbing part ain't so hard," Wayne said. "It's what happens once you get caught that's hard."

"Who says we're gonna get caught?" Billy Miller said, jumping out of the armored car.

"Why, the law will be on you boys like flies on a turd," Wayne said.

"Is that why you didn't put up no fight?" Charley asked him.

"I forgot my gun," Wayne said. "That's why I didn't put up no fight. I ain't fool enough to think I could whip a stout boy like you. Besides, that fella with the hogleg acts like he's trigger-happy. I ain't in the mood to get shot over somebody else's money."

They heard footsteps on the sidewalk, somewhere back in the fog. Charley made a sign for Wayne to shush. Billy held out his hand for the pistol, but Charley wouldn't let him have it.

"I think it's a woman," Billy whispered in Charley's ear.

Charley didn't answer. Whoever was making the footsteps came up even with them, and kept going. They heard a door open and shut. Somebody, maybe a secretary, had just gone into the Kroger Bakery.

"Put the money sacks in the car, we're leavin'," Charley said. "And don't get lost doing it."

"I never been lost in my life," Billy replied.

"I guess that was why you was behind the car when we started this," Charley said.

"Shut up about that," Billy told him. "I just turned the wrong way when I opened the door, that's all."

"Son, would you mind setting me on the sidewalk before you leave?" Wayne asked. "The cracker truck might come along and run me over, if I'm flopped out here in the street."

Charley lifted the old man, and carried him a step or two onto the sidewalk.

"Much obliged," Wayne said. "I hope you'll drag Cecil a little closer to the curb, while you're at it. He's poor company, but I'd still hate to see him get squashed by the cracker truck."

Charley didn't make any promises. He decided Wayne was probably trying to keep him talking until the law showed up. But when he got back to the street, he dragged Cecil part-way up on the sidewalk. Cecil had become semiconscious again, and was moaning and groaning.

It was so murky that Charley ran over the curb when he turned onto Grand Boulevard.

"You'll be the next one hittin' a lamppost," Billy Miller said, hanging onto the door handle.

"Applesauce," Charley replied, driving hell-bent-for-leather into the fog.

4

"I bet this bracelet cost thirty dollars if it cost a cent," Beulah Baird said, holding up her wrist.

Charley kept mum—though, in fact, the bracelet had set him back nearly forty bucks.

"My sister Rose would give her eyeteeth for a bracelet this pretty," Beulah said, turning her wrist a little so the bracelet would catch the light.

"I guess you were born lucky," Charley said. "It didn't cost you no eyeteeth, or any other kind of teeth, neither." They were both naked, laying across the double bed in Beulah's room. Charley had his leg thrown over her, and was propped up on his elbow, watching her face.

"You can get off me anytime you feel like it," Beulah said, trying to twist out from under his leg.

"What if I don't feel like it yet?" Charley said, tightening his grip on her.

"Good Lord, it's five o'clock, and I'm weak in the knees as it is," Beulah said, glancing over at the clock on her dresser. "You boys from Oklahoma got a little too much starch in your systems."

"Ain't no such thing as too much starch," Charley said, grinning.

Beulah grinned back. She had to like the big hick; she hadn't been surprised when he knocked on her door, either; but she *was* surprised by the bracelet. And besides, he was so cute.

"That's easy for you to say, you ain't got to trot over to Ma Ash's and serve supper," Beulah told him. "My knees need to be working till at least after supper, if you don't mind—and after supper, there'll be Wally to deal with."

"I figure it's about time you shoved that donkey off the porch," Charley said.

Beulah giggled. She was even cuter when she giggled, Charley thought.

"I hope you realize that's my fiancé you're calling a donkey," she said.

"He won't be your fiancé long," Charley informed her, rolling off. Beulah immediately hopped out of bed, naked as a jaybird, sat down in front of her dresser, and started fixing her face.

"Why, I guess he will—why wouldn't he?" she asked, a powder puff in one hand.

"Because Billy Miller's gonna kill him for cheatin' at cards," Charley said.

"That won't work, because Wally won his pistol," Beulah said. "He gave it to me to carry in my purse."

"Why would you need a gun in your purse?" Charley asked.

"Some hick from Oklahoma could come along and get fresh," Beulah said, turning to grin at him a moment. "What did you say your nickname was?"

"Choc," Charley replied.

"Choc? What kinda nickname is that?" she asked, screwing up her face.

"Choc, like in Choctaw beer," Charley admitted. "I drank so much back in Akins that I ended up with Choc for a nickname."

"It sounds too hicky to me—I think I'll just call you Charley," she told him. She got up and walked over to her closet. "Don't peek, I'm about to get dressed."

"Why can't I peek, I've done seen you undressed," Charley asked, sitting up in bed.

"That's different," Beulah said. "I don't allow nobody to watch me dress."

"Not even me?" Charley asked.

"Nobody means nobody, buster," Beulah said, slipping behind the closet door.

Leaves were blowing off the tall elm trees in the yard of Beulah's boarding house. Charley sat on the edge of the bed and watched the leaves blow, while Beulah stayed behind the door getting dressed. Now that the fun was over, he felt low. He had meant to head home to Ruby and Dempsey the minute he and Billy Miller split the payroll money, but there was so much more money in the sacks than he had ever expected to see—more than eleven thousand dollars, half of which was his—that he lost his momentum for a few days. He spent a whole day trying to get used to the fact that he had more than five thousand dollars cash money, right in his room at Ma Ash's boarding house.

In the twenty-one years of his life, Charley had never had as much as fifteen dollars cash money in his pocket at one time. Dempsey, their little boy, was nine months old, but Ruby still didn't have a wedding ring—he hadn't even been able to afford one of the cheap ones they sold at the Woolworth's over in Sallisaw.

Having all that cash money was so peculiar for Charley that it paralyzed him for most of a day. He was afraid to take the money with him out into the streets; somebody might rob him, or else he might lose it. But he was also afraid to leave it in his room. He spent a whole morning dividing it into stacks and then hiding the stacks, only to decide fifteen minutes later that the stacks weren't hidden well enough. Pretty soon, he had them back on the bed. He recounted them and then hid them again,

24

in new hiding places that weren't any harder to find than the old hiding places.   :

Charley didn't trust Billy Miller, and the feeling was mutual. The two of them counted the money six or seven times, but neither of them had ever counted that much money before, and neither of them could quite convince himself that the count was accurate. Charley was afraid to leave his room for long stretches because Billy's room was just down the hall from his, and Billy was sneaky.

Beulah came out from behind the closet door in her slip and stockings, and went back to the dresser to finish fixing her face.

"What I'd like to know is how come a country boy who works in a bakery catching bread trays can afford thirty dollars to buy me a bracelet with garnets on it," Beulah said.

"The boss likes me," Charley told her.

"I like you, too, but I wouldn't cough up no thirty dollars so you could buy your girlfriend a bracelet," Beulah said, putting on her lipstick. Beulah was so cute, her face didn't need much fixing, in Charley's view.

"If you spent thirty dollars on me, how much was you planning to spend on your wife?" Beulah asked, giving him a glance in the mirror.

"Shut up about my wife, it don't concern you," Charley replied. He had bought Ruby an eighteen-karat gold wedding ring, a new chenille housecoat with big roses all over it, and some silk stockings. He bought Dempsey a jack-in-the-box and a teddy bear. He had bought himself a fine gabardine suit, just like the one "Legs" Diamond was wearing in the latest issue of *Police Gazette*. It was being altered so the cuffs would hang just right. He was thinking seriously about spending twelve hundred dollars on a new Studebaker car to drive home to Sallisaw. He hadn't really meant to buy Beulah Baird anything, or even to pay her a visit, but then he remembered how cute she looked when she was waving her tail in front of his face, and after a certain amount of remembering, he changed his mind and bought her the forty-dollar bracelet with the garnets on it.

"Well—if you say so," Beulah replied, miffed.

"I say so," Charley retorted. Being reminded of the fact that he had a wife, and a beautiful wife at that, not to mention a nine-month-old son, made him feel unhappy. He should have headed home already, and he felt sure he would have headed home if Beulah Baird hadn't been so determined to flirt with him. But she had flirted with him, and he had taken a strong dislike to her rat-faced boyfriend, and the next thing he knew, he was back at the jewelry store.

"I think you and Billy pulled a job, that's what I think," Beulah said, petulant, coming over to sit on the bed for a minute. She was still in her slip.

"I got a job, I don't need to be pullin' one," Charley said. It amused him that she was so brash. Ruby Floyd had a temper, all right, but most of the time she wasn't brash like Beulah, who would come right out with whatever she was thinking—she didn't care who was listening, either.

"If you're so fond of your job, why ain't you over at the bakery catching bread trays?" she asked. "How come you can loll around all afternoon making me weak in the knees?"

"I'm on vacation," Charley said. "The boss likes me so much, he lets me take off whenever I feel like chasing women."

"You're a liar, you and Billy pulled a job. How much did you get?" Beulah asked, bold as brass.

"I thought you was due over at Ma Ash's," Charley reminded her. "Why are you sittin' here bein' nosey?"

"Wally's a pill, and he can't dance," Beulah said, thinking out loud. "Besides that, he's tight. He wouldn't buy me a thirty-dollar bracelet if he robbed the mint."

"I don't doubt a word of it," Charley said. "He looks like a cheap little skunk, if you ask me."

"I wouldn't mind breaking up with him if I knew a nice fella who was tall, and could dance, and who liked me and wasn't tight," Beulah said, teasing him. Wally Ash had gotten to be a real pain in the neck lately. He was so jealous that Beulah couldn't even go to the five-and-dime by herself without Wally dealing her a fit.

"I know a fella just like that," Charley said, grinning. "The only thing he likes better than girls is Choctaw beer."

"I guess I better go to work," Beulah said, jumping up. "Ma Ash don't tolerate no lagging."

26

"When was you thinkin' about breakin' up with that cheap skunk you're engaged to?" Charley asked her.

"I ain't set a date," Beulah replied. "When was you thinking of going home to your wife?"

"Not for another day or two," Charley said.

5

Charley was careful to give the impression at Ma Ash's that he was still working his shift at the bakery. He put on his work clothes before he left to take Beulah her bracelet, and he was wearing them when he went back to the rooming house for supper. He hadn't picked up Ruby's chenille housecoat yet, or his gabardine suit—Dempsey's toys were hidden in his sock drawer in the bottom of the bureau, and the wedding ring he kept in his pocket.

Ma Ash, though, had an experienced eye. She was a tall, skinny woman, and the veins in her arms stood out as big as ropes. The minute Charley parked himself at the dinner table and reached for the sweet potatoes, she took in the fact that he didn't look the way he usually looked when he got off his shift at the bakery: floury was how he usually looked.

"Did they fire you, or did you quit?" she asked him, straight out. Ma Ash had done a little bit of everything in her forty-two years, so she didn't object to a certain amount of sinning in her boarding house. Her given name was Louise, and she had come to St. Louis from Aurora, Missouri, a one-horse town just southwest of Springfield. Louise Ash was quite a looker when she was a young country girl, and George Barker, the husband of the one and only Kate "Ma" Barker, had taken a shine to her about the time his fourth son was born. George was crazy about Louise; the only problem was his wife: she was just plain crazy. When Kate Barker found out her husband was warming the sheets with the youngest and prettiest of the Ash girls, Louise took the first train out of Aurora, ended up in St. Louis, and had been there ever since. Now every few months, the papers were filled with murders and robberies committed by Ma Barker and her sons—Louise Ash was glad she'd left for St. Louis twenty-five years ago.

Sinning of various kinds was to be expected in a big city, but Ma Ash *did* like to know what sins were being committed in her house. A little gambling or a little whoring didn't upset her— she'd done as much herself—what upset her was the thought that the police might know more about what was going on in her boarding house than she did. When she fixed Charley with her experienced eye, he squirmed and tried to pretend he had his mouth full, when in fact, he had yet to take a bite.

"No, ma'am, they didn't fire me, and I didn't quit," he said. "The boss likes me for some reason."

"So does Beulah, *for some reason*," Wally Ash said sarcastically, though he little suspected just how much liking his girl-friend had shown Charley that very afternoon.

"Shush, Wally—Beulah would flirt with a post," Ma Ash said. "I wasn't talking to you, I was just wondering why Charley looks so clean after a day's work."

"Got moved into the office," Charley said. This time, he did have his mouth full, and if questioned further, he was planning to sound as dumb as possible. It occurred to him a second too late that he was just about as dumb as possible: why would the bakery move him into the office after only three weeks on the job?

"The office?" Ma Ash said, without a trace of a smile. "Why would they do that? You don't look like a big reader to me."

"Well, I subscribe to *Police Gazette*," Charley said. It was a lie—he didn't subscribe to any magazines. But he did buy *Police Gazette* almost every month; at least he did if he had a dime when he happened to be passing the newsstand.

"It's mostly crooks that read *Police Gazette*," Ma Ash observed dryly. "They think they'll learn some trick that will help them stay ahead of the law." She turned and glared at her two sons.

Wally and William Ash looked almost like twins, though they had been born a year apart. Both of them had faces like hatchets, kept their hair slicked down, and wore felt hats that smelled of hair oil.

Wally considered himself engaged to Beulah Baird, and William, not to be outdone, had proposed to her sister Rose several times. Wally had never got Beulah to actually say she'd marry him, but so far as the public knew, they were engaged. If he happened to mention at the dinner table that Beulah was his fiancée, she didn't deny it, though his saying it didn't make her any friendlier, either.

Rose, on the other hand, had turned William Ash down flat several times. She was more interested in Billy Miller, even though Billy Miller seemed more interested in his gun. She went out with William Ash because he had more money and could occasionally be pried loose from some of it.

While Charley was squirming, Billy Miller was feeding his face. He knew Ma Ash suspected him of criminal activity, and he didn't plan to give her the slightest reason to quiz him. When Rose came in with a big dish of corn and another of sweet potatoes, Billy kept his eyes on his plate, though his normal habit was to give Rose a wink, or a little smile, if he could do it without William Ash noticing.

"Shut up!" William Ash said, the minute Rose stepped into the room.

Everyone, even Ma Ash, was startled by this command, since Rose, who was quiet by nature, hadn't uttered a sound.

"Shut up?" Rose said. "I haven't said a word."

William Ash's fear was that Rose would one day turn into a flirt, like her sister—he was determined to nip any signs of flirting in the bud, so determined that in this instance he nipped before there even *was* a bud.

"That's Rose with the sweet potatoes," Wally Ash informed him. "That ain't Beulah—Beulah's the one who gabs."

William ignored his brother, and gave Rose a stern look.

"Stop lookin' daggers at me," Rose said, getting annoyed. "I told you, I ain't said a word."

"Well, don't," William said—he was the kid brother. "Wally don't like no lip from his woman, and that goes for me, too."

"If Wally don't like lip, what's he keeping company with Beulah for?" Ma Ash inquired. "Beulah's about three-quarters lip."

"She buttons it up when I tell her to, though," Wally said.

Charley was trying to stay neutral, hoping everyone would forget about his sudden promotion to office worker, but when Wally made his brag about how well Beulah minded him, he couldn't help but smile.

"What are you grinnin' about, bud?" Wally asked, glaring at him.

"Why, nothin'," Charley said. "I always smile when I'm eatin' first-rate grub, and this is first-rate grub."

"Thanks for the compliment," Ma Ash added. One thing she liked about Charley was that he ate a lot—people who picked at their food annoyed her. She liked a man who would sit down and dig into the meat and the spuds, with no gab. If she had been a few years younger, or Charley a few years older, she would have fired Beulah Baird and hooked up with him herself, which was not to say that she believed a word of his story about the promotion.

"Ma, I don't like this clodhopper," Wally whined.

"Who asked you to like him? He pays his rent," Ma Ash said. "If you don't want to sit at the table with him, go eat in the kitchen."

"You oughta kick him out," Wally said, still glaring at Charley. "Next thing you know, he'll be flirtin' with my girl."

"Wally, can it!" Ma Ash told him. "I'll not have roosters fightin' over hens at my table!"

Beulah came in from the kitchen just as she said it, a pitcher of buttermilk in one hand, and a plate of fried chicken in the other.

Charley couldn't resist a little joke.

"Ma'am, the only hen I'm interested in is this one I'm eatin'," he said, holding up a wishbone he had picked clean. Beulah set the buttermilk down, and the next thing Charley knew, she had stepped over and pulled the wishbone with him.

"Ha, you got the long end, you get to marry first," Beulah said. "I got the short end, I get to make a wish."

30

"You better make the right wish," Wally demanded.

"What if I was to wish you'd drop dead, Wally? Would that be the right wish?" Beulah said. Then she held the platter in front of Charley so he could have his choice before setting it on the table. Charley took a breast and two gizzards; he couldn't resist gizzards.

"Why'd you serve him first?" Wally asked. "If you oblige that hick one more time, you'll be lucky not to get your face slapped."

Beulah walked around the table and stuck her face right in front of Wally's.

"Slap it now, if you're gonna slap it, Wally!" she said.

"Uh, I didn't mean right now," Wally said, wishing he'd never uttered the remark.

"I'll slap her," William Ash said—he was appalled that his brother hadn't risen to such a blatant challenge.

"I'm too much of a gentleman to hit a gal over a piece of chicken," Wally said. "That's kid stuff."

"Kid stuff?" William said. "She's askin' for it."

Charley agreed with that appraisal. Beulah was practically asking to be knocked on her butt.

"Ma, she's slackin'," Wally said, trying to put the best face on the matter that he could. "Tell her to go bring the pie."

Beulah straightened up, and took off her apron. But she kept her eyes on Wally.

"You should have smacked me, kiddo," she said. "I doubt you'll ever be in slappin' distance again."

She handed the apron to Mother Ash, and marched out of the room. Wally turned red in the face, jumped up, and followed her. Billy Miller caught Charley's eye, but Charley kept on eating, as if nothing had happened. It was obvious that Beulah Baird could take care of herself, at least if Wally Ash was all she had to contend with.

"I hope he whups her," William said, trying to be loyal. He didn't believe it would happen, though, and neither did anyone else at the table.

Mother Ash had no interest in her son's squabble with his girlfriend. If Wally and Beulah broke up, so much the better. She meant to keep her boys for herself, even if Wally was a lying little coward and William as dumb as a brick. Beulah Baird was nothing but trouble on two legs, in her view.

The flowered wallpaper in her boarding house might be peeling in a place or two, but her mind wasn't peeling. She saw Billy Miller throw Charley a look about the time Wally went hurrying out of the room after Beulah. Something about Charley Floyd's face made her feel motherly toward him; and at the same time, not so motherly.

"I'd give Billy Miller a detour if I was you, Charley," Ma Ash told him. "He's the kind of fella that burns oatmeal."

"Burns oatmeal?" Charley asked. "What's that mean?"

"It means he'll lead you to trouble, but when the trouble shows up, he won't be smart enough to get you out of it," Ma Ash said.

"Say, why are you pickin' on me?" Billy asked, severely stung. "Ain't I always paid my rent on time?"

"I didn't say you was a bad boarder," Ma Ash told him. "I just said you burn oatmeal."

6

After supper, Charley and Billy sat on the front steps for a while, smoking. While they were smoking, Rose and Willy came tramping down the steps and headed for Sligger's Dance Hall, a few blocks away.

They could smell Rose's perfume for a moment, until the September breeze wafted it away.

"I don't see why anybody'd go out with a lug wrench like Willy," Charley said.

"Money," Billy replied. "I'd bet two bits he bought her that perfume."

Billy was in a low mood because of Ma Ash's insult. Seeing Rose go off with Willy didn't do much to lift his mood.

"Well, you got more money now than he's got," Charley reminded him. "Go buy her a bigger bottle."

"I'm the best dancer in St. Louis, and here I am, sittin' on the porch with you," Billy said. In moments of discouragement, he could think of many solid reasons for feeling sorry for himself.

"I guess Beulah quit her job," Charley said. "That'll take half the fun out of supper."

Charley didn't like being around folks in low moods. Melancholy was like quicksand to Charley—if he got too close, he'd slip down into it himself.

"How come you know so much about robbin' armored trucks?" Charley asked him. He thought if he changed the subject, Billy's humor might return. Billy didn't talk much, but he sure liked gabbing about himself.

"When I was first startin' out, me and my buddy Eugene's first and last robbery was an armored truck. Why rob a bank when all the money's drug around in those trucks, I remember Eugene tellin' me. I was young and dumb, he was older than me and had spent time down in the Booneville Boys' Home, so I figured he'd been around." Billy paused to light a cigarette.

"Well, one morning we headed downtown, waited across the street from the First National Bank until it was light, and up pulls this big armored truck. Before I knew what was goin' on, Eugene ran across the street, yellin' at the driver to get out and hand over the cash."

"Sounds like the nervous type," Charley observed.

"Yeah, he had a callus on his thumb big as a walnut. Eugene was always snappin' his fingers—the more nervous he got, the more he'd snap," Billy told him. "Anyway, I took one step off the curb, when the back door of the truck swings open, and out jumps a guard with his gun pulled."

"What'd you do?" Charley asked.

"Hell, I turned and ran. Eugene was thinkin' the driver was the only fella guardin' all that money. That's how come I knew there'd be somebody in the back of that truck with the Kroger payroll," Billy said, smugly.

Charley's strategy worked; Billy was back to being his arrogant self.

"I thought you was goin' to Oklahoma to see your wife," Billy said. Having Charley living on the same floor as him made Billy nervous. Charley had told him about picking the lock on his hometown post office and making off with $350 worth of pennies. Then Charley had got scared and threw the pennies into a cistern, not two hours before the Feds showed up at the Floyd farm looking for him. If Charley could break into a post office, he could also break into a room at the Ash boarding house. Billy might saunter down the hall to the crapper some morning, and come back to find his money gone.

"Are you tryin' to run me off because you're scared I'll rob you?" Charley asked, remembering his own worries about Billy robbing him.

"If you're such a good lockpick, why couldn't you?" Billy asked. Charley wasn't looking too friendly—spells of unfriendliness came on him real quick.

"I didn't say I couldn't," Charley pointed out. "I could break into your room in about three seconds, if I was in a hurry."

"That's why I'm worried," Billy said. "I ain't good with my hands, like you. I doubt I could pick a lock if I had a week."

"I doubt it, too—this morning, you couldn't even find the front end of the car," Charley said. "I could rob you, but I ain't going to, and you best believe that if you wanna pull any more jobs with me."

"Who says I'd pull any more jobs with you?" Billy said, getting mad. "You just got here. I'm the one who knows how things work, remember?"

"Yeah, but I'm the one tied up both guards," Charley reminded him. "You probably woulda tied one of your feet in with one of the guards' and the next thing you know, you'd be caught."

"That wasn't what we was talkin' about," Billy said. "Why wouldn't you rob me?"

"Because I wouldn't rob nobody I run with," Charley said. "I never will. Your money's as safe as if it was in a bank, unless one of the Ash brothers finds it."

"How about the old lady—she's got keys to all the rooms," Billy said. "I wouldn't put much past the old lady."

"If you got the fidgets, move out," Charley told him.

"I think I will," Billy said. "What about you?"

Charley grinned. "I'll stay put till I see how much fur Beulah scratches off Wally."

7

Charley had had a few surprises in his time, but none that quite matched the one he got the next morning, when Ma Ash walked up to him in the second-floor hall and started unbuttoning his trousers.

Charley was so shocked, he didn't say a word. At first, he thought she must be searching him for dope; Billy Miller had told him she was strict about dope.

But Ma Ash soon found what she was looking for, and it wasn't dope. Charley still had his comb in his hand. He had just finished combing his hair; he had been meaning to walk over to Beulah's place to see if she was up. He was feeling pretty starchy, but he sure hadn't expected to get his pants unbuttoned right outside the door of his room by Ma Ash, his landlady.

"Let's have a look at this ear of corn we got here," Ma Ash said, leading him back into his room. She'd had a wakeful night, and decided toward the end of it that motherly was not how she felt about Charley Floyd. Leon Light, her regular stiff, had been off in Paducah, Kentucky, for two months, visiting his sister and playing dominoes.

Ma Ash was a woman of decision, and her opinion of Leon Light was straightforward: if he'd rather be over in Kentucky playing dominoes, let him. Charley Floyd had a restless eye and might be gone any day. Also, he was stout-built, and stout-built men had always appealed to her more than the skinny sort.

"Can you get undressed, or are you paralyzed?" she asked, as she shoved Charley into his room and latched the door behind them.

"Ma'am, I didn't expect you," Charley said, endeavoring to be polite.

"Let me tell you a secret about screwing women," Ma Ash said.

"What?" Charley replied, even more shocked—he had never heard a woman use such a word.

"Don't go off in the mornin' with your shoelaces tied in double knots—not if you're gonna wear them lace-up shoes," Ma Ash said, hiking her dress. "I could read three newspapers while you're getting them shoes untied, and I didn't come upstairs to read newspapers."

Charley never got his shoes untied, and never got undressed, either. He lost control of his fate. At first, he thought it might be bad luck, but pretty soon he decided it was good luck, and ceased to regret that he hadn't made it over to Beulah's.

He blinked a few times, and when he woke up, Ma Ash was sitting with her legs across him, smoking a cigar. That surprised him, too: she didn't allow smoking at her dinner table.

"This ain't the dining room," she said, when he mentioned this inconsistency. Charley thought it was pretty odd that he was in bed with a woman whose hair was mostly grey, but he kept the thought to himself. At the dinner table, Ma Ash kept her hair in a bun, but she had let it down, and it was long and wild. From behind the smoke of her cigar, Charley could see her dark eyes watching him. He decided she was a little scary. Probably the thing to do was wait long enough to be polite, and then head for Oklahoma. He had no doubt that Ma Ash was way ahead of him when it came to smarts. Billy Miller might be right: she might have her eye on the cash.

"Whereabouts in Oklahoma do you live?" Ma Ash inquired. She knew she had scared the boy, which amused her. He was the kind of pretty boy she could get real sweet on, if she let herself. But in this instance, she didn't plan to let herself, pleased though she had been by his stout build.

" 'Round Sallisaw," he told her. He had just awakened from a short nap and still had sleep in his voice, like a little child.

"A place that size is too small for you, Charley," Ma Ash said. "There ain't enough to think about in them small towns. Fighting with your family is about all there is to do."

Charley had to admit she had a point. There was certainly a lot more to think about in St. Louis than there had been in Sallisaw. Robbing the Kroger Bakery was a big thing to think about, and Beulah Baird was something to think about, not to mention the woman sitting with her legs across his, smoking her cigar.

In Sallisaw, there was Ruby and Dempsey to think about— them, and plowing—and he didn't derive any pleasure from thinking about plowing. Even if he had liked plowing, which he didn't, he'd never be able to plow well enough to please his father, Walter Floyd. The fact was, he could never do anything well enough to please Walter Floyd.

"Tell me about office work," Ma Ash said, smiling at him. She looked younger when she smiled—almost pretty.

Charley felt it was a good time to be cautious. He had no intention of telling the truth, but he wasn't wide awake enough to figure out a good lie, and he knew it.

"Mostly I move boxes," he said, finally.

"Oh, can it!" Ma Ash said. "They wouldn't let a hick like you in an office if you was totin' a desk, and you ain't been totin' no desks, not in the last day or two."

"I've been poorly this week," Charley said, trying to think fast. "They let me have two days off."

He was determined not to mention the crime if he could help it, but before he could make up his next lie, he got another surprise: Ma Ash slapped him in the face, and it was no love pat, either. She gave him the kind of slap Wally Ash would have given Beulah Baird if he had been brave enough.

"You got to learn to lie a lot better, if you hope to be a

crook," Ma Ash said. "You're in the big city now—this ain't Sallisaw."

Charley's cheek was stinging. Ma Ash had smacked him the way his mother used to, if she happened to find a beer bottle under his mattress.

He decided Ma Ash might be dangerous, and that his best move would be to say as little as possible. She was right about St. Louis not being at all like Sallisaw, though. In Sallisaw, older women didn't walk up to him in a hall and start unbuttoning his pants. Younger women didn't either, for that matter. Not that it hadn't been exciting—once he got home, he thought he might encourage Ruby to be bolder. Of course, he would have to be careful not to give her a hint as to how he had learned about such goings-on.

"I guess I never had much to lie about before," Charley conceded. "Beer drinkin's about all there is to lie about back home."

"You've got plenty to lie about now, though," Ma Ash told him. "There's the Kroger job, and there's Beulah, and now there's me."

"What about Beulah?" Charley asked, pretending he hadn't heard her mention the Kroger job.

Ma Ash shook her head, located her underpants, and got up off the bed.

"You're cute, Charley," she said. "But I've had lots of cute. What I find hard to tolerate in my old age is bullheadedness. If you're gonna be a big-city crook, you need a better partner than Billy Miller. If Billy had an umbrella and it was coming a downpour, you'd have to remind him to open the umbrella, or he'd drown."

"He does get flustered," Charley admitted.

"I'll say he does," Ma Ash said. "When you're pulling a heist, you need a partner that's steady. Otherwise, you could end up in Jeff City for about ten years, and cute won't get you nothing in Jeff City."

"What's in Jeff City?" Charley inquired.

"The Missouri State Pen," Ma Ash told him. "The next time you decide to rob an armored car, look me up. I'll show you how to do it smooth, so the guards won't even get a look at you."

Big-city life was certainly different, Charley thought. His

38

landlady, who was forty if she was a day, was standing by the bed with her underpants in her hand, volunteering to be his partner in crime. She made him nervous, but despite that, he had an urge to take her up on it. She certainly looked competent. The problem was, she was so far ahead of him. If they did a job together, she might take all the money and lock him in an armored car or something.

Ma Ash was starting to appeal to him, though: one minute he'd feel the appeal, and the next minute, if he happened to look her in the eye, he wished he had slipped out sooner and hotfooted it over to Beulah's, where life was simpler.

"You better skedaddle home, bud," Ma told him. "Don't spend none of that money till you get at least to K.C., either. If you do, the cops will be on you like flies on a turd."

"That's what the guard said," Charley replied, startled.

"You should've conked that old son-of-a-bitch the second he stepped out of the cab," Ma told him. "He'll be the one to send you to the pen, if they nab you—or maybe I should say, when."

To his amazement, Ma Ash leaned over and gave him a hard kiss.

"Next time you want your corn shucked by a real shucker, come back and see me, honey," she said. Then she went out the door, her underpants still in her hand.

8

The Studebaker was robin's-egg blue, with white leather interior and whitewall tires. It was the prettiest car on the showroom floor. Every time he could think of an excuse to walk down to Kingshighway Boulevard, Charley took a look at it.

Then he started walking past the Studebaker showroom even if he didn't have an excuse, just to look at the car. Lots of nights he dreamed about Ruby and her long legs; but the night after the holdup, he dreamed about the Studebaker. It began to swell up in his mind until he could hardly think of anything else.

The summer he and Ruby got married, Pear's Department Store in Sallisaw had put a beautiful white suit in the window. Charley stopped in front of Pear's to admire the suit so many times that Ruby finally got mad at him.

"If that suit was a girl, you wouldn't be welcome to keep gawkin' at her," Ruby said. Then she jabbed him in the ribs with her elbow. The jab took him by surprise, since most of the time Ruby was easy to get along with. She did have a Cherokee temper, though—she rarely blazed up, but she could sure smolder.

"It's just a suit of clothes, why can't I look at it?" he asked.

Ruby didn't answer, but she kept on smoldering for the rest of the day.

Beulah Baird was nothing like Ruby when it came to window-shopping. Beulah liked nothing better than to wander through the stores, making lists of things some man might buy her someday. She kept the lists in the top drawer of her bureau. The name of the store where the goodies were was penciled in neatly at the top of each page. The afternoon after his visit with Ma Ash, Charley paid Beulah a call, and she showed him her lists. After all, he'd bought her a thirty-dollar bracelet for starters; there might be better things to come. Beulah had told Charley how when she was a little girl, she used to go through the wish books, marking all the items she would order if she just had the money. Wandering through the stores was like looking through those catalogs, only better, since everything was real and right there in front of her.

What Ma Ash called "screwing," Beulah referred to as "fussin'." After she and Charley had fussed a little, Charley amused himself by pretending he was going to buy Beulah this or that from each of the lists. Even though she knew he was probably lying, Beulah's eyes lit up at the idea of presents.

"Goin'-away presents," Charley reminded her. "I got to hit the road."

"What have you got to hit the road with, other than them two big feet?" Beulah inquired.

"A new Studebaker," Charley said.

"Baloney and macaroni," Beulah told him. "If you've got a new Studebaker, where's it parked?"

"On Kingshighway Boulevard," Charley said.

"Then why ain't we in it, takin' a ride?" Beulah asked him.

Something about the way Beulah asked that question put Charley on his mettle. He had been tempted to march into the showroom and price the car several times. All that had stopped him was his shabby clothes—he knew he looked too country to be pricing Studebakers.

That was all about to change, though. His new gabardine suit was waiting for him at the tailor's. He had bought a nice white shirt and a swell red tie to go with it, and he had been unable to resist a pair of black leather gloves.

"Soon as I run an errand, I'll be callin' my chauffeur," Charley said, grinning, as he pulled on his socks.

"You're a liar, and you know it," Beulah said. "You don't own no Studebaker car."

"Who says I don't?" Charley said. "When you get tired of bein' naked, put on a dress. I'll come by, and we can take a spin before supper."

"If you can afford Studebakers, why bother with supper?" Beulah asked. "I quit my job last night, or did that slip your mind?"

"Maybe you did, but I still got to eat," Charley informed her.

"You don't have to eat at that old hag's boarding house—not if you can afford Studebakers," Beulah remarked. "I'll dress up, and we can go to Sala's over on Dago Hill—it's a real nice place."

"Well, what'll we eat?" Charley asked, feeling nervous all of a sudden. He had heard there were restaurants so fancy a fella needed a college diploma just to read the menu.

"IIow about champagne first?" Beulah asked. "We'll worry about food after we see how drunk we get."

"I wouldn't mind some champagne right now," Charley said.

He had a feeling that life was speeding up—he had five thousand dollars in cash, two girlfriends, some dandy new clothes—

why not have a Studebaker, too? It was a new life he was living. In his Oklahoma life, it would take him a year just to earn what his suit cost. In his Oklahoma life, it would take him ten years to accumulate enough cash to buy a Studebaker, even if he saved every cent he made.

But he wasn't in Oklahoma; he was in St. Louis, in Beulah Baird's bedroom. What was real in Oklahoma and what was real in St. Louis was two different reals. In Oklahoma, he had a beautiful, long-legged wife and a fat, happy little baby boy, but his days were spent plowing dusty furrows behind a skinny-assed mule. In St. Louis, he had new clothes, a brash girlfriend, and could go out and drink champagne if he wanted. Why not have a robin's-egg-blue Studebaker, too? All it took was cash, and he had cash.

Even so, nice as he looked in his new suit and white shirt and red tie, his knees were shaking when he finally got up the nerve to walk into the Studebaker showroom on Kingshighway Boulevard. It was like going into a restaurant so fancy that he didn't have enough education to read the menu. What if he asked the wrong question, and they spotted him for a rube? What if he embarrassed himself so much they refused to sell him the car? Beulah was already primping for their big night; if he showed up without the Studebaker, she would laugh in his face and go make up with Wally Ash.

"Twelve hundred smackeroos," the salesman said, when Charley worked up his nerve and priced the robin's-egg-blue Studebaker.

"Admire your suit," he added, feeling the sleeve of Charley's coat. "Can't afford gabardine myself, but I know it when I see it."

The salesman, a short fellow, had a moustache so bushy he had to tilt his head back a little and breathe out of his mouth to get enough air.

"Of course, we have cheaper models," he said.

"I'm not shoppin' for a flivver," Charley informed him. "This car's for my wife, she likes blue."

"You're in luck then, mister," the salesman said, tilting his head back slightly. "We ain't had a car this blue since April. What part of Oklahoma do you come from?"

42

"Sallisaw," Charley said, startled.

"I knew it wasn't Ardmore," the salesman told him. "Down 'round Ardmore, they pick up that Texas drawl."

Charley would never have thought that he'd fork over twelve hundred dollars for anything in his life; a week earlier, it would never have occurred to him that he'd ever have twelve hundred dollars cash money to fork over. It was scary how quick everything could change, but it was also exciting, kind of like the first dip on the big roller coaster he had ridden when he was fifteen, and had hitchhiked to the state fair in Oklahoma City.

Beulah Baird would be so excited when she saw him drive up in the new car, she would practically fly out the window. She might want some "fussin' " right then, and if she didn't, she would undoubtedly welcome it later, after they drank a few bottles of champagne.

Charley decided the salesman's comment about Oklahoma accents was an insult. What right did a car salesman have to be making remarks about how people in Ardmore talked? Charley would have liked to grab him by the moustache and hoist him off the ground, but instead, he did the next best thing, which was to peel off twenty-four fifty-dollar bills, and buy the blue car.

The salesman didn't bat an eye.

"I doubt there's a prettier car in the whole state of Oklahoma," he said, handing Charley a receipt.

"Chicago's my destination," Charley replied.

9

Ruby was putting a fresh diaper on Dempsey, when she heard the door open behind her. She thought it was her mother, coming over to help her do a load of wash. She was already soaking all Dempsey's diapers in the big washtub out back.

"Ma, would you hold Dempsey a minute?" she asked.

"Ma's got both hands full, but I'll hold him," Charley said.

Ruby whirled around, and saw him—she was so startled, she almost dropped Dempsey. The next moment, Charley had his arms around both of them, squeezing them tight. He gave her a big, hungry kiss. Dempsey had just finished nursing, and was slobbering a little.

"Don't let him slobber on your suit," Ruby said.

"Miss me?" Charley asked.

Ruby felt like sunshine was beaming right out of her heart.

"Miss you's all I done the whole time you been gone," Ruby said. She sat Dempsey down for a second so she could throw her arms around Charley and give him a real kiss. Dempsey immediately began to yell. He didn't like being left out, not even for ten seconds.

"Hey, buddy," Charley said, bending down to pick him up. "Looks to me like you've grown."

Ruby felt such a gladness at having Charley back that it blinded her to everything except hugging him, kissing him, smelling him. When he left for St. Louis to look for better-paying work than what could be had around Sallisaw, Ruby'd had no idea what an ache the missing would be. Up till then, she and Charley had not been apart a single night since they married. She knew Charley had left home when he was sixteen and followed the wheat harvest for almost a year, but that was before they'd fallen in love with each other. She'd really had no way of knowing what a month without Charley would feel like. But she knew now, and she didn't plan to put up with it or go through it again.

44

"I got presents," Charley said, with that big grin she had never been able to resist, not since the first time he kissed her behind her pa's barn on her fourteenth birthday. Now Ruby was eighteen. They had married, had Dempsey, and become a family. She didn't want Charley going off anymore, and she meant to put her foot down hard, the next time the subject came up.

It was while Charley was down on the floor showing Dempsey how to work the jack-in-the-box that Ruby's head began to clear. When she first turned and saw Charley, it seemed like every drop of blood in her body had started shooting through her veins at twice the normal speed. It was speeding so fast from happy feelings that it almost lifted her off the ground.

But the first kissing was over, and Charley, big kid that he was, sat engrossed in showing Dempsey how to work his new toy. Ruby came back to earth, and she began to notice things— and as soon as she started noticing things, a clock of worry began to ticktock in her mind.

"Charley, where'd you get that suit?" she asked. "You wasn't wearin' no gabardine suit when you left."

All he'd had in the way of clothes that day he hopped the train was two pairs of work pants and three blue work shirts, which Ruby had washed and starched and ironed herself so Charley would look decent when he went to apply for jobs. He hadn't been wearing a suit, or a white shirt, or a red necktie, all of which he was wearing now.

"Honey, I kinda hate to tell you how I came by this suit," Charley said, looking up at her. "It's a terrible sad story."

"Tell me anyway," Ruby said. The worry clock was still ticktocking, like the big clock her parents had that kept her awake on still nights throughout her girlhood, until the day she left home to marry Charley Floyd.

"My boss gave me this suit," Charley said. "It was his boy's. I guess we're about the same size."

"Why would he give you his son's suit?" Ruby asked.

"Well, 'cause his boy got killed deer hunting," Charley told her. "One of his own buddies shot him by accident."

"Oh," was all Ruby said.

"My boss has taken a shine to me," Charley continued.

"I guess so, if he gave you a gabardine suit," Ruby said, not satisfied. It was when Charley turned his big brown eyes to hers and looked the most innocent that he told the biggest lies. In the year they'd been married, she had caught him in some whoppers—every time she caught him, he would promise not to lie anymore—but Ruby took those promises with a grain of salt. Charley couldn't help making up lies; it was mainly because he wanted life to seem better than it was, or himself to seem better than he was, or something. Ever since he was a little boy, he had always tried to make things sound better than they actually were. Expecting Charley Floyd not to lie was like expecting a drunkard not to drink.

Ruby was young and had little education, but her folks were practical people, and she liked to think she had a certain amount of common sense. Charley told her himself one of the reasons he loved her so much was that she was sensible. The gabardine suit fit Charley like a glove, better than a suit would fit if it was made for someone else.

"This suit fits you real nice," she said, feeling the material. "That boy must have been your twin."

All the way down from St. Louis, Charley had been trying to figure out some lies that would work with Ruby. But Ruby was hardheaded and smart, and fooling her had never been easy. As he got closer to Sallisaw, he began to slide downward, and not just because he had a high-tempered wife, either. In only a few weeks, he had gotten used to having a big city around him. He had forgotten just how empty the land looked, and how dusty and poor the little towns were. It was far easier to leave such country than it was to come back to it, even with a beautiful wife and a jolly little baby waiting for him.

"I got presents for you, too, honey," Charley said quickly, before there could be any more talk about where he got the suit, or how well it fitted him.

When he slipped the gold wedding band onto her finger, Ruby looked pleased, but there was a glint of suspicion in her eyes.

"All the time I was driving home, I was thinkin' about givin' you this wedding ring," Charley said, hoping sentiment would make the glint of suspicion fade away.

But the second he spoke, he realized he had slipped again.

46

"*Driving* home?" Ruby said. "Where'd you get a car? You didn't even have money to buy a train ticket, when you left here," she reminded him. Then she glanced out the window, and saw the blue Studebaker sitting in front of the house.

"That car belongs to my boss," Charley said hastily. "He loaned it to me for a few days so I could come home and see you and Dempsey."

That lie didn't work, either, though it wasn't the lie that rubbed Ruby wrong this time.

"Let you come home for a *few days*?!" Ruby said, coloring. "You mean you're gonna leave us again?"

"Honey, it's the best job I ever had," Charley said, jumping up so he could pull her into his arms and kiss her suspicions away. As he was jumping up, though, he accidentally triggered the jack-in-the-box, and the little clown popped up and whacked Dempsey right in the eye, hard. Dempsey had been trying to peek into the box to see where the clown lived. The minute he got whacked in the eye, he began to yell at the top of his lungs.

Ruby picked up Dempsey and tried to shush him. Charley could tell she was mad.

"Ain't it about time for his nap?" Charley asked—he felt like his grip on family life had slipped considerably in the short time he had been away.

"You're his daddy, you been back ten minutes, and you want me to just stick him in his bed?" Ruby asked. "Why'd you even come back? Why're you here, stirrin' us up, if you're just planning to stay a few days?"

"Ruby, I can't answer every question in the world right this minute," Charley said. "Let's go for a ride—it's a beaut of a car!"

"I can see that lookin' out the window," Ruby replied. "You must have the best boss in the world. First he gives you his dead boy's suit, then he loans you his car so you can drive all the way down to Oklahoma and give your wife and child a few minutes of your valuable time!" She was so mad that Charley could see the vein popping out right next to her eye—the vein that always popped whenever she caught him in a lie.

"We could go to the drugstore and get Dempsey an ice cream

cone," Charley said, trying to ignore the anger in her voice. "You and me could have a soda. They don't make sodas up in St. Louis like they do in Sallisaw."

Ruby relented, finally, and allowed herself to be taken for a ride in the blue Studebaker, mainly because it beat staying home and fighting. Dempsey loved the car; he bounced up and down on the seat. And she had to admit, the leather seats smelled good.

It was a pretty day, and just being with Charley caused her mood to improve. Charley was the only man for her—always had been, always would be, even though she didn't believe a word he said—not about the suit, not about the car, not about the boss, or the job, or anything. Her husband was a liar; if she let herself stay mad about it, she'd be mad twenty-four hours a day.

It was fun to roll down the main street in Sallisaw, watching the farmers and the tradespeople and the roughnecks turn their heads to gawk at Charley Floyd and his wife and baby, in their new car. Ruby's suspicion was that Charley had stolen the car. He was a natural-born thief; after all, he had stolen her heart. But the sight of how happy it made him just to *have* such a car, just to *drive* it, made her push the thought out of her mind. One thing she had already accepted about life with Charley Floyd: she better take the fun when it was there to be taken—there might be more fun tomorrow—but then again, there might not.

Millie Adelson, the girl who waited on them at the soda fountain, had been sweet on Charley once. Most of the young women in Sallisaw had been sweet on Charley Floyd at one time or another. Millie was so distracted by the sight of Charley in his new suit that she dropped two scoops of ice cream right out of her scooper while she was making their sodas.

Dempsey wanted to climb on the counter, and Charley had to threaten to take him outside to get him to settle down. The baby's eye was already puffy from where the jack-in-the-box had whacked him.

"Gosh, Charley," Millie said, breathless. "You could be an undertaker, with a swell suit like that. Lots of folks would be happy just to keel over and die if they'd get buried by a fella that looked as good as you do in that suit."

48

Charley grinned—he loved being complimented on his looks and his attire. But Ruby thought the remark inappropriate. She didn't appreciate women trying to flirt with her husband—in her presence, or otherwise.

"I'd like another cherry in this soda," she said sharply, to remind Millie Adelson to keep her mind on her job.

10

Walter Floyd was shoeing Captain Bob, his best mule, when Charley turned into the long dirt lane that led up to the Floyd homestead in his new blue Studebaker. Walter was lean and wiry, with not a speck of fat on him, and his skin was dark and leathery from years spent on the almost treeless plains. Captain Bob was a big mule, with a tendency to lean on Walter whenever he picked up a foot, to either trim the hoof or fit the shoe. Seven or eight hounds were milling around, competing for the parings from Captain Bob's big hooves. Walter had sweat in his eyes, and four or five horseshoe nails in his mouth.

Bradley Floyd, tall and thin like his father, stood close by. He had been sharpening knives on the grindstone in the barn. They were planning to kill hogs in a day or two, and butchering six hogs was no light task: Bradley wanted to be sure the knives were good and sharp.

"That boy better have the sense to pull up before he scares this mule," Walter said, through his teeth. "Bob's never seen a blue automobile, he might not take to it."

"I never seen one either, Pa," Bradley said, squinting. "I bet Charley borrowed it from somebody and drove it out here to show off."

Mamie Floyd, tall and stately, stepped outside, flour up to her elbows. Her thick, dark mane was pulled back in a fat bun. She was still a handsome woman, with no grey hair on her head, in spite of more than twenty years living on the bleak Oklahoma plains. Bradley, her oldest, was twenty-five today, and she had been up since dawn, making pies for the occasion.

"Ma, it's Charley, maybe he struck it rich in St. Louis!" Bradley said.

Mamie Floyd was used to surprises by now. She had four girls and three boys, and surprises were to be expected with even one child, let alone with seven. And even though Charley had the devil in him, he was her favorite. Charley had a kind of energy, a curiosity and restlessness, that none of her other children had. Seeing him drive up the lane made her think about the first time she took all her children over to Sallisaw, when Charley was eighteen months old. It was hot as blazes, and she had taken the children into the drugstore for a cold drink. In the blink of an eye, Charley had disappeared. They found him an hour later in the back of the hardware store, playing with a pile of nuts and bolts. Mamie knew from then on if she didn't keep a close eye on him, he'd be gone before she could count to three. Then there was the time he stole all those pennies from the post office in Sallisaw, and they told the federal agents bald-faced lies to get him off. Walter told the agents that Charley had plowed all night, when in fact, he hadn't touched a plow the whole week.

"Don't come on my place drawin' a bead on one of my boys!" Walter told the men. The fact that lawmen would dare to set foot on his property was enough to cause Walter's temper to flare up—Walter Floyd didn't welcome interference from outsiders. Neither did Mamie, for that matter, but she recognized that the law was the law.

As Charley maneuvered up the bumpy dirt road, he honked the horn a few times, to scatter the pack of coonhounds his father insisted on keeping. In lean times, when the family got by on mostly gravy and mush, the coonhounds still got fed, and fed plenty. Charley never could figure out how his ma put up with all those dogs.

Captain Bob was acting nervous, and Charley knew there'd be hell to pay if he drove up and spooked the big mule while his pa was trying to shoe him. He braked well short of Walter and his mule, and eased the Studebaker around to the back of the house where his mother stood.

"Hi, Ma," Charley said, looking up at his mother's floury arms. "You makin' me a pie for breakfast?"

"I'm making Bradley a pie, it's his birthday," Mamie replied, smiling; it always made her heart glad to lay eyes on her restless son. "If you're polite, you just might get a slice."

Bradley came over with a big butcher knife in his hand, just as Charley got out of the car wearing a suit the likes of which Brad had never seen in his whole life—he even had on a red necktie.

"Did you turn preacher, or rob a dry goods store, or what, bud?" Bradley asked.

"Nope, I got promoted at work," Charley said, shaking his brother's hand. "Is it hog-killin' day, or were you plannin' to cut somebody's throat?"

"We might kill the hogs tomorrow, if it's chilly enough," Brad told him. "I'm sure you'll be wantin' to help, but you better change clothes first."

Charley ignored the comment, and walked over to where his father was shoeing the mule.

"Hello, Pa," he said.

Walter was fitting the shoe on Captain Bob's left forefoot, and Captain Bob was leaning on him, as usual.

"Push on this mule, I'm tired of holdin' the son-of-a-bitch up," Walter said. "Whose Studebaker?"

Charley pushed against Captain Bob to take a little weight off his father. He was bigger-built than the rest of the Floyd men, and even though he was the youngest boy, he had always been able to hold his own in any squabble with his older brothers.

"Mine," Charley answered. He knew he ought to lie about the car, but he didn't want to. He wanted his pa to know he owned the new car. Walter was always telling him he was worthless, for drinking beer, or for plowing crooked, or for not doing the milking early enough—seeing the blue Studebaker might change his opinion.

"Whose?" Walter asked, squinting through sweat at Charley.

"I own it, Pa," Charley replied. "It's mine."

51

"Don't come 'round here lyin' to me when I'm busy," Walter said. "I don't believe you. That suit you're wearin' cost more than any automobile I'd ever be able to buy."

"It's gabardine," Charley said, pleased that his father recognized what a fine suit it was.

Walter Floyd finished nailing the shoe onto Captain Bob's foot. He picked up his rasp and filed off the nailheads, making sure the fit was proper before easing the big mule's foot back to the ground.

Then he turned, and looked at Charley.

"If you was worth half the price of that flashy necktie, you'd be home helpin' out," he snorted, glaring.

"Pa, I got a job back in St. Louis," Charley explained. "I'm only home for a day or two, but I'll be glad to help out while I'm here."

"Take them tools back to the barn—that'd be a start," Walter said, abrupt. Then he walked over to the Studebaker, opened the door, got in behind the wheel, and honked the horn. His hounds began to bay; several that had been sleeping crawled out from under the house. Walter continued to honk, and the hounds to bay.

"This car ain't so bad," Walter said, when Charley came back from putting the tools in the barn. "I like this horn, I can use it to call my hounds. Your ma pretty near ruint it, though, she got flour on the seats. I suggest you give me this one since it's ruint, and get you another."

He looked out at his youngest boy.

"Or, you can take my flivver, if you're in a hurry and want to just swap even."

Charley knew to walk soft when his father began to josh him. Sometimes Walter joked the most before he got the maddest. One minute there'd be a spark of humor in his dark, flinty eyes, and the next minute those same eyes would glint like ice in a ditch.

"Ma, got any flapjacks?" he asked, hoping to turn the conversation away from his new car—maybe it hadn't been such a good idea to drive out and show it off, after all.

"Flapjacks, are you drunk?" Bradley asked. "Breakfast was

52

four hours ago." He turned, and started back to the barn with the butcher knife.

"No flapjacks, but I could rustle up some eggs," Mamie said. "You're so dressed up it makes me nervous, son. Take off that necktie, at least."

Walter continued to sit in the Studebaker blowing the horn at intervals, while Mamie led Charley inside, and made him grits and eggs. Every time Walter honked the horn, his coonhounds bayed.

"I don't see how you put up with all them hounds, Ma," Charley said.

Mamie had gone back to her piecrusts.

"Those hounds are the least I put up with," Mamie said. The day the federal agents showed up looking for the stolen pennies, she'd had the uneasy feeling that it wouldn't be the last they'd see of the law. Now, Charley was sitting at her kitchen table, shoveling in food like the big kid he was, wearing a suit that the most prosperous banker in Sallisaw would be hard put to afford —not to mention the fancy car her husband was making all the racket in—and Mamie had the uneasy feeling in her stomach again, only this time it felt worse.

"Your pa's mad," she told Charley. That was the first thing she would have to deal with. The law, if it came, would be the second.

"Why?" Charley asked. "All I done was go off and get the best job there was to be had in St. Louis."

"What qualifies you for the best job in St. Louis—you left school in the seventh grade," Mamie said, skeptical.

"I don't know exactly," Charley said, trying to look convincing. "Maybe the boss just likes me—is there anything wrong with that?"

"Not a thing, if it's true," his mother replied.

"Then why's Pa mad?" Charley asked, again.

"Because you're driving a nicer automobile than he drives. He ain't a man who likes to be outdone, particularly by his own children," Mamie replied.

Just then, Walter Floyd stomped in the back door, followed by three hounds.

"Get 'em out! I won't have dogs in my kitchen while I'm cookin'," Mamie snapped.

"No, but you'll have this lyin' whelp in his fancy suit," Walter said. There was a Mason jar full of whiskey sitting in the cabinet. Walter took a glass off a shelf, and poured it full.

"Looks like good moonshine, Pa," Charley said, trying to be mild.

"You don't know enough about moonshine to be the judge, now, do you?" Walter said. His voice had taken on a sarcastic tone, and he had a mean gleam in his eye. He turned on his heel and went down the hall, the glass of whiskey in his hand.

"You still make the best grits, Ma," Charley said, in an attempt to keep his mother soft. "Ruby ain't got the hang of grits yet."

Walter Floyd came right back into the kitchen, the whiskey glass empty. He had a razor strop in his hand. Before Charley could get a forkful of eggs to his mouth, Walter began to flail at him with the razor strop.

"What'd I do, Pa?" Charley protested, standing up fast. The whipping didn't hurt much yet, but his father was in a cold fury —Charley had seen him that way often, and he wasn't likely to stop whipping until his arm wore out.

"I don't know what you done, but I aim to find out!" Walter bellowed, whopping Charley as hard as he could. "You don't come 'round here lyin' to your mother and me about a job, and this fancy suit, and that fancy car, when we know you left home without a cent to your name not a month ago!" He happened to hit Charley a good lick across the face, and before he knew it, Charley had yanked the strop out of his father's hand.

"Pa, I'm grown, you can't whip me no more!" Charley yelled, throwing the razor strop out the kitchen window.

Walter looked as if he might press the attack with his fists, so Charley put up his guard. But after glaring for a moment, his father dropped his hands. He poured himself another glass of whiskey, and went back outside to his hounds.

"I told you he was mad," Mamie said, tense. "Finish your eggs, and get out of here."

"Ma, didn't you hear me?" Charley said, his face beet red

from anger. "I'm grown now. It's *my* business where I got the car!"

"Yes—your business, and the law's business, too, I imagine," Mamie said, looking him straight in the eye. "Your pa and me lied to the law once to get you off. We won't lie for you again."

"Aw, who asked you to?" Charley said, straightening his coat and tie.

"Don't sass me, Charley Floyd," Mamie said. "And I'll tell you another thing. You better never let me see you raise your hand to your pa. He ain't perfect, but he's your father. If I *ever* see you raise your hand to him, you'll not be welcome in this house again."

"I didn't raise my hand to him," Charley said quietly, wanting the last word. He finished the glass of buttermilk he had been drinking, and went out to the car. He could see Bradley through the open barn door, still grinding knives. Walter Floyd was harnessing Captain Bob, getting ready to plow.

Charley honked the horn a time or two, as he turned and drove away.

Bradley waved, and four or five of the coonhounds bayed, but his father did not so much as turn his head.

They were just finishing up the cornbread when Bert Cotton knocked at the front door. Cornbread was one thing Ruby felt confident about—she thought she could make cornbread that was at least as good as her mother-in-law's. Charley seemed to think so, too; he ate most of it, along with white beans, okra, and hominy.

At one point, Charley buttered a piece of cornbread and offered it to Dempsey.

"Don't give him that, he'll choke on it," Ruby said. She took it away from him, but not before Dempsey had smeared himself good with the butter.

"I just wanted him to have a taste," Charley said. "He's big enough to have a taste."

Ruby was about to give her husband a lecture on how easy it was to choke babies, when they heard the knock. Ruby looked out the window, and saw the sheriff's black car, parked right behind the blue Studebaker.

"It's Bert," Ruby said. "What does he want?"

"Probably to flirt with you, I doubt he knows I'm home," Charley said, pushing back his chair. "Either that, or he wants me to go set a trotline with him. We caught that eighty-pound catfish on a trotline. Bert's never got over it."

Ruby felt anxiety rising in her when she saw the sheriff's car, but Charley didn't seem the least bit concerned. He had been pals with Bert Cotton all his life; maybe Bert *was* coming to set up a fishing trip.

"Come on in, Bert. You missed the cornbread, but there's plenty of beans left," Charley said, opening the front door. Bert Cotton was a tall, lanky drink of water, so skinny that if he turned sideways, a fellow would have to look close to spot him. He had left Sallisaw to go work in the oil fields for a while; then, in a wink, he had come home and got himself elected sheriff of Sequoyah County.

"Sorry to interrupt your supper," Bert said politely.

"You ain't interrupting it, you're just in time for it—Ruby's made a cobbler," Charley said. "Get in here, I'm lettin' in flies."

Charley stepped outside, since Bert didn't seem to want to step in. The next thing he knew, Bert had handcuffed him, both hands. He did it so quick and so smooth that Charley felt like a fool. He had walked out his own front door, right into a pair of handcuffs.

"Is this a joke, bud?" Charley asked, feeling anger rise.

Bert looked him right in the eye, perfectly friendly and perfectly firm.

56

"Nope, I'm arrestin' you, Charley," he said.

Ruby was on her way to the door with Dempsey in her arms when Bert said it. When she saw that Charley was handcuffed, she almost dropped the baby. It was as if a hole had suddenly opened up in her life, and she had fallen into it. Solid ground had been there a moment before, but now there was only empty space.

"If this is a joke, I wish you'd waited till I finished supper," Charley told him. "Take these damn things off, and let's go eat."

"We're goin' to the jail, Charley," Bert informed him. "Ruby can bring down a dish of cobbler a little later, if she's a mind to."

At that moment, Charley remembered what the elderly guard had said—Ma Ash had said it, too: The cops will be on you like flies on a turd. He had thought it was just scare talk. But here he stood, handcuffed, and it was one of his oldest buddies that had caught him, too.

"But I ain't done nothin', Bert!" Charley protested. In fact, he had almost forgotten about robbing the armored car, though it had happened only a little more than a week earlier. It felt more like something he had dreamed about than something that had actually happened.

But the handcuffs reminded him it wasn't a dream—there they were, squeezing his wrists.

"You know me, you know I ain't bad," he said to Bert.

"Oh, I never said anything about you bein' bad, Charley," Bert said. "I don't think you're bad, particularly. But I do think you robbed an armored car, up in St. Louis, which is why I'm takin' you in."

Charley turned his face for a moment, looking for Ruby's. She was standing just inside the screen; he could hear Dempsey fussing. The sun was setting, and the screen was golden with light. But he couldn't see Ruby. All he could see was the golden screen.

"It's all right, honey, it's a mistake," Charley said, in the direction of the amber screen. "Bert's just doin' his job. I'll go on down to the jail and straighten this out. Keep the cobbler warm."

"With the evidence we got, she'd have to keep it warm several years at least, before you'll be back to eat it," Bert said. "Ruby, you're welcome to bring a dish on down to the jail—I'm sure it's first-rate cobbler."

Ruby didn't say a word. She knew she ought to say something to comfort her husband; but her throat closed up, and she couldn't speak.

When Dempsey saw his daddy being led away, he began to squall. Charley looked so forlorn, walking across the yard to the sheriff's car, that Ruby could hardly stand it. In just a few moments, he seemed smaller, as if he had shrunk. Tears began to sting her eyelids; she felt like squalling herself.

Then she remembered she had set the coffeepot on the stove. Charley liked strong coffee with his pie. Ruby stumbled back into the kitchen, and moved the coffeepot. Then she sat down at the table, and bawled. Dempsey managed to get hold of a small chunk of cornbread, which he promptly crammed in his mouth. She raked most of it out, but he swallowed a little bit, and choked and sputtered and slobbered until he could get enough air in his lungs to squall some more. Ruby let him squall. All she could think of was Bert's comment about several years passing before Charley would be back to eat his pie.

Several years? She knew there was no way she could stand it. Alone, just her and Dempsey, for *several years*? Thinking about it made her numb in the head—she had gone numb like that when her grandpa died, when she realized she would never see him again.

Dempsey finally stopped squalling, and began to bite on his teddy bear. Ruby had a little coffee herself, and then she dished up a big plate of cobbler to carry down to her husband at the jail. It was vinegar cobbler, with raisins in it, Charley's favorite.

12

"Don't sit over there and sull up on me," Bert said, as he was driving Charley to jail. He had known Charley long enough to recognize when he was mad, and Charley was mad enough to bite.

"You said it to Ruby yourself," Bert added. "I got my job to do."

"You're mighty slick with them handcuffs, bud," Charley said. "If I'd had any idea you was about to pull a trick like that on me, I'da knocked you into next week."

"Stuff like that just adds to your sentence," Bert advised.

"There wouldn't have been no sentence," Charley informed him. "I'd have been gone down the road. You and no other law would've got tin bracelets on me."

Bert didn't answer.

"I think you arrested me 'cause I bought a car that's twice as fast as this jalopy," Charley said. "Since when is it a crime to buy a new car?"

"It ain't a crime to buy a new car," Bert told him. "But it *is* a crime to buy one with money stolen from the Kroger Bakery in St. Louis."

"I never heard of no Kroger Bakery," Charley said. "I been in Kansas City most the time.

"Me and you been friends since the third grade," he added, looking at Bert reproachfully.

"Seems like you was smarter in the third grade, Charley," Bert said. "I'm a sheriff, not a saint, and I can't say what I might have done if I'd been lookin' at an armored car full of money. But one thing I can say is that if I pulled a robbery, I wouldn't be leavin' evidence like this around—at least, I hope I wouldn't."

He reached in his shirt pocket, and pulled out one of the little paper bands that the fifty-dollar bills had been wrapped in. The paper band was orange. The stamp on it read: Tower Grove Bank, St. Louis, Missouri.

"I don't even know what that is," Charley said. "I never seen it before. Why would you arrest me because of a little scrap of paper?"

"Because I found it in the glove box of your new Studebaker," Bert said. "This one, and a few more like it."

"Who asked you to look in my glove box?" Charley said. "I never thought you'd be sneaky enough to search my car."

"You *was* smarter in the third grade," Bert said.

Charley stopped feeling mad, and began to feel sick. He remembered that Ma Ash had mentioned a place called Jeff City, where they put fellows that did crimes in Missouri. He didn't know where Jeff City was, but it was bound to be a long way from Ruby and Dempsey, and Bradley, and Ma and Pa. He began to get a lonesome feeling, even though he was still in his hometown. The lonesome feeling made his stomach feel real empty, all of a sudden.

"I hope Ruby don't forget to bring me some pie," he said. "I could sure use a little pie."

13

After she walked home from the jail and washed the pie dish, Ruby lay awake for many hours, listening to the crickets, and looking at the shadows the moon made on the plains. Now and then, a cloud would block the moonlight, and the night would seem very dark; she wished there could be Charley beside her, with his arms around her, when it grew so dark.

Then the cloud would move on up toward Kansas, and the silvery moonlight would shine into the little bedroom. Ruby scarcely moved, and her eyes were wide open. She could hear

Dempsey's light, regular breathing. He was in a crib across the room—Bradley Floyd, Charley's brother, had made them the crib as a wedding present.

Ruby tried to imagine what several years without Charley would mean. The thought made her so numb that she hardly even cried—now and then, she leaked a tear.

In the jail, Charley had just sat. He looked like a balloon that had had most of the air let out of it. By the time she got there with the cobbler, he had lost his appetite. Bert Cotton ate most of the pie; Charley told her to let Bert have it. When she asked him if he had done the robbery, he just looked at her sadly. He never gave her an answer one way or the other. It was as if he had decided to stop living, in the last half hour, and he was already so far away that Ruby couldn't reach him.

"Ten years, I'd 'spect," Bert said, when she asked him how long Charley's sentence might be, if he got convicted.

Bert was immediately sorry he said it, the way Ruby's face turned pale. Ruby was a girl—just eighteen—and she was a nice girl, too. She didn't deserve to have such misery heaped on her so young.

"It might be less," he said, hoping some color would return to her cheeks. "They might let him out early, if he behaves."

Ruby didn't sleep.

Later, toward morning, she went to the kitchen and lit the lamp. Then she sat at the kitchen table, and drank cold coffee for what remained of the night.

14

The state of Missouri sent two deputies all the way to Sallisaw to bring Charley back to St. Louis. Both of them were big and round. When they marched him onto the train, Ruby broke down. She had left Dempsey with her mother so he wouldn't have to see his daddy handcuffed between two fat deputies. Bradley and Bessie, his wife, had come to the station to see him off, and to help Ruby as best they could. Mamie Floyd had visited him in jail once; she didn't say a whole lot, and neither did he. Walter Floyd stayed home.

"Has Pa been coon huntin' much?" Charley asked.

"Coon huntin' and drinkin'," Mamie replied—that was about the extent of the conversation.

"Hurry back, bud," Bradley said, as they were putting Charley on the train. He felt silly saying it, since it was obvious Charley wouldn't be hurrying back. But Charley was his brother, and he felt like he had to say something.

"Don't worry about Ruby none," he added. "Me and Bessie will see that she don't come to no harm."

Charley just nodded. Bessie had been a good sister-in-law to Ruby. She had her arms around Ruby while Ruby sobbed. A norther had struck the night before, a strong one, and lines of prairie dust were skating along the bare platform.

"Your wife's got some squaw in her, ain't she?" one of the fat deputies said, as the train pulled out. Charley didn't answer. Both deputies chewed tobacco, and they passed an old coffee can back and forth between them, using it as a spittoon.

Ruby had come to the jail four or five times a day. She was so torn up about what had happened that Charley was almost glad when it came time for them to put him on the train and take him north. Ruby had kept wanting him to talk about the robbery —to admit it, or deny it, or explain why he did it, or something.

"I don't want to talk about it," he said, and that was *all* he said. Sometimes at night in his cell, he could almost convince himself that he hadn't really done it—that someone who looked like him had taken over his body for a while, tied up the guards, and taken the money. How could he explain to Ruby how easy it had seemed, and how polite he had been to the guards? It had been such a foggy morning, and the whole thing hadn't taken five minutes. It had seemed so simple. He never dreamed anything could go wrong, even though the guard warned him, and so did Ma Ash. The thought of having to be in jail for years never crossed his mind, or Billy Miller's mind, either, so far as he knew.

But now the train was moving north, picking up speed. Sallisaw was behind them. There was nothing to see out the window but the windy prairie, and now and then, a farmhouse. One of the guards offered him a chew, but Charley shook his head.

"Don't you chew?" the guard asked, surprised at having his offer declined.

Again, Charley shook his head.

"I reckon he'll be chewin' before he sees this part of the country agin," the other guard said. "There ain't nothin' to do in the Jeff City pen *but* chew."

Charley kept his eyes on the floor. He tried not to think about Ruby and Dempsey. He tried not to think about anything.

His insides felt as cold and thick as mud.

15

"Well, you ain't such a pretty boy now, are you?" Ma Ash said, looking at Charley—he was slouched in one of the straight-backed chairs in the ugly, green-walled visiting room in St. Louis City Jail.

"Who ever said I was pretty?" Charley asked.

"I said it, and I doubt I was the first gal you ever heard it from, either," Ma replied, handing him a pack of smokes.

"They sheared me like a sheep," Charley said, ruefully. "If I don't shave quick in the morning, I got more hair on my face than they left on my head."

"Lice," Ma Ash said. "It was in the newspaper. This old jail is crawling with lice."

Charley bristled at that, although the short barber with the fat stogie told him the same story while he was shearing off his hair with a pair of clippers that looked just like those they used to shear sheep down in Oklahoma.

"Lice," the little barber told him. "They like to hide up near the roots."

"I don't have lice, get me?" Charley told him, indignant. "I know enough to keep myself clean."

"You'll have 'em if they don't sentence you quick and ship you out of here," the barber said. He had an enormous belly, and wore an undershirt. The ash from his cigar kept dropping on the undershirt, but the barber either didn't notice or didn't care. Shock after shock of Charley's thick hair fell to the floor. Now and then, the barber took the cigar out of his mouth for a second, and moved it from one side of his mouth to the other, causing more ash to drop off. The ash that made it past the fat man's stomach mingled with Charley's hair on the grimy jail-house floor.

"I never had lice in my life," Charley insisted, first to the barber, then to Ma Ash.

"There's a first time for everything," Ma said. She had on a coat with rabbit fur around the collar.

"There won't be no first time for me gettin' lice," Charley said. "I'd know it if I had any."

Ma Ash grinned. "You're a stubborn little son-of-a-bitch," she said. "Maybe that's what I like about you—that, and the fact you was a mighty pretty boy until you ran afoul of the law and got stuck in this filthy jail."

"I don't intend to be here long," Charley said, realizing that his tone so far hadn't been too polite. Ma Ash was his first visitor. He had been in City Jail nearly a week, waiting for his day in court. Any visitor was welcome, particularly one who was thoughtful enough to bring him smokes.

"You *won't* be here long," Ma said. "But where you're going will make this place look like the Garden of Eden."

Charley kept quiet. He had already heard too many stories about the Jeff City pen. Half the crooks in City Jail had been in Jeff City at one time or another, for one crime or another; they all had stories about what a rough place it was.

"First time I was in Jeff City, I seen a guard jab a crowbar right through a man's foot," an old burglar told Charley. The old man's name was Tommy Pippin. Charley shared a cell with him for two days. The first night, Tommy had been coming off a long drunk, and he had the shakes so bad he had to hold onto the bars to keep from rattling his false teeth clear out of his head.

"Ouch!" Charley said, when he heard the crowbar story. "Why'd he do that?"

"Just took a notion to," Tommy said, still shaking.

"You wouldn't have any snuff, would you?" he asked, a little later.

"Don't use it," Charley replied. "My grandpa uses it, though."

Tommy Pippin considered that information for a moment.

"What's the chance of your grandpa gettin' nabbed?" he asked, finally. "I sure could use a dip."

Ma Ash's deep-set dark eyes were studying Charley closely. "Who's your shyster?" she inquired. His jailbird shirt didn't fit. His wrists stuck out of his shirtsleeves a good two inches. The pants, on the other hand, were too long. They hid his feet completely, and he had been stepping on his own trouser legs when he came into the visiting room. With his sheared head and clothes that didn't fit, he looked about seventeen. Looking at him, as dejected as a boy could be, made some of Ma Ash's motherly feelings come back.

"My what?" Charley asked.

"Your lawyer," Ma said.

"I ain't seen none yet," Charley told her. "Where's Billy Miller?"

Ma Ash snorted. "That little fool hightailed it to Indiana," she said. "He's got a sister in Indianapolis."

"I hope they don't catch Billy," Charley said.

"Listen, bud, your good heart's gonna be your downfall," Ma Ash pointed out. "You need to learn to look after number one. If you don't, you won't last long in this business."

"I ain't in no business," Charley said. "I just made one mistake."

"Yeah, but you're young, you'll make more," Ma Ash said. "I'm older than you, and I'm still making 'em."

"You ain't in jail," Charley reminded her.

"I'm not?" Ma said. "Then where are we havin' this conversation, the Hotel Statler?"

Charley had to grin. "Well, you're in jail right this minute, but you can leave," he said. "I'm gonna be here awhile."

"Who's your judge, have they told you?" Ma asked.

"Judge Whaley," Charley told her.

"Oh, Bull Whaley," Ma said. "He's never heard the word 'mercy,' and if he had, he don't subscribe to it. If the law says he can give you ten years, then he'll give you ten years."

Charley felt scared. He couldn't imagine a month in a place like the jail, much less ten years in a place even worse than the jail. What would Ruby do? Where would she get the money to raise Dempsey? Would they even remember him after ten years? How would he survive that many nights without Ruby to hold him?

"I know Bull Whaley," Ma Ash said. "Back when I had a house, one of my girls used to shuck corn with him on a regular basis. If I can locate her, I'll ask her to put in a word for you. Bully was so sweet on her at one time that he almost left his wife."

"That's the first good news I've had," Charley said. "I hope he's still sweet on your friend."

"I'll have to find her first," Ma Ash said. "Got any plans for when you get out?"

"I ain't even *in* yet," Charley said. "How would I go about plannin' that far ahead?"

"Planning ahead's what you need to do," she said. "Thinking about how rich you could get if you hook up with me might help you keep from going stir-crazy."

Ma Ash was still looking at him with her deep-set black eyes.

66

Despite her hard outside, she had always been pretty soft inside, and it had been a long time since she'd had feelings as strong as the ones she felt for Charley Floyd, even though he was half her age.

"Hook up with you doin' what?" Charley asked.

"Something that pays good, and ain't too risky," Ma Ash said.

Then, to Charley's astonishment, she reached over and squeezed him, right through his pants. There was a guard standing by the door, but the guard didn't notice.

"I'll see if I can find that whore," she said, getting up to leave.

"Thanks for the smokes," Charley said, still embarrassed by what Ma Ash had just done.

"Keep that cob steady," Ma Ash said, winking, as she turned to leave.

16

Elbert Devaney was leading Charley back to his cell after his short visit with Ma Ash, when the desk guard yelled down the hall after them.

"Hold up, Elbert!" the desk guard said. "There's another dame here to see Floyd."

"You're popular with the ladies," Elbert said, a little wistfully. Elbert's right eyeball jiggled rapidly when he was nervous, which he almost always was if he happened to be in the company of a lady. Because of what he called his "nervous eye," and perhaps for other reasons as well, Elbert had never been especially popular with the ladies.

When Charley got back to the visiting room, Beulah Baird was waiting, and it didn't take much brain power to figure out that Beulah was steamed. Her face was redder than her lipstick. Charley was glad to see her, and he couldn't help being amused that she was so mad.

"What was that old whore doin' comin' out of this jailhouse?" Beulah asked.

"What old whore, honey?" Charley asked, looking as innocent as he could with his sheared head, and his ill-fitting clothes.

"Ma Ash—you know who I'm talkin' about," Beulah said. "I oughta smack your face."

"My cousin from Illinois came across the river to see me," Charley said. "Cousin Annie. But she ain't a whore."

"I don't believe you. I nearly run smack into Ma Ash," Beulah told him. "How come I didn't see this cousin of yours, if she was just here?"

"Maybe she's usin' the ladies' room," Charley suggested. If Beulah barged off to look, he could always argue that Cousin Annie had slipped out while Beulah was in the visiting room.

"You're full of baloney, you lyin' hick," Beulah said, her eyes blazing. "Rose told me Ma Ash was sweet on you, but like a fool, I laughed it off."

She stopped talking, and waited for him to respond. But Charley didn't respond. He just assumed a blank look, and sat down in the same chair he had been sitting in when Ma Ash reached over and squeezed him.

"Answer me, Charley!" Beulah demanded. "Are you sweet on her, or ain't you?"

"Honey, I'm in jail," Charley said. "I'm sweet enough on you that I just about go crazy every night I'm in here without you."

It was true, too—at night, he lay awake, either thinking too much about Ruby, or thinking too much about Beulah. Thinking about Ruby was hopeless, since she'd never be able to scrape up the trainfare to come as far as St. Louis. Beulah at least lived in St. Louis; she might be mad as hell, but she was there, close enough that he could smell her perfume. Beulah wore a lot of perfume.

"Here, I brought you some smokes," Beulah said, pulling cigarettes out of her purse. She was calming down a little, and the red had begun to drain out of her face. The remark he made

68

about nearly going crazy from thinking about her was the kind of remark she liked to hear.

"I wish they'd caught Billy Miller instead of you," Beulah said.

"Why have you got it in for Billy?" Charley asked. "Billy don't mean no harm."

"That's all *you* know," Beulah said. "Rose gave in and went out with him a few times, and the next thing you know, the little jerk was two-timing her."

"With who?" Charley asked, curious. Back in Sallisaw, a man was lucky to have one wife, or one girlfriend, or one anything. But up in St. Louis, in the big city, anything could happen. It was like he was living two different lives, one in Oklahoma and one in Missouri—or he had been, until he got caught and stuck in jail. Now, he wasn't really living any life—but still, two women had showed up at the jail to see him. The thought perked him up a little. The company of Elbert Devaney, and old Tommy Pippin, had begun to get him down.

"With some hash-slingin' slut," Beulah said, her voice full of scorn. "My sister won't put up with two-timing men, and neither will I."

"Rose won't have to put up with it unless she moves to Indiana," Charley said. "I hear that's where Billy's hiding out."

Beulah's face, which had just begun to soften, immediately hardened again—Charley realized he had made a slip.

"Who told you he was in Indiana?" Beulah asked. "Not everybody has that information."

Charley decided to be brazen. In his experience, if he had to lie to a woman who had cornered him, as his wife Ruby often did, the best course was to tell the biggest lie he could come up with.

"Why, Billy sent me a postcard," he said. "I got it just before the sheriff hauled me off."

The next thing he knew, Beulah had slapped him as hard as she could. The slap made enough noise that the guard heard it.

"Here, now," the guard said, frowning at Beulah. "You're supposed to visit him, not beat him up. We'll beat up on him ourselves, if he needs it."

"Mind your own business, fatso," Beulah said, furious. The guard was on the heavy side. "I guess I can smack my boyfriend if I want to."

"Not in St. Louis City Jail you can't," the guard informed her. "We don't allow whores to beat up on stiffs, not in this jail."

"Hey, this is my fiancée," Charley said, turning to the guard. "We'd be married already if you boys hadn't got me mixed up with the crook who robbed that armored car. Don't be callin' my fiancée no whore."

"Then tell her to buy a punchin' bag, if she's itchin' to slug somebody," the guard said. He took a plug of tobacco out of his hip pocket, and broke himself off a chaw.

"Honey, get yourself under control," Charley told Beulah, trying to soothe her. "One more slap, and we'll lose our visitin' rights."

"I don't know why I'd wanna visit a two-timin' liar like you anyway," Beulah said. Charley had put his arm around her shoulder, and she shrugged it off. "I'll tell you right now, if I find out you had anything to do with that old whore, you'll never lay eyes on me again."

Charley leaned back, trying to look startled by this threat.

"Beulah, I'd just as soon go blind than to think I'd never see you again," he said.

Beulah hadn't expected him to say anything that strong. The thought of Charley's sad brown eyes going blind brought her temperature down a little.

"Why don't you go peek in the ladies' room—Cousin Annie might still be in there, powderin' her nose," Charley suggested. "If Ma Ash was here, it's probably 'cause one of her fool sons got arrested."

"They ain't arrested. Wally was pesterin' me just this mornin'," Beulah said. "I wish you was out, I need you to sock him."

Charley didn't like the thought of Wally Ash being anywhere near Beulah.

"That chump," he said. "Why'd you ever go out with a chump like that, anyway?"

"Oh, I don't know," Beulah said, flustered. She wanted to sit on Charley's lap and kiss him a few times, but the fat guard was looking right at them, so she didn't dare.

70

"I wish that goon would leave us alone for a minute," she said. "I've been missin' you so bad, I'm all in a fuss."

"Maybe he'll choke on that chaw," Charley said, grinning at the guard. The smell of Beulah Baird's perfume was beginning to liven him up. He could tell she was in the mood to spoon a little, too. Beulah possessed a goodly amount of brass, as she quickly demonstrated by walking over to the guard with a dollar bill in her hand.

"Say, mister, if I give you this dollar, will you turn your back for a few minutes?" she asked.

"Nope," the guard said. "If you give me that dollar, I'll arrest you for bribery.

"You shouldn't of got sassy with me," he added. "I don't accept no bribes from sassy women."

"I didn't mean it when I called you fatso," Beulah said, giving him her sweetest smile. "I like a man with a stout build."

The guard tried to ignore this compliment to his physique, but no man could remain totally immune to Beulah when she turned on her charm. After all, Floyd would soon be off to prison, leaving Beulah behind. She was smiling at him gaily, and standing close enough that he could smell her perfume.

"What's your name, anyway?" Beulah asked.

"Hershel," the guard said. "Hershel Farrow."

"Hershel, couldn't you turn your back for just one teeny minute?" Beulah asked, batting her eyes at him hard and fast.

"Aw, go on and smooch him, if you want to," Hershel said. "More smoochin' goes on in this visitin' room than goes on in a whorehouse in a whole month."

"Hey, don't be talkin' about whorehouses around my fiancée," Charley said. "She's a respectable girl, she don't know nothin' about stuff like that."

"If she's so dern respectable, what's she doin' with a jailbird like you, Floyd?" the guard asked.

But he politely turned his head when Beulah sat down on Charley's lap and began to kiss him. When the visiting time was up, Hershel had to whack his nightstick against the doorjamb three or four times to get the two lovebirds' attention. Beulah finally unpeeled herself from Charley, and allowed herself to be led out. She was crying like the world was coming to an end.

Later, Hershel found himself unable to forget Beulah Baird. Girlfriends came and went all day long in the visiting room of the St. Louis City Jail, but Beulah Baird was special. She had those bright eyes and that sweet smile.

"Why do you think women go for crooks?" he asked Elbert Devaney, after he had returned Charley Floyd to his cell.

Elbert had never given that specific subject much thought, but he had given a lot of thought to the fact that women seemed to like almost any man better than they liked him. Of course, he *did* have a nervous eye, but then lots of men who had warts, or busted noses, or other defects had cute girlfriends.

"Never thought about it," he admitted to Hershel Farrow.

"I wonder if they're built different, crooks," Hershel theorized.

"Built different?" Elbert asked, befuddled. "Built different how?"

"Built different down below," Hershel replied.

"Down below?" Elbert asked, even more puzzled than before. "Down below where?"

Hershel began to regret even attempting to discuss such a complicated subject with someone as brickheaded as Elbert Devaney.

"Aw, forget I ever mentioned it, you idjit," he said.

17

Judge Bull Whaley was surprised to see Lulu Ash sitting at his customary table in the coffee shop of the Great Missouri Hotel. Judge Whaley could not remember how many years it had been since he had encountered Lulu Ash face-to-face, but he knew it was her the moment he stepped through the door of the coffee shop. Not many retired whores would be bold enough to help themselves to a seat at his table. Not many would be smart enough to realize that it *was* his table.

"Good morning, Bull," Lulu said, pleasantly. "You been eatin' too many mashed potatoes."

"I rarely touch a mashed potato," Judge Whaley said. "I content myself with mush now, mostly."

"You didn't grow that belly eatin' mush," Lulu said.

"Smart judges are all fat, Lulu," Judge Whaley said. "Judicial wisdom requires a certain girth."

"I see," Lulu said. "What if I bought you breakfast?"

"I don't want you buying me breakfast," the judge said. "But I am glad to see you. Any news of Nora?"

"Still sweet on her, are you?" Lulu asked.

"No," Judge Whaley said. "I ain't sweet on her—I'm in love with her. That's a far worse condition for a man with my responsibilities.

"I 'bout died when she married. But you know that," he added.

"You could yet, couldn't you?" Lulu asked.

"I mostly feel dead as it is, to tell you the truth," the judge replied. "But I might rise up like Lazarus if I could spend a few nights with Nora."

Lulu Ash said nothing. A waiter hurried over with the judge's coffee.

"You're an unlikely Jesus, Lulu," the judge said. "Maybe you're going to raise me up."

"Maybe I am, Bully," Lulu said. "It depends."

"Oh," the judge sighed. "That's how it is."

"I know where she is," Lulu Ash announced.

"Lulu, I don't care where she is unless she wants to see me," the judge informed her. "If she was in China and wanted to see me, I'd catch the first boat. But if she's across the street and doesn't want to see me, then it's no matter."

"She wants to see you," Lulu Ash said. "You should have left your wife, if you love Nora so much."

"No argument there," the judge said. "I should have left my wife."

"Then why didn't you?" Lulu asked.

"I wish I knew," Judge Whaley said. The waiter came back with eggs, ham, potatoes, and lots of biscuits, all of which he set in front of Lulu Ash.

"It was cowardice, I suppose," the judge said finally, taking a biscuit.

"I knew that anyway," Lulu told him. "It's always cowardice when a man won't choose. I just wanted to hear you admit it."

"I admitted it, now where's Nora?" the judge asked.

"She's handy," Lulu replied.

Judge Whaley sighed again. He had never liked dealing with women, particularly women like Lulu Ash. So far as he knew, Lulu had never given anything away, at least not to him.

"I've got to get to court, what do you want?" he asked.

"I want you to go easy on the Floyd boy," Lulu informed him.

The judge looked around the dining room, which was usually filled with lawyers, other judges, bailiffs, and the like. None were there at the moment, since he tended to be about twenty minutes ahead of the breakfast crowd, in order to have some time to think. But the boys would soon be coming, and none of them would miss the fact that he was breakfasting with Lulu Ash. A newspaperman or two might even show up; they wouldn't miss the fact, either.

"You oughtn't to order such a big breakfast when you're bribing a judge," he said. "You need to bribe him quick and then skedaddle."

"I ain't bribin' you—it's just a simple trade I had in mind," Lulu said. "There's no law against tradin'."

"I expect Nora could find me if she really wanted to see me," the judge said. "If she really wants to see me, I don't need to be making any trades with you."

"If you think it's that simple, then do as you please," Lulu Ash said.

The judge pondered that a moment. Two bailiffs walked in while he was pondering.

"Well, it was a first offense," he said. "I might give him five instead of ten."

"That'll do," Lulu said. "He's a soft boy. He'd never recover from ten."

74

"If he's soft, he may not recover from five," the judge told her. "He may not even survive. I'm not soft, but I'd be hard put to survive five years in Jeff City."

"Yeah, but you're a judge," Lulu said.

"A judge who's crazy about a whore," she added.

Judge Whaley knew it was true. Just thinking about Nora made him want to leave the bench, leave his wife, desert his children. Every form of ruin seemed preferable to a life without Nora Mullins.

Two lawyers came into the dining room. Lulu was finishing her eggs.

"The boys are starting to show up," he told her. "You might show a little consideration."

"Oh, can it!" Lulu replied, annoyed. She hated to be rushed when she was enjoying a good meal. "We ain't doin' nothing wrong. They'll think I'm settin' you up with a girl."

"Which you are, I hope," the judge said.

Lulu finished the eggs, and wiped her lips.

"She lives in St. Charles on Fifth Street, in a white house with blue shutters," she said. "It's the only house with blue shutters on Fifth Street."

"She's not married anymore, is she?" the judge asked.

"Nope, she left that mug—she lives alone," Lulu said, as she got up to go.

18

"It must be the judge's birthday," the bailiff said, as he and Elbert Devaney walked Charley out of court, and back to the jail.

"Why else would he give you only five years?" the bailiff added.

"That's right," Elbert said. "Five years is easy. He coulda given you ten."

"It was my first crime," Charley reminded them.

"Judge Whaley figures once a crook, always a crook," the bailiff informed him. "I'm surprised he didn't throw the book at you."

"You stole twelve thousand dollars," Elbert said. "I've known Judge Whaley to hand out ten years to old boys who never stole but three hundred."

"It isn't how much, Elbert—it's the fact that he used a gun," the bailiff added. "That makes it armed robbery."

"I had a gun all right, but I didn't use it," Charley said. "I wasn't even the one holdin' it."

Elbert liked Charley, who was looking real gloomy, even though he'd drawn a light sentence. He tried to think of something to say that might lift his spirits some.

"You'll only be 'bout twenty-five when you get out," he said. "If you behave, they might let you out a little early, even."

Charley kept walking down the grey corridor. He didn't seem to hear what was being said, and his eyes had a faraway look in them. Elbert would have liked to cheer him up, but when he looked at Charley and saw the faraway look in his eyes, he couldn't think of a single other thing to say.

19

When Billy Miller showed up at the back door of the Ash boarding house, he got a cool reception.

"I'm surprised you got the gall to come slinkin' around

here," Lulu Ash said, looking at him coldly through the screen door.

"Why? I'm still payin' rent, ain't I?" Billy retorted.

"You ain't payin' rent, and I never heard of you," Lulu said.

"What about my clothes?" Billy said, horrified at the thought that something might have happened to his new pin-striped suit.

"I never heard of your clothes, neither," Ma Ash said. "Get along down the street, I don't harbor criminals in my boarding house.

"At least I don't harbor criminals as dumb as you," she added.

"But what about my clothes?" Billy asked, again. He couldn't believe his clothes weren't still living in the Ash boarding house where he'd left them. "I had all kinds of clothes."

"Now you've got no kinds," Lulu said. "I got rid of everything you left in the room. Go to a dry goods store, if you need clothes."

"I hear Charley's in Jeff City," Billy said. He was hoping that if he kept talking, Ma Ash would soften up and invite him in.

"He's doin' five years for being dumb enough to pull a stickup with a stupid little jackass like you," Ma said. "Go away, I told you. I don't want any bulls to see you slinking around my house."

With that, she shut her door, and turned the key in its lock.

"Gosh," Billy said, to no one. His fate seemed harsh. He had come back from Indianapolis because he was tired of listening to his sister and her husband fight. Mostly they yelled, but occasionally, things got out of hand, and they slugged each other, or broke furniture. Billy couldn't take it. He missed St. Louis, missed the camaraderie of the Ash boarding house, missed Rose, missed Charley.

In fact, it was Charley he missed most of all.

With Charley around, life seemed to hold more possibilities. Maybe the next time they pulled a robbery, things would go off smooth.

Ma Ash had made it clear she didn't intend to let him in, so Billy had no choice but to wander down to a barroom. It was chilly, and his overcoat had been one of the things he forgot to take to Indianapolis, he had been in such a hurry to get away. All the time he was there he had meant to go buy a new overcoat, but his sister's fights with her husband demoralized him so much that he mainly sat around her kitchen all day, listening to the radio and playing solitaire.

"Hi, Killer," the bartender said, when Billy walked in. "I thought you moved to K.C. or somewheres."

"Florida," Billy corrected. "I went to see the alligators."

"Okay," the bartender said, though he didn't believe a word of it. The bartender's name was Louie.

"Kill anybody while you was gone?" he asked.

"Can it," Billy said. "And don't be callin' me Killer, neither. The only person I killed was my brother, and that was an accident."

"Accident?" the bartender said. "I thought you shot him over a dame."

"I did," Billy admitted. "It was just an accident we liked the same dame."

"Where's your big friend, the one from Oklahoma?" Louie asked. "I ain't seen him in a while."

"Another accident," Billy said. "He fell down a bread chute at the bakery and busted himself all up."

"Too bad," Louie said. "I liked Charley. He sure could swig down them beers."

20

Trainfare from Sallisaw, Oklahoma, all the way to Jefferson City, Missouri, was seven dollars—not counting meals—and it took Ruby almost ten months to raise it, mainly by taking in washing. On days when she slipped back twenty-five cents or so because Dempsey had to have medicine or something, Ruby almost despaired. Charley's ma and pa had refused to help her, though his brother Bradley did slip her a nickel or a dime here and there. Her own folks were sharecroppers, and they seldom had cash money. Anyway, cotton was down, and they had no money to spare.

At night, Ruby lay alone in the bed she had shared with Charley, feeling like her heart would burst from missing him. Some nights she cried; other nights she lay in bed and looked out the window, feeling dry as dust. She knew she couldn't take any five years without seeing her husband. As it was, every day seemed like a month, and every week like a year. She lost her appetite, and she lost weight—some days it was all she could do to work up a smile for Dempsey.

Ruby had bought a cheap, Indian rule tablet, envelopes, and stamps with her first washing money. It was three months before Charley sent her a letter, since it had taken that long for him to be sentenced and sent to the Missouri State Penitentiary. By then, she had used up practically the whole tablet writing him a letter every few days, telling him about Dempsey, about Bessie and Brad's new baby, about the long, cold nights without him to keep her warm.

Bessie was the one person Ruby could talk to about her loneliness, and her need to see Charley. Bessie was kind. She took Dempsey whenever she could, and let him play with Brad's and her two youngest children. Bayne and Wayne, their nine-year-old twins, would watch the little ones while Bessie and Ruby visited.

"I'd be the same, if it was Brad in the pen," Bessie told her. "I'd lose my mind if I had to be away from Brad."

It was Bessie who agreed to keep Dempsey for a few days, when Ruby finally saved up the seven dollars. Ruby washed and ironed all her clothes, and packed them neatly in her little valise. She had to sit on it to get it closed, it was stuffed so full.

Then the train came, and Ruby got on it. She had never been inside a train before, and was as nervous as a cat. The air smelled like cigar smoke, and it was hot and crowded. Ruby tried to find a bench where she could be by herself, but there were no empties. She barely found a seat before the train started moving, finally sitting down beside a cowboy, who politely tipped his hat when Ruby approached.

"I sure hope this train don't wreck," she said, thinking it would be polite to make a little conversation.

The cowboy, a man of about forty, took a long time to answer. He seemed to be considering all the reasons that might cause the train to wreck.

"It's a pretty good ol' train," he said, after a few minutes. "I don't 'spect it'll wreck."

The cowboy had a saddle propped between his legs. Ruby considered asking him where he was going, but abandoned the notion. She sat and looked out the window, wondering if Charley would look older when she saw him, wondering if he would even be glad to see her. She had sent him a picture of herself and Dempsey in one of her letters, so he wouldn't forget what she looked like.

The cowboy got off in Welch, which was way up by the Kansas line. He didn't say another word, but he tipped his hat to Ruby when he stood up to leave the train.

21

The sight of the Jeff City penitentiary scared Ruby so badly that she almost didn't have the courage to go in. To her it looked like something out of a fairy story, or a bad dream: a dirty, old castle from a long time ago. The thought that Charley, her husband, was inside that dark place upset her so, that she began to shake all over. She had tried to make herself look pretty for

Charley's sake, but it was a gloomy, rainy day, and her spirits were as shaky as her legs.

Everything inside the pen was ugly, too, including the old woman who searched her, and dumped everything in her handbag out on a table. The careless way she did it made Ruby mad. All she had been allowed to bring Charley was a bottle of soda pop and some tobacco and rolling papers. The man at the little grocery next to the jail had told her that was all they'd let her bring him, and Charley even had to drink the soda pop while she was there. No factory cigarettes were allowed, but the clerk assured her that all the inmates learned how to roll their own. The old woman was pulling at her handbag like she meant to tear it apart.

"That's my only handbag," Ruby said. "I ain't got no Winchester in it, if that's what you're thinking."

"You better can the sass, if you want to see your stiff," the old matron said. "This is a prison. We don't tolerate no sass."

When the visiting hour came, there were lots of visitors lined up—mostly older women, mothers whose boys were in jail. Ruby was the youngest woman by several years. The waiting room was grey, and it stunk. Ruby decided the stink must be from all the sadness: she had never been in a place where everybody was so sad. Even in the hospital the night her grandpa died, there had been a few jolly people, but there were no jolly people in the Jeff City pen.

The place where she finally got to see Charley was a big, screened-in room. She and the other visitors were herded into it, sort of like chickens. Then the prisoners began to come in, on the other side of the wire. When she realized she wasn't even going to get to touch Charley, Ruby began to cry—she couldn't help it. She had saved up her seven dollars just to stand in a pen and look at him through chicken wire. How was she supposed to even give him his soda pop through all that wire?

When she saw Charley, he was walking kind of funny, holding one hand behind him as if he was holding a surprise. His hair was cut close to his scalp, which made Ruby feel even sadder. Charley had always been vain about his hair, and he had reason to be—his hair had been thick and soft.

When he finally spotted Ruby, he smiled, and a little bit of life came back into his face. He came over and gave her a kiss through the screen, but he was still holding his hand behind his back, and he walked kind of awkward.

"Charley, what's the matter with you?" Ruby asked, putting both her palms against the screen, to get as close to him as she could.

Charley looked embarrassed, which to Ruby only meant that he looked sweet.

"Got a rip in my pants that's nearly a foot long," Charley said, with a rueful smile. "If I don't hold 'em together, my ass will hang out."

"Honey, that's awful," Ruby said. "Won't they even give you good pants?"

"They're supposed to, but I've been holding my ass in for a week, and I still ain't seen the pants," Charley told her. "How's Dempsey?"

"Fine, he misses his daddy," Ruby said. "I left him with Bradley and Bessie—they miss you, too."

Charley didn't answer. He stood looking at her through the screen with sadness in his eyes, still holding his hand behind him to keep his ripped pants closed. Ruby knew from the look in his eyes that he missed them, too, more than there was any point in talking about.

Later, when she had stumbled out of the dirty old building back into the gloom of the day, the look in Charley's eyes was the one thing Ruby remembered about the visit. The rest had been too brief. Charley and the other convicts had been let into the room with their visitors for fifteen minutes, so Ruby did get to hug Charley and kiss him, hold him close, give him his soda pop and his tobacco—but it seemed like only seconds that they could touch. Then the prisoners were taken back outside the screen again; she and Charley talked a little more, their hands pressed together against the wire. Ruby gave him what news there was, and then he was gone into the darkness of the prison with the other men. It was so brief that Ruby couldn't accept it was over, that months would pass, or even years, before she would see her husband again. She cried so hard that she had to sit down outside the prison on the side of the road, and then she stopped crying, or caring if she could walk or not.

82

After a while, a car stopped beside her and an old man in a black felt hat tipped it when Ruby looked up at him.

"Need a lift to the depot?" he asked.

Ruby nodded, and got in. When the old man let her out at the train station, she thanked him. Her voice sounded like the voice of someone she didn't know.

22

Charley tried to get his mind off Ruby as he walked back to his cell. He felt if he didn't get his mind off her quick, he might go crazy. Touching her for only a few minutes and then having to walk away, back into the grey hall with the grey men, gave him the worst feeling he'd had since he arrived in prison.

Mostly, in his days of imprisonment, Charley just felt dull. For a week or two at a stretch, he would feel almost nothing; he just let the time tick away, doing no more than was necessary, feeling no more than was necessary. Sometimes he thought he had stopped being a human and had become a vegetable—his fingernails grew, and his hair grew, but nothing else happened within him. He waited, like a root, for the time when he would have a chance to see light, and live again.

But Ruby had been in his arms; he had kissed her, and he could still smell her powder. All the life they could still have together was there in her touch, in her eyes, in the feel of her arms. Walking away from Ruby was so hard it made Charley shudder. For a terrible minute or two, he thought he might crack—plenty of cons did crack, on visitors' day. Charley wanted to turn and strangle the guard, although he knew it would just get him shot. He kept clenching and unclenching his fists as he walked. He wanted to kick something, slug somebody, let life surge up in him again. The few moments with Ruby had reminded him that he was human, a man—he wasn't a potato. He wanted his wife.

He didn't crack, though—not quite. His cellmate, Jerry Jennings, a Texan who had robbed a train and then had the misfortune to fall off it and break his hip, sat on his bunk, smoking. Jerry had been in the pen three years, and had never had a visitor. He was so hungry for gossip about the outside world that he started asking questions before the guard had even locked Charley in.

"Was it your ol' lady? How's she doin'? How's your boy?" Jerry asked. "Did she give you any more pictures?" Charley had his picture of Ruby and Dempsey stuck on the wall right above the head of his bunk.

"She don't have no camera," Charley said. "She's barely gettin' by."

He wished Jerry would shut up so he could grip every moment of Ruby's visit firmly in his memory; though, in a way, keeping such a memory lit up too bright might make his time harder to serve. Part of him wanted to remember; part of him needed to forget. He was still shaky with all the pent-up feeling as it was. He wanted to sock the wall, since he hadn't socked the guard.

"So how's your boy?" Jerry asked, again. Charley talked so much about Ruby and Dempsey that he thought it appropriate to ask.

"She said he misses me," Charley told him. "Dempsey can say 'Mama,' and he knows his colors."

"Oh, Lord, it makes me wish my little girl hadn't drowned," Jerry said. Jerry's year-old daughter had drowned in only two inches of water. She had reached down in a bucket to retrieve her clothespin dolly, fell in, got caught, and was dead when her mama found her a few minutes later—her feet were sticking straight up out of the pail. His wife couldn't stand the grief, and had killed herself right after the funeral.

"They oughta given you some better pants, since it was your ol' lady come to visit you," he added. "If it had just been some floozie, it wouldn't have been so bad."

Charley suddenly put both hands behind him and ripped

what was left of the seat out of his pants. He kept ripping until he tore one pants leg completely off.

"Hold it, don't be goin' berserk!" Jerry Jennings said, alarmed. Charley Floyd had been a placid cellmate, and Jerry wanted it to stay that way.

"I ain't berserk," Charley said, dark. "You'll know it if I go berserk."

Then he threw his pants leg out of the cell.

"I expect that's against the rules," Jerry informed him. "If you ain't careful, they'll come and stuff you in solitary—then I won't have nobody to talk to, and neither will you."

Charley didn't answer. He was hoping some ugly guard would come strolling by, with his mind elsewhere, trip over the pants leg, and break his fat neck.

23

"Help you with your valise, ma'am?" the skinny young man with the funny cowlick asked, smiling. Ruby had noticed him earlier, sipping coffee in the little cafe by the depot. The young man was about her age or a little older, and kept glancing at her as she sipped her coffee—that was what made her notice him in the first place.

Ruby didn't know if it was proper to let a total stranger carry her valise onto the train. On the other hand, there was a line of people waiting to board, so what could happen? And her little suitcase was pretty heavy. She had packed every stitch she owned, even though she knew she would only get to see Charley one time, and could only wear one dress. She had wanted to give herself choices; and, in fact, had tried on all five of her dresses before making up her mind.

"Thank you, I'm Ruby Floyd," she said, offering the young man her hand. That was to make sure he saw her wedding ring —the wedding ring and Dempsey's toys were the only things they had got to keep after Charley's arrest. Ruby had hidden the wedding ring in their corn-shuck mattress—otherwise, the law would have taken it, too.

"I'm Lenny," the young man with the cowlick said. He had a shy grin.

Even so, the fact that she was allowing a stranger to carry her suitcase made Ruby feel nervous. Then it turned out the train was so full, there were only two seats left, right together at the rear of the car. Lenny let her choose, so she took the seat by the window, and he took the seat on the aisle.

"It would be nice if you could make a wish and be home," Lenny said, trying to be friendly. "These bouncy old trains upset my stomach."

"I didn't get your last name," Ruby informed him.

"It's Bachelor, Lenny Bachelor," the young man said. Then he blushed. Ruby had to smile at the name.

"So you're a Bachelor, even if you ain't one," she said. He blushed even redder.

"Yep, right now I'm both," Lenny admitted. "Folks kid me about it so much, I doubt I'll ever marry."

"Aw, you oughtn't to let your name stop you," Ruby said. "Folks would forget about it, if you found a nice wife."

Lenny grinned. "I've looked all over Coffeyville, Kansas, and I ain't found one yet," he told her. "I'm a baker, most of the time I'm covered with flour. I expect that counts against me, too."

"Why would it, flour washes off. I'm covered with it, too, when I make biscuits," Ruby said.

She relaxed a little. Lenny Bachelor was easy to talk to, for a stranger. Pretty soon, she relaxed a little more. The rocking of the train as it rolled south through the Missouri hills helped her relax. It had been a strain, going to see Charley. If she ever got home, she felt like she could sleep for a week; though, of course, Dempsey would never put up with her sleeping for a week.

86

She yawned a time or two, and the next thing she knew, the train was screeching to a stop, somewhere in Kansas. Now it was her turn to blush—to her deep embarrassment, Ruby realized she had slumped over against Lenny, and slept with her head on his shoulder.

Apparently, this embarrassed Lenny too, because he blushed again when Ruby woke up and looked at him.

"Guess you were plumb tuckered out," he said, shyly. He had enjoyed having the pretty young woman's head on his shoulder, even though it might look bad to her. He knew she would be shocked when she woke up.

"Why'd we stop?" Ruby asked, looking out the window trying to hide her embarrassment. "I don't see no town."

"Cattle," Lenny told her. "I guess the cowboys had trouble getting them across the train track in time."

Ruby saw that, indeed, a herd of scrawny cattle were meandering across the tracks, up ahead. Several cowboys were waving ropes at them and yelling, but the cattle didn't seem to be in any hurry.

When Lenny Bachelor got off the train in Coffeyville, Ruby thanked him for helping with her valise, and she let him shake her hand again.

"I'm sorry I used your shoulder for a pillow," she said.

"Aw, forget it," Lenny said, blushing again.

Later, as the train chugged on toward Oklahoma, Ruby began to feel real lonely. She wished Lenny Bachelor had been going a little farther. He was nice, even if he did blush a lot, and having someone to talk to kept her mind off Charley.

Ruby stared out at the endless plain. The prairie grass was waving; there was a high wind that day.

Charley still had four whole years to serve. Ruby didn't know how she would stand it.

24

Jody Turpentine, a big dumb lout from Joplin, Missouri, was the name of the guard Charley finally slugged.

"I never heard of nobody bein' named Turpentine," Charley said to Jerry Jennings, the day he found out Jody's name.

"I never either, but it's his name all right," Jerry said. "Don't go joshin' him about it, he's touchy."

"Aw, he's a big ugly screw," Charley said. "I'll josh him if I feel like it."

"It's your noggin he'll crack open," Jerry said, shrugging.

Jody Turpentine liked to pretend he played the drums. He didn't have a drum, but he had a nightstick, and he liked to drum on the bars when he woke up the cons every morning. If he had it in for a certain con, he would stand in front of his cell and drum for ten minutes sometimes.

One of the stiffs Jody had it in for was Charley Floyd. He claimed not to care for Okies in general, which may have been true. But what was certainly true was that he didn't like Charley. Each morning, just when Charley was hoping for five more minutes' sleep, Jody would stand outside his cell, drumming on the bars with his nightstick. His drumming wasn't musical, either—it wasn't anything but noise.

"I'm gettin' my fill of that fat turd," Charley told Jerry several times. "One of these mornings I'm gonna yank that toothpick out of his hands and drum on *him* for a while."

"I'd think over that plan, if I were you, bud," Jerry told him. "They'll stick you so far down in the hole, you won't see daylight again till Groundhog Day."

"It might be worth it," Charley said. "He oughta leave us alone."

"On the other hand, he's got the club, and you ain't," Jerry pointed out. "You'll get out of here sooner than later, if you just ride your own beef."

"Ride my what?" Charley asked. He had never heard the phrase before.

"Just do your time," Jerry explained. "You start beatin' up guards, and it'll be that much longer before you get to see Ruby and your boy."

But the very next morning, Charley was seeing his wife and baby in a beautiful, happy dream: He was trying to teach Dempsey how to pitch horseshoes, even though Dempsey was so small he could barely lift one; Ruby was holding a horseshoe in both hands, waiting her turn. Charley could even see that her long, bare legs—long enough that Ruby could lock them tight around him when they made love—had a chigger bite or two, just above one of her ankles. Ruby hated shoes, and she was always barefoot, though she knew the grass was full of chiggers.

In the dream, Dempsey and the horseshoes faded out, and he and Ruby were walking down the path toward the creek, holding hands. Just off the path was a little patch of grass. If the dream had lasted even another few seconds, Ruby would have had her long legs locked around him.

But before they reached the patch of grass that had often been their little bit of Eden, Jody Turpentine planted himself in front of Charley's cell, and began to drum on the bars with his nightstick.

"Don't you ever wake up on time, Okie?" Jody asked.

Charley got his eyes open wide enough to see that Jody was standing there—scratching his balls with one hand, and woggling the nightstick with the other, making as much racket as he could, for no better reason than he liked to make a racket and interrupt sweet dreams.

"I'm awake," Charley said.

"Yeah, but you ain't up," Jody replied. "Hustle."

When Jody unlocked the cell, Charley waited until Jerry was out and gone down the walkway before coming out himself. Jerry had only a few months left to serve, and Charley didn't want to involve him in any trouble. Jerry was an older man and moderate, but he didn't like Jody either, and there was no predicting what he might do when the fight started.

Jody had reached in his pocket for a fresh tobacco chaw,

when Charley hit him, flush on the point of his jaw. Jody went down so hard he slid across the floor, and split his head open on the bars of a cell ten feet away.

"I told you to leave me be, you son-of-a-bitch," Charley muttered, his teeth clenched as tight as his fists. Jody Turpentine was unconscious, and didn't hear.

Four or five guards came running. They whacked Charley around pretty good, while the cons who had been shuffling off to breakfast stood and watched. Charley didn't really feel the whacking, although he was sore from it for two or three days of the week he spent in solitary confinement. At some point, Jody Turpentine came down and drummed on the iron door of Charley's cell until his arm wore out. Then he yelled a few insults, pissed on the door, and went away. The fact that he pissed on the door didn't matter much, since the whole cell smelled like an outhouse anyway.

Charley's week in solitary was kind of restful; he slept most of the time. Often, he had difficulty sleeping soundly in his own cell, because Jerry Jennings snored with the force of a locomotive most of the time. Night after night, Charley would crawl down and roll Jerry on his stomach, the only position that cut the snoring. Charley would usually get sound to sleep about dawn, a few minutes before Jody started drumming on the cell.

In the hole, Charley could think about Ruby and Dempsey all he wanted, without having to make conversation with Jerry Jennings or anyone else. It wasn't only Ruby and Dempsey he thought of, either. Beulah Baird was much in his thoughts—he had been hoping Beulah would show up on visitors' day, though another thing he was hoping was that she and Ruby wouldn't show up on the *same* visitors' day—or Beulah and Ma Ash, either. It had been a near miss with those two, that day in City Jail, too near a miss. Charley decided he would rather take a whacking from a few screws anytime than have Ruby and Beulah, or Beulah and Ma Ash, or any two women show up on the same visitors' day. What if Ma Ash and his own mother showed up on the same day? He'd never be able to go back to Sallisaw, if something like that happened.

When Charley got out of solitary, he discovered that slugging

90

Jody Turpentine had earned him the respect of cons who had never so much as looked at him before.

"The better people are getting to like you, Charley," Jerry said.

"What better people?" Charley asked. "There's nobody in here but crooks."

"Yeah, but there's crooks that know what they're doin', and crooks that don't know, and never will," Jerry told him. "I'm the second kind. I doubt I could stay out of the pen a year if my life depended on it."

Charley had noticed that Jerry didn't seem to particularly mind being in jail.

"Say, do you like it here, bud?" he asked his cellmate.

"Naw, but I don't care much for the outside, either," Jerry confided.

"Why not?" Charley asked.

"Too many decisions," Jerry said. "I pile up all them responsibilities, and the next thing you know, I get confused, and go do something like rob the store that's right next to the sheriff's office."

"I thought you robbed trains," Charley said.

"I tried, but it's tricky," Jerry confessed. "I wasn't expecting the engineer to hit the brakes so sudden like. That's how come me to fall off and break my hip."

"You should have waited till it was stopped for the mail or something," Charley advised. "Then you could have slipped right on and robbed it with no risk of falling off."

"That's how a smart crook would have done it," Jerry said, wistful. "What I'm trying to tell you is that I ain't a smart crook. I'm what they call mediocre.

"There's plenty of smart crooks here in Jeff City, though," he added.

Charley liked Jerry, and found it sad that he had already resigned himself to being a dumb crook—Jerry would be spending most of his life in a cell in Jeff City, or in another pen in another state. After all, Jerry was only thirty-five. It seemed to Charley that he could improve his technique if he tried.

"You ain't old," he pointed out. "You probably just need to think about a safer type of robbery."

"Well, I've robbed a little bit of everything, and I've always got caught," Jerry said. "I just ain't got the knack." He was beginning to feel forlorn from thinking too much about his own incompetence.

"Applesauce," Charley said, though maybe it wasn't. Maybe Jerry did prefer to be in jail, which was his business, if it was true.

"What makes you think there's so many smart crooks in here?" he asked. If crooks were smart, it seemed to him, they'd still be on the outside.

"Why, there just is," Jerry insisted. "There's old boys in here who've robbed the biggest banks in Missouri. There's two or three that have got away with at least fifty thousand dollars."

Charley found that impressive. It occurred to him that since he had to be in jail anyway, he might as well be learning something.

"Point a few of them big-timers out to me, would you?" he asked Jerry.

"You bet, Charley," Jerry said. "They got their eyes on you already. They know you're sharp."

"Applesauce," Charley said, again. But he was flattered anyway.

25

For nearly a year after her visit to Charley in the Missouri State Pen, Ruby hoped that somehow she would be able to scrape up another seven dollars so she would be able to go see him again. That spring, though, it rained for thirty days and ruined the wheat farmers. Then it stopped raining, and by August the drought was so fierce that it ruined everyone else. No-body could afford to send out their laundry. Ruby traipsed around to every store in Sallisaw trying to find work, but there was no work. She filled in two days a week at the five-and-dime, but the pay was fifty cents a day. By fall, she had given up on ever getting to visit Charley again—seven dollars was more than she was ever going to be able to accumulate. Dempsey got the whooping cough, and his medicine ate up the few dollars she had managed to save. Her parents couldn't help her; the cotton failed, and they faced a bleak winter themselves. Her brothers set traps, and occasionally caught a possum. That, and corn mush and greens, was about all they had to eat. If they did happen to have possum, they always invited Ruby and Demp-sey, though. What little they had, they shared, and the same was true of Bradley and Bessie Floyd. They had managed to keep a little garden going with water from their cistern. Ruby and Dempsey ate with them two or three times a week, regular.

The winter was a low point. Their little two-room house was drafty; Dempsey caught cold after cold. His throat would get so sore he couldn't swallow. Ruby would have to warm milk for him until it got a little better. The doc said he needed his tonsils out, which would have to be done in a big hospital in Tulsa. There was no money for that. Some nights, with the wind howl-ing through the house and Dempsey coughing or burning with fever, Ruby would lie in bed, sleepless, wishing she wasn't alive. Life was just misery and struggle, and more misery and more struggle, so far as she could see. She'd had few letters from Charley, and she didn't know if he even still remembered them —she had only seen him for an hour in almost three years. She tried to remind herself that she and Charley were still married, and that someday he would be a free man and they could be together again, and things would be swell. But in the cold nights, with Dempsey sick and coughing, Ruby stopped being able to believe that things would ever be swell—not for her, not again. She even had to beg a little cough medicine from the druggist; she had no money to pay for it.

Her memories of Charley and their happiness together had faded so badly that she could no longer use them to cheer her-self up. Ruby had used those memories so much that she had worn them out. They weakened and dimmed; occasionally, one would mix for a moment in a dream. But in the daytime, as she struggled to make some sort of life for her little boy, the good times she once had with Charley came to seem unreal. Charley might never be back, and if he did return, he might be somebody she would no longer know, or no longer want. Sometimes, she could still feel angry: for a selfish whim, because he wanted a fancy suit and a big car, Charley had doomed her and Dempsey to a life of loneliness and want. He hadn't considered them, and he didn't deserve them.

In the two years since their train ride together, Lenny Bachelor, the baker from Coffeyville, Kansas, had come to visit her three times. Each visit had been prefaced by several polite letters. Lenny had an aunt in Sallisaw, and stayed with her on his visits. The best part of Lenny's visits was that he was sweet to Dempsey. He loved Dempsey, and Dempsey took to him right away. Lenny always brought a box of doughnuts from the bakery, and some kind of little present for Dempsey besides.

On the third visit, something happened that Ruby couldn't undo, and she started it, not Lenny. She was just plain tired of doing without, of having no one to hold her, and no one to touch. He had gentle blue eyes, and a shy grin—he wasn't all that shy, though, once he got started.

"I'm sure 'nough in love," Lenny told her at the end of that visit, as he was about to leave. "I wish you was free, so we could marry."

"Would you marry me, bad as I am?" Ruby asked, feeling guilty. It was easy to like Lenny.

"Aw, Ruby, you know I would," Lenny said. He had tears in his eyes when he left.

Ruby wouldn't let him even kiss her on the train platform, though. She didn't want talk. Besides, Dempsey was with them. He hated to see Lenny go, and hung onto his leg until the last minute.

That night, Ruby expected her conscience would hurt, but it didn't. She was alone, and it was nobody's fault but Charley's. She had to do the best she could, and she already knew Lenny Bachelor well enough to be sure he was a good man. She could have walked into any feed store in Oklahoma and done a whole lot worse. Besides, he had a steady job, and he was generous with what little he had. She wouldn't have to be begging cough medicine if she was with him. Maybe he could even scrape up the money for the tonsil operation; the one time Ruby mentioned it to him, he had immediately offered to help, though eight dollars was all he had to spare at the time.

For a few days, Ruby wavered. She remembered how sad Charley had looked in the prison visiting room, trying to hold his ripped pants together so he would look decent for his wife. For all she knew, he still thought of her every night. It might be that having her and Dempsey to think about was all that was getting him through; Charley had told her that, in the few minutes they'd had to hug. In the letters she'd got, he had sent his love to Dempsey, and mentioned that he dreamed about them both sometimes.

But that didn't solve the problem of the cough medicine, or the struggle to scrape up food, or the loneliness that was making her feel like an old woman, although she was barely twenty-one. She remembered, too, that when she walked out of the Jeff City pen, she was so full of despair she didn't know how she would make it without Charley.

Bessie Floyd loved her sister-in-law, and sympathized with her struggle. Bradley, her husband, wasn't quite as wild as his brother or his father, but he was wild enough. Bradley's weakness was moonshine. He was sweet when he was sober, but once he siphoned a little corn whiskey into him, he'd pick a fight with anybody, and usually ended up the loser. He had his portion of the Floyd temper—sometimes, when Bradley had been gone for a day or two, laying up somewhere with his jug, Bessie wondered why she had ever married into the Floyds in the first place. She knew Ruby Floyd was probably wondering the same thing—she hadn't even laid eyes on Charley for two years.

So it was no big surprise to Bessie when Ruby walked in one day with a guilty look in her eye. Bessie was not a judge. Folks had to get by, and getting by wasn't always as simple as the Bible said it should be.

"I done something bad with Lenny," Ruby said. "Now I'm in a pickle."

"Does that mean you're pregnant?" Bessie asked.

"No, not yet," Ruby said. "But I'm thinking I may leave Charley."

Bessie had not met the young baker from Coffeyville. Ruby hadn't wanted to insult Charley's family; she had been discreet. All she knew was that Ruby was agitated.

"Charley would kill me if he knew I was even thinkin' about this," Ruby said.

"Honey, stop looking that way," Bessie said. "Charley didn't never mean bad for you and Dempsey—if I run over the dog with the flivver, even if I don't mean to, and even if I love the dog, the dog's still dead. Charley left you in a hard spot, whether he meant to or not. You got a child to think of."

"What if Charley still wants me when he gets out?" Ruby asked. She trusted Bessie's judgment. Bessie was solid.

"I don't know what if," Bessie said. "A person can what-if themselves to death. Grown-up life's largely guesswork, anyway."

Ruby wandered around the kitchen, still agitated.

"Do you love this fella?" Bessie asked.

Ruby picked up the coffeepot; she looked like she needed to throw something. Bessie hoped she wouldn't throw the coffeepot—it was already dented, from a time she had thrown it herself.

"He's likeable," Ruby said, finally. "He's real, real likeable."

"Anything can grow," Bessie said, waiting.

Ruby put the coffeepot back on the stove.

"Anything can shrink, too," Bessie reminded her, after a moment. "Bradley and me have kind of shrunk ourselves a little bit."

"Has he been drinkin' too much again?" Ruby asked.

"Enough, but it ain't that," Bessie told her. "I don't know that it's any one thing, especially. It just feels kinda shrunk."

"Will you hate me if I marry Lenny?" Ruby asked. "I got to make a move. I got to, Bessie. I can't stand no more of this. It ain't good for Dempsey, me bein' so blue all the time."

"I won't never hate you, Ruby," Bessie said. "We been through too much together. We're both married to Floyds, that's enough right there."

"I sure hate to leave you and Bradley, though," Ruby admitted. "You've been a big help to me and Dempsey, my own folks are too hard up to do much."

Bessie walked over, and gave Ruby a hug. She was a skinny girl; Bessie could feel her thin body shaking.

"Life ain't for sissies," Bessie said.

"Aw, Bessie, I don't know anything about life," Ruby said. "I don't know who it's for. I just know I got to do better than I'm doing. I think it would be better for Dempsey."

"You gonna divorce Charley, then?" Bessie asked.

Ruby wasn't sure whether she still loved Charley—or if it was just the *memory* of Charley that she loved. It had been so long since she'd seen him that he had become kind of like a ghost.

But she and Dempsey had to live; she couldn't think about Charley now.

"If I decide to marry Lenny, I guess I'll have to," Ruby said.

26

Big Carl Bevo was treated special from the moment he entered the Jeff City pen. The first time Charley happened to walk past his cell on the way to a meal, Big Carl was sitting on his bunk, eating a steak and reading a newspaper. Two guards were bowing and scraping while he ate, asking him every minute or two if he needed anything.

"What's he done that he gets to eat steak in his cell?" Charley asked Jerry.

"That's Big Carl Bevo," Jerry said. "I expect they'd let him have more than steak, if he wanted it."

"Like what?" Charley inquired.

"Like a whore," Jerry said. "Or maybe two whores."

"What's he done that he's so special?" Charley asked. "I don't see nobody else eatin' steak around this jailhouse. I doubt even the warden gets anything that tasty."

"Well, Big Carl's a lot more important than the warden," Jerry said. "I expect the warden would trot down here and shine his shoes, if Big Carl asked him to."

"Shit in a bucket," Charley said, impressed. "What'd he do?"

"He's kilt three people with his bare hands, for one thing," Jerry said. "Besides that, he pulled the biggest job ever pulled in Missouri."

"How big, and what kind of job?" Charley asked.

"The First National Bank of K.C., that's how big," Jerry informed him. "Ninety-two thousand dollars, and they still ain't found the money. Of course if he hangs, it won't do him no good, but if he can buy his way around a hangin', he can afford all the steaks he can eat."

For the next few days, Charley watched Big Carl Bevo whenever he got the chance.

"I don't think I'd care to associate with him," Charley said. "He's got eyes like a fish."

"He's kilt three people with his bare hands," Jerry reminded him. "If he speaks to you, be polite."

"Why would he speak to me?" Charley asked. "I ain't no big-time crook."

"You never know," Jerry said. "Big Carl hears everything."

"So what?" Charley said. "What would there be to hear about me?"

But to his surprise, that very afternoon, Big Carl stopped him as he was on his way to the mess hall.

"Hey, Choctaw," Big Carl said. "Hold up a minute."

"Me?" Charley said, startled.

"You're the only Choctaw I see," Big Carl said.

"I ain't a Choctaw," Charley said, a little offended. "My name's Charles Arthur Floyd."

"You look like a Choctaw boy to me," Big Carl informed him. "You got some squaw blood in you, I guess. Come on in here a minute."

Charley didn't like being told what to do, not by Big Carl or anybody else.

98

"If I don't go eat, I'll miss the grub," he said.

Big Carl turned his cold fish eyes on Charley.

"Worse things could happen than missin' that slop," he said.

"Yeah, like what?" Charley asked. He was beginning to see red, and he didn't care how many men the old fish-eyed crook had killed with his bare hands.

"Like me having a couple of screws beat the shit out of you before they throw you back in the hole," Big Carl said, waving to the two guards whose job, so far as Charley could tell, was to see that no one annoyed the famous convict.

The two guards slapped Charley around for ten minutes or so, while Big Carl studied a racing form. Charley didn't make a sound the whole time. Big Carl didn't look up when they hustled Charley off to solitary.

After they were gone, he put the paper down, and thought about the green kid Lulu Ash had asked him to keep an eye on. He sure was a stubborn little prick—he could see why Lulu had taken a liking to him. He knew the kid had been watching him, too. Charley Floyd might be green, but he was tough, and kept his mouth shut. The kid had a short fuse, though—if he didn't learn to get a grip, that short fuse would blow up in his face.

In fact, the kid reminded Big Carl of himself, when he was young.

Twenty-four hours later, the same two guards yanked Charley out and hustled him back up to Big Carl's cell. Big Carl was still studying the racing form.

"Hi, Choctaw," Big Carl said. "Are you in a better mood today?"

"No, and you can go to hell," Charley said.

The guards were about to start whacking him again, but Big Carl waved them off.

"You're a pretty tough kid," he said to Charley. "I'm beginning to see why Lulu likes you."

That was another surprise.

"Lulu who?" Charley asked.

"Lulu, the lulu," Big Carl said. "The dame that'll come up to you and grab you by the pecker when you least expect it.

"Does that ring any bells?" he added, when Charley didn't answer.

"Why would it be any of your business if it did?" Charley asked.

Big Carl shook his head. "Aw, scram," he said. "Lulu asked me to look after you, but you're so damn bullheaded I don't know if I can put up with your lip."

"She shouldn't have bothered," Charley said.

"I'll second that," Big Carl said. "You're a Choctaw boy with bad manners. Go eat slop, if you can't be nothing but rude."

"You had me beat up, remember?" Charley reminded him.

"Beat up?" Big Carl said. "Son, that was just practice. If I'd had you beat up, you wouldn't be standing here yappin'."

"That don't mean I liked it," Charley said.

"Lulu's got a soft spot for you," Big Carl said. "She told me to school you a little. Lulu's an old friend. I wouldn't like to see her get hurt by some rude Choctaw boy—get me?" Big Carl said, sharply.

"How could I hurt Ma Ash?" Charley asked. "I'm in the pen."

"You'll be out one of these days, though," Big Carl said. "You might two-time her or somethin'. You wouldn't know it, but she's got a pretty big soft spot."

"I'm married," Charley informed him. "I doubt I'll ever see Ma Ash again."

Big Carl shook his head again. "I'm gettin' disgusted with this line of blab," he said.

He didn't say any more. Charley strolled on down and got in the mess line. He hadn't had a bite while he was in the hole, not even water.

When Jerry Jennings saw Charley at the back of the chow line, he dropped back to wait with him.

"What happened to you?" he asked. "I thought you'd escaped."

"Big Carl had me beat up," Charley said.

"Uh-oh," Jerry said. He turned white.

"Why?" Jerry asked, when he got over the shock.

"Don't ask me." Charley shrugged. "I'm too hungry to think about it right now."

100

27

Dear Charley,

I never thought the day would come when I'd be askin' you for a divorce. But I guess it's silly to think you know how life's gonna be, because you don't.

Dempsey and me are livin' on charity now, a little from Brad and Bessie, and less from my folks. I been goin' it alone ever since they took you off, and I guess I just ain't strong enough to go it alone no more. It ain't fair to Charles Dempsey, for his Pa to be gone and his Ma to have to work so hard just to make ends meet.

I need to divorce you, Charley. And there's somethin' else. I've met a man here. He loves me, and he's sweet to Charles Dempsey. He takes him fishin'. He even bought him one of them little baseball gloves.

He wants to marry me, Charley. I expect I'll marry him, once the divorce goes through. I guess we'll move to Kansas. He ain't you, but Ma says it ain't common to find a man who'll be good to another man's child.

Here's a little piece of coloring Dempsey did with his crayolas. Don't forget him, he's a fine little fellow.

I'll always love you, Charley.

I expect this is about the best I can do.

Love,
Ruby

Charley didn't like what he was reading in the letter—Jerry couldn't help but notice. He took a long time to read it; right away his face began to sag. Then his whole body seemed to sag. At one point, he let a page or two drop out of his hand, and was a long time picking them up.

When Charley had read the letter a few times, he folded it carefully and put it under his pillow. Then he sat on the edge of the bunk for quite a while, just staring.

"Bad news?" Jerry asked, finally. He could stand only so much silence, especially the heavy kind that filled the cell when Charley Floyd got morose.

"Mind your own business," Charley said. He seemed to barely have enough energy to speak the four words.

Jerry knew he ought to shut up, but he was too anxious.

"I hope your ma didn't pass away," he ventured. Jerry remembered the day Charley had gotten the letter telling him his pa had been shot dead on the main street in Sallisaw. Old Man Floyd had gotten in a dispute with a man at the hardware store over some lumber he had taken from Floyd's cotton gin. Old Man Floyd walked out of the store in a high temper, and the man followed him out and killed him with a rifle, on the spot. The jury acquitted the killer, too; evidently, they felt he had good reason to be afraid of Old Man Floyd.

Charley cried a little about his father, but mostly he got mad. He told Jerry several times that once he got out, he meant to take revenge on his pa's murderer. Jerry had no doubt that he meant it, too. Charley was not a man to make idle threats.

But his reaction to this letter was worse. The news, whatever it was, seemed to take the life right out of him. He sat on the edge of his bunk for an hour or more, blank, no expression in his face at all.

Jerry tried hard not to chatter; he was aware that his chatter irritated Charley at times. But the weight of sadness in the cell became too much to bear.

"Your boy ain't sick, is he?" Jerry asked. "He didn't drown, like my little girl, did he?"

"He didn't drown," Charley said, finally. "He's movin' to Kansas."

"Well, Kansas is a good state," Jerry said. "They've got that big pen up at Leavenworth. It's a federal pen."

Charley was thinking about Ruby—her smile, and her dark hair, and her long legs. He remembered once when they were courting, and they had set off for a camp meeting. Ruby's pa had even loaned them the wagon, because it was preaching they were going to hear. They didn't make it to the preaching, though. They stopped the mule about a mile from the camp meeting, close enough that they could see the lights from the tent and hear the hymns. Now and then, they could even hear the preacher, yelling out his sermon. But he and Ruby weren't in the mood for preaching; they took their clothes off, used them for a pallet, and made love during the whole camp meeting. They were still doing it when the lights went off in the tent. They were like alley cats that night, yowling and scratching. The wagon rocked so, that the old mule swished his tail and flicked his ears.

Wagons began to pass near them as the worshipers headed home across the prairie, and Ruby got worried that somebody would see them naked, or figure out what they were doing. But they rested for a while, hunkered down in the wagon, until all the folks were gone. Then, with only the moon to see them, they made love until nearly morning. Charley could still remember how cool the plains breeze felt, on his and Ruby's sweaty bodies.

The next day, he fell asleep plowing and let the furrow go crooked. His father yelled at him when he saw the furrow.

That camp meeting evening seemed like a long time ago. It felt like something that could only have happened in another life. Many a time in his cell, Charley had thought about Ruby in the wagon.

That was happiness.

Now she was leaving him, taking Dempsey, and marrying another man. He didn't blame her; he had left her alone for nearly four years, with no money and no support. But Ruby was still his one true love.

There was no use supposing he would ever be that happy again.

28

"Another ten years, and the Feds will have guns," Big Carl said, cutting his steak. "When that happens, crooks like us won't have a chance.

"You'll live to see it, but I won't," he added—needlessly, Charley thought. Big Carl was due to swing at dawn. He hadn't been able to buy off anybody high up enough to issue one more appeal.

Now he was eating his last rare steak, washing it down with straight gin. He had offered to order up a steak for Charley, too, and any other time he would have jumped at the chance for a good piece of beef. This particular evening, though, he couldn't muster much appetite.

Big Carl was all right, Charley thought, once you got to know him. He had taught Charley a lot about how the rackets worked, and he had instructed him about how to approach a bank if he had robbing it in mind.

"Don't believe everything you read in the papers," Big Carl had told him. "Not all crooks are yellow, and crime *does* pay— you just gotta stay smart."

He stopped, and lit a big cigar. The two guards rushed over, trying to light it for him—he waved them off, annoyed.

"Always case the joint first. You gotta know if there's a guard inside, and how many suits work in the back," he told Charley. "You gotta look sharp when you're robbin' a bank. You wanna look like all the money in there belongs to you, like you got the right to take it. Wear the best suit you can buy, don't go in looking like a mug.

"Be sure to take a hostage or two, and don't rough anybody up, if you can help it," he said, between puffs on the smelly cigar. "You can let 'em go, once you're home free."

Charley listened to Big Carl, more out of respect than a need to understand what he was talking about. Once he got out of the pen, Charley had no intention of ever going back. Robbing banks wasn't exactly the profession he had in mind for himself, once he was free.

Big Carl kept puffing and kept talking.

"You gotta know your partner better than your gal. Don't ever run with anybody who isn't a stand-up guy."

Big Carl finished his cigar and sat up, his hands on his knees. He looked Charley hard in the eye.

"Listen and listen good. Choler is why I'll be swingin' from the end of a rope—my bad temper's bought me nothin' but trouble," Big Carl told him. "If I taught you anything while you're in here, it's to keep a cool head—don't let nobody make a sucker out of you. The biggest suckers are the ones who go off half-cocked, they make the worst mistakes."

Now Big Carl had only a few hours to live, a fact which bothered Charley more than it seemed to bother Big Carl. While he ate his steak, he studied the racing form.

"I'll miss the horses," he admitted, looking thoughtful for a moment. "They're pretty, horses. I could watch a horse race any day.

"I hope you'll tell Lulu I done my best to school you," Big Carl said, a little later. "Lulu's a good gal. She used to be an A-number-one crook, too."

"Is that right?" Charley asked. "Did she ever kill anybody?"

Big Carl chuckled.

"That's between me and Lulu, son," he said. "She had an eye for business, that's for sure. Lulu could have been richer than Rockefeller, if she'd put her mind to it."

"Why didn't she put her mind to it?" Charley asked. He was becoming more and more curious about Ma Ash.

Big Carl chuckled again. "Money don't interest her as much as peckers do," he said. "She likes to run boarding houses."

"I'd rather be rich as Rockefeller, myself," Charley said.

"You ain't Lulu, though," Big Carl reminded him. "There's a reason she likes to run boarding houses—that way, there'll always be a pecker or two around to grab if she feels like it.

"I'd have been richer myself, if I hadn't liked the horses so much," he added, as he ate the last bite of steak.

When the guard came to get Charley, Big Carl Bevo scarcely looked up. The last Charley saw of him, he was still studying the racing form.

29

Charley walked up to the diner and then stopped. It was just a dirty little cafe by the side of the highway, but he was afraid to go in. He hadn't seen anyone but cons for nearly four years. He'd gotten out early for good behavior, but he was afraid he might have forgotten how to talk to normal people. He knew he must look like a criminal, in his ugly prison suit. Folks would take one look at his suit, and his prison haircut, and know exactly where he'd been for the last few years.

He was hungry, though, not to mention nervous. He thought a cup of coffee might settle his nerves. A cup of coffee was about all he could afford. They'd only given him ten dollars when they let him out. He was a far piece from home, and would have to walk it, more than likely. He had to make his money last.

"How do you like your java?" the counterman said, when Charley finally worked up his nerve to go in and take a seat.

"Black," Charley said. He was sure the counterman knew he had just got out of jail.

As he was sipping his coffee, trying to make it last, a big, elderly trucker with a moon face and scraggly grey hair came in and sat down right next to him at the counter. The trucker gave Charley a friendly look.

"Howdy," he said. "How long you been out, son?"

" 'Bout three hours," Charley said, keeping his voice low.

"It shows, huh?" he added.

"Sure does. You look like you been livin' in a closet," the trucker replied. "So what? A few days out in the weather, and you'll be as good as new."

The trucker slapped the counter with a big hand.

"How about a little service here?" he said.

The counterman was in the kitchen, but a skinny little waitress hurried over, pulling a pencil from behind her ear.

"You're a loud bastard—what'll it be?" she said.

"Coffee, ham, two eggs sunny side up, plenty of biscuits, and no cussin'," the trucker said. "The same for my friend here."

"You payin'? I know he ain't good for it," the waitress said.

"Hell yes, I'm payin'," the trucker told her.

He slapped Charley on the back, much as he had just slapped the counter.

"You need somethin' to stick to your ribs," he said. "Where's your home, son?"

"Sallisaw," Charley replied.

"Say, down in the Oklahoma hills?" the trucker asked. "You're in luck. That's the way I'm headin'."

The skinny waitress brought their coffee. After a cup, Charley began to feel a little better. When the food came, he felt better still.

"Eat up now, I don't like to lag," the trucker said.

Charley ate up, while the trucker talked.

It rained all afternoon, while the truck roared on south through Missouri. Charley sat hunched against the door, saying very little. Once they got into Oklahoma, he began to get the scared feeling he'd had outside the diner—the feeling that he was branded as no-good. He began to wish he could live in the truck forever, going on down the road. At home, everybody knew he was a jailbird. He'd be lucky if his own family wanted to take him in, or even see him.

"I was never in the pen," the trucker said. He could see plain enough that the boy was gloomy.

"I been in jail plenty of times, though," he added.

"What was your crime?" Charley asked, looking out the window.

"Bustin' heads," the trucker said. "Most of them needed

bustin', too. I hit one ol' boy so hard he didn't wake up for three days. If the ol' fart had died on me, I guess I'd been bound for the pen, too. But he finally woke up. Then he cheated with a married gal, and her husband shot him. Kilt him dead.

"The stupid son-of-a-bitch never had no sense," he added. "I 'spect he's about as well off dead."

"I doubt he'd see it that way," Charley said.

It was after dark when they approached Sallisaw. Charley wasn't feeling any better. He kept picturing people staring at him on the street—of course, it was dark, and there wouldn't be many people on the street. But the no-good feeling wouldn't leave him.

"You got family in Sallisaw, son?" the trucker asked.

"My ma," Charley said. "And my brothers and sisters."

"Got a wife?" the trucker asked. "I bet it would sure feel good gettin' home to a wife, after bein' in the pen a spell."

Charley didn't answer; not that he disagreed with what the old trucker said. If he still had Ruby to get home to, he wouldn't be feeling so bad.

But Ruby and Dempsey were gone, and the closer the truck got to Sallisaw, the worse Charley felt.

When the trucker slowed down, right in front of Pear's Department Store, Charley was feeling so bad that he thought he might throw up. He realized he wasn't ready to come home—he started to open the door of the truck, but he stopped.

The trucker, whose name was Sam Campbell, saw that the boy wasn't happy to be home. He didn't say anything. Sallisaw was the boy's home; if he didn't feel like getting out, that was his business.

Charley felt so confused that his head began to throb. He wanted to see his ma. He wanted to see Bradley. He would have liked to sit out by the barn with Brad and have a few bottles of Choctaw beer.

But he felt low as a worm—he felt like dirt. He was home, but he didn't feel he had any right to be there. Ruby was gone, and Ruby was right. He didn't deserve a wife; he didn't even deserve a family.

"I've heard there's work down around Seminole, in the oil fields," he said, finally. "You think I could get on?"

108

"A big strappin' boy like you? You bet you could get on," Sam Campbell said. "But what about your folks? I thought you wanted to see them."

"Not today, I guess," Charley said, sitting back. "Better to come home with money in my pocket. I'd rather just ride on down to Seminole, if that's okay with you."

"That's fine, son," Sam said.

Charley hunkered back down in the seat and stared out the window.

As they drove out of Sallisaw, the rain streaking down the windshield matched the tears that wet Charley's face.

Book Two

1929–1931

1

"Five dollars a week to sleep on the floor with a bunch of goons?" Charley said, stunned. "I don't even get a bed, and you want five dollars a week?"

"That's for inside," the landlady said. "I got two spots left on the porch—they'll be three dollars a week. If you just want to sleep in the yard, it's a dollar a week."

"I'll try the yard," Charley said. "I didn't know lodging was this costly down in Seminole."

"This is a boomtown, mister," the landlady said. "I got to make hay while the sun shines. Once this oil plays out, you can rent the whole town for five dollars a week."

"When *does* the sun shine here, ma'am?" Charley asked. "It sure ain't shined since I got here, and I been here all day."

"We're having a rainy spring," the landlady admitted. "That's what makes the porch such a good investment."

It wasn't raining hard, but it was drizzling. Charley had already spent five of his prison dollars on some work clothes, including a slicker. Then he had to spend two more dollars on some overshoes—the wagons and buggies in the streets of Seminole were up to their hubs in mud.

"If you think that's mud, wait till you get out to the fields," the dry goods salesman said. "This is like a sandy beach compared to the fields. It's muddy enough out there to swallow an ox."

Charley was painfully aware that he was down to three dollars. He didn't relish the prospect of sleeping in the soggy yard, though, even if he did have a slicker.

The landlady hadn't yet unlatched the screen door. She didn't offer to show him the room where he could sleep on the floor for five dollars a week.

"This is a take-it-or-leave-it town, bud," she informed him. "We got a hundred boomers a day showin' up here. If you don't take it, somebody else will."

"I'll try the porch," Charley decided. "Do I have to pay the whole week's rent in advance, or could you trust me for a dollar of it?"

The landlady, Myrtle Bolen, unlatched the screen and stepped outside to take a look at the boy standing on her porch. He was a good-looking boy, though he had a prison haircut and sad eyes.

"I reckon you'd steal, but I doubt you'd cheat," she said. "Gimme two dollars. I'll spot you meals till you get work."

That night, the wind shifted; sheets of rain slashed the porch. Even so, twenty men slept on it, some of them not as lucky as Charley—at least he had his slicker. Thirty or forty men slept in the yard. In the middle of the night, two roughnecks got in a fight—the winner nearly suffocated the loser by pushing his face down in the mud and holding it there. Two men had to scrape out the loser's nose with their pocketknives, while he gasped for breath through his mouth.

All night long, wagons full of roughnecks and pipe slogged through the streets, big lanterns swinging from the back of each. The mule skinners cursed the mules that pulled the wagons. Sometimes a wagon would stick and all the roughnecks would have to jump out, in mud up to their thighs, to try and get the wagon moving again.

Charley slept an hour maybe, but at least, thanks to his slicker, he kept fairly dry. He had to wait for twenty minutes before he could get a place at the breakfast table, though. When he finally got a spot, he was so hungry he ate seven eggs and a dozen biscuits.

Ten minutes later, he got work driving a pipe wagon. The wagon was stuck a block from the boarding house; the driver had evidently had enough. The foreman, who had worked twenty hours straight in the rain, had nodded for a minute on the wagon seat. When he woke up, he didn't have a driver, a fact which put him out of temper.

"Sir, could I catch a ride out to the fields?" Charley asked, mistaking the foreman for the driver.

"Can't you see this goddamn wagon is stuck?" the foreman snapped, irritated.

"It seems to be," Charley said, trying to be polite.

"Can you drive a mule team?" the foreman asked. "I got no use for mules myself, and they generally refuse to obey me."

"You bet I can drive a mule team," Charley said. Of course, he never had driven a mule team, but he had plowed behind Captain Bob.

"If you can drive this one, you not only got a ride, you got a job," the foreman said. "I think that fella who quit was Canadian. I knew I oughtn't to have trusted no foreigner."

Charley was so thrilled at the prospect of work that he jumped right up on the wagon seat and let out a screech he had learned from a Choctaw preacher who lived in a little cabin near the Floyd farm. It was an old war cry of the Indian days—Charley thought it might work on the mules, and it did. They were so startled, their ears all tipped straight up. They lurched against the harness and got the pipe wagon moving again.

"What kind of yellin' was that?" the foreman asked, impressed. He found a whiskey bottle in his coat pocket, and offered Charley a swig.

"Indian yellin'," Charley said. He accepted the swig, and handed the bottle back to the foreman.

"I guess them mules didn't want to be scalped," the foreman said.

2

Whizbang Red worked with two other whores in a tent behind the barbershop. She spotted Charley for a jailbird from his haircut—but Whizbang was feisty, she didn't care.

"I been in a few clinks myself," she said. "What kinda job did you pull?"

"Just a job," Charley said. He liked Whizbang the minute he laid eyes on her. She had bright red curly hair, lots of it, and her skin was the color of sweet milk.

"When's the last time you had a gal?" she asked, once their visit was concluded. "You didn't need a whore, you needed a bucket."

"Aw, applesauce," Charley said. "What's a cute girl like you doin' workin' in a tent behind a barbershop?"

"It beats Alaska," Whizbang told him. "Ever been there?"

"Not yet," Charley said. "What's up there besides bears?"

"The two-legged variety," she said, the corners of her big blue eyes wrinkling with a smile.

"What's your real name?" Charley asked.

"June," Whizbang said. "You're kinda cute, when you smile."

"So are you. I'll be smilin' a lot more now that I've met you," Charley admitted.

"Don't lose your job," Whizbang said. "I might decide I want a bigger tent."

"I'm an expert mule skinner," Charley bragged. "I won't lose my job."

He lost his job that very afternoon.

An old man who had once been a blacksmith in Sallisaw, Curley Miller, happened to be the new foreman at the site where Charley delivered pipe. Charley was helping the crew unload the pipe, trying to keep the mud from squishing down into his overshoes, when Curley Miller spotted him.

"Hey, ain't you Walter Floyd's boy?" Curley asked. "Ain't you up from 'round Sallisaw?"

116

"Yes, sir," Charley replied. Since Curley Miller was home-folk, Charley thought he might be about to get promoted.

"Wasn't you up in the pen somewheres in Missouri?" Curley asked.

Charley was struggling with a length of two-inch pipe—he pretended he didn't hear the question.

"Answer me!" Curley bellowed.

Charley squinted up at the old man. "Yes, sir, but I paid my debt. I'm workin' honest now."

"Not for me you ain't," Curley Miller snarled. "I don't employ no cons. Draw your pay and scat."

Charley was wearing a hard hat to protect his head, in case somebody up on a rig dropped a hammer or a wrench or something. He started to walk off with the hard hat still on his head.

"Hold on," Curley Miller said. "Hat's company property."

Charley took the hard hat off his head and sailed it as far as he could, out into a field of swamp mud.

Then he went and drew his pay, and paid Whizbang a surprise visit.

"I think I'll just call you June," he said. "Whizbang's too much of a mouthful. You oughta give up whizbangin', anyway."

"Give it up? For what?" Whizbang asked, a twinkle in her eye.

"To travel the world with me," Charley told her. "You're too cute to be a tent whore in a boomtown."

"Pays like Christmas, though," Whizbang said. "Another six months, and I can retire."

"Retire to what?" Charley asked.

"Whatever I wanna retire to," she said.

"Where could we go on our travels?" Charley asked. The fact was, he'd gotten tired of Seminole—tired of the drizzle, the mules, the porch, and the oily mud.

"I'm gonna stay here and enjoy Christmas," Whizbang said. "What about Colorado?"

"What's so great about Colorado?" Charley asked.

"Denver's got real nice air," Whizbang remarked.

"Are you a Colorado gal?" Charley asked.

"Nope, I'm from Spokane, Washington," the redhead said.

"I'd enjoy Colorado if you'd come with me," Charley said. "I get blue when I travel alone."

"I get blue when it ain't Christmas," Whizbang informed him. "I doubt you could afford me as a steady thing."

"What if I told you I was the best bank robber in America?" Charley asked.

"What if I told you I was Clara Bow?" Whizbang responded, grinning.

"You got more tongue than you got sense," Charley said. "Stop waggin' it, and let's hit the road."

"Nope, I like my tent just fine," she said. "Go on up to Colorado and rob a few banks. Buy a nice Studebaker and come back through. If you showed up in a slick car, I might hook up with you permanent."

"Last time I bought a Studebaker it didn't work out," Charley admitted. "This time, I think I'll try a Buick."

3

Charley had been in Pueblo, Colorado, long enough to walk three blocks, when a cop pulled up beside him in an old police car that wheezed like a sick bull.

"Where you think you're goin', bud?" the cop asked.

"I just got here," Charley said. "I was on my way to find a hotel."

"Get in," the cop said. "You won't need a hotel. You can stay in jail."

Charley left Seminole with nearly two weeks' wages in his pocket, some of which he had used in Albuquerque to clothe himself properly. He had bought a suit, two shirts, and a necktie, and was wearing the suit, one of the shirts, and the necktie when the bull pulled up beside him. Of course, the suit wasn't as nice or as expensive as the one he'd had made in St. Louis right after the Kroger job, but he did think it made him look respectable.

The Pueblo cop evidently didn't agree.

"Say, is it a crime to walk down the street in this town?" Charley asked. "That's all I'm doin'—walkin' down the street."

"I didn't say you done a crime," the cop said in a dry tone. "I just told you to get in."

"What if I don't want to ride in no police car?" Charley said.

"Get in, son," the cop said. "Consider it an invite.

"The jail and the hotel ain't far apart," he added. "If we decide you're an honest citizen, you can stroll right over and take a room."

"Is it the haircut?" Charley asked, as they were pulling up to the jail.

"What haircut? What about haircuts?" the cop asked. "What's a haircut got to do with anything?"

"It's a prison haircut," Charley announced.

"Son, I ain't interested in your hair," the policeman said. "We don't allow no loiterin' in this town—there's an ordinance against it. That's why I brought you in."

"What the hell's loiterin'?" Charley asked. "I never heard of it. I was just walkin' down the street, lookin' for a hotel and hopin' for a job. Does that amount to loiterin'?"

"You talk too much," the cop said.

Charley left his necktie on for the mug shot. He didn't smile for the jailhouse photographer, though. He didn't want anybody to think he enjoyed being arrested for loitering.

"How are folks supposed to find work if they ain't even allowed to walk down the street?" he asked the sheriff when the sheriff came in.

"No little criminal from Missouri oughta expect to find work in Colorado," the sheriff said. "We'll let you go in the morning. I want you to skedaddle out of here. We got enough crooks here without bringin' 'em in from out of state."

"I been workin' honest in Oklahoma," Charley said. "I can be just as honest in Colorado.

"I kinda like the mountains," he added.

He did like the mountains. Just looking at the Rockies awed

119

him. He had grown up fishing and hunting in the Cookson Hills, but the Cookson Hills were just bumps with trees on them, compared to the Rockies.

"Hike on up to Wyoming," the sheriff said. "Wyoming's a state that don't mind riffraff, and they got plenty of mountains."

"I ain't riffraff," Charley replied. "Does one mistake make a fella riffraff for life?"

The old patrolman who had brought Charley in had developed a liking for him—partly, it was the bold way the boy spoke up for himself.

"I doubt he's bad, Jake," he said to the sheriff. "I could haul him down to the cafe and see if they need a dishwasher."

"Naw, he's just a road boy," the sheriff said. "I got nothin' against him, I'd just rather he settled in Wyoming."

"I'll sleep in the hotel, if you don't mind," Charley said. "I got the money, and I earned it honest."

Jake, the sheriff, softened a little.

"If you'd rather pay out good money than bunk for free, then help yourself," he said. "Me, I'd take the free bunk."

"I've a powerful lack of affection for jails," Charley said.

On the way to the hotel, Charley considered how muddled life had become since he got out of prison. He didn't remember it being so confusing before he got sent to the Jeff City pen.

The sheets on the bed in his little hotel room were dusty, but he had a good view of the peaks. He got undressed, lay down, and looked out the window. The moon came up long before Charley finally fell asleep.

It was chilly in the morning when he came downstairs. Jake was sitting in the coffee shop sipping coffee.

"There's that boy who'd rather pay out good money than bunk free," the sheriff said to the waitress.

Charley hiked out to the highway shivering from the chill. He held up his thumb, and the very first flivver coming down the road stopped for him. He'd made up his mind in the night to take the first ride he was offered. If the car was heading north, he'd try Wyoming. If the car was headed south, he might try Texas for a while. Big Carl had run a club in Fort Worth once; he told Charley Texans were friendly, by and large.

The flivver was being driven by a rancher bound for Amarillo,

120

Texas, on his way to finish up a big cattle deal. The man was a drinker, and he immediately asked Charley if he wouldn't mind driving.

"The difference between drinking on horseback and drinking in an automobile is, if you drink on a horse you just get lost, but if you drink while you're drivin' you get killed," the rancher observed. He then proceeded to drink until he passed out. When Charley stopped for gasoline, it was all he could do to wake the rancher so he could pay for the gas.

They reached Amarillo the next morning, not long after sunup. The rancher was in a sorry state. He had consumed three bottles of whiskey during the drive.

"It's ugly down here in Texas, but cattle are cheap," he said, when Charley got out.

The wind was blowing twice as hard as it had been in Pueblo. There was so much dust that Charley's teeth felt gritty. He was walking near the railroad track looking for a diner or someplace that had eats, when a police car pulled up beside him.

"Where you goin', bud? Get in," the cop said.

"I'm just looking for a place to get breakfast," Charley said. "Is that a crime in Texas?"

"It depends on the fella that's lookin'," the cop replied. "There's lots of crimes, son. If we look hard, we can probably find one for you."

Charley got in the car. At least he was out of the wind and the grit.

"You could be a vagrant," the cop said, looking him over. "There's laws against vagrancy."

"I might have to learn to fly," Charley said, annoyed.

"What's that?" the cop asked—he thought he hadn't heard the boy right.

"Flyin'—it's about the only thing there ain't a law against," Charley answered. "If I walk, I get arrested for vagrancy, and if I stand still, I get arrested for loiterin'. What's that leave but flyin'? There's more crimes than I ever heard of in this country."

"You mean flyin' in an airplane?" the cop asked, looking puzzled.

"Just flyin'," Charley replied, shaking his head. "Flyin', any way I can."

4

"Ma, can I have some flapjacks? I know it's late," Charley said. He had walked off the highway an hour before, as hungry as could be. At first, the familiar kitchen felt unfamiliar to him, it had been so long since he sat in it. But after a cup of coffee, he began to relax. The only thing new in the kitchen was a radio, which mainly seemed to crackle and make static. His ma didn't look any older. Bradley had left for the fields long before. When Charley had walked up the dirt road to the house, he'd barely been able to keep from turning around and going back to the highway. He knew he had disgraced the family name; he didn't even know if his mother would let him in the door. He was afraid he might turn out to be as unwelcome at home as he had been in Colorado, or Texas.

"How many can you eat, son?" Mamie asked, smiling at him. While she worked at the stove, she watched her son. To her, he still looked like a young boy—to her, he still looked soft. Sometimes the pen made a man mean, but Charley didn't look mean. He looked like a hungry boy, eager for the taste of his mother's flapjacks.

"Where all'd you go, Charley, after you got out?" she asked.

"Worked in the oil fields awhile. Got any sausage?" Charley said. The taste of flapjacks and syrup reminded him what a good cook his ma was.

He didn't want to tell her about Colorado and Texas. She might not believe he had been arrested for no reason.

"This sausage is spicy, now," Mamie warned him. "That's the way your pa liked it."

"Can we go to Pa's grave?" Charley asked.

"Sure," Mamie replied, a little surprised by the request.

"I wish me and Pa'd had a better talk the last time I seen him," Charley said.

"Your pa was touchy—too touchy," Mamie said. "That's

what got him shot. He lost his temper and scared that old man so bad, he shot your pa."

"He didn't go to jail for it, neither," Charley said. "I went to jail, and I never hurt a soul."

That afternoon Charley, Bradley, and Ma Floyd rode out to the little cemetery where Walter Floyd lay buried.

"Pa would have been out with his hounds tonight. It's a good night for coon huntin'," Bradley said.

"What happened to the hounds?" Charley asked. He'd had a sense that something was missing besides his pa, when he walked up the road to the house—what was missing was the baying of his pa's hounds.

"I got rid of all of them but Pete," Mamie said. "I put up with hounds my whole married life."

Charley stood looking at his father's grave. It had been rainy when Walter was buried; the grave had sunk several inches. The sunken, sad way the grave looked made Charley get a lump in his throat.

The day was windy, and it had turned drizzly. The wind blew wet leaves against the windshield of the flivver as they walked back to the car.

"If anything happens to me, put me next to Pa," Charley said.

"Don't be talking sad, son," Mamie said. "Burying a husband's hard, but burying my child would be too hard. I'd rather go next, the way the Lord meant it to be, than to take on a grief like that."

"I just said *if*, Ma," Charley mumbled, sorry he'd said it.

Being home made Charley think of Ruby. In the late afternoon, he took a nap and dreamed about her. For supper, his ma made a vinegar cobbler, which had always been his favorite.

After supper, they sat in the kitchen, listening to the drizzle.

"That radio has more crackle to it than a passel of hens," Mamie said, standing up and turning it off.

Bessie had come over to see Charley. She had gotten pretty fat, but Bradley didn't seem to mind. Charley didn't either. Bessie was jolly, most of the time.

"So Ruby lives in Coffeyville?" Charley asked.

123

"Yeah, Coffeyville—that fella she married is a baker, I believe," Bradley said.

"I met him once," Bessie added. "He seemed like a nice man."

Charley was quiet.

"He's a baker, I think," Bradley repeated.

"You said that, shut up!" Charley snapped, his temper getting the best of him. "I don't care what the son-of-a-bitch does. I just wondered where Ruby was living."

"She brings Dempsey down when she can," Bessie said. "Ruby tries to keep in touch."

"Not with me, she don't," Charley said. He felt bitter. What business did Ruby have coming to see his folks, if she had married a baker? What business did she have keeping in touch?

His ma seemed to pick his thoughts right out of his head.

"Ruby will always be family to us, Charley," Mamie said. "It ain't her fault you got sent to the pen."

"Aw, who said it was?" Charley replied.

"She didn't have money and couldn't get work," his mother told him. "She had it hard, son. Don't you be blaming her for marrying—it was the only out she had."

Charley didn't answer, but he didn't like it that his own family took Ruby's side.

"I would have waited for her till hell froze over," Charley said.

Bradley snorted.

"You better not be laughing at me, bud," Charley warned. "What's so damn funny?"

"The notion of you waitin'," Bradley said. "Waitin' to you means only havin' a new gal ever' week or so."

Charley jumped up and was about to slug his brother, when Mamie stepped between them.

"Sit down," she said. "There'll be no fisticuffs in my kitchen."

"We'll step outside! You heard what he said, Ma," Charley said.

"No," Mamie said, firm. "You settle down now—and keep your mouth shut, Bradley! Your brother's only been home one day. Looks like you two could get along for one day."

"All I done was say the truth. Charley ain't the waitin' kind," Bradley said, disgusted.

124

"Just 'cause I don't get you tonight don't mean I won't get you one of these days, bud," Charley said. But his mother had her eye fixed on him, and it was her kitchen. He sat back down.

"Don't go sniffin' around Ruby," Mamie Floyd said.

"But I want to see Dempsey—ain't I got a right to see my own son?" Charley asked.

"Of course you got a right. But you can see Dempsey down here," Mamie said. "I'll go fetch him, or Bessie can. But leave Ruby alone. She took a hard situation and made the best of it. Don't be troublin' her."

"I guess I ain't popular nowhere no more," Charley said, hot under the collar. "At least you still like me, don't you, Bessie?"

"I still like you, Charley," Bessie said.

"Yeah, but she's sweet-natured, she likes everybody," Bradley said.

"I'll speak for myself if you don't mind, Brad," Bessie said, surprising everyone.

5

"It's none of your business, you nosey little prick," Lulu Ash said, her eyes blazing. "You keep up with your corn shucking, and I'll keep up with mine."

"Good Lord, I just asked," Charley said, subdued. "You was the one who told him to look me up in the pen."

"That don't give you an invitation to pry," Lulu said.

"When's the last time you seen him?" she asked a little later, when she'd stopped being annoyed.

"The night before he swung," Charley told her. "He offered me a steak, but I didn't have no appetite. I liked the man."

"I bet he drank gin to the end," Lulu said. "I never figured

Big Carl would swing. He was a smart fellow, but he had one bad habit."

"What was that?" Charley asked.

"Killing people," Lulu replied.

"I heard he killed three," Charley informed her. "That's what my buddy Jerry said."

"That was with his bare hands," Lulu said. "He shot a few, and threw one stiff out a window. I'd say he killed nine or ten, not countin' niggers."

Lulu's memories of Big Carl Bevo went back a long way, but she didn't intend to share many with Charley. He had been her first pimp, for one thing; that was in Louisville. He was rough at first, but once he figured out he could trust her, he became a solid friend. In Chicago, he had taught her how to do abortions —when he brought her a girl who needed one, it was usually Big Carl that paid the fee. They tried Philadelphia for a while, but neither one of them liked the people. He set her up in her first house in St. Louis, but then he killed two colored fellows who rubbed him the wrong way, and that ended that. They tried being lovers, but Lulu soon discovered that he preferred her as a business partner. It didn't sit well at first, but once she accepted it, every job they tried together made money.

Lulu had no intention of going into matters of that sort with the randy kid who was sprawled across her bed, though it did please her that he had been interested enough to track her down all the way to Kansas City. She'd had to pack it out of St. Louis in a hurry because her two brick-headed sons, Wally and William, had managed to get crosswise with Sal Licavoli, the head of the St. Louis mob. And relations with Judge Bull Whaley had deteriorated. Evidently, he had developed habits Nora couldn't tolerate, so she kicked him out, after which Bull decided Lulu had set him up in order to get her young stiff a short sentence. Bull Whaley was a vindictive man, and so was Licavoli; two powerful men on the prod in one town made life too hectic, so Lulu packed up and headed west.

Charley was mighty glad he found Ma Ash. He had no idea what he was going to do in the world, and thought she might help him with a notion or two. So far, all she had done was

126

unbutton his trousers again, but he sure wasn't going to kick about that. He found out Beulah was in K.C. somewhere, with her sister Rose. He meant to sidle over to Beulah's place when opportunity offered, but so far, Ma Ash had barely given him time to catch his breath.

Lulu Ash knew exactly what the big kid on her bed was thinking. She'd just put out what she had, and the little bastard was already thinking about that yappy little whiff, Beulah Baird, who was no more than a cute floozie with nice legs. That was the way it was, with younger men—in a way, it amused her; and in a way, it didn't.

"If I was to let it happen, you could be my downfall," she said, to give him something else to think about. "I could get mighty sweet on a young stiff like you."

It was true, too; it was her heart she'd had the urge to put out when she opened the door and saw Charley standing on her porch, all weary from the road, with eyes as sweet as sugar.

Something in Lulu couldn't hold out against a sweet boy like Charley. She was only a breath away from being in love with him, foolish and dangerous as that was. But it had always been that way with Lulu; young men with sweet, sad eyes had been her downfall more than once. It was why Big Carl had finally stopped doing business with her.

"Smart as you are about jobs, it looks like you'd be smarter about stiffs," he'd told her bluntly. "What's the point of setting up a racket and raking in dough if you're gonna throw it away for some little jerk with a hard-on?"

"I can't be smart all the time, it's too lonesome," Lulu told him. "What are you complaining about, anyway? I ain't slipped up on the business end, and are we raking in the dough!"

"You might slip up, though," Big Carl said. "You ain't tough enough to go to the top in this business. I expect you should stick to running whorehouses in K.C. or somewhere."

Charley had dropped off to sleep. Lulu couldn't keep her eyes off him, or her hands. Big Carl had probably been right. She was running a whorehouse in K.C., just like he'd told her she should.

At least it wasn't lonesome.

127

6

Bill "the Killer" Miller was hanging around the secretarial college when Charley located him. The secretarial college was in a gloomy old brick building in downtown Kansas City. Bill was dressed dapper, in hopes of appealing to some of the young women who were upstairs learning shorthand and typing.

"I guess you're a part-time pimp now, you little fart," Charley said, walking up behind Billy.

Billy jumped about two feet, and then turned around and pumped Charley's hand.

"I missed you, bud," Billy said, briefly overcome by emotion.

Despite himself, Charley was glad to see Bill Miller. There was something about the guy that he liked, though he had never expected to find him standing around a secretarial college in K.C., trying to pick up dissatisfied secretaries in hopes of turning them into whores.

"I missed you," Billy said, again.

"Applesauce," Charley said. "If you missed me that much, why didn't you confess? Maybe they'da put us in the same cell."

"I wouldn't have got off as light as you," Billy explained.

"Why's that?" Charley asked.

"You still had most of the money when they caught you," Billy said. "That's why they went light on you."

Charley decided not to tell him about Ma Ash and the judge.

"What happened to yours?" he asked. "Have you got it hid somewhere?"

"I lost every cent of it in a poker game," Billy said. "The stiff I was playing cheated."

"The stiffs you play always cheat," Charley mentioned.

Just then, two girls with bobbed hair came clipping out of the secretarial college. The western Missouri breeze was blowing hard.

128

"There's two skirts, you better get to work," Charley said. "Both of them look like they'd make good whores."

"I'll ask them if they've got change for the streetcar," Billy said, setting his fedora more tightly on his head. Too many times as he was about to speak to one of the would-be secretaries, the breeze had whipped his hat off, forcing him to chase it. Few girls would accept a pimp who had to chase his hat.

A lot of the time, Billy didn't really care whether the girls became whores or not; in most cases, he would have been happy enough with just a date.

"Say, either of you ladies got two dimes and a nickel?" Billy asked, approaching them boldly.

"What if we have?" the taller of the two asked. She was a good head taller than Billy Miller.

"Why are you always hanging around here, you little twerp?" the other girl asked. She was a redhead.

"Do you think we're loose, is that the game?" she asked.

Charley strolled over—he thought he ought to assist his friend. That very day, Ma Ash had bought him a swell blue suit. She also bought him shirts, neckties, and shoes; she even picked out his socks. As a special indulgence, she allowed him a pair of black gloves.

"Big Carl was right," she said. "If you decide to pull a bank job, you need to dress like you belong in a bank."

Ma Ash even bought him some white cotton handkerchiefs, and showed him how to fold them so they'd fit in the pocket by his lapel.

With his new suit and a green necktie, Charley felt smart enough to help Billy out with the girls. He tipped his hat when he approached, a detail Billy had neglected.

Billy rarely tipped his hat—in his view, that only encouraged it to blow away.

"Good afternoon," Charley said. "I hope my pal ain't been rude."

He gave the girls a big smile, and both of them smiled back.

"Him? I didn't even notice him," the redhead said. "Is he your kid brother, by any chance?"

"Say, I'm older than him by a long shot," Billy said. He was more than a little insulted.

"I wouldn't be mentioning long shots if I was as short as you," the taller girl retorted.

"How about dinner?" Billy asked, thinking a bold invitation might turn the tide in his favor.

"Dinner? You barely come up to my kneecap," the girl said. "I'd have to ask the waiter for a high chair, if I went out with you."

"Don't listen to him, he runs off at the mouth," Charley said. "My suggestion would be that we find a place that ain't so windy."

"Where would that be?—this is K.C.," the redhead said.

"Don't you girls live in a boarding house?" Charley asked.

"Yeah, but it's respectable, we ain't allowed gents," the taller of the two said.

"Who says we ain't respectable, I'm a college graduate," Billy said. It was a lie he often resorted to when all else seemed to be failing.

"I bet, the college of low altitude," the redhead said. Both girls giggled, and even Charley had to smile, although he knew Billy hated to be ridiculed about his height.

"You girls wouldn't be from Tulsa, would you?" Charley asked.

"Nebraska," both girls chimed.

"We're going to be secretaries long enough to marry our bosses—then we'll be rich and have maids," the redhead informed them.

The girls let Charley and Billy take them to a soda fountain and buy them malts, but that was as far as the evening went. They even refused to allow the fellows to board the same streetcar.

"You ain't working out as a pimp, Billy," Charley said, while they waited for the next streetcar. "Maybe we ought to pull a job. Only this time, we'll do it right."

"What kind of job?" Billy asked.

"Maybe a bank job," Charley said. "Ma Ash will help us plan it."

"I could use the money, that's for sure," Billy said.

130

"I don't suppose you still have the gun, do you?" Charley asked.

"I lost it in a poker game," Billy said. "The stiff I was playing cheated."

7

Charley had expected Beulah to be a little miffed that he hadn't looked her up sooner, but he did not expect her to black his eye with a shoe.

Nonetheless, he barely had time to get "Hello" out of his mouth, before Beulah whacked him in the eye with a shoe. She put some muscle behind it, too. Charley couldn't remember taking a worse lick since Pa's mule kicked him.

"What was that for?" he asked, trying to assume an innocent look.

"That's because I hate your cheatin' guts," Beulah said. She flailed at him again, but this time he was ready. They wrestled awhile, and he finally got the shoe away from her.

"I been waitin' and waitin'!" Beulah said. "But no, you'd rather stay over there and screw that old whore.

"You must have screwed her good, or she wouldn't have bought you no suit," Beulah added, just before she burst into tears.

Charley got a lie out as quick as he could.

"I would never do a thing like that, honey," he said. "I thought of you all the time I was in the pen. You never came to visit me one time."

"If I had, you'd have had two or three girls there ahead of

me, I bet," Beulah said. "You're a cheatin' liar, Charley, not a word you say is the truth."

It was more than an hour before Charley could work his way back onto kissing terms.

"You better not poke no dick at me, not in my mood," Beulah warned him, despite the kissing. "I'm mad enough to stab you with a fingernail file."

Charley milked his eye for all it was worth. In fact, it was already swollen nearly shut.

"It's a good thing you wasn't carrying no high heels," he said. "If you'd whacked me with a high heel, it would have gone plumb through my brain."

"I wouldn't have done a bit of damage, because you don't have no brain," Beulah said. "That dick you're so proud of is all the brains you got."

"Aw, Beulah, let up, it's been years since I seen you," Charley said. He was beginning to feel sorry for himself. Beulah was cuter than ever; she just wasn't as friendly.

"You're lucky I even opened the door. I don't have to put up with no two-timing jerk," Beulah said, her chest heaving. Charley was as cute as ever, but the thought of Ma Ash made her steam.

"Aw, Beulah," Charley said, again.

"Aw Beulah what?" she asked. "Give me one reason why I shouldn't whack you in the other eye."

"Then I'd be totally blind," Charley said. "Is that a reason? I was gonna take you dancing, but now I can't see to dance."

Beulah remained silent.

"Let's go down to Oklahoma, me and you and Billy and Rose," Charley said, suddenly inspired.

"Oklahoma? Why would we wanna go there?" Beulah asked.

"For the adventure," Charley said. "Me and Billy might pull a job. You and Rose could shop while we work."

"Yeah, and the next thing you know, me and Rose will be in jail for life, and you and Billy will be doing what you please," Beulah said. "Billy's got a brain the size of a pea, and the rest of him ain't much bigger."

"But I'm gonna do the plannin' this time," Charley assured her. "Bill the Killer won't do nothing but take orders."

132

"I thought you was goin' straight," Beulah reminded him.

"I meant to," Charley said. "But I tried, and it didn't work. I tried Colorado and Texas both, and I got arrested so quick I didn't even have time to mess up my shoeshine."

"That's 'cause you look like a crook," Beulah said. "Where would we go to pull this job?"

"I told you, Oklahoma," Charley repeated. "We'll find some little town where the law's lazy."

"Forget the law, what about the shoppin'?" Beulah reminded him. "Why would me and Rose want to go to Oklahoma to shop? They got better stores right here in K.C."

"Partly you'd be goin' for the fun of it," Charley told her. "There's other things to do besides shop."

"Not many," Beulah said. She stuck a foot in Charley's face.

"Smell my dirty feet," she demanded.

Charley shoved her foot away. "Why would I want to smell your dirty feet?" he asked. "I need to find some ice to put on this eye. I can't see a thing."

"I'm still mad about Lulu," Beulah said. "Why would you want to have anything to do with a stinky old bitch like her?"

"Will you can it?!" Charley said, getting a little steamed himself. "We got to plan this job, and thanks to you I ain't got but one good eye to do it with. I'm sick of arguing about Lulu Ash."

"Oh, now you're even callin' her by her first name," Beulah said, feeling her temper rise again. "I guess that means you two are on real familiar terms."

"Can it, I said, before I black *your* eye!" Charley snapped.

"Oh yeah? Black it if you're so bold!" Beulah said, shoving her face up in his.

Charley remembered that she had done the same thing to Wally Ash in the dining room of Wally's mother's boarding house. Everyone had made fun of Wally for being too weak to slap her. Now she had just put him in the same position, only fortunately, they were alone.

"I have no intention of hitting you," he said, stiffly. "Can't you take a little teasing?"

Beulah grinned, and gingerly attempted to raise his bruised eyelid to see what the eye itself looked like.

"You ain't a bit tough, Charley," she said. "You ain't a bit tough."

"You might be wrong about that," Charley said. "Just because I'm sweet on you don't mean I'll put up with all your sass."

"Well, so far you've put up with it," Beulah said, still trying to get a look at his eyeball. When she did, she was shocked by the effects of her own violence.

"Gosh, your eyeball's all bloodshot," she said. "I got in a good lick, didn't I?"

"If Billy asks what happened, tell him a mule kicked me," Charley said.

8

Lulu Ash laughed so hard when she saw Charley's shiner that he began to get a little hot. Then it made him miss Ruby. All these city women did was slug him, or laugh at him.

"What'd she hit you with?" Lulu asked.

"A shoe," Charley admitted. "That ain't what I came to talk about."

"No, I bet it ain't," Lulu said. "You're too easy to get along with, sonny. You'll always be lettin' a woman lead you around by the nose."

"If I do, it won't be nobody I know at the moment," Charley informed her. "You was gonna tell me about how to pull a bank job. Big Carl told me some, but he said you knew as much about it as he did."

"More—he wasn't no bank robber," Lulu said. "He robbed the First National and took that ninety grand, but then they

134

caught him. Me and one of my johns robbed six banks in Indiana, and nobody ever laid a finger on us.

"They was small-town banks, we didn't get much, but it was a living," she added.

"We're leaving tomorrow," Charley said. "I guess we'll head for Oklahoma. Got any advice?"

"Arrive about an hour after the bank opens, or else about an hour before it closes," Lulu said. "There's a rush when a bank opens, and another when it closes. It's best to hit a bank when things are a little slack, and the tellers are yawning."

"Okay," Charley said. "I need to buy a gun, though. Billy lost mine in a poker game, along with his share of the Kroger payroll job."

Lulu opened a bureau drawer and rummaged around under some of her lingerie. Then she handed Charley his old pistol, the one Bill Miller had used to cover the guards that morning in the fog.

"Why, this is my gun!" Charley said, astonished. "I traded a five-gallon jug of moonshine for this pistol years ago."

"I kept it for you," Lulu told him.

"Aw, thanks," Charley said. His face lit up at the sight of the gun. It reminded him of home. The old farmer who traded him the gun was named Leroy Starr—he had a big thirst for moonshine.

"You ain't thinkin' of shootin' your missus with it, are you?" Leroy asked, when he handed Charley the pistol. It was a hot day. Mr. Starr had been digging a corner posthole, and his shirt was sweated through.

"Why, no, why would I shoot Ruby?" Charley asked, taken aback at the thought.

"I ain't acquainted with your wife, son," Leroy Starr said. "But I've come close to shootin' mine with it a few times, I can tell you.

"I guess you can take it," he said, finally. "I can shoot my wife with the shotgun, if it comes to that."

"Hope you like the moonshine," Charley said.

"Say, how much do I owe you for it?" Charley asked, looking at Lulu.

"It's a gift, Charley," Lulu said.

When he left, handsome as could be in his new suit, Lulu stood by the window and watched him go. She cried a little. Boys like Charley were her weakness, and she was getting too much in love with him—foolish for a woman her age. But he had given her such a sweet kiss for keeping his pistol for him. What could she do but fall?

9

"If they catch us, Rose and me got our story worked out," Beulah said, as they drove into Earlsboro. "We'll say you're white slavers, and you give us dope and brought us to Oklahoma against our will.

"Rose is under age, it might work," she added.

"Don't break no traffic laws—that's important," Billy Miller said.

"I thought we come here to shop," Rose said. "Shop for what, cornbread? I doubt this dump even has a five-and-dime."

"It's got a five-and-dime, and a dry goods store, too," Charley assured her. "It's a decent little town."

"I'm sure it is, if you like cornbread," Rose said. "Me, I'm a city girl from way back."

It depressed Charley that nobody in the car had a good word to say about Oklahoma. To him, it seemed like a nice fall day. The sun was shining, and the wind wasn't blowing too hard, and the leaves were pretty. Despite all this, his three companions had griped the whole way from Kansas City. Their yapping was beginning to get on his nerves. He was starting to wish he had left them in Kansas City, and robbed the bank by himself. He could just leave the motor running, dash in and dash out. Lulu Ash warned him against being greedy, anyway.

"Just look at it as a living," she said. "If you can get more than a few hundred and the law don't wing you, you're ahead."

They pulled up in front of the dry goods store just as it opened, and let the girls out. The bank was right across the street.

"Don't spend too much money," Charley warned them. "We ain't robbed the bank yet."

"We'll be lucky if we can spend two bits in this burg," Beulah said.

Billy Miller stroked his gun while the two of them smoked and waited. It was his own gun this time, but the sight of Billy rubbing it made Charley nervous.

"Suppose the law comes along and sees you rubbin' that gun?" he said.

"I got cat's eyes," Billy said, grinning. "I'd hide the gun, or else I'd plug the lawman."

"You go shootin' a lawman, and it's curtains for both of us," Charley said. "Don't shoot no lawman, or anybody else if you can help it.

"There's a big difference between a robber and a killer," he added. "And don't you forget it."

Folks went in and out of the bank, old ladies and merchants, mostly. It was Wednesday, a slow day. Lulu had explained that Mondays and Fridays were the busiest days at a bank. She thought it wiser to do the holdup in the middle of the week, though Charley argued that maybe Fridays were better, because Fridays were paydays and the tellers would have lots of money for paychecks.

"Here come the girls," Billy said, finally. Charley was on pins and needles waiting.

"All we could find was fingernail polish," Beulah said. "I'm thinking of painting my nails purple—they say it's the rage. What would you say to that, Charley?"

"I'd say you're an idjit," Charley said. "Pipe down—you're gettin' on my nerves, and Billy's too."

"Gosh, I was just bein' a girl," Beulah said. "Can't a girl even be a girl?"

"Yeah, but couldn't there be such a thing as a *quiet* girl?" Charley asked.

When it finally came time to rob the bank, Charley and Billy got out, leaving Beulah at the wheel.

"Straighten your necktie," Charley said, as they were crossing the street, their pistols in their pockets.

Just as they got to the bank, a tall cowboy in a white Stetson and brown boots with narrow tips arrived at the door a step behind them. Charley politely held the door for him.

"After you, sir," he said.

" 'Preciate it, mister," the cowboy replied.

Once inside, the cowboy went up to one teller—Charley chose a teller two windows down. There were only three tellers in the bank, and one of them was gone.

"This is a stickup," Charley said, only to hear what sounded like an echo, to his left. He stopped talking, and turned to the cowboy, who was looking at him a little oddly. Charley decided it must have been nerves, so he faced the old-lady teller and tried again.

"This is a holdup, give me your money," he said again. But again, there was the echo—it was like there was a choir of two, robbing the Earlsboro Bank. Charley looked back at the cowboy, and the cowboy was looking at him.

"Say," the old-lady teller demanded. "You crooks better decide which one of you is robbin' this bank. There ain't money enough for both of you to rob it. We're about to go under as it is."

"I'm robbin' the bank, ma'am," the cowboy said firmly. "I don't know what this city slicker thinks he's doin'."

"No, that's gettin' it backwards," Charley said. "*I'm* robbing the bank. This cowboy needs to go shoe his horse or something."

"Sir, I was here first—had my gun out before you even got to the teller's window," the cowboy pointed out.

"That was 'cause I was polite and held the door for you," Charley reminded him. The cowboy's cool demeanor was beginning to irk him.

Bill Miller was standing over by the window, watching the street.

"Shoot him and grab the money," Billy said. "We got to hot-foot it out of here."

"Would you mind tellin' me why?" Charley asked Billy, irritated that a smooth-looking job had suddenly gotten complicated.

Charley looked at the cowboy, and the cowboy looked at him.

"I guess six bits is better than nothin'," the cowboy said. He reached through the window and grabbed all the cash he could scrape out of the cash drawer. Charley did the same. The two tellers didn't make a move.

"Let's go, bud, there'll be another day tomorrow," the cowboy said, seeing that Charley seemed reluctant to leave.

"We're supposed to take hostages—they can stand on the running board," Charley said. He was trying to follow Big Carl's instructions precisely, but the arrival of the cowboy flustered him—he had almost forgotten the hostages.

"Say, that's an idea," the cowboy said, grinning. "I would have thought of that myself, eventually."

He waved his pistol at the two tellers.

"Come on, ladies, we've appointed you hostages," he said.

"Can I get my hat?" one teller asked. "I get an earache if I go off without it."

"Charley, the sheriff's coming, I may have to shoot somebody," Billy said.

"I told you not to use no names!" Charley said, annoyed by the incompetence of his partner.

"Come ladies, time's awasting," the cowboy said.

"What about my hat?" the teller insisted.

"Grab it!" the cowboy demanded.

Beulah was standing across the street, looking at a pair of shoes in the window of the dry goods store, when Charley, Billy, and the cowboy rushed out, herding the two tellers in front of them.

"Get over here, pronto!" Charley said. "You was supposed to stay behind the wheel."

Beulah hurried back. They all piled in the car, with the two elderly tellers on the running boards.

"I don't think we need the hostages," Billy said. "All they're doing is blocking my aim."

"Nobody told you to aim—the sheriff ain't even noticed us," Charley said, pulling away slowly so as not to attract attention.

Bobby Jars, the sheriff, was walking along thinking about how much he liked cracklins. He was planning to kill his pig in a day or two if the cool weather held, and he intended to make at least a bushel of cracklins. Bank robbery was the farthest thing from his mind.

He thought it was kind of strange that Mrs. Dean and Mrs. Johnson, both tellers in the bank, would be riding down the street on the running board of a black car, but Sheriff Jars saw no reason to be too concerned about it—both old ladies were a little off, anyway.

Old Man Jessup, an ancient, nosey fart who spent most of his time spitting and whittling on a bench in front of the feed store, was out of place this morning. He was on a bench by the bank—an annoyance. People who wanted to visit the bank wouldn't appreciate having to wade through a pool of his tobacco juice.

"I'm votin' against you next election, Bob," the old man said, without provocation.

"Why? I ain't arrested you, though I'd like to," the sheriff said.

" 'Cause you're too damn ignorant to stop this bank robbery that's just took place," Old Man Jessup said. The car was stopped a few blocks away so the hostages could step off the running boards.

"Bank robbery?" the sheriff said, surprised. He tried to pull his pistol out of its holster. The holster had a fancy catch in it which was supposed to release the pistol instantly when he pulled on it. Only this time, it didn't. The pistol felt like it was welded to the holster. By the time he finally got it out, the black car had proceeded on its way.

"Pshaw, they let those women loose," Old Man Jessup said. "They could've carried the women all the way to Chiney and I wouldn't have cared."

"China," the sheriff corrected.

"Those old biddy hens don't like me," Old Man Jessup said, watching apprehensively as the two tellers approached. "Two to one they try to make me move."

140

Sheriff Jars had stopped thinking about cracklins. The election was only two months away, and now he had let the bank get robbed.

"A citizen's got the right to sit anywheres he wants to sit," the old man said, spitting discreetly beside his bench. The two women looked stirred up, to him.

"Mr. Jessup, I hope you change your mind about that vote," the sheriff said.

10

The cowboy tipped his hat to the two old ladies when they stepped off the running board.

"Thanks for your time, ladies," he said.

"Ma'am, hope you escape the earache," Charley said, not to be outdone when it came to politeness. He also tipped his hat, a courtesy Billy Miller neglected.

"Tip your hat, where's your manners?" Charley said.

"Him? Manners?" Beulah said, smirking.

"Shut up, I was watchin' the sheriff," Billy said. "Why's this cowboy in the car with us? All he done was interfere."

The cowboy tipped his hat again, this time to Beulah and Rose.

"Mornin', ladies," he said. "You both sure are dressed pretty."

"Say, I like this bozo," Beulah said.

Despite himself, Charley liked the man, too. Billy Miller was right—all he had done was butt in—but there was something real likeable about him. He seemed in a perfect humor, and just having him along made things jollier.

"Ain't you got a horse or something, cowboy?" Charley asked.

"I had a car," the man said. "I think I'll just leave her sit. That sheriff might get his gun out of his holster, eventually."

"So what's your moniker?" Beulah asked. "I'm Beulah, and this is Rose. The little shrimpy guy is Bill 'the Killer' Miller."

"George Birdwell," the man said, shaking hands all around. "If you folks would just be kind enough to carry me about a hundred miles up the road, I'd be obliged."

"We ain't takin' you no hundred miles unless you chip in for the gas," Billy announced.

"Who died and made you boss?" Charley asked. "Shut up if you can't be polite."

"I'd be happy to provide the gasoline," Birdwell said.

"What do you think about women who paint their fingernails purple?" Beulah asked. "I'm thinking of trying it."

"Bob better not try it, that's what I think," Birdwell said.

"Who's Bob?" Rose asked.

"My wife," Birdwell replied.

"I thought Bob was a boy's name," Charley said. "I never heard of a woman named Bob."

"You have now, bud," Birdwell said. "Bob's sweet as honey, I miss her right this minute."

To everyone's surprise, the man's eyes misted up at the thought of his wife. Once he thought about it a few seconds, Charley sympathized. His own eyes had often misted if the thought of Ruby happened to cross his mind.

"Say, how many jobs have you pulled?" Charley asked. He remembered how calm and collected the cowboy had been when he entered the bank.

"Six and a half, if you mean banks," Birdwell said, with a grin. "Earlsboro would have been seven, if you hadn't come along and grabbed half the loot."

"It looked like a cozy little bank," Charley observed. "We had no idea you had your eye on it, too."

The first hundred miles passed quickly. Beulah made good her threat to paint her nails purple—it put Charley off, but she defied him. George Birdwell had only taken up bank robbing recently; he mostly traveled the rodeo circuit. He'd been all over

142

the West, competing in rodeos, and he had many stories to tell. Although he mentioned several times how much he missed his wife, Bob, he didn't ask to get out. He had a bottle of whiskey in each coat pocket, and shared them with the crowd. Billy Miller got tired of driving and gave the wheel to Charley, who kept rolling along in the general direction of Illinois. Before he had driven twenty miles, everybody else in the car fell asleep. During the night, Charley pulled off a time or two to nap, but mostly he kept driving. Big Carl had emphasized that it was wise to put as much distance as possible between himself and the scene of the crime.

When dawn came, Charley was feeling pretty yawny, but they were on the delta of the old Mississippi. Billy Miller and George Birdwell were awake, but the girls were sound asleep.

"We're nearly to the river, let's stop and eat a catfish," Billy suggested.

"Let's cross it and then eat the catfish," Charley said. "I'm more in the mood for flapjacks, anyway."

George Birdwell was tipped back comfortably in his seat with his hat brim pulled down against the glare of the rising sun.

"What river might that be, boys?" he asked. "I ain't been payin' too much attention to the scenery."

"Why, the Mississippi—what river would it be?" Charley asked, surprised.

"Whoa, horses, whoa!" Birdwell said, sitting up. "This is where I dismount."

"Why?" Charley said—he had come to like the man, and felt disappointed at the thought of him leaving.

"I got a powerful superstition against crossing big water," Birdwell said.

"But we was gonna work Illinois for a while," Charley said. "There's lots of nice banks east of the Mississippi. You'd be welcome to come along."

"No, thanks—I appreciate the offer," Birdwell said. "You're welcome to the banks. I wouldn't cross no big water for a hundred banks."

Bill Miller was glad to see the cowboy go. It wasn't that he disliked him, particularly. It was mainly that there wasn't room in the car for anyone with such long legs.

"But how will you get back?" Charley asked, when they let Birdwell out by the side of a long field.

"If I can't steal a horse, I guess I'll ride my thumb," Birdwell said. "Adios, folks." He grinned, and tipped his hat.

"Give my regards to the ladies," he added. "I got qualms about purple fingernails, though."

When Beulah woke up, Charley repeated the remark. Partly it was to irritate her, but partly he meant it. He thought women ought to be proper in their attire.

"Why would I care what some cowboy thinks about my fingernails?" Beulah asked. "Where is George, anyway?"

"He left," Billy told her. "My guess is, he couldn't stand your yappin'."

"Oh, can it, you little creep," Beulah said. "I can't help it if I got somethin' to say!"

11

The Sylvania job would have gone off smooth if it hadn't been for the hostage. The only woman in the bank when they started the robbery was the bank president's wife, and she was so fat that when Charley helped her up on the flivver's running board, the car tipped to one side.

"I don't think this is gonna work," Charley said. "No offense, ma'am, but I think we may have to do without a hostage, this time."

"Get in here, people are lookin'," Beulah said, pointing at a hat in the window of the dry goods store. "Rose, make a note of this store."

"Make a note of the store?" Billy said. "Why?"

144

" 'Cause there's a cute hat in the window, and I may want to come back and buy it," Beulah informed him.

Just as Charley took the wheel, a deputy sheriff rounded the corner a block away, and drew his pistol. Billy was in the back seat. The deputy fired once, and Billy knocked out the back window and cut him down with the Tommy gun. Charley saw the man sprawl against a building as he gunned the car.

"Hey, you moron, why'd you knock out the window?" Beulah shrieked.

"Because he's been itching to kill somebody ever since I met him, and now he has!" Charley said, bitterly.

"He was shootin' at us!" Billy said, plaintively.

"He only shot once," Charley said. "He couldn't have hit us in a week. You couldn't wait to use that Tommy gun, could you?"

Billy felt sick at his stomach. They'd had the Tommy gun three days; a mug they met in a chili joint in Cincinnati sold it to them. They had taken it out and fired it into a riverbank a few times, but Billy really hadn't got the hang of the gun. When he knocked out the back window of the car, the gun seemed to shoot itself. He'd had a bad dream once: some bull had shot at him, and he was able to watch the bullet go into his head, right between his eyes. When the hick deputy popped at them with his pistol, Billy blasted away, not expecting to hit much. It was a surprise to see the deputy flung back against the building like a rag doll.

"If I didn't have to drive, I'd climb back there and beat the tar out of you!" Charley said, hot. "Now we're in the soup for sure."

"Yeah, and there's glass all over this car," Rose said. "If I cut myself, you'll be sorry."

"Gee," Billy said, feeling blue, "I guess I ain't got a friend in the world."

He felt like going back to Indiana to watch his brother-in-law and sister slug one another and break furniture. It beat staying with Charley, when Charley was hot.

"You'll make lots of friends in the clink, if you don't swing," Charley informed him. He roared around a corner and had to swing into a ditch to keep from smashing an old man poking along in a wagon. The car bounced when he cut back onto the road.

"Will you slow down?" Beulah said. "I didn't come to Ohio with you to get smashed in a car wreck."

"This is a getaway car, get it?" Charley told her. "A getaway car is supposed to go fast. Otherwise you don't get away.

"They won't let you wear no purple nail polish in the Ohio pen, I'll bet you that," he added.

"Charley, are you still mad at me about that?" Beulah asked. "If you are, you need to get over it."

"This may surprise you, Beulah, but I got bigger things to worry about right this minute than your nail polish," Charley said, sarcastic.

"Billy, I'm lettin' you out at the first bus station I can find. You need to take a powder until things settle down," he added.

"Maybe the deputy didn't die," Billy said, forlorn. "Maybe I just winged him."

Nobody answered.

"I can't imagine why we bought this Tommy gun," he said, a little later. "It's too much gun for these small-town holdups."

"I wish George Birdwell had come with us," Charley said.

"That cowboy?" Billy said, indignant.

About that time, it began to snow, forcing Charley to slow down.

"Now every cop in the state will be looking for a black Ford with a smashed-out window," Charley said, disgusted.

"It's snowing on me," Rose said, astonished. "It's snowing right into this car."

Billy Miller felt more and more friendless. Not a single person would even look at him, but he knew Charley was still hot, from the way he was gripping the steering wheel. He was squeezing it so hard, his knuckles were white.

"I've had bad dreams about freezin' in snowdrifts," Beulah said. "Can't we stop and get a room?"

"It just started snowing five minutes ago," Charley said. "There ain't no snowdrifts, and we ain't stoppin'."

"I wish you wouldn't talk rude to me, Charley," Beulah said. "I get blue when you talk rude."

"I hope it snows all night," Charley said. "It'll cover up that window Billy smashed out."

146

"Yeah, but it'll cover me up, too," Rose said. "I'll be the one in the snowdrift."

"Yeah, her and me will be the ones in the snowdrift," Billy piped up.

"Charley, you act like this is all my fault," Beulah said. "But it ain't my fault. I didn't tell you to rob that bank, and I didn't shoot no deputy."

Charley's face was as dark as the starless sky. "You bought that purple nail polish, though," Charley said, grim. "Things have been goin' downhill ever since."

12

"I never even heard of Sylvania, Ohio," Charley said. "This is a case of mistaken identity, I don't even have a bank account."

The fat detective with the sap hit him in the head so hard that he fell out of the chair. Charley was on his hands and knees on the dirty floor, seeing lights in his head. The lights were red, like an Oklahoma sunset in the fall.

"I hate stubborn crooks," the detective said. "Kick him, Asa. See if you can knock loose a rib or two."

Asa, a big bull of a cop, kicked Charley three times. Charley stopped seeing lights in his head, and saw nothing. When he came to, they had propped him in the chair again. Charley was afraid to lean back for fear he'd vomit, and afraid to lean forward for fear he'd tip out of the chair.

"Mistaken identity," he slurred.

"No, we got the identity straight," the detective said. "You're Charley Floyd, and you done four years in the Jeff City pen, over in Missouri, for robbin' an armored car. Your partner got away that time, and now he's got away agin. He must be a few degrees smarter than you, bud."

"I don't know who you're talkin' about," Charley insisted. "Where would I get a partner?"

He and Beulah had been in bed in a cheap rooming house, when the goons broke in. Beulah had been trying to cheer him up, and she had been having no luck.

"Charley, I took the nail polish off," she said, holding her fingers up for him to see.

"It won't bring that deputy back to life," Charley said. The deputy had been killed instantly—they heard that on the radio in an eats joint they stopped at. Billy Miller had caught a bus to Louisville, where he had a cousin. Rose decided to go with him, even though he wasn't particularly nice to her.

"Some kind of boyfriend's better than no boyfriend at all, I guess," she said, giving her sister a kiss just before she boarded the bus.

Charley threw the Tommy gun into the Ohio River.

"That's a hundred dollars wasted," he said.

"Charley, don't you want to fuss around some?" Beulah asked, about five minutes before the goons broke in.

"I'm wearing my blue slip," she added.

"Big Carl said that once the killin' starts, it never stops," Charley said. "He was a man who knew what he was talking about, too."

"I'm a woman who knows what she's talking about, too," Beulah informed him. "Big Carl's dead, and the deputy's dead, but my pussy's alive, and it's right here in bed with you."

Charley didn't say a word—he just looked out the window. It was still snowing.

But the cops found the car anyway. They wouldn't even give Beulah time to dress. She had to put her coat on over the blue slip when they took them to jail.

"If I was to miscalculate and hit you too hard with this sap, it would crack your noggin wide open," the fat detective said. "Your brains would run out like egg yolk."

He gave Charley a little bit of a whack, to remind him what the sap felt like. Charley saw the red lights again.

"Start over about your partner," the detective said. "What did you say his name was?"

"Mistaken identity," Charley said. "If I hadn't taken a wrong turn down in Kentucky, I wouldn't even be in Ohio tonight."

The big bull kicked the chair over. Charley went skidding across the floor, and hit the wall.

"Maybe we oughta go slap that little chickadee around for a while," he said. "She might squawk pretty good if her feathers get yanked. This hick's too dumb to make good conversation."

Charley kept mum. He wasn't worried about Beulah. If they aggravated her, she'd call them a few names they hadn't been called before. Beulah might be a flirt, but she was solid—she wouldn't give their game away.

The bull kicked Charley in the face as he left the room.

"Sleep tight, Oklahoma," he said.

13

Bessie Floyd brought Ruby the news. She and Bradley had driven up to Coffeyville for a square dance. She told Brad she needed to get out more or else go crazy, so he agreed to take her to the dance. They brought Millie, their little six-year-old, so Dempsey would have a cousin to play with. Lenny and Bradley were in the back yard, pitching horseshoes, when Bessie handed Ruby the clipping from the newspaper:

Charles "Pretty Boy" Floyd Sentenced to 15 Years
for Sylvania, Ohio Bank Job
Accomplice Escapes

"Pretty Boy?" Ruby said. "Where'd Charley get a nickname like that?"

"You got me," Bessie said. "Maybe some newspaper guy made it up."

"I bet Charley hates it," Ruby said, frowning.

Bessie and Bradley had driven all that way to visit; Ruby didn't want to let them down. But inside she felt like cold dough. The thought of Charley being behind bars in a prison for fifteen years was a thought she couldn't bear. Dempsey would be a grown man before his daddy got out; more than likely, he'd be married and have a baby or two of his own. Charley would have missed his whole raising: father and son would be two strangers.

Bessie saw that Ruby was sad. She held out her arms to Ruby, for to Bessie, she still seemed like a girl. At least Lenny was nice; he was just a little solemn. He wasn't a cutup like Charley. But he wasn't in jail, either.

"Aw, Bessie. Why'd he have to do it?" Ruby said. "Why couldn't he have been satisfied with things like they was?"

Bessie didn't answer. She had no answers when it came to Charley Floyd.

"We was so happy, Bessie, that year Dempsey was born," Ruby told her. "I never wanted nothin' but to be with my husband."

Just then, the men trooped in from horseshoe pitching.

"Dern, Brad must have been born with a horseshoe in his hand," Lenny said. "He hit five ringers. I barely throwed that many ringers my whole life."

Lenny saw that Ruby was tearful, but he didn't say anything. Part of Ruby wished he would say something; part of her wished he would complain that she didn't really love him—at least if he complained, she would know that *he* knew her feeling for him wasn't all it should be. Lenny was so sweet, and so kind to her and to Dempsey, that she couldn't *not* love him some—still, just the mention of Charley Floyd's name, or a headline in the newspaper, made her realize the difference between what she felt for Lenny and what rose up inside her when she remembered her time with Charley. When she was hit with the difference, as she just had been, she felt too sad to be around anyone. She missed Charley almost more than she could stand—but at the same time, she felt so sorry for Lenny that it was all she could do to face him, much less pretend that everything was okay.

"Bradley's pitched horseshoes ever' spare minute since I've known him," Bessie said. "I could barely get him to stop long enough to court me."

Before Ruby could say a word, Dempsey came running into the kitchen purple in the face, Millie right behind him. The two of them had been playing Chinese checkers in the bedroom.

"He swallowed a marble!" Millie informed them. "I told him not to put them in his mouth, but he just kept on doin' it!"

Lenny grabbed Dempsey, and promptly turned him upside down. Ruby tried to get her finger in Dempsey's mouth so she could scrape the marble out, while Bradley pounded him on the back. Lenny began to shake him up and down; Brad kept pounding. Later, nobody could agree on which tactic worked, but the marble popped out and rolled under the stove. Ruby rocked Dempsey in her lap for a while, until he quit crying and caught his breath.

"It's a wonder children ever live to get grown," Bessie said.

"I guess that'll teach you not to swallow marbles," Ruby told Dempsey.

"I didn't swallow it, it rolled down my throat," Dempsey informed his mother. Then he went outside to pitch horseshoes by himself.

14

Both the bulls were mad at Charley because he won their ham sandwiches in a poker game. It happened while the train taking him to prison lurched across Ohio in the middle of the night.

"I don't see why we gotta tote you to the pen at night anyway," Earl said. He was the fat bull.

"It wasn't my idea," Charley replied.

"It's cheaper at night, Earl," Luke told him. Luke was the skinny guard.

"The state of Ohio don't believe in wastin' no money on transportation," he added.

"I wouldn't mind playin' some more cards," Charley said. "Maybe you'll win your sandwiches back."

"Wouldn't do us no good if we did, you already et 'em," Earl said. "Now me and Luke will have to get by till breakfast on chewin' tobacco."

"Serves you right for playin' cards," Charley told them with a grin. "You're lawmen, you ought to know better than to gamble with an outlaw like me."

"It's funny that a train trip would cost less at night," Earl said. "It's the same distance, night or day, way I see it."

"We could play for your next year's wages," Charley said. "If I win, you could send the money to me at the pen."

"You didn't have to eat both them sandwiches," Earl said, morosely. "You could have et one, and let me and Luke split the other."

"I'm goin' to the pen," Charley said. "I may not get a decent sandwich for fifteen years. Your old lady can make you another one tomorrow. When you see her, compliment her on the pickles, those were tasty."

To his surprise, Luke began to cackle hysterically. He was given to fits of various sorts, but Charley had never heard him laugh so hard.

"Say, what's so funny?" he asked. "All I did was give Earl's old lady a compliment on her pickles."

"I get a fit ever' time I think of pickles," Luke replied.

"Why?" Charley asked. "What's so funny about pickles?"

"Shut up, Luke," Earl said. "This man's a convict. We ain't supposed to entertain him—we're only supposed to haul him to the pen."

Charley waited, hoping somebody would let him in on the joke involving pickles, but nobody said another word. He had to sit between Earl and Luke, so he couldn't even look out the window. After a while, when Luke had stopped laughing and caught his breath, Charley stood up.

"Where you goin', bud?" Earl asked.

"Thought I'd jump the train," Charley said. "If there ain't gonna be no more card playin', I might as well."

"Jump the son-of-a-bitch," Luke said, grinning. "A stunt like that'll break your thievin' neck."

"Yeah, go break your neck," Earl told him. "It'll save the state of Ohio your room and board for the next fifteen years."

"I'd rather take a piss than break my neck, if you don't mind," Charley informed them.

"Take one for me while you're at it," Luke said. "I hate pissin' on a bumpy train."

The commode was in the next car. As soon as he was out of hearing, Earl leaned over to Luke.

"You wasn't gonna tell that joke about the man who put the dill pickle up his wife's twat, was you?" he asked.

"No, I never heard no such joke," Luke said. "I was gonna tell a better one, I bet."

"Tell it now," Earl suggested.

"Naw, it's too long," Luke said. "I'll keep it to myself till Charley gets back."

Charley went into the washroom and washed himself good in the washbasin. He hated feeling dirty, and the night train was anything but clean. It smelled like throw-up, from all the drunks who had puked on the floor.

Once he had freshened up, Charley walked out of the washroom and on back to the caboose. The conductor was there, sprawled out on a bench, asleep with his mouth wide open. An empty whiskey bottle rolled around on the floor. Charley went on out the back door of the caboose to the little platform at the end of the train.

He looked around. He couldn't see a light anywhere; he only saw the dark forest on both sides of the track. In a way, that was good, since the forest would hide him. Ohio wasn't empty, and he was sure he'd find a farmhouse somewhere—maybe he could steal a file out of a barn and file off his handcuffs.

The jump wasn't as bad as he'd expected. He went off his feet and scraped one hand pretty good, but he didn't break his neck. He watched the train until it rounded a bend in the forest and was out of sight. He would have preferred to walk along the track until he spotted a town or a farmhouse—it would be a lot easier on his clothes, but he knew easy traveling was a luxury he could not afford, not right now. Sooner or later, even Earl and Luke would figure out that he'd jumped the train. Once they figured it out, there would be pursuit.

Charley loped down the track a few hundred yards in the opposite direction from the train, and then turned off into the woods. He nearly stepped on a possum before he had gone twenty feet from the tracks. Seeing the dumb little creature reminded him of the time Ruby had tried to cook one, not long after they were married. Something went wrong, and the possum meat turned out so oily that they had to throw it away. Ruby cried for an hour, thinking it meant she was a failure as a wife.

"Honey, you ain't no failure as a wife," he told her. "You're just a failure as a possum cook.

"You do fine with pork chops," he added, in an effort to cheer her up.

As Charley picked his way into the dark Ohio woods, he couldn't help thinking about Ruby, and her long legs, and her sweet smile, and her cooking. He might only be a handcuffed convict who'd jumped a train, but it was his firm intention, before his life ended, to find Ruby wherever she was, and eat some more of her pork chops.

15

Earl got uneasy about Charley long before Luke did. Luke took life as it came, but Earl was a worrier.

"It's takin' that crook a long time to piss," he observed. "What if he did jump the train?"

"Aw, he didn't jump," Luke said. "I 'spect he's takin' a long crap."

"It's a mighty long one, if that's what it is," Earl said, ten minutes later.

Luke didn't respond. He was lost in thought.

"You sure you never heard that joke about the man who put a dill pickle in his wife's twat and left it there a week and it come out sweet?" Earl asked. "Then the old boy started givin' these sweet pickles to his buddies and they got a taste for 'em, never suspecting the truth."

"What truth?" Luke asked. When he was lost in thought, it was hard to get the simplest point across to him.

"I think I'll check the washroom," Earl said.

"Help yourself," Luke said. He was engaged to a woman who wanted him to buy the wedding dress, a thirty-dollar expenditure, and he was trying to get easy in his mind about whether or not she was marrying him for his money. Her name was Yvonne, not a common name in the part of Ohio Luke was from.

Earl checked the washroom, and found no Charley. Then he checked the caboose, where he found a drunk conductor, but no Charley. Then he became alarmed, and began to run back and forth through the cars, pistol drawn, yelling for Charley Floyd. A yarn salesman, sound asleep in the first car, threw up his hands in alarm when he saw a bull standing over him pointing a gun.

"I didn't do it!" he said.

"Go back to sleep, you idjit," Earl said, disgusted. "I ain't lookin' for you."

When Luke was finally persuaded that the prisoner had made a bold escape, he had another fit: a fit of panic. If he got fired over such an escapade, he wouldn't be able to afford Yvonne's wedding dress, nor would he have the money she was going to marry him for.

Earl convinced the engineer to stop the train, and he and Luke jumped off and ran back up the track a long way, hoping to bump into the prisoner. Their hope was that he had indeed broken his neck and would be lying there dead, leaving their futures secure.

But there was no sign of Charley, and they were finally forced to wake the conductor and wire the local authorities. The engineer was against any kind of wait. He didn't like having to stop his train in a remote region in the dark.

"What if his henchmen jump us?" he asked Earl.

"Hell, they'd have to find us first," Earl told him. "I ain't got a clue where we are, have you?"

"Yeah, we just passed Mattville," the engineer said.

The conductor was the only one who could approve a wire, and he was so soused they couldn't get him fully awake. When he did finally regain a semblance of consciousness, he failed to grasp the seriousness of the situation.

"There's bears in them woods, maybe they'll eat him," he said, when it was made clear to him that a dangerous prisoner had escaped.

Then he got into a heated argument with Luke, insisting that bears were far more of a danger to the general populace than bank robbers.

"Bears are always eatin' drunks," he insisted.

"Yeah, but Charley ain't drunk," Earl said.

When the Mattville sheriff arrived, Luke was unlucky enough to let slip the awkward fact that Charley had told them he meant to jump the train.

The sheriff's name was Colley Colliers. He was a dignified man who didn't appreciate incompetent performances on the part of law officers. Six hounds milled around his legs while he stood on the railroad tracks, trying to take the situation in. Two deputies and three deer hunters had followed him out to the train. The deer hunters had come along for the excitement.

156

They were hoping Colley would deputize them before the shooting started, but he mainly seemed irritated by their presence.

"You mean he *told* you he was gonna jump the train, and you let him?" he asked Earl.

"Sheriff, we thought he was joshin'," Earl replied.

"I'da thought he wouldn't of told us, if he meant to do it," Luke added.

"You boys don't have the firewood to fuel much thinking," the sheriff informed them bluntly. "When you take a prisoner to the pen, you have only one rule to keep in mind—you don't let him out of your sight till you get him to the pen! If that means standing in the washroom with him, that's what you do!"

Just then, they heard something cross the track fifty yards or so down the tracks. Two of the deer hunters lifted their rifles and blazed away. One of the deputies was about to follow suit, when the sheriff yelled.

"What do you vigilantes think you're shooting at?" he demanded to know. "When I need random gunfire, I'll ask for it."

"I believe I hit him, Sheriff," one of the deer hunters proudly announced.

"Probably a bear," the conductor said. "These woods are full of bear."

"How the hell would you know, Shorty?" the sheriff asked. "I've lived here all my life, and I've never seen one bear."

The group walked on down the way, swinging lanterns, and found a Jersey milk cow, stone dead on the tracks.

"Uh-oh," the deer hunter said.

Sheriff Colley Colliers shook his head.

"Amateurs are the bane of my existence," he grumbled.

16

When the landlady knocked on the door and told her she had a telephone call, Beulah had been about to jump into bed with Beauregard Evans, her new boyfriend. Beauregard had already undressed and was sitting on top of the covers with his dick sticking straight up in the air.

"I can't come right now, tell 'em to call back, please," Beulah said. She wished Beauregard would have the decency to cover his pecker with a pillow or something, but Beauregard was a cardsharp—he had few, if any, manners, but he did have dash.

"They said it's about your mother," the landlady said, through the door.

Beulah knew then it was Charley. Her mother was dead, and had been for five years. Beulah read in the newspaper about Charley's daring escape, and she knew she'd be hearing from him—she just didn't know when. The telephone was all the way down on the first floor, at the end of the hall.

"Oh, my God, did she have another stroke?" Beulah said, thinking quick.

"He just said it was about your mother," the landlady said, again.

"I gotta go talk, it's Ma, she might be dying," Beulah said, grabbing her robe. "I'll be back in a minute, I gotta find out how she is."

Beauregard looked annoyed, which didn't surprise Beulah. He leaned over and grabbed his pants—Beulah thought maybe he'd leave, which wouldn't have broken her heart—but all he did was pull his pocket watch out of his pants pocket and prop it on a pillow. He didn't say a word. The man meant to take her at her word—he wanted her back in one minute.

Beulah tied the robe, flew down the stairs, and ran down the hall to the telephone.

Charley was calling from a bus station in Akron, standing on one foot and then the other for fear some cop would spot him.

He thought Beulah would never get to the telephone. Several times, he nearly hung up and bolted. He had nipped the money to make the call from the cash register of a small cafe across the street. He couldn't wait forever, though he had no place to go. Early that morning, he had broken into a blacksmith's shop and used a file to get the handcuffs off. He had also stolen a shirt and a pair of pants off a clothesline. They didn't fit too well, but he couldn't walk around Akron in prison stripes.

"What took you so long?" he said, when Beulah finally got to the telephone.

"Charley, I was about to go out on a date," Beulah informed him. "I'm keeping him waitin' right now."

Charley saw red instantly. He'd been freezing and starving for three days, crawling through the woods and sleeping in ditches, and now Beulah was trying to rush him because she had a date, probably with some slick bozo whose middle name was pussy.

"Tell your damn date to go to hell!" Charley said, through clenched teeth. "Whose girl are you anyway?"

"Why, yours, I guess," Beulah replied, startled at how mad he sounded. "I didn't even know if you were dead or alive— what's it hurt to dance a little?"

"I'll dance on your head!" Charley said. "I'll bounce you across the sidewalk a few times if you don't get rid of that mug and get up to Akron quick. Find Billy, and make him drive. Bring Rose if you want."

"That little jerk's been two-timin' my sister, I don't know if she'll speak to him, much less ride in a car with him," Beulah said.

"Where is Akron, anyway?" she asked. "Why can't you come to Cincinnati?"

"Because I'm the most wanted man in the state of Ohio, that's why!" Charley said. "I've had nothin' to eat for three days except a piece of pie, and I swiped that. Don't stand there askin' questions, just get Billy and get a car and come get me. I'll be somewhere around the bus station."

"Honey, I miss you," Beulah said. "I really miss you."

"Miss you, too—folks are lookin', I gotta hang up," Charley said. "Get up here, don't let no grass grow under your feet."

"Grass don't ever grow under my feet," Beulah said before

hanging up. But that wasn't the way Beauregard Evans saw things—he was red-in-the-face mad when she got back to her room. He yelled at her, called her a two-timing whore, slapped her face, and even yanked her hair a few times.

"Keep your hands off me, you masher!" Beulah screamed. "Get your drawers on and get out!"

The landlady didn't like loud fusses. She started banging on the door, which was probably all that saved Beulah from getting slugged.

The landlady, Mrs. Temple, wasn't exactly a prude, but she did have her standards.

"Can't you find a quiet boyfriend?" she asked Beulah, as Beulah and Rose were leaving.

"I'm going to get a quiet one right now, he's up in Akron," Beulah said. "He's real sweet, Miz Temple, you'll see."

"You shouldn't have mentioned Akron," Rose told her, as they waited for Billy Miller to show up with the car. "The cops know you go with Charley—what if they come 'round asking questions?"

"Oh, mind your own business, Rose," Beulah said, flustered.

17

"You go flirt with the clerk," Charley told Beulah.

"That fool? He looks like he's got chicken pox," Beulah told him. They had only been in the dry goods store a few seconds. Billy and Rose were out in the car. Charley was still sore as hell at Billy because of the deputy; Billy still maintained it was self-defense. The drive had been tense.

"I can't rob no bank in clothes like this," Charley said. "Hurry up and do it while he's the only one in the store."

As soon as Beulah had the pimply clerk's attention, Charley grabbed a suit, a white shirt, and a tie. He ducked into a dressing room and changed in thirty seconds. When he peeked out, Beulah had the clerk's undivided attention. She was trying on hats, and when the clerk went back into the storeroom to bring out more hats, Charley slipped away. He couldn't resist taking a nice pair of gloves that were in a case not far from the door.

Charley walked briskly across the street to the little bank, strolled in, and smiled at the teller, a freckle-faced girl of about twenty.

"Miss, this is a stickup," he said. He didn't even have to show the gun.

"Oh, Lord, mister, I wish you'd picked another bank," she said, shaking.

"Miss, you won't be harmed," Charley said, pleasantly. He took what cash he could reach, and left. When he jumped in the car, there was no Beulah.

"I bet she's still tryin' on hats," Rose said. "You know Beulah."

"Damn her, I just robbed the bank—what'd she think we come here for?" Charley said, exasperated. "Go get her, Rose, and make it snappy."

"Listen, buster, you're the one told me to flirt with the clerk," Beulah said, when Rose finally got her out to the car. Billy drove, while Charley counted the money. It was a little over six hundred dollars.

"I didn't tell you to flirt with him into next week," Charley said. "What did you think I was doin', pickin' daisies?"

"You could've been flirting yourself, for all I know," Beulah said, pouting.

They found a rooming house in Bowling Green. It had ugly brown wallpaper, but it was on a quiet street—a little too quiet, to suit Beulah and Rose. It rained all afternoon. Billy Miller was in a stiff temper because he hadn't been allowed to participate in the robbery.

"Can it, I didn't want you machine-gunnin' the teller," Charley said.

"I ain't even got a machine gun!" Billy protested. "You could of let me watch the street, at least."

"I did—you just watched it from inside an automobile," Charley said. "Stop your yappin', this was a bread-and-butter job. We needed livin' money, that's all."

"So next time can I go in?" Billy asked.

"If you're good," Charley said.

"What if I ain't?" Billy said, annoyed by Charley's attitude.

"If you ain't, we'll just have to shoot you," Charley replied. He didn't smile when he said it, either.

Beulah and Rose had spent most of the afternoon filing their nails, and listening to the radio.

"Say, ain't you Mister Sunshine," Beulah said, looking at Charley.

Charley kept looking out the window at the grey sky.

"Getting a word outa you is like pulling a tooth," Beulah said.

"Who asked you to pull a tooth?" Charley snapped.

He got up and walked into the bedroom. A minute or two later, Beulah followed. She approached Charley timidly.

"Charley, are you just blue, or did I do something?" she asked.

Charley sat on the bed, looking out the window at the Ohio rain. He could look so sad sometimes that it made Beulah want to cry. She got kind of desperate when Charley looked that way.

"Can't you tell me what's the matter? What have I done now?" Beulah asked.

"Nothin'," Charley told her. "Nobody's done nothin'."

He breathed out a heavy sigh.

"Sometimes I miss Oklahoma, that's all," he said.

Beulah felt like crying.

"I guess it's a faded love we got going here, if you could have me to fuss with and still miss a sorry place like Oklahoma."

"What's so sorry about Oklahoma?" Charley asked, defensive.

"Nothing, if you like hot, dry, and ugly," Beulah said.

"Shut up about Oklahoma!" he snapped. "That's only part of it."

"So what's the other part?" Beulah asked.

"I don't like bein' hunted like a damn varmint," Charley said.

Later, they kissed and made up, but Charley couldn't shake

162

his blue mood. When Beulah was out of the room, he would sneak looks at the picture of Ruby and Dempsey he'd kept since the day he got out of prison. Looking at the picture made him wonder how life could turn out so different from what a person thought it was going to be. Ruby looked so sweet—and Dempsey was such a good, cheerful little boy. They were still his family; they always would be.

There were times when he couldn't afford to look at the picture—if he did, he'd break down and sob.

18

Few barbers had the patience to deal with Charley, and the barber in the Bowling Green, Ohio, barbershop was no exception.

"Could you even up them sideburns, sir?" Charley asked. He was studying the haircut closely in the mirror.

"Mister, they *are* even," the barber said.

"Not quite," Charley informed him. "The one on the right looks longer to me."

"It ain't, unless I'm goin' blind," the barber replied.

"Don't argue with him, he's stubborn," Billy Miller said. He'd been finished with his haircut for about ten minutes.

"Your eyesight could be fadin' a little," Charley said. "The one on the right's longer. Not by much, but it's longer."

The barber held his temper with difficulty.

"Whatever you say," he said. "In this barbershop, the customer is always right."

"Even when he's dead wrong?" Billy remarked.

"Aw, shut up," Charley said. "Why don't you run outside and see if you can keep the girls from spending all our money?"

"I'd rather wait till the barber gets teed off enough to cut your throat," Billy replied.

The barber pretended to level the sideburns, though he knew they were perfect.

"It would take a surveyor to get them sideburns more even," he said, finally.

"The right one's still longer," Charley insisted. "You didn't even cut any more off it."

"I was just *leveling*, sir," the barber said, stiff.

After the barber gave him a final combing, Charley reluctantly got out of the chair, and paid the man.

"You ought to think about gettin' some specs, sir," he told the barber. "Your eyesight's fadin'."

"I need a new wallet," Billy said, once they were out on the street.

"What for? Once Beulah and Rose get through in that store, you won't have nothing to put in it," Charley said. "I'm gonna go over and drag them out."

Zibe Castner, the deputy sheriff of Bowling Green, knew the flivver was suspicious the minute he saw it. He was sitting in a diner finishing his coffee when he looked across the street and saw two swells in a strange car pull up to the curb and get out. The driver was a big, strapping fellow; the passenger was short, and strutted about like a banty rooster. After they strolled off down the sidewalk, Zibe finished his coffee and darted over to examine their flivver. It had Missouri plates, which was uncommon in itself. Then he headed in the same direction as the two men, glancing in storefronts as he went, hoping to catch a glimpse of them at close range. At the barbershop, he took a quick peek through the window and saw the big man who parked the car sitting inside, getting a haircut. The man looked like Pretty Boy Floyd to Zibe—the man who had embarrassed every law enforcement officer in Ohio by escaping from a train as it was taking him to the pen.

Zibe saw Floyd, or the man he suspected was Floyd, come out of the barbershop with his squatty little companion. The two crossed the street, and went into a department store.

164

Zibe was relieved; he figured that meant he didn't have to collar the two crooks. He could trot around to the jail and get Sheriff Galliher, who would no doubt be happy to reinforce him.

Unfortunately, when he burst into the jail with the news, Sheriff Galliher was engrossed in the latest issue of *Spicy Detective*, his favorite magazine.

"Chief, I got somethin' hot," Zibe Castner said.

"Leave me alone, Zibe," the sheriff said. "Nothing could be hotter than *Spicy Detective*. That's what the word 'spicy' means —hot."

"There's a car with Missouri plates parked in front of the barbershop," Zibe said. "Two men just left the barbershop and went into the department store."

"So what?" Galliher said, not taking his eyes off the magazine. Zibe couldn't blame him, really; *Spicy Detective* did have some pretty racy illustrations.

"It's no crime to get a haircut," the sheriff added. "It's not even a crime to be from Missouri, it's just bad luck."

"I think it might be Pretty Boy Floyd," Zibe blurted out. "I'm just about sure."

That changed the sheriff's attitude pronto. He dropped the magazine on his desk, and reached for his pistol.

"Let's go catch him," he said. "If I was to arrest Pretty Boy Floyd, they'd probably give me a free subscription to *Spicy Detective*."

By the time Charley and Billy got across the street to the department store, Beulah had already piled up seven or eight things she wanted to buy. Rose, who preferred to look, was trying on a hat.

Beulah gave Charley's new haircut a close look. Then she gave him a peck.

"Charley, you're cute when you're all spiffed up," she said. "Only your sideburns are too short."

"That's what the barber tried to tell him," Billy said.

"Beulah, you could spend money in your sleep," Charley said. "Hurry up and pay, we need to move."

"What's the rush?" Beulah asked. "Me and Rose want to look in that big store down the street."

"I might buy a new hat if the girls are gonna keep shoppin'," Billy said.

"Give it a pass," Charley told him. "You look dumb enough in your old hat."

"You don't ever say nothin' nice to me," Billy said, feeling sorry for himself.

It had been a cloudy day, but the sun broke through just as the four of them stepped out of the department store. Charley was carrying all of Beulah's packages, a bulky load.

"This stuff would fill a boxcar," he said, but he was joshing. Sunshine always picked up his spirits. Beulah was cute, there was no getting around that—and he had come to like her sass. There were far worse things in life than traveling around with a sassy girl who had swell legs.

Charley started down the street toward the car, his arms full.

"We won't be long," Beulah said, as she, Rose, and Billy started across the street.

"Take your time," Charley said. "Tryin' to keep up with you has worn me out. I might curl up in the car and take a nap."

Just as he said it, Sheriff Galliher and Deputy Castner stepped out from behind a small milk truck that was parked on the other side of the street. Both of them had pistols in their hands; Charley saw them before Billy did.

"Just a minute, sir," Galliher said to Billy.

"Look out, Bill!" Charley said, dropping the packages so he could get at his pistol.

Bill "the Killer" Miller had his mind on his new hat. He was thinking along the lines of a grey fedora—he thought he looked dignified in grey. Maybe Rose would like him better if he had a new hat.

It wasn't that Rose was mean; it was just that lately, he'd had a harder and harder time getting her attention. A new grey fedora might help.

Then Charley yelled, and Billy looked up to see a tall cop aiming a pistol at him. Billy immediately yanked out his gun and fired, but he missed and hit a car. Then he felt himself falling backwards, and the sky above him began to swirl. He looked down at his stomach and saw blood on his shirt, which annoyed

166

him. He looked up and saw Beulah, who seemed to be falling, too, blood on her face. Billy wanted to help her, but he couldn't move. His shirt was ruined, that was for sure—all he could see when he looked down was blood. He heard guns going off, but he didn't know who was shooting. The street rose up toward the sky, and both were swirling so fast that Bill "the Killer" Miller had to close his eyes.

When Charley saw the deputy shoot Billy, he hit the man with three quick shots, and turned his gun on the sheriff. But as he did, the sheriff took cover behind a car. Charley shot again, and missed.

"Stay put," he yelled to the girls just as Billy fell, but the girls took off running, screaming at the top of their lungs. Beulah had only taken two steps, when the sheriff fired again, and Beulah went down.

"I'm shot!" she cried, trying to get to her feet. Charley saw blood running down her cheek. He also saw that the sheriff had good cover, which meant that his own best bet was to run. People were pouring out of storefronts, wanting a glimpse of the action.

"I'll come back for you!" he yelled, hoping Beulah heard him.

Then he began to run, as he had never run in his life. He ducked around an old lady, and jumped clean over the hood of a car. He glanced over his shoulder and saw that the sheriff was after him—but then the sheriff bumped into Rose, and had to slow down so he could hand Rose over to some vigilante. Charley knew it was his chance—he raced two blocks in record time, digging the car keys out of his pocket as he ran. By the time he got the door open and the car started, the lanky sheriff, no lagger himself, was only a block away. Charley whirled the flivver around, and took off in the other direction.

Out of town—fast—was where he needed to be.

19

The little diner was at a dirt crossroads about a mile from the Kentucky River. Smoke came out of the chimney. There were no cars in front, so Charley decided to risk it. He had been driving for nine hours, trying to stay alert, keeping on the smallest roads he could find. He needed coffee; some ham and eggs wouldn't hurt, either.

There was no one in the diner but an old waitress, and an even older man. The waitress was smoking a cob pipe. The old man had a devilish look in his eye; he wore the kind of cap railroad men wore.

"When I was a boy, women didn't stick pipes in their mouths," he said, as soon as he had Charley for an audience.

The waitress turned, and stared the old boy down.

"When you was a boy, they hadn't even invented pipes," she told him. "You oughta stay out of other folks' business and concentrate on growin' some new teeth—your first batch is about all dropped out."

"Let 'em go, I'll gum it. Bad as the food tastes around here, it don't matter," the old geezer retorted.

"Take a stool, sonny," the waitress said. "I ain't had a customer that looks as hungry as you in a long time. What'll it be?"

"How about a pot of coffee and three eggs fried hard?" Charley said. The food smells in the diner made him feel weak from hunger.

"Ham with the eggs wouldn't hurt," he added.

"Sausage with eggs might hurt even less," the waitress said. "I got some mighty good sausage."

"Yeah, from a nigger's pig," the old man said. "I'd rather not graze on no nigger's pig."

"Why not?" Charley asked. "A pig's a pig, so far as tasty goes."

"Shut up tryin' to lose me business," the waitress snapped. "Go on home to your wife."

168

"She might take after me with a hatchet," the old fellow reported. "I'm safer here, even if the food's poison."

There were two pieces of pie on a plate behind the counter. Charley felt so hungry all of a sudden that he decided to eat his dessert while his meal was cooking.

"Which one of them slices of pie is freshest?" he asked.

"You crawled into the wrong hole, if you expect fresh pie," the old man said. "That piece of pumpkin there was cooked last Thanksgiving, and that piece of vinegar pie's been here since April."

"I'll take the vinegar," Charley said. He ate it in three bites, and it tasted fine. The waitress set the coffeepot on the counter. He helped himself to some java.

While Charley waited for his eggs and sausage, the old man looked him over carefully, from head to toe.

"Stop starin' at the customers, Jake, I've warned you about that," she said. "Folks don't like to be stared at when they're eatin'.

"He looks like a nice boy, leave him be," she added.

"How would you know, you just laid eyes on him," he said. "He could be Pretty Boy Floyd, for all we know."

"Yeah, and you could be Jesse James, but you ain't," the waitress replied.

"I'm from Iowa," Charley said.

"Howdy," the old man said. "I never met nobody from Ioway. Docs it rain over there in Ioway?"

"Why, yes, now and then," Charley replied. The waitress plopped him down a plate of hard-fried eggs and hot sausage.

"I guess if you can trust anybody, you can trust a fellow from Ioway," the old man observed. "I've heard Ioway's a good state."

"I wouldn't move for a million dollars, I know that," Charley said.

"Kentucky's full of crooks," the man said. "I never cared for Kentucky."

"Why didn't you move away, then?" the waitress asked. "All us around here would of had peaceful lives if you'd moved to a different part of the world fifty or sixty years ago."

"Somebody oughta take a two-by-four to your skull," the old man said. "If I couldn't cook no better than you, I'd at least have the decency not to go 'round poisoning folks."

"These are tasty eggs," Charley said. "Real tasty sausage, too."

A minute after he said it, Charley suddenly lost his appetite. He couldn't even swallow the bite of hard-fried egg he had just put in his mouth. It was as if the tasty eggs had turned to sawdust. He managed to wash the bite down, but it took two or three swallows of coffee.

What cost him his appetite was the memory of Billy Miller lying flat on the street, a big splotch of blood spreading across his stomach. Billy wasn't moving, either. His pistol had fallen out of his hand; his eyes looked straight up in the air.

All the way down to Kentucky, for nine hours, Charley had pointed his mind toward the next curve in the road. He didn't think about the deputy he had shot three times. He thought about Ruby and Dempsey; he thought about coffee and eggs. He thought about horseshoe pitching with Bradley, and his ma's flapjacks. He drove fast, but he took care not to wreck.

Between one bite and the next, the memories came. The old man kept talking, but Charley stopped hearing what he said. The waitress was looking at him funny, but he didn't care. His mind took him back to Bowling Green. He remembered that Beulah fell. He didn't know if she was alive or dead, or if the deputy was alive or dead, or Billy. He might be a wanted killer now; he might never see Beulah again. The day had turned sunny, just before the lawmen jumped them. He had gotten over feeling annoyed about his haircut. Then, before Billy and the girls could even get halfway across the street, the shooting started, and by the time it was over, the whole world had changed.

Charley had one bite of sausage left. He had been taught to clean his plate, and he felt he ought to. He poked his fork into the sausage, and started to put it in his mouth, but he never got it there. His hand stopped working in midair; he put the fork down. When the waitress picked up the coffeepot and poured more hot java, he didn't stop her, but he didn't lift the cup, either. Everything had stopped working except his memory, and what he remembered took his appetite.

"Are you okay, son?" the waitress asked. "You look peaked all of a sudden."

Charley just sat there. He didn't know how to answer.

"He ate that pie too fast," the waitress said to the old man. "He ate it in three bites. Maybe it made him sick to his stomach."

"The pie had nothin' to do with it," the old man said, taking out a tin of snuff. "What got his stomach was that nigger pig."

20

Charley made it all the way to Kansas City by keeping to the back roads. Lulu had been expecting him, much to his surprise. She was standing on the back porch of her house when Charley pulled into the alley.

"Leave the motor running," she said, walking out to the fence. "Get in the house, I'll hide the car."

"What's the matter?" Charley asked. At times, he forgot he might be a wanted fugitive; then there were times the thought sneaked back into his mind. Driving into K.C., he had been thinking of Lulu, and her habit of walking right up to him and unbuttoning his pants.

That wasn't the mood she was in when she came out to the alley and hustled him into the house.

"What do you mean, what's the matter?" Lulu asked, incredulous. "You killed a deputy sheriff, what do you think's the matter?"

The death of the deputy sheriff was one of the things Charley had a hard time remembering. The shoot-out on the street in Bowling Green had lasted all of fifteen seconds—it had been so sudden he had to strain to convince himself that it had happened at all. It didn't connect to life—or to what had *been* his life.

By the time Lulu got back from hiding his car, Charley was so upset he looked as if he was about to cry. More and more things he didn't want to think about kept popping, unbidden, into his brain. He remembered that Billy Miller looked like someone had poured a bucket of blood on his shirt; he remembered the blood all over the side of Beulah's face when she fell. He had to do something to get his mind off the bad memories.

Lulu saw that the boy was a nervous wreck. He had always been shy—but this time, when she came through the door, he tried to put his hands on her.

"None of that," she said, giving him a stiff frown. "I've got a new boarder, and he's jealous."

"If he's just a boarder, what's he got to be jealous about?" Charley asked.

"Oh, all right then, a new boyfriend. Is that plain enough for you, Oklahoma?" Lulu said, flaring up.

Charley's face fell even further. He felt completely let down.

"I guess I thought I could count on you," he said.

"I hid your car, didn't I?" Lulu said. "You're in my house, ain't you? I could go to the pen for what few years are left of my life, for harboring a cop killer. But I'm harboring you, ain't I?"

Charley nodded weakly; he looked disoriented, and confused.

Lulu snorted. "If you ain't sure, then leave. Here's your car keys."

"I'm tuckered out from drivin'," Charley said. "I don't want to leave, I'm sorry if I was rude."

"You can't chase all over the countryside with your little floozie and come back expecting me to be a sucker for that cute grin of yours," Lulu informed him.

"I said I was sorry," Charley said. He was too weak to argue. "Beulah may be dead, for all I know."

"No, she ain't, haven't you read a paper?" Lulu asked.

"I been keepin' to the back roads. There ain't many paper stands along them roads," Charley said.

"Beulah's in the hospital, expected to recover," Lulu told him. "Rose was in custody for a while, but they let her go."

172

"What about Billy?" Charley asked. "He looked real bad the last time I saw him."

"He didn't live—neither did the deputy," Lulu said. "They both died, right there on the street."

"We wasn't even robbin'—hell, we brought money to that town," Charley said. "Beulah and Rose spent nearly forty dollars."

"The last thing I'm interested in is Beulah Baird's shoppin' habits," Lulu said. "The fact is, you killed a cop. Big Carl swung, and he never killed no cop."

"The man had a gun pointed at me," Charley said. "They jumped us for no reason."

"They jumped you because they recognized you—who give you that haircut?" Lulu asked. Charley looked numb. Annoyed as she was with him, she couldn't hold up the stiff frown. He was a boy in trouble, bigger trouble than he knew.

"A barber in that town where Billy died," Charley said.

"I've got a room in the basement, behind the boiler," Lulu said. "Get down there and stay down there. I'll bring you some grub after a while. If the cops figure that out, you can squeeze up the coal chute and hoof it."

"How long before you can feed me?" Charley asked. "I ain't had no grub since Kentucky."

"Three hours," Lulu said. "I'll have to wait till my beau goes off to his card game."

"I wish you didn't have a beau," Charley said. "I don't know what to do next. I never meant to kill nobody."

"Meant to don't matter now. The deputy's dead," Lulu said. "Scat, get on down to the basement. I'll see you later."

"Got any clean clothes that might fit me?" Charley asked. "I ain't changed in days."

Lulu remembered how meticulous Charley was about his appearance, almost like a woman. He wouldn't even wear the same shirt two days in a row, if he could help it.

"Edward's about your size," she said. "I'll see if I can sneak you down some duds."

"Who's Edward?" Charley asked.

"My beau, who do you think?" Lulu replied.

21

"You ate enough spuds to sink a tugboat," Lulu said. "Being wanted ain't killed your appetite."

"I told you, I ain't had a thing to eat since Kentucky," Charley replied.

He felt out of sorts. The little room behind the boiler was hot as August in Akins. Lulu's new boyfriend's clothes were a size too small for him—his wrists stuck out of his shirt, and his ankles stuck out of his pants. But at least they were clean.

"I ain't had cobbler this good in forever," he added.

Lulu knew Charley was disappointed because of Edward, her new stiff. Charley had no right, of course. But when had that ever stopped a jealous man from being jealous?

In a way, his brooding touched her. He wanted her, and he wanted every other woman, too—but at least he wanted *her*. Lulu couldn't find it in her to stay mad at him. She liked him a lot; probably she even loved him. But neither feeling really improved the odds against him. Charley was a wanted killer now; pussy or no pussy, life would never be the same for him again.

"We need to think ahead, Charley," Lulu told him. "I can't keep you in my cellar but a few days. Where can you go hide out for a while?"

"Why, Oklahoma," Charley said. "Folks in the hills will hide me. They know I ain't bad."

Lulu grabbed Charley's face with both hands and jerked him so hard, he heard his neck pop.

"Look at me," Lulu said. "Look at me, and listen hard. You don't want to hear this, but you are a killer. That man died, and his name wasn't Lazarus."

"Stop sayin' that, Lulu—it was him or me!" Charley pleaded. "It was him or me."

"That don't change a thing," Lulu explained. "He's dead, and

174

you're the killer. I believe you didn't want to kill nobody, and I know you wish you hadn't. But you did, and if they catch you, you'll swing, just like Big Carl. You can't fart around anymore, Charley."

"Why are you jumpin' on me?" Charley asked. "I didn't mean for none of this to happen. It just did."

Lulu looked at him and sighed.

"You'll be sorry if I lose my patience," she said. "I ain't jumpin' on you. What I'm tellin' you is, it's time you grew up. You gotta keep your head, because if you don't, the law will catch up with you and jerk it right off the top of your neck."

The only good news Charley'd had since he left Bowling Green was that Beulah was alive, and was going to be okay. But he was in a hot little basement in Kansas City, with a smelly furnace two feet away, and an old woman he should have left alone a long time ago telling him he had to be careful, when he knew it better than she did. It was when things got gloomy that Charley began to miss Ruby and Dempsey the most—and things were about as gloomy as they could get.

"I wish I had a home to go to," Charley said, feeling sorry for himself.

"A home to go to? And do what?" Lulu asked.

"Who's this Edward?" Charley asked.

"Don't be changing the subject on me," Lulu said. "Edward's my business, not yours. Go home and do what, I asked you?"

"Go home, and be home," Charley replied.

"I read you got four hundred dollars out of that bank job you pulled the day before the shootout," Lulu said. "Four hundred dollars don't go far, when you're wanted."

Charley put his face in his hands. He had no idea what he'd do if he went back to Oklahoma. Ruby was married, and she and Dempsey were gone, living in Kansas. His brother Brad and his sister-in-law Bessie were there. Maybe Beulah would like to bunk with them for a while after she got out of the hospital, until she got better. But he wasn't about to mention that thought to Lulu.

"You could get by robbin' banks if you had a good partner," Lulu said. "A partner who's smart and could make a plan."

"George Birdwell," Charley said, remembering the cowboy from Oklahoma. "He'd make a good partner. We robbed the same bank at the same time, once."

"Go find him, then," Lulu said. "That car needs to sit in a garage for a few months. I'll get you a different car."

"So who's Edward?" Charley asked, again.

"Aw, let up!" Lulu said—but she smiled when she said it.

22

When Bob Birdwell saw the car coming up the lane toward their stock pens, she grabbed the shotgun out of the pantry, and shooed the kids into the storm cellar. It was tornado weather, dark clouds boiling out of the southwest sky—the kids would have to go to the storm cellar pretty soon anyway, even if she didn't have to shoot the fellow in the car.

"Ma, there's black widow spiders in the storm cellar," Little George complained. Little George never had been able to tolerate bugs of any kind.

"So what, you're bigger than they are," Bob told him. "Step on 'em and squish 'em."

"Ma, they ain't on the floor, they're on the *ceiling*," Little George pleaded. "I can't squish 'em. What if one falls on my head and bites me?"

"You'll die, then," Laura Bell, his sister, said unsentimentally. Laura Bell was the spitting image of her mama, skinny as a twig, and just as cute. "Black widows are poison," she added.

"I'm poison too, when younguns don't mind," Bob said. "If you ain't down in that cellar in ten seconds, I'll have Daddy get out the razor strop when he comes home."

176

That threat rarely failed. The kids took off for the storm cellar carrying Baby Jessie, who was yelling her head off.

The car came around the stock pens, and stopped. Bob gave some thought to the possibility that it might be a cattle buyer, coming to see the eighteen yearlings that would soon be for sale. Maybe he got wind of the yearlings, and came out to make a bid.

The minute the tall fellow stepped out of the car, Bob recognized him: it was Pretty Boy Floyd. George had given her a full description. He had also told her repeatedly that Charley Floyd was a mighty good fellow, but Bob kept the shotgun cocked anyway. George Birdwell trusted everybody in the world, and it was sure to be his downfall someday, in Bob's view. She herself trusted no one, except Baby Jessie, who was too young yet to lie. Little George, on the other hand, came out with a lie a minute, although he was not quite five.

One of the roan yearlings was sniffing at the headlight of the car, which Mr. Floyd—if that was him—didn't appreciate.

"Git!" he yelled.

Bob walked out to the back gate, shotgun at the ready.

"That yearling don't understand English," she said. "He only understands stick. Whack him on the snoot, and he'll quit slobberin' on your car, mister."

Charley saw a fair-skinned, freckled woman with light brown hair cut like a boy's, pointing a shotgun at him. The woman was so skinny he could practically count her ribs through her dress. Though her dress was pretty, she wore big clodhopper shoes with the laces dangling loose. George had assured Charley that Bob, his wife, was the most beautiful woman in Oklahoma, which was a lie. Nonetheless, there was something about Bob Birdwell that appealed to Charley on sight.

"I don't have a stick," Charley pointed out.

"You should have come armed," Bob said. "Yearlings in this part of the country don't speak English."

"If George was home, he might not demand you point that shotgun at me," Charley said, a winning grin spread wide on his face. He had not moved any closer to the gate.

"George is seldom home, and even if he was, he don't tell me where to point my shotgun," Bob said. "I'll point it at anybody I don't trust. I don't know you, so I don't trust you."

"I came to see George," Charley informed her. "I'm Charley Floyd."

"That's right, the fella who meddled on the Earlsboro job," Bob said. "That's reason enough to shoot you right there. I don't like meddlin' from strangers, and neither does George."

"Ma'am, it was pure accident," Charley said. "We just walked into the same bank at the same time. It wouldn't happen again in a hundred years."

"Not if I shoot you, it won't," Bob said. "Maybe you'd be interested in buyin' some of our yearlings."

"Let me make a proposition," Charley said, smiling. He was liking Bob Birdwell more and more. She was different, that was for sure. He couldn't help but think that Ruby would like her, too.

"A what?" Bob asked.

"A suggestion," Charley explained. "Shoot the yearlings, and I'll buy you."

"That's a thought," Bob said, cocking her head sideways— she liked the big boy's style.

To his surprise, she pointed the shotgun up in the air, and fired both barrels. It was an old twelve-gauge, and the kick knocked her back a step or two.

"Them crows was out of range, if that's what you're shootin' at," Charley informed her. He pointed to a flock of crows a mile away, flapping along in front of the gathering storm.

"Oh, I wasn't shootin' at nothin' in particular," Bob told him. "I like to fire the gun once in a while, to scare off anything mean that might be lurkin'.

"I hope you ain't mean, Mr. Floyd," she added. "I can't afford to waste no more shells today."

"Call me Charley, ma'am," Charley said.

The wind began to whoosh hard enough that it was rocking the flivver. The clouds rolling in were dark as pitch.

"It's looking real stormy," Charley said. "Would you and George have a cellar, by any chance?"

"Yep, the younguns are already in it," Bob said.

"Hope it don't blow my car away," Charley said.

"I'd druther it wouldn't blow the fence down, neither," Bob said. "Our yearlings might wander off."

In the storm cellar, Bob smoked a skinny little cigar—Charley remembered that George Birdwell had smoked a few just like it, on the trip east after the Earlsboro job.

The three children huddled next to their mother like little possums. When Charley tried to talk to them, they looked shy, and ducked their heads.

"Where is George?" Charley asked.

"Over in Altus, rodeoin'," Bob said. "He's riding broncs, I 'spect."

"If I had a cute family like this waitin' for me, I'd give up the broncs," Charley confided.

"Yeah, but you ain't George," Bob said. "George is a rake and a ramblin' man. He shows up every now and then, whenever he decides it'd be nice if I had another baby to keep me busy. Otherwise, he's off and gone."

The storm blew itself out in twenty minutes, and the clouds moved on toward Missouri. It had rained hard for a few minutes; Bob's little possum children found a mud puddle, and began to splash in it.

"Are you a drinkin' man?" Bob asked, as she stirred up some cornbread.

"By happenstance, I have a bottle in the car," Charley said. "I'd be glad to share it with you, if you'd like."

"I'd like," Bob said.

In fact, Charley had started boozing every night, from loneliness. It turned out that Bob Birdwell frequently did too, for the same reason. She fed Charley and the kids a big supper, and then the two of them drank until the bottle was empty.

"You used to could get good moonshine 'round here, but them days are past," Bob said. "You lookin' for George 'cause you aim to pull a job?"

"I never got to know George real well, but I liked him," Charley explained. "He invited me to visit, so here I am, taking him up on it, and he ain't even home."

"That man would rather rodeo than eat," Bob said. "He's broke ever' rib he's got and most of his other bones, too, but he won't stop.

"You can bunk on the couch if you like," she said, catching Charley in a yawn.

"Don't you have a family?" she asked, as she was spreading Charley a quilt.

"I had one a while back," Charley said. "I don't have them now. My wife divorced me, took my little boy, and married again."

"Aw, that's a shame," Bob said. "You don't seem so hard to get along with."

"It wasn't that," Charley said. "I was in the pen almost four years. Ruby couldn't tough it out."

Bob looked at him thoughtfully. "Are you the cheatin' type, Charley?" she asked.

Charley was embarrassed by the question. Bob Birdwell was an odd one. All evening, he had been wanting to ask her why she didn't tie her shoelaces, but he never quite got the question out.

"Cheatin' type?" Charley asked, pretending ignorance.

"I mean, do you run with whores?" Bob asked. "Nothin' personal. I just wondered."

"Well, I ain't a preacher, I'll put it that way," Charley replied.

"George runs with whores," Bob said, shaking her head. "I can't break him of it."

She looked sad when she said it—Charley didn't know what to say.

Then she went to put her children to bed. Charley took off his shoes and lay back on the quilt. The last thing he remembered, he was thinking about Ruby's long legs. He didn't wake up till he heard Bob Birdwell's coffeepot perking, early the next morning.

Bob had tiptoed in and put a blanket over him, in the night.

23

Charley got a big surprise when he walked into the little Altus hospital. Whizbang Red was sitting in the waiting room, crying, and she looked older.

"Hello," Charley said cautiously—he was glad to see her, but he wasn't sure she would remember him.

"Charley?" she asked, evidently not sure it was him.

For a few seconds, neither of them could think of what to say next.

"Here, sit down, pardon my manners," Whizbang said. "My boyfriend got hurt in the rodeo—I ain't myself."

"Your boyfriend?" Charley said, trying not to let disappointment creep into his voice. It seemed his bad luck with women was becoming a pattern. "Your boyfriend ain't George Birdwell, is it?" Charley asked.

Just as he said it, a frantic-looking couple burst through the door—the man, a leather-skinned roughneck, was carrying a little girl, who looked terrified.

"Where's the doc, Sissy's got an eraser stuck up her nose!" the woman said, frantic.

Whizbang pointed to the swinging door, and the couple kept right on going.

"I hate hospitals," Whizbang said. "All you see is bunged-up folks."

"Is George Birdwell your boyfriend?" Charley asked, again. He figured Whizbang had lost track of the question, as a result of the interruption.

Whizbang nodded—she was feeling tearful again.

"He's in there right now. I'd be with him, but the doc chased me out."

"What happened?" Charley asked.

A bronc pitched him into the fence," Whizbang said. "He broke his collarbone, and one of his ears kinda got knocked loose.

"I wish he'd give up the rodeo, but I don't have much sway over him," she added.

"I doubt anyone has much sway over George," Charley said. He was trying to cheer Whizbang up.

"If anybody does, it sure ain't me," Whizbang admitted. "I didn't know you and George was friends."

"I barely know him, but I like him," Charley said. "He invited me to visit, so here I am."

George strolled through the swinging door just as he said it. Except for his bandages, he looked like he'd stepped right out of a bandbox. He had a fresh bandana around his neck, and his Stetson was perfectly creased. His boots were even shined.

"Why, Charley boy, howdy-do," Birdwell said. He grabbed Charley's hand with his good one, and shook it vigorously.

"Honey, is your ear okay?" Whizbang asked. "I can't see it for all them bandages."

"I think they sewed it back on pretty straight," George said. "Red, this is Charley. Charley, Red."

"We introduced ourselves," Charley said. He thought it unnecessary to refer to their former association.

"Let's sashay on out of here," Birdwell suggested. "I've inhaled about as much of this antiseptic as I can tolerate."

George and Red were installed in a small room at the hotel in downtown Altus. The lobby and the hallways were full of saddles and chaps, and the whole place smelled of saddle soap and ointment. Three moody-looking cowboys were sitting in the small lobby, smoking. All three of them looked as if they'd just been in a fight.

"This palace is where the rich rodeo hands stay," George informed him, once they were in the dusty little room.

"The mattress on that bed ain't no thicker than a steak," he added.

"If this is for rich cowboys, where do the poor ones stay?" Charley asked. "It smells like something died in here."

"Dern, I didn't realize he was so finicky, Red," George observed, with a grin. "You know the way to kill that smell?"

"I have no idea how to kill it, Mr. Birdwell," Charley replied, holding his nose.

182

"The way to kill it is to get drunk—call me Bird, please," Birdwell said. "That's what all my friends call me."

"A better way to kill it is to leave Altus," Red said. "Why do we have to stay, George? Why can't we head on back to Seminole?"

"Leave?" George asked. "Why would I leave when I still might win the bronc riding?"

"Honey, you broke your collarbone," Red reminded him. "You can't be riding no bronc with a broken collarbone."

"Go wash your face, you got tear tracks," George said. Red headed in the direction of the little sink over in the corner of the room.

"Hungry, Charley?" Bird asked.

"I could eat," Charley admitted.

The next thing he knew, they were sawing at tough Oklahoma beefsteaks in a joint called the Dew Drop Inn. The place was filled with cowboys and whores.

"This steak is so raw, I can hear it mooin'," Charley complained.

"The rodeo's in town, bud," George said. "They don't have time to do no well-done cookin'."

"Where'd you two meet up?" Charley asked, meaning Birdwell and Red.

"Waurika," Whizbang said. "Some bulls were draggin' me in. Bird walked up and pretended he was my husband, and I've been in love with him ever since."

"I can see why," Charley said. " 'Course, I'd defend you, too, if I seen some bulls slappin' you around."

He thought it best not to refer to his visit with Bob. For all he knew, George hadn't even told Whizbang he was married. Whizbang Red looked sad every time she let her eyes linger on George Birdwell. Maybe she already knew her dream was a hopeless one.

Charley felt sorry for Red. He thought she was in the same boat with him. He wasn't going to get over Ruby, and Red wasn't going to get over George.

As for George Birdwell, the notion of getting over someone didn't apply—he had no intention of doing without anybody. A little fiddle band struck up "Red River Valley," and Bird immediately yanked Red out of her chair, and headed for the dance floor.

"I can't stand dawdlin' over food, when I can be kicking up my heels," Bird said.

Charley sat and watched, wishing Ruby was there. Ruby loved to dance. So did Beulah, for that matter. He wondered if Bob Birdwell was much of a dancer. She would have to tie her shoes if she got on a dance floor; if she didn't step on her own shoelaces, somebody else would.

Birdwell insisted that Charley take a turn on the dance floor with Red. He was glad to, although his own stepping was a little rusty. But the place was so full of cowboys and whores, he couldn't dance two steps in a straight line if he'd wanted to.

While they were dancing, Charley got blue. The blue spells were coming more and more often now, and he would just sort of lose his energy when they hit. He'd be driving down the road, and all of a sudden get so blue he would have to pull over. Sometimes, even putting his foot on the brake took more energy than he had.

Red was no moron; Charley's mood got so heavy, he could hardly pick up his feet.

"What's wrong, hon?" Red asked. "You look like you ain't got a friend in the world."

"Do you ever get the feelin' that you've made one too many mistakes?" Charley asked her.

"Had it all my life," Whizbang replied. "So far, it ain't stopped me from makin' more, though."

"Meaning George?" Charley asked.

"George is just George," Red said, glancing across the crowded dance floor to catch a glimpse of the man she loved.

"I can't help lovin' him, Charley," she added. "I can't help lovin' him, though I know he won't be true."

Charley was relieved when the number ended.

"Ever rodeo, Charley?" Birdwell asked, when Charley brought Red back to her seat.

"Rode the milk cow once, that's the extent of it," Charley told him.

"You oughta try it sometime," Bird said, with a grin. "If you're lucky, maybe you'll break your collarbone, too."

184

24

"We could rob that nice little bank over in Enid, and drive off smooth," Birdwell told Charley.

"How do you know we could drive off smooth?" Charley asked. They were back in the dusty hotel room with the bad smell. Whizbang was sound asleep—when she was awake, she looked older; but when she slept, she had the look of a little girl.

" 'Cause I know the sheriff over in Enid," Birdwell informed him. "He visits his girlfriend regular, and his girlfriend lives six miles out of town."

"What about deputies?" Charley asked. "It was a deputy I had to shoot, up in Ohio."

"They ain't got no deputy in Enid," Birdwell assured him.

"Are you sure, Bird?" Charley questioned. "I can't afford no mistakes, this time."

"They ain't got no deputy 'cause he drank lye and died," Birdwell said, getting a little impatient with so many questions. "It was in all the papers—Red will tell you."

"They could've hired another deputy," Charley pointed out. "We better make sure. I don't want to look up and see some fat cop pointing a gat at my head. That's another thing, Bird—why do you suppose so many cops are fat?"

"Bud, you worry too much," Birdwell told him, ignoring the question. "Now, that ain't to say we shouldn't plan, I'm a firm believer in plannin'."

"Why'd that deputy drink lye?" Charley inquired.

"Thought it was moonshine," Birdwell said. "He drank half the jug before he realized his mistake."

"Uh-oh," Charley said suddenly. "We need to check the back door."

"What back door?" Birdwell asked.

"The back door of the bank in Enid," Charley said. "I thought you believed in plannin'."

"Except on days when I break my collarbone," Birdwell said,

with a twinkle. "All I believe in is booze and pussy, on those days."

"I can take a hint," Charley said. "I'll go bunk in my car."

Birdwell cast a fond eye at Whizbang Red, who was sound asleep and snoring lightly.

"You can bunk where you want to," Birdwell said. "I was thinking of going out on the town, myself. I don't aim to sleep my life away."

Charley had been thinking about rolling back over to the Dew Drop Inn himself, and having another dance or two. He had noticed a pretty little brunette that all the cowboys wanted to dance with. Now that he had warmed up by dancing with Red, he might try to get a dance with the brunette whore.

"What about Red?" Charley asked.

Birdwell cocked an eye in Red's direction and grinned.

"Looks to me like Red's asleep. Anyway, me and her ain't married," Birdwell said.

"You don't say?" Charley said. "Let's go."

They arrived back at the Dew Drop Inn only to discover that there had been a large-scale fight. Half the tables were smashed, and several cowboys nursed swollen eyes and busted lips. The brunette whore was sitting over in a corner with sawdust on her skirt, crying her eyes out.

"Aw," Charley said. "I think I'll go try to cheer up that little lady."

"I was having the very same thought, only I seen her first," Birdwell said.

"Oh, can it, Bird," Charley said. "You can't pull that on me this time. I got as much right as you do to rob a bank, and I got as much right as you do to try and cheer up that gal."

"On the other hand, I'm cuter than you," Birdwell said, doing a little dance step for the lady's benefit. "She might cheer up quicker if she had someone real cute to entertain her."

"I know you're dandy, but I expect I'm cute enough," Charley said.

Rather than argue the matter further, he walked over to the whore, and offered his handkerchief.

"Ma'am, can I be of assistance?" Charley asked.

186

When the whore looked up, Charley had to admit she wasn't quite as pretty as he had been picturing her in his head.

"Go stick your dick through a knothole," she said. "Who asked you to butt in?"

"I told you you wasn't cute enough," Birdwell said. He had strolled up behind Charley. He smiled his most winning smile, and tipped his hat to the whore.

"Gimme that six bits you owe me, George," the whore said.

"What six bits?" George asked, looking as innocent as a four-year-old—or trying to.

"That six bits you never paid me in Muskogee," the whore said. "You know what six bits. I ain't a sucker like Red, I'm a workin' girl."

About that time, a bowlegged old cowboy with a blotchy face came up, and took a wild swing at Charley. The cowboy was so drunk he missed completely, and wandered out onto the dance floor. He swung at the first dancers he came to, but he missed again. A big fellow with a paunch stopped two-stepping long enough to pop the old man in the jaw, flattening him.

"Oops, Old Man Taylor oughtn't have bothered Winfield," George observed. "Winfield will box him if he has to."

"Where's the six bits, George?" the brunette whore insisted. "Pussy costs just as much in Muskogee as it does anywhere else."

"I can still remember when you thought of something besides money, Flo," George said. But he dug the money out of his pocket, and gave it to her.

"I only come over here 'cause you was crying," Charley told her. "I didn't invite no insults."

"I'll cry if I want to, cornbread!" the whore said, acidly.

"This place ain't as friendly as I thought it was," Charley mumbled. "I wish I'd stayed at the hotel."

"We can cruise on out of here," Birdwell said. "There's a place over in Lawton that stays open all night. Maybe the whores ain't so grouchy, over in Lawton."

"Let's drive," Charley said, heading for the door.

25

Charley arranged to meet the train in Tahlequah. He thought it was safer than having Rose bring Beulah all the way to Sallisaw. Bob Birdwell had done him the favor of wiring the trainfare up to Ohio the day before he and George pulled the bank job in Enid. George might talk casual, but when it came time to work, he was all business. The two of them were in the Enid bank less than two minutes, and got away with nearly three thousand dollars in small bills. The sheriff, as George had predicted, was visiting his girlfriend, and no deputy had been hired to replace the one who drank the lye.

Beulah still had a bandage over one eye. Tears leaked out from under the bandage when Charley spoke to her, and took her in his arms.

"Oh, Charley," Beulah said, hugging him tight. "I thought I'd die from missing you."

"Honey, we got to scat," Charley said. "Somebody from 'round Sallisaw could step off this train and recognize me. I got an aunt lives in Tahlequah."

In the car, Beulah clung to Charley, shaking like a leaf, while Birdwell drove.

"It's a long way down from Ohio," Rose said. Other than that, she didn't say much, but Charley could tell she was glad to see him.

"These little gals need a rest," Birdwell said. "Let's take 'em home to Bob."

"Does Bob run a hotel?" Beulah asked. Her one blue eye, the one that wasn't bandaged over, looked scared.

"You've lost weight, looks like," Charley said. He was not used to Beulah being so subdued. Usually, Beulah made all the conversation—all he had to do was grunt once in a while.

"Getting shot in the head kinda takes your appetite," Beulah replied.

188

"I guess it would," Charley admitted. It shocked him that Beulah had lost so much of her brass. He missed her yapping, among other things. He wasn't sure that going to Bob Birdwell's was such a good idea. Bob Birdwell didn't impress him as being the kind of woman who welcomed carloads of company.

"Maybe we ought to take them on to Brad and Bessie's," Charley said. "They're expecting us, and Bob ain't."

He had decided Beulah and Rose ought to stay with Brad and Bessie while Beulah recovered from her injury. That way, they'd at least be in Oklahoma, and he'd get to see them. Birdwell acted like he didn't hear Charley's remark.

Charley was apologetic when they drove up to the Birdwell farmhouse. It was clear that Bob had no idea her husband was even in their part of the country. She was doing a big washing on the back porch, scrubbing the clothes on an old scrub board, and putting them through a wringer. The kids, meanwhile, were in the back yard, throwing mud pies at one another.

"It's a good thing I'm a washin' fool," Bob said, when the car drove up. "I'll barely get this load done before I'll have to start scraping the mud pies off those tykes."

Her shoes still weren't laced, but at least she was in a welcoming temper. There was a ham bone and butter beans on the stove. Bob complimented Beulah and Rose on their frocks.

So far, though, Charley had not seen Bob even so much as look at her husband. The kids looked at George, though. The two that could walk jumped in his arms, mud pies and all, and George gave them both big kisses before he picked up Baby Jessie.

"George, stick some money under the churn before you leave," Bob said, as she was dishing up butter beans. "Our hens ain't layin', I'm gonna have to start buying eggs."

"Buyin' eggs? When you live on a damn farm? I never heard of such expense," George said. He looked grouchy at the thought of having to shell out for eggs.

Bird never said another word to Bob during the visit—nor did Bob say another word to Bird. About an hour later, just before they left, Charley saw George slip two bills into the sugar jar.

"I thought you was supposed to put that money under the

churn," Charley said, as he and Bird stood on the porch smoking, waiting for Beulah and Rose to finish prettying themselves up.

"What money?" Birdwell asked.

"You was supposed to put Bob's egg money under the churn," Charley said. "But you didn't, you put it in the sugar jar."

"If that woman thinks she's gettin' money out of me to buy an egg, she's got another think a'coming," Birdwell said. "If I ever start giving her money for things like eggs, she'll bleed me dry in a month."

"Eggs don't cost much, do they?" Charley asked.

"You pay for the hen, you're supposed to get the dern eggs free," Birdwell said, sounding huffy.

"If Bob went off and bought a bunch of worthless hens, that's her lookout," he added.

Charley didn't know what to say.

"What about the money you put in the sugar jar?" Charley asked. "What was that for?"

"That's for me to know and you to wonder about," Birdwell said, still in his huffy mode.

The four of them were about to get in the car, when Birdwell suddenly changed his mind and decided to stay with Bob and the children. Charley was taken aback—they had planned to take Beulah and Rose to Bradley's house, and then pull another bank job to help pay for Beulah's doctor bills. Bird wanted to go over to Frederick, and rob the bank there.

"But it's your car," Charley pointed out. "Mine's down at Brad's."

"Come back and get me in a day or two," Bird said.

"I don't understand," Charley said. "I thought we had a plan."

"We did, till Bob got it into her head to squander all our money on eggs," Birdwell said.

"What if I give her money for the eggs?" Charley offered. "It can't be that much. Then we won't have to change our plans."

"Who asked you to spoil my wife?" Birdwell said.

"Gosh, I thought you loved her to pieces," Charley said.

"I do, but I may stop if she keeps on wastin' money," Birdwell said. " 'Night, girls. You hurry up and get well, Beulah, and

190

don't let nobody black your good eye." He kissed the Baird sisters on the cheeks.

"I don't aim to, I usually do the eye blacking myself," Beulah told him. "I blacked Charley's once, with a shoe."

Bird went back in the house, still looking huffy.

"I don't get it," Charley said, shaking his head, as they pulled out onto the highway. "All he talks about is how much he loves his wife, and then the only time he even speaks to her, it's to complain about a little egg money."

"You don't understand women, Charley," Beulah observed. "How much farther is this place we're looking for?"

"We ain't looking for no place, I'm takin' you to my brother's house till you get well," Charley said. "You think I have to look for my own brother's house?"

"Shut up, it's just an expression," Beulah said.

Charley felt confused. He wished women were simpler. Even Ruby wasn't simple, really—it was only when he was far away, imagining her, that she seemed simple. At home, close up, he never knew when she might burst into tears, or when a fight might break out.

"If he loves Bob so much, why doesn't he show it?" Charley asked. "He didn't even look at her when we drove up."

"If I hadn't so much as looked at you when you stepped off the train, how would you have felt?" he asked.

"I'd have slapped you silly. So would Rose, wouldn't you, Rose?" Beulah said to her sister.

"I expect," Rose said.

"The point is, I ain't Bob Birdwell," Beulah said. "Maybe she don't like her husband paying attention to her in public.

"That don't mean he don't pay her attention in private," she added.

Back up the road, in the privacy of the Birdwell bedroom, Bird and Bob were paying one another some urgent attention. Bird had barely been willing to wait for the children to be put to bed before he started paying Bob her share of attention.

"Why do I love you so much, you skinny little hussy?" Bird asked Bob, during a respite.

"Because I keep your dick slick," Bob said.

191

"That's one reason, but there might be others," Bird allowed.

"I doubt it, sweetie," Bob replied.

26

"They're real kind," Beulah said with a sigh—she was referring to Bradley and Bessie. "Rose thinks so, too."

Rose, at the moment, was down in the kitchen with Bessie, peeling pears.

"This is a decent room, ain't it?" Charley asked. He was almost at his wit's end with Beulah. He had even gone to Tulsa and bought her presents, but Beulah just wouldn't perk up.

"I don't care much for the wallpaper, but it's a decent room," Beulah said. She looked out the window at the view, which was bleak. It was wintry and grey, no leaves on the trees. Bradley's old milk cow was standing in the mud, licking a calf. A black pig was standing by the trough, waiting for Bessie to bring it some slop.

"Then what is it?" Charley asked. "Why don't you ever smile? What would it take to get you to be your old self?"

Beulah shrugged. She was in an old flannel gown, sitting up in bed. Some days, she scarcely got out of bed at all.

"I don't have no idea," she confessed. "I just feel blue."

"Everybody feels blue sometimes," Charley said. "You think I don't?"

"Why would you feel blue, Charley?" Beulah asked. "All you got to do is run around with George Birdwell and rob banks. You robbed one just yesterday."

"That wasn't much of a bank," Charley said. "We only got seven hundred dollars."

"That's seven hundred more than anybody's handed me lately," Beulah said.

Charley lay on the bed, and put his arms around Beulah, tight. The doc had taken the bandage off her eye the week before, and the eye looked fine to him. There was a little scar on her temple, but it wasn't bad. Beulah's eyes were just as blue and pretty as ever—only now, instead of a twinkle, they looked as if big tears were about to form in them. Charley missed the twinkle, even if it was a mean twinkle most of the time.

Charley slipped his hand under the covers. He tried a kiss and a feel, but Beulah didn't respond. She kept looking out the window.

"You need a shave," she said. "Your whiskers are all scratchy."

"Why shave?" Charley asked. "Why do anything? All you do is lay here. I can't make you laugh, I can't get you excited, I can't even make you mad. If you're gonna be like this, I might as well grow a beard. At least it'd be something to do."

Beulah smiled a tiny smile when he said that.

"Charley, are you frustrated?" she asked.

"Yeah, I'm frustrated!" Charley told her. "I want my girlfriend back."

Beulah put her hand on his cheek.

"Was I a good girlfriend, Charley?" she asked.

"Hon, you were the best girlfriend in America," Charley replied. "You were cute as pie, and you still are."

"If I was such a good girlfriend, why'd you screw that old whore?" Beulah asked.

"Who says I did—can't you let that go?" Charley asked. "I've heard enough about that."

"Ha, got your goat," Beulah said, showing some life.

Charley didn't answer.

"I didn't mean to start an argument," he said. "I just want you to perk up. Ain't there nothing I could buy you that might help?"

He thought he was making some progress, but then, to his horror, two big tears rolled out of Beulah's eyes. She put her face against his neck, and clutched him to her.

193

"You shouldn't have taken me no place where I'd get shot, Charley," she sobbed.

"Honey, how was I to know that deputy would pop up with a gat?" Charley said. This was another matter they had been over several times.

"You shouldn't have anyway," Beulah insisted. "Me and Rose are just little chippies—we ain't bank robbers. If that bullet had been aimed even a teensy bit better, I'd be dead. I'd have died right there in the street."

"But it wasn't, and you didn't," Charley pointed out, as he had several times before.

"You don't know, you never been shot," Beulah said. "Gettin' that close to dying makes a person different. Sometimes I feel like I did die, and all this is just a dream or something."

Charley gave out a heavy sigh, and rolled away from her.

"Honey, you didn't die," he said. "The doc says you're fine. All you need to do is perk up."

"Docs don't know everything," Beulah informed him. "Why don't you go feed that stupid black pig, and leave me alone."

"I don't own that pig, it ain't my job to slop it," Charley told her. "Why don't you bounce your ass out of that bed and go help Bessie with the pears, like Rose is doing?"

"I'll help when I feel like it," Beulah replied. "Go shave and stop pestering me. I'm getting well the best way I can. Bringing me off down here to the sticks didn't help, I can tell you that."

"I don't want to hear no complaints about Oklahoma," Charley said, pointing a finger at her. "You ain't givin' Oklahoma a chance."

Beulah had grown up in South St. Louis, right smack dab in the center of the city. Any time she'd spent in the country had been on drives between the big cities, like St. Louis and Chicago, or St. Louis and Kansas City. Life in the Oklahoma dust bowl was a far cry from the bright lights and dance halls of K.C. and downtown St. Louis. The dirt and boredom was something she didn't think she could ever get used to, even if she never recovered from her gunshot wound.

Beulah looked annoyed. "Charley, will you just go away?" she said. "Go dig a hole or something. I'm here, ain't I? I'm giving

Oklahoma a chance. What do you want me to do, dance with the milk cow?"

"By God, if that's how you feel, I guess I'll leave," Charley said.

Later, Beulah got her bathrobe on and went down to the kitchen and read stories to Annie Lee, Bessie and Bradley's youngest girl. Annie Lee was four.

"Annie Lee, you got the prettiest hair," she said, stroking the child's blond curls.

Bessie came in with an armful of stove wood just in time to hear Beulah compliment Annie Lee on her hair. Bessie smiled —she couldn't look at her daughter without smiling. The boys were a different matter; at least they were when they were being devils.

"There's still a biscuit or two in the oven," she told Beulah. "You could have some of that plum jelly with them."

"I'll eat, directly," Beulah said. "I guess Charley went off mad."

"Well, he went off," Bessie agreed. "He didn't speak to me, so I don't know how mad he was."

Beulah looked around the poor little kitchen, with the wood stove that was barely holding together. The kitchen was clean and smelled good, because Bessie was a good cook, but it didn't take much of an eye to figure out that the Floyds were poor. They relied mostly on the vegetables Bessie had put up during the summer, with a little fatback for seasoning.

"Charley, why don't you give them some money?" Beulah asked, the second day she was there, when she was settled enough to begin noting the poverty.

"They're your kin," she added. "You rob banks—give 'em some money."

"They got their pride, Beulah," Charley told her. "They like to do for themselves. They won't even take but fifteen dollars a month for boarding you and Rose—and I had to beg 'em to take that."

To Beulah, it seemed a bleak life: Brad a slave to the land all day, Bessie up before dawn and still cooking or scrubbing or sewing after sundown, money so scarce that the kids were only allowed to wear shoes from November to April. The bigger children sometimes went off to school barefoot, even with frost on the ground.

But Charley was right: Brad and Bessie had their pride—the most she had been able to do for them was let Bessie have a little of her toilet water one night, when Brad and Bessie had gone to a barn dance.

Bessie put the wood down by the wood stove, gave Annie Lee a little kiss, and Beulah a little squeeze. Beulah had been reading Annie Lee the story of Jack and the Beanstalk.

"I just love your sister Rose, she's got such a sweet disposition," Bessie said, sitting down across from Beulah and Annie Lee. "She's out there right now, getting her feet muddy, trying to help Brad get that new calf to suck."

"Rose is a worker," Beulah said. "She's always put me to shame. I'll sit around painting my nails, and Rose will be down in the kitchen scrubbing an oven or something."

Bessie laughed. "Well, somebody's got to read stories to Annie Lee. Lord knows I seldom have the time."

"Bessie, would you tell me if I'm a burden?" Beulah asked. "If I am, I'd rather hitch a ride to the bus station and just go."

"Honey, what gives you the notion that you're a burden?" Bessie said. "Me and Brad love havin' you and Rose. It's good for the kids to have new people in the house once in a while, and it's a help to me and Brad, too.

"If we stay to ourselves too much, all we do is sit around and fight," she added, getting up and walking over to the sink.

"Charley wants me to be cheerful like I used to be," Beulah said. "He thinks I can just perk up because he says 'Perk up.' "

"It don't work that way, does it?" Bessie said. "The minute I get a little hot, Bradley tells me to calm down. It makes me want to crack him with a piece of firewood."

"I wish I could perk up," Beulah said. "I never was the mopey type. But I never got shot in the head before, either. I think it changed me inside. Sometimes I wonder if I ever will be jolly again."

"You'll be jolly again," Bessie assured her. "Maybe not right away. But in a year or two, I 'spect you'll be fine."

196

"A year or two? Gosh," Beulah said. "Charley Floyd won't put up with no two years of moping."

Before she could stop herself, Beulah burst into tears.

"Don't drip on the book," Annie Lee said, yanking it out of Beulah's hands.

Bessie took Beulah's tears in stride. She put down the dishrag, walked over by her chair a minute, and put her arms around Beulah's shoulders.

"Charley's just a man, honey," Bessie said. "He ain't a bad one, as men go. He's always offering to help his family out. He's got a good heart—he's always took up for Brad, and he takes up for me like I'm his own sister."

"Do you think he loves me, Bessie?" Beulah asked, gasping and trying to get her breath and dry her tears.

"Aw, he loves you—you oughtn't to be doubtin' that," Bessie said. "You think he'd go to all the trouble to bring you down here to get well, if he didn't care?"

"But he might stop—I ain't pretty anymore, and I ain't very warm to him, either—something's gone wrong with me, I don't know what." Beulah sobbed; then she began to cry even harder. Bessie pulled up a chair, and began to stroke Beulah's hand.

Annie Lee, tired of so much bawling, got up and went outside. She tried to pitch the kitten into a mud puddle, but the kitten meowed and ran off to the barn, to hide in the hay.

Bessie didn't say anything. She just let Beulah cry.

"You're no burden, Beulah," Bessie said, after a while. "You and Rose wouldn't be burdens if you lived with us for the rest of your lives. It'd just mean we had a bigger family, which I'd like."

"You would?" Beulah asked.

"I was one of fourteen kids," Bessie informed her. "We had cousins livin' with us, and everyone else you could think of— hired help, and neighbors' kids, and widows, and I don't know who all. I miss it. I get to feelin' lonesome around here, even though there's the bunch of us, countin' you and Rose."

" 'Course, I got lonesome at home, too," Bessie added. "I may just be the lonesome type."

"That's what I think about Charley," Beulah said. "He's got that lonesome look in his eyes, and it's worse since he shot that deputy. I don't know what to do. I love Charley to pieces, but I can't love him enough to take that lonesome look out of his eyes."

"Ruby couldn't, either—if you don't mind my mentioning her," Bessie chanced.

"No, mention her," Beulah said. "He'll hardly say her name around me. It's because he's still in love with her, I guess."

Bessie didn't answer.

Beulah didn't know if she should press Bessie. She had always been curious about Ruby, and still was, but she felt it might not be good manners to be asking questions of Bessie, her former sister-in-law. Beulah was a guest, and she wanted to use good manners, if she could manage it.

"I keep thinking I ought to leave him," Beulah said. "If I left him, maybe he'd go get Ruby back, and she'd do a better job at getting him to feel less lonesome."

"Ruby's married to a decent man, and I hope she'd have more sense than to leave him and go running around with Charley," Bessie confessed. "That's hard for me to say, because I love Charley. But he's a wanted killer, and even if he wasn't, I doubt Charley Floyd could stay home and be happy with any woman for very long."

"He thinks he could—all he talks about is having a home somewhere," Beulah said. "Shoot, I'd try it with him if that's what he really wants—at least I'd try if I ever get over the mopes."

Bessie shrugged. "Men mostly want what they don't have, Charley's no exception. When he had a home, and a wife and a child, he couldn't wait to run off to the big city and get in trouble. I guess part of him wants to settle down, but then part of him can't tolerate settlin' down, either."

"I wonder how we'd do if we got married?" Beulah wondered. It was a hope she had been nursing for a while.

"If you could manage to keep him home, I guess it could be fun," Bessie said. "I got my doubts that anybody could keep old meanderin' Charley home for much of a stretch."

"I expect you're right," Beulah admitted. "But if I can ever get my spirits up, I might give it a try.

"Where's that plum jelly?" she asked, getting up and grabbing a cold biscuit out of Bessie's oven.

27

"Lenny, don't box with him when I'm trying to get him ready for school," Ruby scolded.

"Tell him to quit. I'll be glad to quit—I'm the one gettin' whipped," Lenny said, as Dempsey pummeled him with lefts and rights. One right went slightly astray, and knocked a box of cereal off the breakfast table. Dempsey was doing his fancy footwork and stepped on the box of cereal as he was dancing around, throwing punches at Lenny.

"That's enough, Dempsey! Stop it!" Ruby said. "Just stop it."

Both her husband and her son were cutups, which she didn't usually mind. The problem was that they were apt to be at their friskiest right before breakfast, a time when she would have liked to sit quietly and saucer a cup of coffee. Her brain got off to a slow start some mornings, and having Lenny and Dempsey punching at one another like prizefighters, knocking cereal off the table, didn't help it pick up speed.

"Well, off to work," Lenny said, leaning over to give Ruby a peck. "Try not to beat up nobody at recess, Mr. Dempsey."

"I *will too* beat up somebody at recess!" Dempsey predicted —though usually, he was timid at school, and didn't get in fights. It was only in daydreams that he beat people up.

"Lenny, could you bring home a few doughnuts from the bakery?" Ruby asked, looking up at her husband. Lenny was the sweetest guy in Coffeyville, Kansas, that was for sure. He didn't know how to take care of himself at all. It made Ruby feel sorry for him.

" 'Course—you want the glazed?" Lenny asked.

"Just doughnuts, all kinds, any kinds," Ruby said. "You decide."

Lenny gave her another peck, and left.

"Charles Dempsey, do you think you could clean up that cereal you spilled?" Ruby asked.

"It's all squished, Mama," Dempsey said. "You can sweep it with the broom."

"Okay, go get me the hairbrush, your hair's one cowlick after another this morning," Ruby said.

While Ruby was trying to smooth down Dempsey's hair, there was a knock at the front door. Ruby was still in her bathrobe and gown; she had a suspicion that it was a vacuum cleaner salesman who had been pestering everybody in town for the past week. Ruby had already turned him down twice, and didn't have any patience left to waste on the man.

"Dempsey, would you get the door?" she asked, giving his hair a final brush. "If it's a salesman, tell him to go away, we don't want any."

She was about to put the coffeepot back on the stove to warm the coffee a little, when Dempsey came back into the kitchen with a funny look on his face.

"What's the matter?" Ruby asked.

"It wasn't the vacuum cleaner man," Dempsey said.

"Who was it, honey?" Ruby asked, stooping down in front of him.

"It's my daddy," Dempsey said.

"Oh, did he forget something?" Ruby asked, assuming he meant Lenny. Dempsey had called Lenny Daddy for the past month or two.

"No . . . I don't mean Lenny," Dempsey said. "It's my *daddy*."

Ruby thought it was some tease Lenny and Dempsey had thought up to pester her, just as she was trying to get Dempsey off to school. It seemed to take longer every morning, but once it was accomplished she could look forward to an hour of peace and quiet before she had to start dealing with the chores of the day.

She jumped up from the table, ready to give Dempsey and Lenny a piece of her mind: then she saw Charley, standing in her front door, in a stylish blue overcoat.

The shock hit Ruby so hard that she felt weak in the legs. She didn't know what to say or do. She had imagined such a moment —Charley coming back—but when she was imagining it, she handled it well, she kept it under control, she did the sensible thing.

But this wasn't imagining; Charley was standing in the open door. One more step, and he would be in her home. It wasn't old feelings coming back; it took only one look in his eyes to make her know that she still loved him: the feelings had never gone away.

"Come in, shut the door, somebody might see you—oh my God, did Lenny see you?" Ruby asked—Lenny was so jealous of Charley's place in her past and Dempsey's that if he had seen Charley coming up the walk, he was probably already down at the sheriff's office, turning him in.

"He didn't see me, Ruby—I parked in the next block," Charley assured her. "He went on to work."

Ruby quickly turned her attention to Dempsey. It was too unsettling to look at Charley.

"Dempsey, you're going to be late for school if you don't hurry," she said.

Dempsey's face fell.

"But I don't have to go to school today," Dempsey said. "Daddy said I didn't."

For a moment, the swirl of feelings inside Ruby focused and became anger.

"Oh, Daddy did, did he?" she said. "You two must've got acquainted real quick, if he's already telling you what you can and can't do."

Charley knew he probably shouldn't have told Dempsey such a thing—but it was something he couldn't resist. He saw the red anger spots on Ruby's cheekbones, and the heat in her eyes. He tried grinning; maybe it would help.

"Don't you bust in here after all this time and start giving

201

orders, Charley!" Ruby said, her eyes flashing. "I ain't raising no outlaw. Dempsey has to go to school like other children."

"Mama, can't I miss one day?" Dempsey asked. "Daddy's here."

"No, you can't, Charles Dempsey," Ruby said. She grabbed his coat and stuffed him into it.

Charley looked at his son and shrugged. "Mama's the boss," he said. "You go on to school."

"Will you be here when I get back?" Dempsey asked.

"I sure will," Charley said, avoiding Ruby's eyes when he said it.

Even so, Dempsey was reluctant to leave. He took a step or two and stopped, turning around and looking at his father, hoping his mother would relent.

"Charles Dempsey, GO TO SCHOOL!" Ruby commanded, pointing down the street.

Charles Dempsey shuffled off, looking sad. He looked over his shoulder several times, but he kept his feet moving, and proceeded in the general direction of the school. It was a windy day; leaves swirled around him as he walked.

Ruby quickly shut the door, but she and Charley stood by the living room window, watching Dempsey until he turned the corner. Ruby was afraid to speak. Feelings rose and swirled like a tornado inside her, a tornado that might pick her up and toss her into a fence or a wall.

"What was the point of that?" Charley asked, finally. "I ain't seen him in more than five years. It wouldn't hurt him to miss one day."

"Whose fault is it that you ain't seen him?" Ruby inquired. "Where was you, that you didn't see him? I would've sent him to your folks anytime, if you'd just asked."

They looked at one another in awkward silence.

"I guess I didn't feel I had the right to ask you anything, honey," Charley replied.

"Don't call me honey!" Ruby snapped. "I got a decent life here, you can't just open the door and walk in after all this time and start in callin' me honey—like none of what I been through mattered at all."

202

"Can I have a cup of coffee while we're arguin'?" Charley asked. "I drove all night to get here."

Ruby started to tell him to hike it to a cafe and buy himself a cup, but the words wouldn't come out. She turned and went back to the kitchen, with Charley a step behind her.

"I've had dreams about your coffee," Charley admitted, as he sipped a cup. "You ever have dreams with smells in 'em? I have, lots of times."

Ruby decided the thing to do would be not to look at him. If she didn't look at him, the tornado might set her down safe. He could drink his cup of coffee, and then he could go.

"Pardon me, but I have to get busy with the dishes," she said —she was determined to stay calm. She took the coffeepot off the stove and carefully set it in the icebox. She carried several plates to the sink, and then carefully took her apron out of the cupboard. She put the folded apron in the oven, at which point she happened to glance at Charley, who was grinning his infuriating grin.

"Excuse me, honey," he said, as he pushed his chair back from the table and got up. "Are we gonna have that apron with grits or potatoes?"

"You shut your smart mouth, Charley!" Ruby blurted, but before she could say anything more, Charley shut her mouth by kissing her. He just stood up and kissed her, smack on the lips. He had her bathrobe open, too. She felt his warm hands, hands she had missed for years. Then the tornado rose and lifted her so high she forgot about safety. Charley was the storm; what she felt for him was swirling, faster and faster.

There was a hole in the sleeve of her bathrobe, and her elbow got stuck in it while he was trying to get the bathrobe off.

"What's wrong with your elbow?" he asked, as they were doing a sidestep toward the bedroom.

"Nothin', it's just an elbow," Ruby murmured, between kisses.

28

"I saved to buy those curtains," Ruby said, pointing. "I saved to buy these pillowcases. I saved to buy Dempsey's coat."

Charley smiled. "You was always the practical one, honey," he said.

Ruby sat up in bed, turned, and smacked him hard. "Don't call me honey when you ain't even listening to what I'm trying to say," she said. "I was tellin' you what I went through to see that Dempsey had a decent life. You can't walk in here and screw me, and just make up for five years."

"Maybe not, but I gave it a good try, didn't I?" Charley said.

Ruby tried to smack him again. Charley covered his head, and let her pound on his arms for a while.

"I bet you saved for this mattress, too," he said, between blows. "That was real thoughtful of you. When a fella's only got one shot, it's nice to have a decent mattress, don't you think?"

Ruby gave up, finally, and lay back down beside him, as close as she could get.

"You never did listen to me, Charley," she said. "If you did, nothin' bad would ever have happened, and we'd have six kids by now."

"You might have six, but not me," Charley teased. "I'd arrange to take a powder before I'd get stuck raisin' six brats."

Ruby raised up on one elbow and gave him a stern look, though she knew he was teasing her—they'd often talked about having a big family, before he'd gone off to St. Louis and then to jail.

"You better consider bein' less cocky if you expect me to run off with you," she told him. "Why would I run off with you anyway? It'd mean leaving everything I saved for."

"I thought we'd go to Arkansas," Charley said, putting his hands behind his head and looking up at the ceiling. "They got a real sleepy attitude toward the law, over in Arkansas. We could get us a house in Fort Smith somewhere, and eat a lot of cat-fish."

"You better answer my question, Charley," Ruby warned. "The fact we're in this bed at this moment don't mean quite as much as you think it means."

"Shut up fussing, Ruby, my God," Charley said, exasperated. "We belong together—you know it and I know it. I don't care how many damn pillowcases you saved up for, that's all in the past. We got the future to think about now."

"Well, I'm gonna think about mine and Dempsey's, that's for sure," Ruby said, testy. "You best give yours some thought, too."

"I have," Charley said, reaching for her. "Let's enjoy a little more nooky, and when Dempsey gets home, we'll head for the Arkansas line."

Ruby couldn't resist him—it was so easy with Charley—it was honest pleasure, something she had missed for so long she could hardly believe she was having it again.

Afterward, though, she felt sad for Lenny. Lenny was real sweet, and it wasn't bad; it was just that she always knew she had to try, whereas with Charley, the pleasure came, unbidden and unstoppable.

When she told Charley she wanted to go say goodbye to Lenny face-to-face, Charley got real edgy.

"Naw, don't do that, honey, just leave him a note," Charley said, as they were packing the car. "It'd be easier for him that way."

"Macaroni," Ruby said. "Easier for you, maybe. You're afraid he'll talk me out of it."

"He might," Charley said. "After all, he's a saint, and I ain't. You could decide you'd rather have a saint."

Ruby continued to fill the car with her things and Dempsey's.

"We're packing this car—I'm going with you," Ruby said. "I'm going with you, and I ain't gonna look back."

"Then why not just leave the man a note?" Charley insisted. "After all, you told me in a letter you was divorcin' me."

Ruby stopped packing, and turned to him, hands on her hips and fire in her eyes.

"I ain't a coward, Charley," Ruby said, looking at him hard. "I done the best I could. This man was decent to me, and he was a good, kind father to Dempsey. Lenny never once laid a hand on our boy—if he needed to be spanked, I spanked him. I owe him an honest goodbye. It'll kill him, but I can't help it."

Charley didn't say anything—what could he say?

"I'm gonna do it face-to-face—not with no note," Ruby said, again.

They finished packing the car. When Dempsey got home from school and realized they were leaving with Charley, he lit up like a Christmas tree. Ruby hurried him into the back seat of Charley's car, and they left.

Then they drove downtown, and parked about a block from the bakery where Lenny worked. Charley let Dempsey sit in his lap and pretend to drive, while Ruby walked down to the bakery.

"Is Lenny coming?" Dempsey asked his father.

"I don't think Lenny's coming, son," Charley replied.

"Daddy, are we going far away?" Dempsey asked. He had a sense that a big adventure was about to take place.

Lenny was covered with flour when Ruby walked into the back room of the bakery. He was kneading a huge, forty-pound lump of dough. Ruby strode in briskly, trying to feel business-like. But she didn't feel businesslike at all; she just felt sick to her stomach. She and Lenny had never had a bad fight. Once in a while, she would get up on the wrong side of the bed and try to pick one with him, but Lenny wouldn't fight back hard enough to make it interesting. The worst he would do was bicker a little bit and look hurt.

The second Lenny looked at Ruby, he stopped kneading the dough and just stood there—he had something rabbitlike in his look that made Ruby want to club him on the spot, even though she loved him for his sweetness and his gentle ways. She made herself look him right in the eye.

"Charley came back," she said. Then she took a deep breath and said the rest, all at once.

"Dempsey and me are going away with him. They're in the car now, waiting. It ain't fair, Lenny. You've been as sweet to me as any man could be, and you've been just as sweet to Demp-

206

sey. I hate having to hurt you, but I can't help this. I belong with Charley, that's just the way it is."

Lenny stood there, his hands in the dough up to his elbows. He looked at Ruby with the rabbit look, a dull, numb anguish in his eyes.

"I thank you for all you've done," Ruby said, her voice shaking.

"I don't want your goddamn thanks, Ruby," Lenny said, a shaking in his own voice. "I wanted to live with you the rest of my life."

"I know, honey," Ruby said softly. "I know."

She gave him a little kiss, then she turned and left. Lenny never took his hands out of the dough.

When old Mr. Crocker, the owner of the bakery, came into the back room a little later, Lenny was sobbing. Tears ran off his cheeks and down his arms, right into the dough. The surface of the dough was shiny with tears; they were even dripping off the kneading bench, onto the floor.

Old Mr. Crocker was shocked: he would never have expected such behavior of Lenny—he had always been a steady man.

"Why, look here, son!" he said, in his shock. "Now you've ruint that whole batch of dough. We'll be behind all day."

Lenny took his hands out of the dough, turned his back on Mr. Crocker, and dropped to his knees. He sobbed so hard that Mr. Crocker could see his back shaking.

Old Mr. Crocker hardly knew what to do. His wife was in the beauty parlor next door, getting a permanent—he had a sudden urge to run and get her. She was better in such situations than he was. His wife was from a crying family and had experience, since her mother and all six of her sisters would cry if they popped a button, or dropped a nickel through a crack in the floor. His wife would know what to do with Lenny. But she was in the beauty parlor, and she wouldn't appreciate being disturbed. They had been married forty-six years; Mr. Crocker thought he could make that judgment with confidence.

Finally he decided against disturbing Ella. Lenny wasn't sobbing quite as hard now; perhaps he would be able to calm down of his own accord. Mr. Crocker had no idea what was wrong.

Perhaps the boy's appendix had burst, or perhaps he had just learned that his ma had shot his pa, or something. Such catastrophes were not uncommon, and either one would explain the sobs.

Old Mr. Crocker walked around the kneading table and looked at the forty pounds of ruined dough. It looked as if Lenny might have punched it a few times with his fists, as well as crying all over it.

He decided that despite the ruined dough, his first comment might have been too harsh. What was a lump of dough, if the boy's father had been shot and killed by his mother?

"Now, that's all right, son," old Mr. Crocker said. "That's all right. We can always make up some more dough."

29

Ruby was dead silent for almost a hundred miles. Charley and Dempsey tried to josh her, but it didn't work. She looked straight ahead down the road, not responding to either one of them, not speaking. Dempsey jumped up and down in the back seat, something that would usually have brought an immediate reprimand. His mother just ignored him.

"Ain't you gonna make him stop jumping?" Charley asked.

Ruby said nothing.

"He oughtn't to jump in the car. Sit down, son!" Charley finally yelled.

Dempsey sat down for five minutes, and then started jumping again.

"Honey, say something," Charley pleaded. "I can't do nothing with this child."

"Start learning, buster—you're his pa," Ruby said, taking a nail file out of her purse. Charley looked over at her nervously. She was stony. Maybe she was planning to stab him with the nail file. A man he knew in prison had an eye gouged out by a nail file, and it had been wielded by the man's wife.

"What'd I do?" Charley asked. "What'd I do?"

Ruby turned, and looked at him coldly. You idiot, you know what you did, was what Charley construed the look to mean.

At supper, in a little cafe just across the Arkansas line, Ruby finally broke her silence. They ordered catfish, and Dempsey started throwing hush puppies at a little boy sitting next to them. When he threw the third hush puppy, Ruby grabbed him and gave him a hard shaking.

"I've taught you better, Dempsey," she said. "We don't throw food."

"He was looking at me!" Dempsey protested.

"Go apologize to that couple, Charley," Ruby instructed.

Charley was taken by surprise. "Me?" he asked.

"Ain't your name Charley?" Ruby whispered, through clenched teeth.

"Why me? I didn't throw nothing," Charley said.

Ruby looked at him.

"You haven't got any easier to live with, you know that?" Charley said. He was getting hot under the collar.

"Lenny didn't have much trouble living with me," Ruby said. "If I'm too hard to deal with, you can take us back to Coffeyville."

"No, Mama—I want to stay with Daddy," Dempsey said.

"Then you two go and apologize to that nice little boy and his ma and pa," she said. "Go on, before I lose my patience with both of you."

"Let's go, bud—Ma's mad at us," Charley said.

Charley led Dempsey the three steps to the other table. The little boy, a redhead, was eating one of the hush puppies. His parents, both tired, looked up wearily.

"Sorry, folks," Charley said. "My boy's been cooped up in the car all day, I guess he couldn't hold his mischief in no longer."

"Where you folks from?" the tired woman asked. Her husband

was mad at her because the food was taking so long to come, although it was her husband who ordered.

"Sallisaw," Charley said. "We're bound for the Arkansas flats."

"I didn't know it was flat around Fort Smith," Ruby said. "I had the notion it was hilly."

"It is," Charley said.

"Then why did you tell that woman we was bound for the flats?" she asked.

"Can't I say anything right?" Charley asked. "Every time I open my mouth, you jump down my throat."

"If you said something true, maybe I wouldn't," Ruby informed him. "It doesn't have to be smart . . . just true."

"I feel like hanging myself in the barn," he said.

"What barn? You ain't got a barn!" Ruby pointed out emphatically.

"I guess I could find a goddamn barn and hang myself in it if I tried—there's thousands of barns in Arkansas!" Charley said, so loudly that everyone in the restaurant jumped.

Dempsey burst into tears, and so, after a moment, did the little redheaded boy who was eating Dempsey's hush puppies.

Ruby smiled.

"Got your goat, didn't I?" she said.

Charley threw some money on the table to pay for the catfish, and stormed out the door.

"Mama, Daddy left!" Dempsey said, upset. "Go get him, please? Please?"

"It's all right, honey, he won't go far," Ruby said, calmly. "Put your coat on."

Charley stood behind the car, smoking, when Ruby and Dempsey came out. Dempsey looked worried, until he saw Charley—then he beamed.

"Hi, Daddy," he said.

"Hi, bud," Charley replied. He let out a sigh.

"Charley, stop feeling sorry for yourself and get in the car," Ruby said. "I may let up on you. The worst may be over."

Charley got in the car, but he continued to look stiff.

"Daddy, can I help drive?" Dempsey asked. "I like sitting on your lap."

"It's getting dark, son," Charley told him. "You can help me drive tomorrow."

By the time they reached the Arkansas River, Dempsey was sound asleep, curled in the back seat under his little coat.

"Let's get a house with an upstairs, when we get to Fort Smith," Charley said. "Remember how we used to talk about how we'd raise our kids in a two-story house?"

"I remember," Ruby said, in a friendly tone. Then she scooted across the seat, and leaned her head against Charley's shoulder.

"I remember all that stuff we used to dream about," she said. "Reckon there's a chance some of our dreams can still come true?"

"Well, we can get a two-story house," Charley said. "That'd be a start."

Suddenly, Ruby felt a great tiredness come over her—it was as if she'd had to stay awake for five years in order to guard her child. But now, Charley had come back, and she could rest. She took Charley's free hand in both of hers.

She started to tell him she loved him, but before she could get the words out, Ruby fell sound asleep.

Book Three

1931-1933

1

Ruby was painting their new name on the mailbox when she saw a policeman pull in the driveway across the street from them. The sight unnerved her, but she went on painting the name on the mailbox anyway. After much discussion, Ruby and Charley had decided to call themselves the Hamiltons. They even told Dempsey that he had to remember his new name.

"Okay," Dempsey said. Both his parents looked solemn when they made the request, so solemn that he felt he shouldn't ask why his name had to be Hamilton when they moved into their new house. Dempsey didn't really care what his name was. He had a room of his own, and it was upstairs, and there was a swing in the back yard, and his father had promised to take him fishing in the river.

The policeman noticed Ruby painting the name on the mailbox—she smiled at him; he tipped his cap to her briefly, and then went on into his house. He was a heavy man, and walked slowly, as if he were tired.

Ruby forced herself to finish painting the name on the mailbox, but the minute she got back in the house, she shot up the stairs two at a time to wake Charley. He had been putting one of their new beds together, but had lost interest and was taking a nap on the mattress.

"Charley, wake up, there's a cop next door," Ruby said.

Charley had just gone to sleep. He sat up, his hair tousled, and tried to collect his wits.

"Next door which way?" he asked, wondering if he had managed to get a pistol up to the second floor. He and Ruby had put Dempsey in his new school, and then spent a whole day buying furniture, and kitchen stuff, and whatnot. The whole two-story house was filled with beds and couches and lamps and frying pans and rugs and curtains, most of the stuff not yet fully unpacked. Charley had gotten a big kick out of seeing how happy Ruby looked while they were buying the furniture, but he got far less of a kick out of unpacking it and arranging it. He had several guns with him, but he had no idea where they were—still in the car, probably, and the cops were next door.

"Not next door, across the street," Ruby corrected. "It scared me so bad I got mixed up."

"How many are they?" Charley asked, digging in a box of soap and washrags, hoping he might have stuck a pistol in it for some reason.

"How many what?" Ruby asked, confused.

"How many cops are next door? Get a grip," Charley said.

"*You* get a grip, you ain't even got your shirt on," Ruby said. It always ticked her off when Charley told her to calm down. The least little upset, and he acted like she was a raving maniac.

"How many cops are next door?" he demanded. "You started this conversation, what do you think it's about?"

"Don't yell at me," Ruby said. "There's just one cop, and he's across the street. I think he may live there."

Charley sighed, and then he flopped back onto the mattress.

"Why'd you wake me up, then, if that's all the news?" Charley asked. But he wasn't really mad. He was barefoot, and he stuck his foot up under her skirt, and tried to feel her with his toes.

"Don't do that!" Ruby said, jumping back. "Your feet smell. What are we gonna do about the policeman?"

"Nothin'," Charley said. "Cops have to live somewhere. There's no law saying a cop can't live across the street from a bandit."

"But what if he recognizes you?" Ruby said. "He might see a poster or something."

Charley just yawned. "Across the street from a cop is probably the safest place to live," Charley said. "It's the last place anybody would expect to find me."

Ruby wasn't satisfied. "I still think we oughta move," she said. "I'll be a nervous wreck in a week, wondering when he's gonna recognize you."

"You'd worry on a clear day with the doors locked," Charley said, reaching for her with his hand this time. Ruby eluded him, and began to unpack the soap.

"If the doors were locked and you were on the inside, I'd have plenty to worry about," she said. "Gettin' pregnant, for one thing."

Charley had been looking cheerful and sort of silly—his hair was all cowlicks—but he turned gloomy the minute she made the remark about getting pregnant.

"I wish we could have another kid," he said. "I wish we could have five or six. Dempsey deserves some brothers and sisters— we had 'em."

Ruby felt melancholy, too. There was a time when they could have had five or six children—they both would have enjoyed a big family, she thought. But that time was past. Charley could wake up any day and find himself bound for prison, or worse. Ruby could never watch him drive off calmly, even if he was just going to get smokes—she could never be sure he'd come back alive. There was a thousand-dollar reward posted for him already, and the bounty would only go up if he kept robbing banks, which she knew he would: it was what he did. It wasn't a choice anymore. Charley couldn't get a real job, like everybody else—it was too late. She wasn't foolish enough to think he would change, just because she and Dempsey had come to live with him.

"Let's just enjoy Dempsey, Charley," Ruby said, sitting on the mattress beside him. "Let's just enjoy this time together."

Later, Charley looked out the window and noticed the policeman changing a flat on the old police car. He immediately went downstairs, crossed the street, shook hands with the man, and helped with the jack.

"Thanks, Mr. Hamilton," the policeman said, shaking hands again when they finished. "I ain't mechanical, changing tires is about the extent of it."

"Call me Charley," Charley told him.

2

On the day they were supposed to go fishing, Dempsey was the first one up. He quickly put on his clothes and slipped downstairs to the kitchen, just on the off chance that his mama or his daddy might be there. But they weren't. The sun wasn't even up; there was mist in the back yard. His daddy told him they would go out and dig worms, first thing, and they had even got an old coffee can and put some dirt in it, for the worms to live in.

But his daddy wasn't up. Dempsey's new pole, with the line and the cork and the hook already fixed, was leaning up against the back porch. It was annoying that his parents were sleeping so late. Dempsey tiptoed back upstairs, just to make sure his daddy wasn't shaving, or his mama brushing her teeth. His daddy wasn't shaving, and his mama wasn't brushing her teeth, either, so he very carefully pushed open the door to their bedroom, and peeked in.

When Dempsey peeked into the bedroom, he saw that his mother and father were still asleep, their arms around one another. The rising sun had just begun to shine through the bedroom window, covering them with light. Dempsey was a little disappointed; it was the day his daddy had promised to take him fishing, emphasizing how important it was to get up early and be at the river just as the sun was coming up.

Now the sun *was* up, and they weren't even at the river yet. But his mama and daddy looked so peaceful and so happy, sleeping in the sunlight with their arms around each other, that Dempsey decided to let them sleep. Maybe they were extra tired from staying up too late or something.

He went back downstairs, and found a biscuit in the oven. The biscuit was left over from supper, but Dempsey ate it anyway. There wasn't much else to eat. Then he found his worm can with the dirt in it on the back porch, and took it down the steps. He meant to dig for worms. There was a spade in the garage, which he carried into the back yard. To his annoyance, he discovered that the grass in the back yard was really tough grass. He wasn't strong enough to push the spade through it. He got it through a little ways, but not deep enough to get to the worms, and when he tried to pry some dirt up, all he got was grass.

While he was struggling with the spade and the tough grass, he heard the screen on the back door slam. He looked up, and there was his daddy, with some fishing boots on and his shirt unbuttoned.

"I see an early bird, trying to be the one to get the worm," Charley said, taking the shovel from Dempsey.

"Daddy, we're late," Dempsey pointed out. "The sun is up already."

"Don't worry about it, son," Charley said. "I heard on the radio that the fish are sleepin' late today. We'll be there by the time they're ready for breakfast."

His daddy had no trouble with the grass—he pushed the spade right through it, and the second spadeful of dirt he dug up had seven fat, squirmy worms in it. Dempsey pulled one worm apart, trying to pull it out of the dirt, but his daddy said not to worry about it, they could use both parts of the worm for bait.

At the river, two old men were already fishing, floating quietly in a little boat.

"Daddy, why don't we have a boat?" Dempsey asked. "If we had a boat, we could go out where the fish live."

"It's just one of those things we ain't got around to yet," Charley said. "I expect we'll round us up a boat one of these days." He had brought a little .22 single-shot with him, in case Dempsey wanted to plink at turtles, or bottles, or any good target that might be floating by.

After only a few minutes of fishing, Dempsey's cork went out of sight in the brown water, and when he yanked on his pole a small, fat, shiny fish came out of the water, attached to his hook.

"It's a perch," his father said. "Perch are bony. Let's throw this little feller back, and see if we can't hook a big old catfish."

"Where will he go now?" Dempsey asked, when he had pitched the little fish back in the river.

"He'll go home and tell his ma an expert fisherman named Dempsey Floyd caught him and let him go," Charley said. He had forgotten the thermos of coffee he had meant to bring, and was feeling a little empty.

"Dempsey Hamilton," Dempsey corrected. "I'm not Dempsey Floyd anymore."

"Sharp thinkin', buddy," Charley said. "You're Dempsey Hamilton, all right."

"Daddy, will I ever be Dempsey Floyd again?" Dempsey asked.

"Well, maybe," Charley said. He was glad Ruby wasn't there to hear the conversation. Dempsey's confusion about their names, which Charley couldn't blame him for, sometimes set her crying.

"I like Dempsey Floyd better," Dempsey confessed. "That's the same as my Uncle Bradley and my cousins."

"Yep, it is," Charley admitted. "But they live in Oklahoma, and we live in Arkansas. It's better to be Dempsey Hamilton while we're over here in Arkansas."

Just then, Dempsey's cork went way under, and when he tried to pull the fish out of the water, nothing happened. He pulled and pulled, but it was all he could do to keep the fish from pulling him into the river.

"You must have hooked Old Grandpa Catfish," Charley said. "It's gonna take both of us to get this monster to the bank."

He grabbed the pole, and with the two of them pulling, they did get the monster to the bank, only it wasn't Old Grandpa Catfish, it was a snapping turtle as big as a washtub. He had an ugly green shell with mud on it, mean little red eyes, and a snapping beak that scared Dempsey every time the big turtle snapped it.

"Oh boy, that's the end of this fishing trip," Charley said. "This old devil looks like he wants to eat us both."

"Daddy, I'm scared," Dempsey said, staying as far away from the turtle as he could get. "Can't we shoot him with our gun?"

"Be like shooting mud," Charley said. "He's got a brain the size of a pea—we could shoot a whole box of shells into him, and I doubt he'd die."

"What will we do?" Dempsey asked, looking at the ugly monster.

"Want to put him in the trunk and take him home to Mama?" Charley asked. "Mama could use him for a pet."

"No!" Dempsey said. "I don't want to take him home!"

"The next best thing is just to cut him loose and let him go," Charley said, getting out his pocketknife.

Just about that time, two elderly colored men with fishing poles came walking along the riverbank in the clear sunlight. When they saw that Charley was about to cut the line and let the big snapper go, they hurried over.

"Mister, could we have 'im?" one of the old men asked.

"Why, sure—take him, if you can handle him," Charley offered. "He may take you."

The old colored man chuckled. "No, sir," he said. "We take him. He ain't gonna take us."

The old man quickly stuck his foot under the big turtle and flipped him over, and when he did, the other colored man grabbed the turtle by the tail and began to drag him up the bank.

"You men know what you're doin', looks like," Charley said, admiringly. "What are you gonna do with him now that you got him?"

"Eat him, boss," the old man said. "Makes good eatin', Old Man Turtle."

Then he followed his friend.

"Might make good eatin' to them," Charley told Dempsey. "Wouldn't make good eatin' to me. How about you, Dempsey? Want to eat a snappin' turtle?"

"No thanks!" Dempsey said firmly.

3

Charley was buying smokes and rubbers at a drugstore on the main street in Fort Smith when he happened to glance at the magazine rack, and noticed his name on the cover of *Police Gazette*. There was a mug shot taken when he was booked in Ohio, and underneath, in big letters: "PRETTY BOY FLOYD KILLS AGAIN!"

Before paying for the smokes and the rubbers, Charley pretended to browse through the magazines for a bit. He bought *Good Housekeeping* and *Photoplay* for Ruby—she loved movie magazines, and was always looking for tips on how to make her housekeeping more efficient. Then he bought *True Detective* and *Police Gazette* for himself.

"Thanks, Mr. Hamilton," the clerk said. "Ain't seen the missus lately."

"That's because I keep her home," Charley said, winking at

the boy. "Mrs. Hamilton is so pretty I can't allow her out on the street."

"You're right about that, Arkansas is nothin' but mashers," the boy said.

Charley drove to the river, and parked near the spot where he and Dempsey had caught the turtle. Then he read the article. Two cops had been gunned down in a little town outside Kansas City, and a witness claimed to have seen a gunman who looked exactly like Pretty Boy Floyd.

For a time, Charley felt such apprehension that it was all he could do to keep from jumping in the river and trying to swim across. If he drowned, so much the better. He had been in Fort Smith the day of the killing, helping Ruby paint the garage. He was nowhere near Kansas City, and hadn't gunned down any cops. But there was his name, on the cover of a popular magazine. What if Dempsey was over at a friend's house, and the kid's parents read *Police Gazette*? What if one of the parents mentioned Pretty Boy Floyd, and Dempsey suddenly blurted out that Floyd was his name? Dempsey was only seven, and Floyd *was* his name.

For a while, Charley felt hopeless. He could lead an honest life for the rest of his years, never robbing another bank, and it still wouldn't keep some newsie from printing lies about him. The more lies, the bigger the reward for him, dead or alive. Sooner or later, the lies would bring the cops, or a bounty hunter, or a sheriff who could shoot a deer rifle, and it would be all over.

"If I was a king, I wouldn't allow no newspapers or no magazines, either," he said to Ruby that night in their bedroom. Ruby was putting cream on her face.

"I'm glad you ain't king, then," Ruby said. "I couldn't do without my movie magazines. Every once in a while, I need to know what Mary Pickford's up to."

"You won't find it out from no magazines, because magazines don't print the truth," Charley said. "Every word of them is lies."

Ruby turned, and looked at him. He had been dark during supper; he hadn't said two words, and he didn't want to read Dempsey his bedtime story, or tell him one, either. Sometimes

Charley made up bedtime stories about Sam Bass, or Jesse James, or other outlaws, all about them hiding in caves and racing their horses over the hills and prairies and having gun battles with Indians, or Texas Rangers, or one another. Charley loved those stories as much as Dempsey, and he would keep telling them as long as Dempsey would listen.

"Tell me the Starrs, Daddy," Dempsey would plead, after supper.

"I told you the Starrs last night, son," Charley would say.

"Then tell me the Daltons," Dempsey pleaded. "Tell me Jesse."

Charley usually would relent and tell Dempsey about Jesse, since Jesse was both's favorite. But tonight, Dempsey'd had to be content with his mother reading him a story about Daniel Boone.

"Charley honey, are you blue tonight?" Ruby asked.

Charley didn't answer. In a way, he was sorry he had made the remark about the magazines. He didn't want Ruby to know about the story in *Police Gazette*. But Ruby was free, white, and twenty-one—she could walk into the drugstore and buy the magazine herself. She couldn't keep away from magazines; sometimes it annoyed him that she would sit at the breakfast table, reading a movie magazine, when she could be talking to him about something serious, or at least taking care that the biscuits didn't burn.

"Why ask? You ain't gonna answer," Ruby said, thinking out loud.

"It was a stupid question. You can see I'm blue," Charley replied.

"I can see it, I can even smell it," Ruby said.

"Applesauce," Charley said. "You can't smell no such thing."

"Sure I can. You smell like a wet sock when you're blue," she said, hoping a little joshing would bring him out of his sulk.

"So what, you smell like grease right now from that gook on your face," Charley said.

Ruby shrugged. "Keeps me beautiful," she said. "You wouldn't bother with me for ten seconds if I wasn't good-looking."

224

"I might if you wasn't so bossy," Charley informed her.

Ruby shrugged, and let it go. She went to the bathroom, brushed her teeth and combed her hair. When she came to bed, Charley handed her a copy of *Police Gazette* with his picture on the cover, and a big headline about him killing two policemen.

"Every word of that story is a lie," he said while Ruby was flipping pages, trying to locate the story itself.

"Shut up and let me read it," Ruby said. "No wonder you're blue."

She found the story and read it.

"It *is* a lie!" she said. "That was the day we bought the radio. You wasn't nowhere near Missouri."

"Now do you believe me about magazines?" Charley asked.

"I believe you about this piece of junk," Ruby said, throwing the magazine across the bedroom. Then she retrieved it, and read the story again, her chest heaving.

Charley didn't say a word. He lay in bed, smoking. Ruby's eyes flashed, as she reread the story. But then she stopped looking so mad.

She began to look scared.

"Charley, are you sure every word of this story is a lie?" she asked.

Charley didn't want to answer.

"You might as well tell me," Ruby said. "If any of it's true, I need to know. I'll find out sometime, even if it's not till they come to get you."

Charley took a long time to answer.

"I haven't been wanting to talk about this," he admitted.

"No, I guess you wouldn't," Ruby said, taking his hand. She moved closer to him on the bed.

"I killed that deputy in Ohio," Charley confessed. "He shot first—it was him or me."

"What about that one agent in Kansas City?" Ruby asked, her voice low.

"I don't know about him," Charley said. "It's a maybe."

Ruby looked at him, puzzled.

"What's a maybe?" she asked.

"Five or six people were shooting. We were trying to get to

225

our cars," Charley said. "The man popped up right in front of me with a gat in his hand. I thought I just winged him. He kept shooting, and I kept running. Next day, the papers said he died. But lots of people were shooting. I didn't think he was bad hurt. Somebody else might have put one or two bullets into him after I did, I don't know.

"But I didn't kill no two policemen in Missouri last month," he added. "You know that."

"I know that, Charley," Ruby said, quietly.

They lay silent for several minutes. Ruby turned off the bed light. A shaft of moonlight fell across the bed. She looked to see if Charley was asleep, but his eyes were wide open.

"What are you thinking about, sweetie?" she asked.

"How hard it is to stop things, once they start," Charley said. "I never wanted to kill nobody. I never would have, either, except that it meant survival. I gotta survive, don't I?"

"Killing ain't right, Charley—no matter who's doing it—but I don't think I could stand it if you were dead," Ruby said. She hugged him tight, and put her face against his neck.

"Let's don't think about it," Charley said. "Let's go on a picnic tomorrow. We'll take Dempsey to the river. We'll get inner tubes and do some floating. We'll have some fun."

"That's a fine idea, let's do it," Ruby said. But she couldn't stop the scared feeling. She wanted to lie on top of her husband, to protect him from the scared feeling she felt. She snuggled as close as she could get to Charley, and put her leg over him.

Charley turned his face toward her. "We could have some fun right now," he said, a smile working its way into the corners of his mouth. "How about it, honey?"

"How about it?" Ruby replied.

226

4

The picnic went fine, until Dempsey caught the fishhook in his lip. It was his best day ever as a fisherman, and he wasn't willing to quit, even though it was almost too dark to see the cork. He had caught seventeen perch and two small catfish in the course of the day, and he wanted to catch just one more. Three of the perch and both the catfish were big enough to eat —his mama had promised to cook them, if his daddy would clean them.

No one could quite figure out how Dempsey threw his line in such a way as to make the fishhook catch his lip. One minute he was fine, and the next minute he was screaming. Charley was cleaning the five little fish when it happened, and Ruby was carrying the remains of the picnic to the car. It had cooled off after sundown, enough so that she had goose bumps on her legs.

"Hold still, son—hold still," Charley said. "You ain't dead, it's just a fishhook."

"Now you know what a fish feels like," Ruby told him between screams.

"Don't tell him that, there's nothin' wrong with fishing," Charley snapped.

"No, except that you can get fishhooks in your lip," Ruby remarked.

"Get the flashlight!" Charley said.

"What flashlight, we didn't bring it," Ruby said. "We didn't plan on staying after dark."

"Get it out! Get it out!" Dempsey yelled.

"Son, I can't see well enough to get it out," Charley said, cutting the line. "We'll jump in the car and be home in a minute. Then we'll get it out.

"Put a towel around him so he won't bleed on the seat," he told Ruby, but while Ruby was trying to fix the towel, Dempsey started jumping up and down, screaming again. He bled on the seat.

Dempsey whimpered most of the way home. Charley nearly ran over a dog, trying to hurry.

"Slow down, he ain't gonna bleed to death," Ruby said.

"Sorry, my nerves are on edge," Charley said. "Stop whimpering, son."

When they pulled into the driveway, a car with Oklahoma plates was sitting at the curb. It looked familiar, but Dempsey was making so much noise and Charley was so distracted, he couldn't place it.

When they went up the back steps, with Ruby carrying the groaning Dempsey, they saw the glow of two cigarettes over near Dempsey's swing. Charley jumped, wishing he had a gun —but then he placed the car: it was Bob Birdwell's old flivver.

"Don't shoot, pard," Birdwell said. "It's just us Okies."

"My God, George," Charley said. "Dempsey's got a fishhook in his lip, this is Ruby, come on in."

"Hi," Ruby said. "We're a mess, we had a picnic, but there's some fried chicken left if you're hungry."

When they turned the kitchen light on and saw how much blood Dempsey had dripped onto his shirt, both Charley and Bird became visibly faint.

"I can't stand the sight of blood," Birdwell said, turning white.

"You boys go clean the fish," Bob Birdwell said, taking charge of the situation. "Me and Ruby will take care of the doctorin'."

The two men quickly went out the back door.

Ruby held Dempsey more or less still, while Bob sized up the situation.

"That fishhook won't come out—it's got to go on through," she concluded. "If you get a little wire cutter, I can snip that hook off."

"Go ask Charley, I'm confused," Ruby said. "This has got me so shaken up, I can't remember up from down."

Bob didn't waste any time. She found the wire cutter herself, and snipped the hook. Then she took Dempsey's chin in her hand.

"Yell, Dempsey," Bob said. "Yell as loud as you can. Pretend this is a hog-callin' contest. See if you can call the furthest hog."

Then she winked at him, and pushed the hook on through his lip, blood dripping everywhere. Ruby felt a little faint herself, but she held Dempsey still. Then Bob quickly pulled the straight part of the hook through Dempsey's lip. Dempsey screamed so loud that Charley and Birdwell, way out in the yard cleaning fish, both jumped and cringed. In a few seconds, his screams subsided. Bob even got some iodine on the wound before he noticed.

In a few more minutes, Dempsey's cries subsided, and he went to sleep in his mother's lap.

"No fun getting a fishhook in the fat part of your lip," Bob said, grinning at Ruby. "What he don't know and we do, is that there are worse things."

Ruby wasn't quite sure what Bob meant by that, but she was sure she liked Bob, skinny and crazy as she appeared. Once Dempsey stopped screaming, the men came in, looking abashed. Ruby thought Charley still seemed as if he might puke, but he soon recovered enough to eat six pieces of cold fried chicken, and two slices of vinegar pie that Bob Birdwell had brought for them.

"Ruby, you're plumb beautiful," Birdwell said, gallantly. "I don't know why they keep calling Charley Pretty Boy. Who would ever think his mug was pretty?"

"Well, I do, sometimes," Ruby ventured. She was shy around strangers—on the other hand, she was glad for the company. Charley was so annoyed about her not bringing a flashlight on the picnic that there would have been a fight if the Birdwells hadn't turned up. It was just the kind of little thing that started their worst fights.

"See, Bird?" Charley said. "I don't have to be pretty enough for you. I only have to be pretty enough for Ruby."

Bob went out to the car, and came in with a jug of moonshine. Charley carried Dempsey upstairs and put him to bed, and then the four of them got drunk. Ruby rarely had guests in her house, and it made her nervous. She was afraid she would forget something proper, and offend her guests. She might forget to put washrags in the bathroom. For most of her life, she hadn't even had washrags, just pieces of flour sack cut into squares. Her father hadn't believed in spending good money on frills.

"Wash your face with your own two paws," he used to say. "It's just your face."

Ruby and Charley had a guest room, but they hadn't been expecting any guests, and hadn't bought a bed for it yet. The guest room was filled with Dempsey's toys.

"Let's give 'em our bed," Charley whispered. "We can make a pallet."

Once Bob Birdwell got thoroughly drunk, she began to sing "The Wabash Cannonball," her favorite song. She got up and danced around the kitchen, pretending she was playing the fiddle while she sang.

"I run around naked sometimes when I'm drunk," she confessed. She had on her clodhopper shoes, laces untied and all.

Charley winked at Ruby. He thought Bob Birdwell was a real character. Ruby was glad Bob was drunk; maybe she wouldn't notice if some little something like washrags was overlooked.

Then Ruby got sick at her stomach, and ran outside to throw up by the trash barrel. She didn't want her guests to hear her heaving.

Later, when she and Charley were almost asleep on their pallet on the floor, they heard a thumping sound from upstairs in their bedroom.

They raised up on their elbows to listen.

"Are they having a fight?" Ruby wondered. She had never heard a sound quite like the thumping.

Charley listened a minute longer—then he grinned.

"It ain't a fight—listen to them bedsprings zing," he said.

Before Ruby could get to sleep, she grew melancholy. It was fun having the Birdwells, and she was especially grateful to Bob for getting the fishhook out of Dempsey's lip. If Bob hadn't done it, she herself would have had to. Charley couldn't have managed it without losing his lunch.

Still, Charley had talked to her many times about Birdwell's expertise as a bank robber. It seemed to be his profession, just

230

as it seemed to be her husband's. If the Birdwells had driven all the way to Arkansas, it was most likely because George wanted Charley to help him pull some bank jobs. Charley would do it, too. They were running pretty low on money.

It meant Charley would leave, and she and Dempsey would be alone in a place where she had no friends. Bob Birdwell wouldn't be staying with her; Bob had already let it be known that she wanted to hurry back to the farm.

Later in the night, there was more thumping from the bedroom.

"Why do they have to thump?" Ruby asked, rolling over. "We don't thump."

Charley slept through the Birdwells' second session. The next morning he got mildly irate when he saw that in the course of the Birdwells' lovemaking, George had dented the wall behind the Floyds' bed by butting it with his head.

"Dern, George, can't you screw a little lower down on the mattress?" he asked Birdwell, while the women were frying sausage and making coffee.

It was George Birdwell's practice to ignore all criticism, though occasionally he would deign to reply to one by saying something particularly wise.

"Trouble hangs on a woman's skirts, bud," he said. "Plenty's hung on Bob's. Do you want to do a little banking with me tomorrow, or not?"

"How far's the drive?" Charley asked, grinning. It was a crisp morning, and Charley felt good. Dempsey's lip had bled on the pillowcase a little, but he had bounced out of bed full of mischief. He seemed no worse for wear.

"I was thinking we might hit one of them nigger towns," Birdwell said, referring to the several colored townships sprinkled across the Oklahoma plains.

"Those niggers are prosperous," he added.

"You can carry out that plan by yourself, if that *is* your plan," Charley said.

"Why?" Birdwell asked, surprised to have his suggestion rejected. In his view, it was a prime suggestion.

"Every nigger I've ever met could shoot the eye out of a

squirrel," Charley said. "They have to shoot good, or they'd starve to death. They wouldn't have no trouble plugging two white boys."

"Okay, then let's rob Ardmore," Birdwell said. "Ardmore's nearly in Texas, but it's prosperous. If we don't get enough there, we can cross the river and rob Henrietta or somewhere close."

"Let's leave Texas to Bonnie and Clyde," Charlie said. "I expect we can survive doin' jobs in Oklahoma."

As soon as breakfast was over, Bob Birdwell got in the flivver and left. She had not spoken to George all morning.

"Them kids had better not forgot the pig," was her parting remark. "I gave them plain orders to slop the pig."

Birdwell and Charley lolled around all day, playing cards. George threw the football with Dempsey for nearly an hour. When he really drew back and threw, he could shoot the football almost out of sight.

That night, George took the pallet, and Ruby and Charley went back to their bed. They didn't do any thumping, or any zinging, either. Ruby was in a low mood. Charley went to sleep immediately and started snoring, but Ruby lay awake for two or three hours, looking out the window at the moonlight. The uneasiness she'd felt the night before about Birdwell's arrival had lingered throughout the day, and on into the evening.

The next morning, she was hanging out a load of wash when Charley and Bird got in the car and left. They were laughing and cutting up, like boys going to a fair. Charley strutted over, and gave Ruby a big kiss—George Birdwell came, too, to thank her for her hospitality. He tipped his hat, real courtly. Ruby didn't kiss back when Charley kissed her; she felt too low.

When the car drove away, she began to cry.

5

Robbing two banks in one day was a bank robber's dream—Charley and Birdwell soon got so slick that they were able to do just that. The second robbery was in the small town of Atoka, and baseball season had just started. As soon as they got the money safely under the back seat, they blazed out of town at top speed, passing a ballfield on the way.

"I ain't seen a ball game in a while," Charley remarked. "That bank was way down in the middle of town. I doubt folks at the ball game even know it's been robbed."

"I doubt it, too," Birdwell said. "When I was pitching baseball, I once struck out ninety-one batters in a row."

"Ninety-one batters?" Charley said, skeptical. "Bird, that's a lie."

"It was eleven batters, at least," Bird amended. "I can't remember the figures, but it was a good many batters."

They drove out of town a few miles, took off their coats and ties, rolled up their shirtsleeves, and went back to the ball game. There were no bleachers, so they sat on the fender of the car. The game ended in the sixth inning because the community only possessed one ball, and a big, blond-haired boy hit it so hard it sailed out to the highway, landing in a truck that happened to be passing by.

The game had been close up to then, and the spectators looked gloomy.

"It ain't just the game that's over," Birdwell said. "It's the season—they lost their ball."

"Shucks, I love baseball," Charley said. "Let's buy 'em some balls and drop 'em off in front of the bank, next time we come through."

"Okay, Robin Hood," Bird said. "They say charity begins at home, though."

"Not at my home, it don't," Charley said, morose himself over the abrupt end of the ball game. "Ruby hardly ever makes

233

biscuits anymore. I like makin' a pot of spaghetti once in a while, or a pie, but that don't mean I like to do the cookin' all the time."

When they drove out of Atoka, Birdwell was in high spirits, but before they had driven ten miles down the highway, Charley's mood darkened even more. They passed a little shack of a farmhouse, with a family on the porch. Charley glared at them for a moment, and then looked wistful.

"Reckon we'll ever be normal, Bird?" he asked.

Birdwell, who was driving, cocked an eyebrow at him.

"I don't know about you, bud," Birdwell said. "I *am* normal. I been pretty much normal ever since I was born."

"Applesauce," Charley said. "You ain't a bit normal."

"We just watched a ball game," Birdwell pointed out. "Ain't that normal?"

"Not if you rob a bank first, it ain't," Charley said. "If all we'd done was watch baseball, that'd be normal."

"But robbin' the bank was normal, too," Birdwell insisted. "We're bandits—bandits gotta rob something, and banks are a helluva lot easier than trains."

"How would you know?" Charley asked him. "The James boys robbed trains, I guess we could too, if we tried."

"I did try, once," Birdwell told him. "That damn train wouldn't stop. The engineer didn't have the imagination to figure out I was trying to rob him.

"Banks ain't moving objects," he added. "That's why I favor banks, and there's another thing to consider."

"What?" Charley asked.

"Most normal folks is bored shitless," Birdwell informed him. "They just sit around the house watchin' the grass grow, yellin' at each other, mostly."

"Well, I wouldn't," Charley said. "I seldom argue. I'd like to stay home with Ruby and Dempsey from now on and be normal."

"What's stopping you, chum?" Birdwell asked. "Go on back to Fort Smith. Maybe if you pretend you're an insurance salesman long enough, some sucker will walk up and buy a policy from you someday. Then you'll have a new career."

234

"I ain't no insurance salesman," Charley said. "I have to make money, and lots of it. My family's gotta live."

Birdwell cackled.

"In other words, you're just a working man's bank robber . . . just doing it for the money, huh?" he said.

"Well, sure . . . ain't you?" Charley asked. Some days he thought he had his partner figured out, and other days he had to admit, he didn't have a clue.

"Not me, chum!" Birdwell said. "I'm a pure bandit. I don't scorn the cash, but I do it for the thrill and the publicity."

"The publicity?" Charley asked.

"Sure," Birdwell said. "Everybody likes to see their name in the paper."

Charley didn't say much for the next ten miles or so.

"Well . . . I guess I'm a bandit too, then," he admitted. "But you're happy about it, and I ain't. Don't you feel like a low hound when you have to run off and leave Bob and the kids?"

"Not hardly," Birdwell said. "I might miss the tykes once in a while, but I can find a skirt most anyplace I go, and that always helps."

"You mean like Whizbang?" Charley asked.

Birdwell, for once, looked just the slightest bit unhappy.

"No, not like Whizbang Red," he corrected. "Me and Red, we're thick. I just meant a skirt."

"Don't Bob get mad?" Charley inquired.

"Why would she?" Bird asked. "Do I look like I'm fool enough to tell my wife everything I do? It's all me and Bob can do to get along four days at a stretch. If I didn't leave, she'd run me off— and she has, too, plenty of times."

"On account of what?" Charley asked.

"On account of general orneriness," Bird said. "Bob irritates me. If I'm home three or four days, we fight like alley cats.

"Ruby looks like she could scare up a temper herself," George added. "Don't you and her ever scrap?"

"Mostly about my leavin'," Charley said. "Ruby don't like it when I leave."

"Retire, and stay home for about a year," Birdwell suggested. "She might begin to see the benefits of a solitary life."

"I doubt it," Charley said. "Ruby ain't like Bob."

Just then, Birdwell turned the steering wheel so hard, Charley almost ended up in his lap.

"You nearly hit that chicken!" he said.

"Aw, who asked that imbecile hen to stand in the road anyway?" Bird replied, indignant.

6

"I ain't stealin' your husband, Bessie, I just gotta get out now and then," Beulah said, as she and Bradley got ready to head for the honky-tonk.

Most nights now, Beulah and Bradley headed for the honky-tonk, while Bessie and Rose stayed home.

"If you was to steal him, I doubt you'd keep him long," Bessie replied, giving Bradley a black look—it was one thing to be a good brother to Charley; it was another to go hoofing with his brother's girlfriend every night or two, while Bessie stayed home with the kids. In this case, two of the kids had whooping cough, so there was no question of her going.

Bessie didn't allow herself to get too mad, since Rose was so helpful and so nice. Rose didn't ask if she could help; she just pitched in, and she was competent, too. Rose could cook just about anything. Bradley had even come to prefer her flapjacks to Bessie's, which was okay with Bessie. She had cooked enough flapjacks to last her two lifetimes.

"I think Bessie's mad and trying not to show it," Beulah commented, as she and Bradley bounced along the dirt road toward the honky-tonk.

"Not likely," Bradley said, in his dry way. "She shows me

plenty of mad. She's got ways to express it that you wouldn't know about."

Beulah grinned. "Tell me about 'em," she said. "I might want to use 'em on Charley, if he ever shows up again."

It had been two and a half months since Charley had been to see Beulah. She had long since lost patience, but she was still recovering from her head wound, and didn't feel confident enough to leave. Sometimes, just walking along, she would begin to lose her balance and would go teetering off at an angle, until she hit a fence, or a building, or another person—whatever happened to be in the way.

Despite persistent questioning, Bradley refused to go into detail about Bessie's acts of revenge.

"If I was to talk about how mean she is to me in private, it'd spoil the evening," he said.

In fact, he had begun to look forward to his little outings with Beulah, though there was nothing to them but drinking and some hug-and-shuffle on the dance floor. Going out with Beulah was a relief from the *real* problem he had to cope with, which was his mounting passion for Rose, the quiet sister. He and Rose had exchanged a few glances—no more—but an ache was there, in Brad. Some nights, it was all he could do to keep from sneaking down to the girls' room, and crawling right on top of Rose Baird. There was just something about her that he liked.

Meanwhile, his wife was getting more sour by the day. Part of him wished Charley would come and take the girls away, since it would ease the home situation. But part of him didn't want anything of the kind. That part kept wanting to sneak down to the girls' room, and crawl on top of Rose.

The honky-tonk was a tar paper shack that had once belonged to an old Cherokee chief who possessed the ability to coax tumors out of people. He could also coax them out of horses, but rarely out of dogs or other livestock. Seventy-five or eighty of the tumors the old Indian had coaxed out were lined up in Mason jars behind the counter that served as a bar. The names of the folks or the animals the tumors had come out of were written on the lids of the jars, though most of the people had long since died of other causes. In any case, the honky-tonk was a rowdy place where most customers had something better to do than sit around puzzling over names on jars full of tumors.

Beulah danced frantically almost from the moment she stepped into the doorway, mainly to keep her mind off the tumors. She didn't like having to entertain herself in a place where there were parts of people in Mason jars, as if the parts were string beans, or stewed tomatoes. She could just as well have been getting drunk in a speakeasy in St. Louis, or Kansas City, where there were well-dressed stiffs with money in their pockets, as opposed to greasy roughnecks with big smears of oil all over their clothes.

But oil had been discovered in the next county, not six miles away, which is why the old Cherokee's shack had to be quickly converted into a honky-tonk. The oil came and then went, and those who were off the mark quickest with honky-tonks raked in the most profit.

At some point in almost every drunk, Beulah would lose her high spirits. They would spiral down, like a bird that had been winged. Sooner or later, she'd end up staring drunkenly at Bradley, who would be staring drunkenly back.

"Why don't he come, Brad?" Beulah always asked. "Why does he just leave me sittin' here, if I'm his girl?"

Brad loved dancing with Beulah. She could outdance Bessie six to one. But he had begun to dread the part of the evening when Beulah looked at him with her big, brimming eyes, and asked him why Charley didn't come. Bradley didn't have the heart to tell Beulah that Charley was back with Ruby, living in Fort Smith. Bessie knew it, and so did Rose, but no one had the heart to tell Beulah, not while she was so wobbly from her head wound that she was apt to go wandering through mud puddles, or walk in front of cars. The funny part was, her wobbling didn't affect her dancing—Beulah would wave her arms and kick up her heels with the best of them, way better than any woman who was apt to show up at Daddy Jim's honky-tonk, near Akins, Oklahoma.

"That Charley, he's a rambler," Bradley said, his standard description. It was true enough, too. Beulah might pine, but one day Charley would show up, smooth as custard, and Ruby, wherever she was, would be the one pining for a while.

Just as Bradley was about to suggest a little more hug-and-shuffle, a roughneck standing right behind Beulah gave Brad a challenging look.

"I hear they raised the bounty on that murderin' brother of yours," the roughneck snarled. "For three thousand dollars, somebody'll bag him like an old fat coon."

A second later, the man hit the floor. Bradley wasn't large, but when he fought, he uncoiled like a spring. He hit the man so hard he felt like he had jammed his own knuckles halfway down his fingers.

The man was out, cold as a mackerel, but before Brad could stop her, Beulah whacked the man herself with the chair she had been sitting in.

"Hey, gal!" Daddy Jim yelled. "Don't be usin' my furniture for no club, that chair's for sittin'."

Daddy Jim wasn't fond of Beulah. Despite his profession, Daddy Jim had a Baptist streak in him, and he could tell from looking at Beulah that she didn't conform to the Baptist creed.

This time, though, Daddy Jim had miscalculated. Beulah was in such a high fury that she kicked the counter over, spilling several drinks, and came after *him* with the chair.

"You old gut!" she said. "Don't tell me what to do!"

"I own the place, don't I?" Daddy Jim said, trying to grab the chair. He had always been confounded by female anger; he rarely mustered a solid defense, and this occasion was no exception.

"Who cares?! I've seen noodles that would make a better dick than yours would," Beulah yelled. Then she dropped the chair, and began to grab jars of tumors off the shelves and throw them at the crowd.

"Shit, she's throwin' them cancers at us!" one roughneck hollered.

Nobody left, though. Daddy Jim was unpopular with the oil crowd—he had the only honky-tonk within easy driving distance of the oil fields, and because of this advantage, he kept his prices high.

Beulah only threw five or six of the jars, and none of them hit anybody. The roughneck Brad had slugged was still out cold, and he wished he had a tub of ice water to soak his fist. It was going to be hard to plow with his knuckles jammed.

Once Beulah got her steam up, it was slow to subside. She stalked around the room for a few minutes, looking for somebody to kick. Most of the roughnecks could hardly wait to get back to the fields so they could repeat her remark about the noodles. It was the opinion of some that Daddy Jim's reign had ended—he would never be able to live down a remark like that. Speculation was that he would have to move at least as far as Waurika to enjoy any peace.

By the time Beulah and Brad made it home, Beulah had gone to sleep, her head on Brad's shoulder.

It didn't help Bradley's spirits to see Bessie standing on the porch, waiting, when they drove up.

"Hi, hon," he said, when he stopped. "Beulah had a little too much to drink."

Bessie just looked at him, silent as the night.

7

"Maybe I'm just homesick!" Charley yelled. "Can't I be homesick, like anybody else?"

"How can you be homesick for Tulsa?" Ruby yelled back. "You never lived in Tulsa a day in your life. You can't be homesick for a place you never even lived!"

"I'm homesick for *Oklahoma*! The town don't matter," Charley explained. "I just want to be back in Oklahoma. What's so bad about that?"

"If I have to make you a list, I'll make you a list, you dumb-

240

bell!" Ruby said. "The banks in Oklahoma put up that three-thousand-dollar reward for you—that's the biggest reason right there!"

"Aw, honey, you know they'll never catch me," Charley said, though with diminished conviction. "I'm way too slick for the Oklahoma bulls."

"What if there's one that's slicker than you, Charley?" Ruby asked. "All cops can't be as dumb as you think they are, or they'd never catch anybody."

"Sure they would," Charley protested. "A lot of crooks are dumb, too. Plenty of 'em are dumber than the cops."

"Charley, I like it here!" Ruby protested. "This is the first nice house I ever lived in. Dempsey's in a good school, and folks in the neighborhood think we're respectable. I can sleep through the night most nights and not wake up in a cold sweat, worrying about you."

Charley looked out the window. He had a lump of hurt and anger in his chest the size of a basketball. Ruby never wanted to do anything he did. All he had to do was make the simplest proposal—like moving to Tulsa—and in five minutes, he'd stirred up a fight. He never won the fights, either. Ruby had been the smartest girl in her class in Sallisaw. She could outargue him by a wide margin, and she always did. The thought of being agreeable and letting him make the big decisions never seemed to occur to Ruby. He was the husband; he made the living—why couldn't he make a decision once in a while?

"Charley, you and George robbed so many banks in Oklahoma that the bankers doubled the insurance rates," Ruby reminded him. "They're laying for you there. Why can't we stay here in Fort Smith and live a peaceful life?"

"We can, if you don't care about me being happy," Charley said, looking mournful. "I'm from Oklahoma, I ain't from Arkansas. I want to live in my own state. Can't you understand that?"

Ruby had been in the process of scrambling eggs when Charley suddenly came downstairs, took his seat at the table, and with a big grin on his face, announced that they were moving to Tulsa. The news shocked her so that she had stopped making

241

breakfast. All that was on the table was coffee, and Dempsey would be down any minute, ready for some food. With a sigh, she let the argument drop, and scrambled the eggs.

Charley promptly added fuel to the fire by announcing to Dempsey that they were moving to Tulsa in two weeks.

"Why, Daddy?" Dempsey asked, as shocked by the sudden news as his mother.

"Well, because we're from Oklahoma," Charley explained. "Why live in Arkansas if you're from Oklahoma?"

"Daddy, I got friends!" Dempsey said. "I don't wanna leave my friends, they'll miss me."

Charley hadn't meant to reveal that he'd already rented a house in Tulsa. He intended to hold that revelation for a while. But when both his wife and his son decided to be stubborn and selfish, he lost his temper and blurted it out.

"I don't care what either of you want, I make the decisions in this family—I'm the man!" Charley asserted. "I took us a house yesterday, and it's a nice house. Nicer than this one, for that matter."

Dempsey dropped his forehead onto the table, as he sometimes did when he was sad. He didn't cry, but he didn't lift his head, either.

"Aw, now he's gonna be a crybaby!" Charley said, annoyed that his whole family was determined to be as uncooperative as possible.

"Don't say those words! I ain't no damn crybaby!" Dempsey protested, lifting his head.

"See there, now he's cussing," Ruby said.

"This is the goddamnedest situation I ever heard of!" Charley said, throwing down his napkin.

When they heard his car roar out of the driveway, Dempsey and Ruby looked at one another, shrugged, and sighed.

"Eat your sausage, honey," Ruby said. "You don't want to be late for school."

8

Later in the day, in a speakeasy outside Tulsa, Charley managed to locate Whizbang Red. Since Charley found out that Whizbang was in love with George, there had been no commerce between them. But in the lull between bank jobs, George was off doing the rodeo circuit again, and Red, so far as Charley could tell, was leading a lonely life.

He felt a little guilty because he knew he should have been visiting Beulah, not Whizbang. But if he did visit Beulah, she'd stick to him like wallpaper and beg him to take her away, which he couldn't do, not yet. He felt the need of some solid advice, or at least some relaxed company, and Whizbang fit the bill.

"If it was me, I'd move Beulah to Tulsa and leave your family where they are," Whizbang advised. "Your family's happy, and Beulah's not. Why move the happy ones?"

Charley knew that made sense, but it still wasn't the answer he wanted to hear. There seemed to be days when nobody in the world wanted to give him the answer he wanted to hear. He'd think of something sensible, and then everybody he knew would jump on him, and give him a million reasons why it wasn't sensible. Tulsa was a big town; he would be as safe there as he was in Fort Smith. Why not move?

"At least you got money in your pocket, honey," Whizbang said. "Look at me. I'm down to about six dollars, and old worthless George ain't doing a thing about it. He's off riding broncs, which he's a bit too old to be doing if you ask me."

"I'm mad at him, too," Charley said. "He's just as hardheaded as you women. What makes everybody so hardheaded this time of year?"

"Living," Whizbang said. "Want a little nooky, hon?"

Charley did, for some reason; but he felt awkward.

"Aw, Red, I don't know," he said. "What if George shows up?"

"What if he does?" Whizbang said. "Nooky's nooky, and I'm down to six dollars."

"No, you ain't," Charley said, handing her a hundred-dollar bill. "I meant to give you this when I came in. This house is a shack, and it's drafty. Go get you a nice, warm hotel room. You oughtn't to be working in no shack this time of year."

"It beats that tent in Seminole," Whizbang reminded him. "I hate to take your money like this. You sure you ain't horny?"

"I need to go see Ma," Charley told her. "I ain't seen her in a while. I was meaning to use you as my mother today, but I guess it ain't your job."

"I had a tyke once—you didn't know that, did you, Charley?" Whizbang asked. She had a sad look in her eyes, a sadness that went beyond the weariness that was always in her face—except when she looked at George Birdwell, her true love.

"Boy or girl?" Charley asked.

"Boy," Whizbang said. "He'd be about the same age as your boy Dempsey. He died of rheumatic fever in Burkburnett.

"I never did have no luck in Texas," she added.

After a little while, Charley got up and left.

9

When he got to the farm, Charley discovered that his mother's favorite nanny goat had given birth that morning. It was so cold she had herded the nanny and the four little goats into the kitchen to keep warm.

"Goats ain't especially good mothers," Mamie told her son. "This one's never had much interest in her offspring. If I left her out tonight, she might wander off looking for a billy and let these little mites freeze."

"Aw, I doubt she'd be looking for a billy this soon," Charley said. The kitchen was warm, and it was good to be home. He felt like going up to his old bedroom and having a little nap. It seemed like he had driven all over Oklahoma, looking for someone who would agree with him about something. Now he was at his mother's house, still looking.

"She might look for a billy so she could butt him," Mamie said. "She's ornery. Sometimes she'll butt, just to butt—I'm the same way."

"I guess that means I'll have to step lively or I'll get butted myself, is that it?" Charley asked.

"That's it," Mamie said, looking her son right in the eye. Despite all that had happened, he looked so young to her that it was all she could do to resist him.

"What have I done now?" Charley asked. "I come by hopin' there'd be a bite to eat."

"You can eat," Mamie said. "There's a ham bone on the stove, and some spuds. While you're picking at the ham bone, I have a little bone of my own to pick with you."

Charley sighed: argument everywhere. He dished himself up some spuds, and a big slice of ham. If he was going to be chided, it might as well be on a full stomach.

"You need to get those young women away from Bradley," Mamie told him bluntly. "Your brother's a married man."

"Ma, that's why I took 'em there," Charley protested. "Beulah got shot in the head. She needed a quiet place to rest up."

Charley had given little thought to the situation since delivering the girls. But all of a sudden, he began to feel uncomfortable. He knew Beulah was very sweet on him, but he also knew she was a flirt.

"You mean Beulah's after Brad?" he asked.

"No, the other one's after him," Mamie said. "The quiet one."

"Rose?" Charley asked, shocked. This news silenced him.

"Rose?" he said again, after a moment. "Rose never bothers anybody."

"Be that as it may, you need to get them out of there," Mamie said. "Bessie Floyd will only tolerate so much, and when she gets tired of it, some fur is going to fly."

"Uh-oh," Charley said.

Having made her point, Mamie decided to change the subject. In a way, there wasn't but one subject left to talk about.

"Charley, do you ever mean to change?" Mamie asked, rubbing a little milk on the mouth of one of the young goats. She dipped the end of a rag in warm milk; the nanny wasn't being helpful. If she wanted to save the kids, she was going to have to teach them to suck.

"Change what?" Charley asked. "I didn't mean to start no trouble at Brad and Bessie's. I'll go get the girls if it's a problem."

"It's a problem, but it ain't the main problem," Mamie said. "What I mean is, do you intend to change your profession, or are you just gonna go on robbing banks until you get shot down?

"Now, the banks didn't have no mercy when it came to robbing me and your pa," she added. "But mercy ain't the point, or whether the bankers are crooked, or none of that."

"What's the point, then?" Charley asked.

"Death," Mamie informed him. "That's the point."

"Ma, I don't want to talk about this," Charley said. "I can't do nothing about it, so why talk?"

"You could move to California," Mamie suggested. "Lots of folks around here are thinking of pulling up stakes and heading west. They say oranges grow on trees, out in California."

"Ma, I'm from Oklahoma, I'm tryin' to get Ruby to move to Tulsa with me right now," Charley said. "I don't want to go no further away from here. I'd be so homesick way out in California, I'd probably die. I don't care if the oranges do grow on trees, it ain't as good as bein' home."

Mamie sighed, and began to instruct another of the kids with the rag and the warm milk.

"Don't expect me to bury you, then," she said. "When they shoot you down, don't expect it, because I just plain ain't up to it. Maybe Brad can bury you. I don't want to see it."

Charley hadn't expected this kind of talk when he came in the door; all he'd wanted was something to eat, and some advice from his ma about Ruby.

"Ma, can I go take a nap?" Charley asked. "I don't want to talk about this. It ain't as easy to change as you might think."

"I agree with that," Mamie said, dipping her rag in the milk. "Doin' right ain't never been easy."

She looked up at him, and shrugged. "Go on up and rest, son," she said. "You look tired."

She watched her boy as he headed up the stairs.

"I hope I go first . . . that's all I hope," Mamie said, to the nanny goat.

10

Dempsey couldn't take his eyes off Bela Lugosi. Although his mother and father were sitting on both sides of him, holding his hands, Dempsey had never been so scared in his life. Even when the big white owl flew out of the outhouse in his face, he hadn't been *this* scared. His mother knew it, too, but his daddy, who didn't seem to be scared of Dracula at all, was watching the picture show, and not paying attention to how scared Dempsey was.

"I told you we shouldn't have brought him," Ruby whispered to Charley. "It's too scary for a little boy."

What Dempsey didn't like about Dracula was his white skin, and his scary eyes, and his cape. Dempsey could easily imagine how horrible it would feel if a man like that, with white skin and sharp teeth, bit him in the neck. Then all his blood would be gone, and he'd be dead.

Their house in Tulsa was only six blocks from the picture show, which was why they went to the movies so often. Dempsey knew the way perfectly. On Saturday afternoons, he was sometimes allowed to walk the six blocks with one of his friends to see the cowboy pictures. His mother didn't like the cowboy pictures much; she had seen enough cowboys when she was growing up, she said.

This night, though, Dempsey insisted on being carried home. His father tried to talk him out of it, but Dempsey was so scared that he clung to his father's legs until his father finally agreed to carry him piggyback.

"Dempsey, it was just a movie," Charley said, exasperated. "There ain't no such thing as vampires."

"There are, too," Dempsey said. "I saw him." Then he hid his face. He didn't look up once, all the way home, for fear he'd see a bat in front of the moon, and it would be Dracula.

"I told you! He's too little for these scary movies," Ruby said. She was keeping pretty close to Charley herself.

"You *told* me you told me!" Charley snapped. "Shut up about it. You two can go to the movies by yourselves from now on, for all I care."

Dempsey had to be shown three times that the windows to his bedroom were locked, so no bat could get in. His shade had to be pulled down as far as it would go. Even these precautions were only enough to keep him in his bed five minutes. His parents had hardly got under the covers when Dempsey appeared, wanting to sleep with them.

"No, bud, you kick like a mule when you're asleep," Charley said. "It was just a movie, no vampires are going to get you. Go back to your own bed."

Dempsey refused to obey. He climbed under the covers at the foot of the bed, and huddled there between his mother's legs and his father's. In his mind, he saw a big bat—it was just outside the window. As soon as everyone went to sleep, it would come in through the window, and bite his neck until all his blood left, and he died.

"I'm taking him back to his bed," Charley said. "We got a right to live our own lives, don't we?"

"Charley, just let him stay till he goes to sleep," Ruby whispered. "Then we can move him."

Ten minutes after they moved Dempsey back to his own bed,

248

he began to scream. Before they could get him awake enough to calm him, he began to throw up. Charley got more and more annoyed, but Dempsey was out of control, and there was nothing he could do about it.

Ruby held her son, and rocked him in the new rocking chair in their bedroom.

"I'll just rock him, Charley," Ruby said. "You go on back to sleep, honey."

"How can I sleep with him puking?" Charley asked. "I never seen so much fuss over a damn picture show."

"He's a little boy, Charley," Ruby said. "Little boys have a right to be scared."

Charley raised the shade one more time to show Dempsey there was no black bat stuck to the window, waiting to get in.

"See, bud, no bats!" he said, lowering the shade again. But while he was in the process of lowering the shade, something registered that caused him to forget about bats.

"Turn off the light," he said to Ruby.

"But honey, it'll only make him worse," Ruby said. "Can't we leave the light on till he's all the way asleep?"

Charley turned off the light himself, and went back to the window. At the end of the street, he saw the moonlight flash on the fenders of two cars. Directly across the street, he thought he saw a hat on a hedge. It was a normal hat, but it wasn't normal for it to be on the hedge. Most likely it was the head of whichever cop was standing there watching his house.

Fortunately, while Dempsey was puking, Charley had put on his pants and his shoes. He was nervous about getting splinters in his feet, and always put on his shoes when he got up to pace around.

"Jesus, Ruby, it's a raid!" Charley said, racing for the stairs. "There's a hat on the hedge!"

He didn't even take time to give Ruby or Dempsey a goodbye look. If they already had the house surrounded, he'd have to shoot his way out. He kept a Tommy gun on the top shelf of the pantry, out of Dempsey's sight. He grabbed two pistols and his overcoat out of the closet. When he slipped out the back door, he expected lights and bullhorns, but the night was quiet. He got to the car and waited a minute, a pistol in each hand—the

Tommy gun he stuck in the front seat. He thought he could hear voices, but they were down near the end of the street, where he had seen the two cars parked.

It was lucky the Tulsa house had no garage. It meant he didn't have to start the car and back out. All he had to do was push it down the alley to the next street, which he did. It was so quiet he began to wonder if he had been seeing things. Maybe he was like Dempsey—only instead of seeing bats, he was seeing cops.

Charley had no sooner had the thought than two cop cars purred past the alley, their lights off. He hadn't been seeing things: the cops were coming. As soon as the two cop cars turned the corner toward the front of his house, Charley hit the starter and the car started quiet. He eased out of the alley and zigged a block, then went through another alley. He was four blocks away, still traveling down alleys, when he heard the sirens, back in the direction of his house.

It made him mad—the bulls would scare Dempsey and Ruby out of their wits, coming in to catch him with horns blasting. At least it would take Dempsey's mind off Dracula for a while. He didn't like the idea of cops seeing his wife in her nightgown, or of his little boy being carried off to the hoosegow. But Ruby and Dempsey hadn't done anything; the bulls couldn't keep them long.

Ruby could jump on him all she wanted about taking Dempsey to scary movies, but if he hadn't taken his family to see *Dracula*, the evening would have turned out much worse. If they had just gone to sleep, the cops would have caught him in his bed.

Forty miles out of Tulsa, Charley stopped at a diner and had some eggs. The news of his escape was already on the radio.

"That Pretty Boy, he's a slick one," the old waitress said.

"Ain't he, now?" Charley replied, as he sipped his coffee.

11

To Ruby's surprise, the Tulsa detective started crying while he was asking her questions. He looked at Dempsey, who was asleep in her lap by this time—they had been in the police station two hours—and tears began to leak out of his eyes. His name was Detective Jessup. He was fat, and he had a grease stain on his pants leg from having to change a tire while he was on his way to work. Ruby was mad as hops when they brought her in, but she was finding it hard to stay mad at Detective Jessup—he looked too sad.

"Now, Bob," the skinny detective said. "Now, Bob." He patted Detective Jessup on the back awkwardly.

"Bob, if you need to step out of the room a minute, that'd be fine," the skinny detective said. His name was Flax. It was embarrassing to him that his partner had begun to shed tears while interrogating a suspect. This had been going on for over a year now, every time they hauled in some crook's family. Bob Jessup would hold up for an hour or two, and then he'd break down.

"Miz Floyd, if you need a ride when this is over, I'll take you home," Detective Jessup offered, as he turned and slowly left the room.

"Is that allowed?" Ruby asked. She had never been inside a police station before, except to visit Charley when Bert arrested him and put him in the Sallisaw jail—she didn't know what the rules were. This one stank of tobacco juice from several spittoons that hadn't been emptied in a while.

"It's allowed," Detective Flax said. "We brought you in, we can take you back. I wouldn't want you to have to catch no streetcar this time of night."

"What happened with Bob, his boy drowned over a year ago," Detective Flax revealed. "He ain't been the same since. His boy was about the size of your son. I guess that's what got him started downhill."

251

"That's horrible, losing a child," Ruby said. "I don't think I could stand it."

At first, Ruby hated Detective Jessup. He kept his cigar in his mouth the whole time he was arresting her. The cigar smoke stung her eyes. Dempsey threw up again, this time all over Detective Flax's shoes, but he was so busy searching the house that he didn't pay much attention.

Dempsey was scared at first, but then he thought it was interesting that so many policemen were in the house. At one point, there were six, plus the two detectives. At least they allowed Ruby to get dressed, but every time she said she didn't know no Pretty Boy Floyd, Detective Jessup leaned over, blew smoke in her face, and said, "Don't believe ya, don't believe ya," three or four times.

When the police came pounding up the stairs, Ruby was so flustered that she forgot her name was supposed to be Hamilton. She recovered quickly, though, and didn't really get mad until they insisted she come to the station. When they put handcuffs on her, Ruby's temper blazed up.

"This child has to go to school tomorrow!" she insisted. "I can't be keeping him up all night just to sit around some smelly old police station."

"You can if you're arrested," Detective Flax informed her. He had noticed the vomit on his shoes, and even on one of his socks. He had searched the house up and down, and didn't find anything except a lot of movie magazines and eight or ten issues of *Police Gazette*.

"Are you gonna arrest a *child*?" Ruby asked. "Why would you arrest a *child*?"

"Damaging personal property," Detective Flax said. "The little brat threw up on my brogan."

"That's because the Dracula bat came and nearly got all the blood out of my neck, and I was almost dead," Dempsey told him.

On the ride to the jail, Dempsey started telling Detective Jessup about Dracula the vampire.

"He's very bad, he bites people in the neck and they don't have no blood no more," he said.

252

Detective Jessup didn't respond to that opening, so Dempsey tried another.

"Ever catch a snappin' turtle, mister?" Dempsey asked him.

"Shut up, Dempsey, he ain't interested in listenin' to you," Ruby said.

"You didn't answer me about the snappin' turtle, mister," Dempsey said, confidently.

"I've never caught no snappin' turtle, but I once caught an armadillo," the detective said.

"An armadillo?" Dempsey said, amazed. "Whoever heard of an armadillo being in the water?"

"I wasn't fishing in the water," the detective said. "I was fishing in the weeds."

He said it with a poker face; Dempsey didn't know whether to take the remark seriously.

"Whoever heard of fishin' in the weeds?" he asked, just as they got to the police station. Even before he got inside the jail, Dempsey was getting excited. Nobody in his whole school had ever been in jail; it would be something to talk about at recess.

"If you want to catch badgers, you gotta fish in the weeds," Detective Jessup informed him. "You won't catch many badgers fishing in water tanks."

"What do you do if you catch a badger?" Dempsey asked. "Do you throw him back?"

"Not me, I take my badgers home and teach 'em to play the ukelele," the detective said. Even Ruby had to smile at that one, mad as she was.

"Ain't you ever heard a badger play the ukelele?" Detective Jessup asked.

Dempsey had to admit he had never heard such a thing.

"Niggers eat snappin' turtles," he said, in an attempt to hold his own. "I bet you didn't know that."

After the conversation with Dempsey, the steam went out of Detective Jessup's questioning. He kept it up, but his heart wasn't in it.

When Ruby went out of the smelly little room where they questioned her, with Detective Flax carrying a sleeping Dempsey, Detective Jessup was sitting over in the corner, crying.

"Now, Bob," Detective Flax said, subdued. "We gotta take this little lady home."

"God, I miss talkin' to kids!" Detective Jessup sobbed, tears running down his cigar.

12 .

"Wow, that's a gun if I ever seen a gun!" Turnip Breath said, looking at the brand-new Tommy gun Erv Kelley had just anted up for.

Turnip Breath's real name was Willie Locust, but he was known around Clebit, Oklahoma, as Turnip Breath, because of his habit of munching turnips the year 'round, much as sane people might eat apples.

"You can cut ol' Charley Floyd down like a weed, with a weapon like that," Turnip Breath assured his boss.

"Get out there and get that car, and be sure you wipe the windshield dry," Erv instructed. "Folks around here been drivin' off with wet windshields lately just 'cause you're too weak-minded to finish what you start."

Over the cash register in the filling station, Erv had tacked the reward poster for Charley Floyd. Three thousand dollars was a goodly sum; bringing Charley in alive, if possible—dead, if necessary—would take away a little of the sting of having to relinquish the sheriffship of McCurtain County, something Erv Kelley'd had to do only a few months ago. He had been a popular sheriff, too, catching four bank robbers and a murderer in his one short term. Winning reelection would have been easy as snapping peas, but Erv gave up, and bought the filling station instead. It was lose the sheriffship, or lose Amity Bates, the

254

cutest blonde in McCurtain County, and also one of the most resolute. Erv had not even so much as been allowed to give Amity one kiss until she had his solemn promise to give up law enforcement.

"I ain't about to lay awake nights for a whole lifetime, wondering if some drunk's blown your guts out with a hogleg," Amity declared. "I got too much pride to put up with behavior like that."

Since marrying Amity the previous July, Erv had discovered that his little bride had too much pride to do most of the things he had expected her to be doing—Amity had nerve storms if he even suggested doing some of those things—but she was the prize of the county in Erv's eyes, and he was hopeful that Amity's nerve storms would subside once she got more reconciled to married life.

Still, all that money the bankers put up for the capture of Charley Floyd was hard to get off his mind, which was what prompted Erv to strike a deal for the purchase of the Tommy gun. If he was to drag in Pretty Boy Floyd and come marching home with three thousand dollars in his pocket, Amity's attitude toward marriage might improve dramatically. With that kind of money to throw around, Erv would have more to look forward to than a life of wiping windshields, changing flats, and reading oil sticks.

When Willie came back from wiping the windshield, he was eating a turnip, his third of the morning. He wanted to hold the new Tommy gun so bad he could taste it, even while eating a turnip. There were plenty of turnips in Clebit, Oklahoma, but only one Tommy gun, and the Tommy gun was right there in Erv Kelley's filling station.

"Rat-a-tat-tat, rat-a-tat-tat," Willie said. "When you going after Charley?"

"Why would I tell you?" Erv said, looking at Willie, who had a face that looked like a turnip itself, if viewed from the right angle.

"Because," Willie replied. It seemed to him sufficient reason.

"You got a mouth like a sieve, and you eat like you have nine assholes," Erv said, those being two of the milder criticisms he could make of Willie Locust, his one employee.

"Yeah, but I ain't aiming to eat Charley, I'd like to watch you mow him down like a weed," Willie said.

"He got loose from 'em in Tulsa, I figure he'll be going to his brother's one of these days to pick up his girlfriend," Erv said. "He must like the little gal, or he wouldn't have packed her all the way down to Bradley Floyd's to get well."

"Is his brother a nice fella?" Willie asked. "I've heard he's not bad."

"He ain't—I cut hay with Bradley twice," Erv said.

"I doubt he'll appreciate it if you mow his brother down like a weed," Willie said.

"Stop talking like that," Erv Kelley said. "I ain't aiming to mow nobody down. If you point a Tommy gun at some crook and give 'em time to take a good look at it, you won't have to mow 'em down. Most crooks would rather surrender than be cut in two by a Tommy gun."

"Charley Floyd don't aim to be taken alive, though," Willie reminded him. "It says that in all the stories."

"Stories are one thing, and starin' down the barrel of a Tommy gun is another," Erv said.

"Let me go with you," Turnip Breath said. "I won't ask for none of the reward. I just wanna see you catch him."

"You can't be eatin' no turnips, if I let you come," Erv Kelley said.

"Okay," Willie agreed.

"Why not?" he asked, a little later.

" 'Cause they don't call you Turnip Breath for nothin'," Erv said, looking at him sideways.

Erv had been a track star, a football star, and still played on the town baseball team. He was fast on his feet, and the best-looking man in Clebit, by a long shot. Willie often wondered what it would be like to be as handsome as Erv Kelley. He knew that he himself was nothing much to look at. All his life he'd had to rely on smarts.

Two days later, stretched out in some wet weeds right by the gate to Bradley Floyd's farm and holding a ten-gauge shotgun Erv had told him to keep ready in case the Tommy gun failed to work, Willie began to get the sense that he had somehow mislaid his smarts. It was drizzling rain, foggy, and cold. Worse yet, their quarry was actually there—through the drizzle, they could see Pretty Boy Floyd himself, loading suitcases into a green Pontiac. Two young women were running in and out of the house, carrying clothes to the car.

"How'd they get so many clothes, living way out here?" Willie asked.

"Be still—how many times do I have to tell you not to talk?" Erv said. He himself felt confident. Within a few minutes, he was quite sure, he would have captured the most wanted outlaw in Oklahoma; maybe the most wanted anywhere. Charley Floyd was dressed in a suit and tie, and didn't appear to have a care in the world. Once he got the suitcases in the car, he stood talking to his brother and sister-in-law. Bradley wore overalls, and Bessie, whom Erv knew slightly, was holding hands with him. That surprised Erv a little—Amity wasn't at all eager to hold hands with him.

Willie "Turnip Breath" Locust was wishing he had stayed put and run the filling station. He would rather be reading oil sticks and wiping windshields dry than lying in a ditch holding a shotgun, waiting to be plugged by Pretty Boy Floyd. For some reason, his confidence in Erv Kelley had evaporated. Previously, he had assumed that Charley Floyd would be the one killed, but somehow his thinking on the matter had reversed itself. Now he assumed that he and Erv would be killed, and within the next few minutes, too. The young women were both in the car; Charley was just handing some money to his sister-in-law.

Then Charley got in the car, and started it up. The car made a circle, then moved slowly down the muddy road toward the gate, which was closed to keep Bradley's milk cows from wandering off. A couple of milk cows were standing not thirty yards away, looking like they would eagerly wander off if someone would only open the gate.

"I'm gettin' nervous," Willie admitted.

"Why?" Erv whispered. "We got him just where we want him."

"I might shoot a girl," Willie said. "I'd rather not shoot a girl."

"You ain't shootin' nobody!" Erv reminded him, emphatically. "I'm gonna do the shootin', if there is any. He'll have to get out and open the gate, then he'll drive through, and then he'll have to get out again and shut the gate. When he starts to latch the gate, he'll have to put his shoulder into it—that's when I'll stand up and arrest him."

"What if he lets one of the girls open the gate and then shut it?" Willie asked. "They ain't doin' nothin', why couldn't one of 'em jump out and do it?"

Erv didn't bother to answer. He was thoroughly sorry he had allowed Willie to come. It would have been better just to have done the job himself. He had brought Willie along to make conversation, but Willie had been too cold to talk and hadn't said two words during the whole night. Now, just when it was time to concentrate on the task at hand, Willie would start jabbering. The best course seemed to be to ignore him.

The gate the car had to pass through was a barbed-wire gate, stretched tight, and Bradley Floyd was known for keeping his farm, including his fences and gates, in good repair.

Charley Floyd stopped the green Pontiac a few yards from the gate, and got out to open it. He moved carefully, so as not to get too much mud on his shoes. One of the milk cows started over, but Charley picked up a stick and threw it at her. The cow stopped.

When Charley got back in the Pontiac, Erv switched off the Tommy gun's safety catch. Charley was whistling "The Wabash Cannonball" when he got out of the car the second time. He was a good whistler. Charley picked up the gate and got ready to latch it, not suspecting a thing.

The second Charley put his shoulder against the gate stick, getting ready to put the wire loop over the top of the stick, Erv Kelley stood up, his Tommy gun at the ready.

"Leave the gate go, Charley," Erv said. "Get them hands up, or this game's over."

"Drive, Beulah!" Charley yelled. Then he finished shutting the gate, looking at Erv steadily as he did.

Erv had always heard that Charley Floyd was fast, but he had been the best sprinter in the region himself and supposed he didn't have to apologize to anyone when it came to speed. The puzzling thing wasn't that Charley was on the running board of the car in a flash, or that the car was moving toward him, or that Charley had produced a gun from somewhere and was

258

firing it at him; the puzzling thing was that he himself had slowed down—stopped, in fact. He'd had his finger on the trigger of the Tommy gun before he called out to Charley, and the safety was off. But Charley Floyd was on the running board of the car before the Tommy gun fired its first round. Erv thought he hit Charley in the side, but before he could be sure, he himself was spinning around. He was facing down the road; his head went down and up; he confused the earth with the sky for a moment—all before the Tommy gun began to spit a continuous stream of bullets, as it was supposed to. The stream wasn't spitting at Charley Floyd, though. As Erv turned and turned, trying to get his feet straightened out—trying to face toward the oncoming car—the machine gun spewed up dirt as it cut a circular furrow into the ground, a furrow deep enough, it seemed to him, to plant corn in, or even a spud. He couldn't stop the gun —it jerked so he could scarcely hang onto it, spitting bullets into the ground in a circle around his feet.

His eyes began to get filmy, as the gun kept jerking. It was as if Turnip Breath had started washing his eyes as he would a windshield. But then Willie had got weak-minded and wandered off to check the oil or something, leaving a slick, soapy film over his eyes. The film made it hard to see Charley, or the car. Soon, the film made it hard to see anything. Erv was glad when the Tommy gun stopped firing. Then he saw something green and wet, so close to his head it was almost touching his eyeball.

Erv Kelley thought it might be grass—grass wet with rain— but the film on his eyes was so thick that he couldn't be sure.

13

"Good God, it's Erv Kelley!" Bradley said, looking down at the dead man.

"Oh my God, he killed Erv!" Bessie shrieked. They had both run down to the gate through the mud when they heard the shooting. Charley was pointing a pistol at a little turnip-faced man who had been hiding in the ditch. The little man was as wet as if he had swum a river, and he was shaking badly in anticipation of being killed.

Beulah and Rose were crying hysterically, and Charley looked stunned. The dead man's Tommy gun had cut a circle in the grass at his feet. He had stumbled out of the circle when he fell. Brad had opened the gate again, and two of the milk cows had walked through it while they were all looking down at the dead man. After staggering around, Erv Kelley had fallen on his back. They could all see that Charley had hit him twice—dead center —in his chest.

"Shut his eyes, shut his eyes, can't you?" Bessie said, covering her own.

Charley squatted down, and closed Erv Kelley's eyes.

"Who was Erv Kelley? I never heard of him," he said.

"He was sheriff for a while," Bradley said. "I farmed with him a little. Then he give up being a sheriff, and opened a filling station with Turnip Breath here."

"Turnip Breath?" Charley said, looking up at the young man.

"Willie's my real name," Willie admitted. "Turnip Breath's just my nickname."

Charley felt weak in the legs, glad for an excuse to squat. Always before, he had kept running when he'd shot someone. Erv Kelley was the first man he had killed and actually looked in the face. It took the strength out of his legs, looking at him, because there it was: death.

"Charley, you're hit!" Beulah cried, choking off her tears abruptly. "There's blood on your pants."

"He just nicked my hip," Charley said, still looking at the dead man. He had been a good-looking fellow; now, he was dead as a fallen deer.

"You're lucky that's all it was," Bradley said. "Them Tommy guns will cut a man in two."

"He didn't know how to shoot it—he should've practiced," Charley said, standing up. "Tommy guns'll get away from you if you don't hold 'em firm. Look at the ground he plowed up."

"Erv just bought that weapon last week," Willie said. "I doubt he could afford the ammunition to practice. The filling station business ain't been good lately."

"It still beats the bounty-hunting business," Charley said, walking back to the car. He felt a sadness so deep, he didn't think he would be able to drive.

"Beulah, if you're calmed down, would you drive?" he asked.

"Mister, I'd be glad to drive," Willie volunteered.

Everyone looked at him in surprise.

"Drive me where, to the hoosegow?" Charley asked. "I just killed your boss."

"Oh, no, Mr. Floyd," Willie said. "I ain't got no job now. Nobody in Clebit's gonna hire me because of the turnips."

"Turnips?" Charley asked.

"He eats turnips, day and night," Brad said. "That's why they call him Turnip Breath."

"I've always considered turnips to be harmless," Charley said. "Maybe I'm wrong."

"They are," Willie said. "Folks just got funny ideas about 'em, I guess."

Charley sighed. "What do you think, girls? Wanna take this fool along?"

"I don't care who we take, Charley, I just wanna leave," Beulah said.

"What about Erv?" Bessie asked. "Are you just gonna drive off and leave us with this, Charley?"

"What else can I do, other than surrender?" Charley asked. "I'm sorry—I'm mighty sorry. But he jumped up pointing that Tommy gun at me while I was shutting the gate. If he'd been more experienced, he would have cut me down. Once he started shootin', it was kill or die."

"What if they think Brad done it?" Bessie asked. "The law's got it in for us anyway because of you."

Charley looked at his brother.

"They do watch us pretty close now, Charley," Brad said.

Charley raked around in his suitcase until he found a tablet and a pencil that he used to play tic-tac-toe with Dempsey. He sat in the front seat of the car, and wrote on the tablet:

I, Charles Arthur Floyd, killed this man in self-defense. I regret my action but had no choice. My brother and his family are innocent of this killing. They were elsewhere at the time.

Charles Arthur Floyd

Charley handed the letter to Bessie.

"Give 'em that, when they come," he said. "I'm sorry to have brought this trouble."

"You always bring trouble, Charley," Bessie said, with some bitterness. "Being sorry don't change it—it's still trouble."

"Bessie, hush," Bradley said, feeling worse by the minute.

Willie Locust still stood in the wet weeds, with his hands up.

"Put them hands down," Charley said. "Somebody'll come along and hang out a washing on 'em if you don't."

"Much obliged," Willie said, lowering his hands. He had been careful not to look at Erv's body.

Charley noticed a sad look cross Brad's face when Rose finally dried her eyes and got back in the car. It occurred to him then that Bessie might have some reason of her own to jump on him. But they were leaving, and there was nothing he could do to make it up to her. Bessie had a long memory; maybe it never would be made up.

Willie drove; Rose sat in the front seat with him.

"Where we goin', Mr. Floyd?" Willie asked.

"Kansas City, and step on it," Charley said.

When Charley mentioned Kansas City, a light flickered in Beulah's eyes—the first light Charley had seen there in months.

"Will you take me dancin', Charley, when we get there?" Beulah asked, hopeful—she could see Charley was upset.

262

Charley looked out the window. Dancing with Beulah in Kansas City was the last thing on his mind.

"I suppose, if my hip don't seize up," he replied.

14

Beulah clung so tight once they got to Kansas City that the only way Charley could even get breathing space was to give her a wad of shopping money. He made Willie Locust drive her. Willie was constantly underfoot, too, but he drove competently and ran so many errands for the girls that they wouldn't have allowed Charley to fire him, even had he been so inclined. Willie had never seen a city before; he hadn't even been to Tulsa. For the first few days, he did nothing but gawk. He'd even gawk at a fireplug, which annoyed Beulah.

"Stop gawking at that fireplug, you hick," she told him.

"Yes, ma'am, 'scuse me," Willie said. City life scared him, but not as badly as Beulah Baird scared him. When she said jump, he jumped—though often, it seemed, in the wrong direction.

When Beulah counted the wad of money Charley gave her, she began to develop suspicions. Not a word had been said about Lulu Ash, a suspicious fact in itself. Beulah was not one to mask her doubts, either. She had been about to march out the door and get in the car, but she changed her mind and marched up to Charley instead. He was standing by his dresser, picking out a necktie for the day.

"What'd you forget?" he asked, trying to ignore the suspicious look on Beulah's face.

263

"I forgot to tell you what happened to the tomcat when he went up the wrong alley," Beulah said.

"What tomcat, and what alley?" Charley asked, pretending to give the ties a close study.

"What happened was, the tomcat got strangled with a polka-dot necktie," Beulah informed him. "I put up with your wife. But I won't put up with that old whore, I don't care how much money you give me."

"Gosh," Charley said. "You mean Ma Ash? I doubt she's even still in this town."

"Keep doubtin' it!" Beulah said. "I didn't get shot in the head, and then squat down there with Bradley and Bessie in a cotton patch for six months, to see you mess around with that old bitch."

Fifteen minutes later, Charley was sitting in Lulu's kitchen, drinking homemade whiskey. Since the Erv Kelley killing, he had found liquor harder to resist. There were lots of times when he wanted to cut his mind off. Beulah could help him cut it off for a few minutes, but whiskey cut it off longer.

"You should have stayed here and run hootch with me," Lulu said, looking him over.

"Why should I, you don't look rich," Charley said.

"Sass me, and I'll slap your puss," Lulu said. "You're lucky I even let you in the door. Every cop in seven states is waiting to haul you in."

"You notice they ain't hauled me in yet," Charley said. "Ever been to Canada?"

"Yeah. Not much fun to be had in Canada, all that cold takes the humor out of folks," Lulu said. "Why?"

"Where would you go, if you was me?" Charley asked. "I gave Beulah a hundred and fifty dollars so I could sneak off and visit with you for a few minutes. Why do you have to be so stiff? All I want's advice."

Then Lulu did slap his puss. "It may not be all I want," she said, reaching for his pants.

"We're in the kitchen!" Charley told her. "Anybody could walk in!"

But nobody did.

264

"I wouldn't go to Canada," Lulu said, when she got around to giving him advice.

"Why not?" Charley asked. "I've heard it's a big place."

"That's right—a big place with smart cops," Lulu said. "They'd nab you in a wink."

"Well, forget that, then," Charley said. "What would you do in my spot?"

"Go back to Oklahoma and rob ever' bank in sight," Lulu said. "Spook 'em. Convince 'em bullets can't kill you."

"Yeah, but bullets *can* kill me," Charley said. "What if one does?"

"You'll have been a bandit to the end, at least," Lulu said. "You'll have a big funeral."

"Lulu, I ain't ready for no funeral," Charley said. "I ain't old enough."

"But you ain't green no more, are you, baby?" Lulu said, touching his face. Despite herself, something in her softened whenever Charley looked at her with those lost-looking brown eyes. It was her old problem with men, picking the wrong ones every time—men that were taken; men that wouldn't stay put. Every year, as she got older, she told herself she'd learn, do a better job of picking who she softened for. Better to take up with an older fellow, someone she wasn't likely to be in love with, or even to be so dog-in-heat about, than to keep letting young swaggerers like Charley Floyd grab her heart and leave it bruised. Why don't you learn, Lulu? she asked herself, even as she rubbed the stubble on Charley's cheek.

"That's four killings they've put on you," she said.

"I never done but two of them, and it was kill or be killed both times," Charley said. "I don't believe I killed that agent here. I did wing him, but I think Luther Ott was the one that plugged him solid."

"Don't matter, they've scored it to you," Lulu said. "You oughtn't to even be in this town."

"Maybe not, but Oklahoma's boiling," Charley said. "If you don't advise Canada, where can I go?"

"Try Chi," Lulu said. "Chi's a big town."

"Oh, Chicago, you mean," Charley said. "I've heard it's

windy in Chicago. I get them bad earaches if too much cold wind blows on me."

"I hear you've got a runt driving for you," Lulu said. "Where'd you pick him up?"

"Oklahoma," Charley said. "That's Turnip Breath. He was working for Kelley. When I plugged his boss, he was out of a job. Now he's working for me."

That night, an old beau named Ernie Branch showed up at the boarding house, drunk, and tried to paw her. Lulu slapped him hard, and locked him out. Then she went up to her bedroom, and broke down crying. She didn't want to accept Ernie Branch any longer. Charley Floyd was in town, but he wasn't here with her. He had been so blue about the killings that she made him three ham sandwiches to try and cheer him up. But Charley had a wife, and a girlfriend, too—how was she going to cheer herself up? She was forty-eight. Pretty boys would be coming around less and less in the years ahead. If they caught Charley, he'd swing. She wouldn't even have him to visit in jail, not for very long. One minute she'd be wishing she had never met him; the next minute she'd be missing him so bad she'd have to hug the pillow to keep from shaking. Foolish, foolish, she thought. Old women should leave handsome young men alone —that was the wise way. But when had she ever cared to be wise?

Charley came to see her seven more times. The day he left for the last time, he had a desperate look. He had decided to go back to Oklahoma.

"Why, if it's boiling?" Lulu asked.

"It's home," Charley said. "If I went to Chicago, I'd just get them earaches."

"That's better than gettin' a necktie with a fatal fit," Lulu said; then she wished she hadn't. She had no place safe to send him —why mention hanging?

"I'll see you in the funny papers," Charley said, trying to grin as he was leaving. He was misty in the eyes, though.

"Keep hightailin' it, baby," Lulu said. "Keep leadin' the chase."

Charley tried again to grin, but the grin came out crooked.

266

15

Bob Birdwell and Beulah Baird hit it off immediately. Beulah hadn't been in the Birdwell house two minutes before they started drinking gin, and dancing to the radio. Bob danced in her big shoes with the laces flapping. George Birdwell was nowhere to be seen, and the kids seemed to scream from morning till night.

"The only thing to do is scream louder," Bob said, so she and Beulah screamed louder. Rose was mopey; she had been, ever since leaving Bradley.

"How long do you think Bird will be gone?" Charley asked. "Staying around here with you screeching hens will soon drive me daft."

"You was born daft, honey," Beulah informed him. "It's a good thing you're cute."

"Don't be calling me cute—that's a girl's word," Charley said, annoyed. Beulah had recovered a little too much of her spirit, in his view. He couldn't give an opinion on the weather, or even the time of day, without her contradicting him, or sassing him in some way.

"He's cranky 'cause he's broke," Beulah informed Bob. "Soon as him and George rob a few banks, he'll be his old jolly self."

"I don't know when that'll be," Bob said. "George run off with a whore."

Charley decided this was a good conversation to keep his two cents out of. Rose was in the kitchen, sipping coffee. As Charley walked in, he saw her pour some whiskey in the coffee. A little of the coffee sloshed out on the oilcloth tabletop.

"I hope you ain't turnin' into a drunk like your sister," Charley said, lightly.

"I been drinking ever since we left Brad's," Rose admitted. "It don't help much, but it helps some."

"I guess you and Brad were pretty thick," Charley said cautiously.

"How'd you know?" Rose asked.

Before Charley could answer, Turnip came in. Charley had shortened his nickname, for convenience. Now everybody called him Turnip. He had been under the car for some reason, and oil had dripped on his hair.

"Hey, girls, we're rich, Turnip struck oil," Charley said, trying to inject a little humor into the situation.

"It's just a dribble," Turnip said, embarrassed by his own clumsiness—nobody else had oil dripping into their ears.

"Go dribble it outside, I won't have oil on my floor," Bob said.

"I'll go live in a tree, if I can find one," Turnip said. He considered Bob Birdwell to be overly fastidious, but he went back outside and scrubbed the oil off his head with an old sack he picked up near the windmill.

Meanwhile, back in the kitchen, Charley found himself under attack by both Beulah and Bob, who had become surprisingly drunk in a very short space of time.

"All men are jerks, particularly you," Beulah said. "Every single man in the world is a jerk, but you're King Jerk."

"Hold on, now," Charley said. "Why would I be the King Jerk?"

"Because you screwed that old whore in Kansas City, I know you did!" Beulah shrieked. "I hate you!"

She screamed the last comment as loud as she could. The three little Birdwell children had been watching from a hallway, quiet as mice, but when Beulah screamed, they scampered off.

"So what, George's probably screwing one right this minute," Bob Birdwell said. "She's a redhead. I seen her once at a rodeo. I'd like to wrap her in barbed wire and roll her off a cliff."

At that point, Rose Baird burst into tears.

"Stop it, Brad's no jerk!" she said. "Brad's sweet!"

Charley began to wish he were home with Ruby and Dempsey. At home, he had only one woman's temper to contend with. Here, he had three, two of them drunk and the third heading in that direction. Even if Ruby was out of sorts, he

268

could go out in the yard and throw a football around with Dempsey.

Knowing that the Birdwells' larder was apt to be either bare or else filled with eccentric foods he didn't care for, like beets, Charley had brought spaghetti, which he could cook better than passably, he felt.

"If the river was whiskey, you gals'd have to learn to swim," he said. "Get out of the way. Me and Turnip will do the cooking. Maybe you won't hate me so much on a full stomach."

"I'll hate you, full or empty," Beulah proclaimed, but in fact, her anger wore itself out a few minutes after supper. She curled up with Charley on the couch, and slept like a baby. Neither of them stirred until midnight or so, when George Birdwell tromped in, his spurs jingling. He dumped a saddle on the kitchen floor.

"Where's Bob, is she in a high fury?" he whispered to Charley.

"She's your wife, go ask her yourself, you skunk," Charley said, shaking Bird's hand. There was something about George that made folks glad to see him—Charley, especially. Turnip was sleeping on a pallet in the corner, snoring like a buzz saw.

"Who's that little feller with the snore?" Bird asked.

"We call him Turnip," Charley said. "He does the driving, while me and Beulah fight."

Bird stood on one leg and took one boot off; then he stood on the other leg and took his other boot off. There was a baseball bat leaning against the fireplace. Bird picked it up as he headed for the hall.

"What's that for, it's a little late for a ball game," Charley said.

"That depends," Bird said. "I'm so good-lookin', I might have to beat Bob off."

"I doubt it, bud," Charley said.

"Yeah? You don't know her like I do," Birdwell informed him.

16

Beulah insisted on going with them to rob the Sallisaw bank. Rose stayed home with Bob Birdwell to help her clean out the chicken yard. Doing rural chores made Rose feel closer to Brad, whom she pined for desperately.

"Rose may end up married to a clodhopper yet," Beulah said, putting on lipstick. "Rose is the slow one. She ain't glamorous and witty, like me."

"You can take your wit and shovel it down the coal chute," Charley said. "If some deputy shoots you in the head again, maybe you won't be so witty."

"Aw, Charley, you know I make you laugh," Beulah said. "If I wasn't around, you wouldn't crack a smile once a month."

The idea of robbing the Sallisaw bank had been Birdwell's. Charley half liked it and half didn't. It seemed a little too much like showing off. But on the other hand, why not?

"It's your hometown, Charley," Birdwell insisted. "You've robbed five or six banks not thirty miles away. The homefolks are gonna get their feelings hurt if they're left out."

"I guess," Charley said.

But he dressed to the nines—even wore spats—and shined up his Tommy gun anyway. He even made Willie "Turnip" Locust wash his hair under the pump, nearly freezing the young man to death in the process.

"Well, don't be gettin' dripped on when you're crawlin' under the car," Charley warned. "We don't want our driver lookin' like he works in a garage.

"I want you to go in a store and buy yourself a nice cap," he added. "Do it before we rob the bank. There's no excuse for dressing like trash in this line of work."

"What about me, I could use a new chapeau," Beulah said. "I haven't bought a stitch of clothes since we left K.C."

"Beulah, you own enough duds to dress the Ziegfeld Follies," Charley said.

Birdwell had been unusually silent on the way into town, thanks to a spat with Bob, during which he had gotten slapped twice. Now that it was too late, he was annoyed by his own restraint.

"I don't know why I didn't slap that gal back," he said.

Charley had developed a healthy fear of Bob Birdwell—a woman of strong opinions, to say the least.

"If I were you, I wouldn't go slappin' her back," Charley advised.

"Why not? Who's the damn boss, her or me?" Birdwell asked.

"I don't have an opinion, and I ain't venturin' no guess, either," Charley replied.

The first person Charley spotted when they parked on the main street in Sallisaw was his grandpa Earl Floyd. He was sitting with two other toothless old-timers on the spit-and-whittle bench next to the drugstore.

Birdwell, too, was dressed to the nines, in a white suit, a 30X beaver Stetson, and a new belt buckle. Charley carried the Tommy gun, and Birdwell brandished a pearl-handled .45 that was supposed to have once been the property of Buffalo Bill.

"Grandpa, what are you doin' here this early?" Charley asked.

"Come to see you rob 'er, Charley," Earl Floyd said. "That bank's been open ten minutes, you best get started."

"Give 'em hell, Charley," one of his companions said, gumming a plug of wet tobacco.

"Next time, let's advertise," Birdwell said, put out at the thought that the law might know their plans. "Place a notice in the paper, so the boys with the handcuffs won't be late. How'd the news get out?"

"Somebody told somebody, I reckon," Earl Floyd said. "I heard it at the hardware store, myself."

"You and your big mouth," Birdwell said, to Charley. "I'm surprised they didn't scratch up a parade."

"Bird, I never told a soul—why would I? Do I look dumb?" Charley asked.

"No comment, bud," Bird said. "Let's whip up, before the posse shows."

"Honk if there's trouble, Turnip," Charley said, as they hurried into the bank.

"I'll take a few hundred, if you got it to spare after the robbery, Charley," Earl Floyd said.

"He's a forward old bastard, ain't he?" Birdwell observed.

Charlene Gordon was the only teller doing business when Charley and George strode in. Charley recognized her at once. He had taken her to a dance or two before he met Ruby. She had been a lively girl then, but now, she just looked sad.

"Morning, Charlene," Charley said. "I'd be obliged if you'd hand over the money as quick as possible."

"Aw, Charley, don't rob us," Charlene stalled. "We're about to go under as it is."

"Now, Charlene, just 'cause we kicked up our heels together once don't mean you can play on my sympathies," Charley said.

"That's right, lady—we didn't come here to engage in conversation," Birdwell said. "Just give over the money."

"You knew about the tractor flippin' over and killin' Bill—we was married eight years," Charlene said.

"No, I didn't, Charlene. Sorry to hear it," Charley said.

Just then, a young couple who went to the same church as Brad and Bessie popped in the door. Charley knew their first names, but was at a loss for their last.

"Why, hello, J.W.," he said. "Mornin', Bea. I'd be much obliged if you'd step behind the window there with Charlene."

"Is this a robbery, by any chance?" J.W. asked.

"Shut up, J.W., it ain't none of our business," Bea badgered. It was well known in the community that Bea treated her husband like a puppy.

"I just asked," J.W. said, with a pained expression.

"If it is, we'll read about it in the papers," Bea said, as they quickly scooted behind the teller's cage.

Birdwell, meanwhile, was raking bills into a sack as Charlene looked on, an unhappy expression on her face.

"This job's the only way I got to feed my younguns," she reminded Charley.

"We ain't meanin' to take every cent, Charlene," Charley told her.

Then, two farmers and an old lady came through the door. Charley at once tipped his hat to the old lady.

272

"Howdy, Miz Waggoner," he said. "How are you, Mr. Stevens . . . is that Mr. Prideaux there with you? How you all doin'?"

"Poorly, I got the rheumatism," Mr. Stevens said. "What'll you take for that Tommy gun? I could shoot me a pack of wolves if I had me a Tommy gun."

"Can't spare it, sir. Could you please stand over there?" Charley directed. Even as he said it, a short cowboy named Red stomped in.

"Hi, Red," Charley said. "Would you mind just standing over there with the crowd? We won't be but a minute more."

"I got stock that needs tendin' to, though, Charley," Red replied.

"Won't be but a minute," Charley repeated.

Birdwell was filling his third sack; even though, the gathering crowd began to vex him.

"What is this—a robbery, or a town social?" Birdwell queried.

"Little of both," Charley said, grinning. He was hoping Bird would get into the spirit of the thing.

"If this bank goes under and me and my younguns gotta live on the road, I'll curse your name, Charley," Charlene said, grim.

"Charlene, just get in touch with Brad if there's trouble," Charley told her. "I'll see that your younguns don't suffer."

"Okay, Robin Hood, let's get movin'," Birdwell said. "This is hard work, I don't do it for charity."

Just as he said it, a man with a camera burst in. Birdwell leveled the pearl-handled .45 at him.

"Who's this drummer?" he asked.

"Don't shoot him, Bird, it's John Elmer," Charley said. "He runs the local paper."

"Charley, could I get one shot?" John Elmer asked. "We ain't got no fresh picture of you."

"Okay, but just one," Charley said. "I'll stand here, in front of the folks."

Birdwell, a little jealous that Charley was getting so much attention, glared at his partner.

"Come on, Bird—I want you in this," Charley said, trying to appeal to Birdwell's vanity. It worked; George stepped right into the picture. He adjusted the set of his Stetson and smiled, just as John Elmer popped the flash.

"Thanks, Charley," John Elmer said.

Beulah was incensed when she discovered Charley and Bird-well had had their picture made without asking her to be in it.

"I didn't even get to shop. The least you could've done was invite me to be in the picture," Beulah said. "It's gonna cost you, Charley. I don't know what, but it's gonna cost you.

"Bonnie Parker gets her picture in the paper all the time," she added, fuming.

As they tooled on out of Sallisaw, Charley was trying to imagine how mad Ruby would be if he had his picture in the paper with Beulah on his elbow, let alone robbing a bank.

"These little banks don't keep enough hundred-dollar bills," Birdwell observed. He always counted the money as soon as he could. "We mostly got tens, and tens add up slow."

"Shucks, I was gonna give some to Grandpa," Charley said. "I completely forgot. I wonder what he thought of the robbery?"

"He was asleep when we drove off," Turnip said. "He slept through it, I 'spect."

"At least he got to see the Tommy gun," Charley said. "His eyes lit up when he seen it."

"Mine might light up if I seen a diamond bracelet," Beulah said.

Charley didn't answer—he kept his eyes on the road.

"Don't pretend you didn't hear me, Charley Floyd," Beulah said. "You shouldn't have left me out of the picture."

"The only reason I did was because some G-man might see it and come down here just to flirt with you," Charley said, thinking fast. "You're a damn sight prettier than Bonnie Parker any day."

"You think so?" Beulah said, softening a little.

"You bet," Charley said. "You're the cutest thing in the Red River Valley."

"I still might want that bracelet," Beulah replied.

17

It snowed on Dempsey's birthday. Even so, he put on his earmuffs, and his big coat, and a pair of mittens his Grandma Mamie had knitted for him, and he went out in the snow to wait for the mailman. His mom was in bed, coughing. She'd been sick for two weeks, but there was going to be a birthday party anyway, with a cake and candles.

The wind was cutting that day. Dempsey's feet almost froze before the mailman came driving up in his little pickup. There was so much snow on the windows of the postman's pickup that the windshield wipers would barely go up and down. Dempsey had been stomping around in circles, trying to keep his feet from turning to ice. His mama had assured him that his daddy wouldn't forget his birthday; he would send a package, or at least a card. Dempsey wanted to be right there waiting for his daddy's package, snow or no snow.

"Howdy, son—if you're an Eskimo, why didn't you build us an igloo?" the mailman asked.

"I don't know how to build an igloo," Dempsey told him. "It's my birthday. Do you have anything for me?"

The mailman was an old fellow with one eye that didn't see. Dempsey had always wanted to ask him why his eye didn't see, but he wasn't sure if it was polite to ask about such things, so he held back. One of the mailman's ears was bright red from the wind—he had to leave one of the windows down in the pickup so he could reach out and keep the snow off his rearview mirror.

"Well, I've got somethin' for a Dempsey Hamilton," the old man said. "Would that be you, sonny?"

Dempsey felt a moment of confusion. Sometimes he was one, sometimes the other. In Arkansas, he had been Dempsey Hamilton, but now that they were settled in Tulsa, it seemed to him his name might be Floyd again—he wasn't sure.

The mailman was untying the tarp that covered all the packages in the back of his little pickup. He had to blow on his hands a few times to get his fingers working well enough to untie it. Dempsey sympathized—his own feet felt like stumps of ice, and despite his woolly earmuffs, his ears were letting cold air into his head. He knew he'd be lucky not to get an earache, in which case his mama would have to hold a sock filled with hot corn-meal against his ear until it stopped hurting.

The mailman finally got the tarp off and lifted down a big, big package. Though Dempsey had hoped his daddy would send a good present—a punching bag, maybe, or a BB gun, or even a .410 shotgun—he had not expected a box as big as the one the mailman lifted out of his pickup.

"Want me to tote it to the door?" the mailman asked. "Be all you can do to lift it, sonny."

"No. I'll scoot it," Dempsey said. "Thank you, mister."

"It's from my daddy," he added, proudly. "He remembered my birthday."

Then he began to push the box up the icy sidewalk toward the front door. It was so big it wedged in the door. He had to crawl over it, and run to the bedroom to get his mama to help him. His mama was still coughing; she didn't look well.

"Mama, Daddy didn't forget," he said. "A big package came."

That was good news—the only good news. Ruby had worried all night about how she was going to find the energy to make Dempsey a proper birthday. Two or three times she dreamed that Charley appeared, to help her with the cake, and the games. She knew it couldn't be, though. Coming to Tulsa would have been far too dangerous. But at least she could dream; and at least a package had come. It meant Charley still thought of them.

Sometimes, when her spirits were lowest, Ruby wondered if he *did* still think of them, or if she was just fooling herself.

The package was tied with such heavy twine that Ruby had to get a butcher knife to cut it. While she was sawing at the twine, Dempsey stood on one foot, and then the other.

"Mama, are we Floyd now, or are we Hamilton?" Dempsey asked. "Sometimes I can't remember."

Ruby stopped sawing and looked at her son a moment, all

276

eager for his present, his woolly earmuffs hanging around his neck.

"All you have to remember is that I'm your mama," she said, looking serious. "The names don't matter. I'm Mama, and I always will be—you and me are mother and son."

"Oh . . . all right," Dempsey said. She looked like she might cry when she said it. Dempsey didn't want her to cry. He wanted her to cut the heavy twine so he could find out what his daddy had sent him for his birthday.

Ruby was beginning to fear that she had pneumonia, or even TB. She couldn't seem to get her lungs clear, and she didn't have any strength. It took half an hour to get Dempsey's present unpacked. It turned out to be a fine, hand-tooled saddle, just Dempsey's size, with a bridle, and a quirt, and a pair of little spurs, and a pair of furry chaps. The note with the birthday card read:

For my little cowpoke—when I come home, we'll buy a pony.

Love,
Your Daddy

"Mama, it's just what I wanted," Dempsey said.

"I know, honey," Ruby said, pleased. All Dempsey's favorite picture shows were cowboy shows. He spent half his time popping a cap pistol.

"I hope Daddy comes home real soon," Dempsey said.

"So do I, honey," Ruby said.

"I need that pony," Dempsey said. "I need that pony real bad."

18

Every time the door to her hospital room opened, Ruby had the hope that it might be Charley. There had been no word from him since Dempsey's birthday; the cold weather hung on, and her cough got worse. Finally, her sisters persuaded her to go to the doctor, and the doc listened to her chest for a minute, and then put her in the hospital. At least it was pneumonia, and not TB.

"At least, nothing!" her ma said, when she found out. "Pneumony will kill you quicker than you can swat a horsefly."

Her ma and her sister Janie moved into the house to look after Dempsey. Ruby worried constantly that they wouldn't do a good job. Until she went to the hospital, she had not been separated from Dempsey a day in his life, except to visit Charley when he was in the Jeff City pen. Of course, she knew her mother and her sister were competent to take care of one child —her sister already had three kids of her own—but Ruby worried anyway: she couldn't help it.

The other thing Ruby worried about was money. Usually, Charley would send her money through Brad. But since the death of Erv Kelley, it had been too dangerous for him to go anywhere near Brad. The money had stopped coming. Ruby had less than five dollars when she went to the hospital. She had no idea how she'd get the cash to pay for her treatment, much less to keep groceries on the shelf after she got out.

Worse, though, was that she had no idea where Charley was, no idea what he was doing. He could be in Canada for all she knew; he had often talked of trying Canada. She read the Tulsa papers every day, hoping for news that he'd pulled a bank job and gotten away. If she could just get a picture in her mind of where Charley was, she thought she might feel better. Not knowing what part of the country he was in, or if he was even *in* the country, kept her awake nights, worrying.

When her ma brought Dempsey to the hospital, he was subdued. They had strapped the saddle his daddy had sent him for his birthday over a trunk. Dempsey would sit on it for hours—with his chaps and spurs on, his quirt in his hand, staring out the window, pretending to be a cowboy.

"My daddy's gonna buy me a pony pretty soon," Dempsey said, to anyone who commented on his saddle and his cowboy attire.

Then, to Ruby's surprise, a cowboy stepped right into her hospital room one morning, when she still had a thermometer in her mouth. They had put a mustard plaster on her chest the night before, and she hated the smell of it. Her hairbrush had fallen off her bedside tray, so she hadn't even had a chance to brush her hair, when George Birdwell came tiptoeing in. He had on cowboy boots, and a blue coat, and his Stetson was creased as neat as if it had just come out of a hatbox.

"Oh, George, where'd you come from?" Ruby asked, feeling tearful.

"Me? I just flew in from the Panhandle," George said. He flapped his arms briefly, pretending he was a bird.

"How come you're laid up?" he asked. Nothing seemed to get George Birdwell down.

"I took pneumonia. How's Bob?" Ruby asked.

"Mean as ever," George replied. "She wants you and little Charley to come live with us, once these horse doctors turn you loose."

"We might do that," Ruby said. "It's lonesome living by ourselves. The cops watch the house all the time. I guess they think Charley will be dumb enough to drive up and let himself get caught."

Then she remembered that Bird was wanted—there was a reward on his head, too. They were known to be partners in crime. It touched her that Bird had thought to come see her, despite the risk.

The old lady in the next bed was wheezing so loud, two nurses ran in from the hall to tend to her.

"That poor old soul sounds like she's got a piece of barbed wire stuck in her craw," Birdwell said. "Where's your purse?"

279

"Hanging on that chair," Ruby said. "Why?"

"Bob and me thought you might be short," Birdwell said, sticking a wad of bills into her purse.

"Short ain't the word for it," Ruby informed him. "Busted's more like it."

"This'll tide you over till your dashing young husband shows up," Birdwell said. "I see some law out front. Think I'll squeeze out the back door and gallop off."

"Are you on a horse, George?" Ruby asked, thinking the man must be crazy. Why would a wanted outlaw ride up to a hospital on a horse?

George gave her a big grin, and then a kiss.

"Don't, you'll catch pneumonia," Ruby said.

"I ain't horseback, but I've had plenty of nags that could outrun that flivver I'm driving," George said. "You get well, Ruby. I'll send Bob after you and Dempsey, if you'll just say the word. Bob's bought too many hens. She could use somebody to help her gather eggs."

Then he tipped his hat to the nurses, and left. The old lady with the bad wheeze died later in the day.

When they brought the paper the next morning, the first headline Ruby saw was about George Birdwell robbing a bank in a little town west of Tulsa. The robbery had occurred only a few hours before he had showed up at the hospital with the wad of money. In the night, she had counted it—it was nearly four hundred dollars. It made her feel a little better about Charley; at least he had a good friend. She had no doubts that part of the reason Birdwell robbed the bank was to help her out with her hospital bills.

When she told Dempsey they might go live in the country with Birdwell and Bob, Dempsey immediately jumped on his saddle and began to quirt the trunk.

"That's fine, Daddy can bring my pony there," he said. "If we're living in the country, I can ride him a long way, can't I, Mama?"

"You sure can, darlin'," Ruby said, smiling at her boy.

19

Viv Brown didn't look around, but she knew a car was following her along the street, hanging back a little. Viv assumed it was one of her beaux, Rodney Black, the only suitor she had who would be dumb enough to follow her along the street as she was walking home from the newspaper office. She only lived six blocks from the offices of the *Muskogee Blade*. In the spring and summer, she rode her bicycle to work; but in the winter, she usually walked.

Rodney Black's parents had more oil money than they could spend in three lifetimes, but it didn't make up for the fact that Rodney had buck teeth, and a nervous laugh that he laughed every two seconds or so. He had been pestering Viv for a year—she had gone out with him three times, and all three times she had come home with a headache from having to listen to his nervous laugh.

The one good thing about Rodney was that he was so shy, he had never even tried to hold her hand, much less kiss her. If there was one thing she knew about men, it was that she didn't enjoy kissing them if they had buck teeth.

When Vivian was safe on the front porch of her rooming house, she turned, meaning to wave at Rodney as if she had just that minute noticed him. But she had been wrong: a woman with frizzy hair was driving the car. Viv was relieved; just having Rodney in the neighborhood made her nervous. She had never seen the woman before. The woman had pulled up in front of her house, and was looking right at her.

"May I help you?" Vivian asked, thinking maybe the woman was hoping to get a room in the boarding house.

"Are you the girl who writes for the newspaper?" Bob Birdwell asked.

"Yes, I'm Vivian Brown," Viv said. "Who are you?"

"Don't get nosey," Bob said, but she grinned when she said

it. Her nose wrinkled when she grinned, and her eyes were merry.

"What can I do for you, then?" Viv inquired. She was trying to write a short story for *Redbook*, and wanted to get right to work if the lady in the flivver had nothing important to say.

"Are you the newspaper reporter gal who's been sendin' letters to Bradley Floyd?" Bob asked.

Viv jumped like somebody had stuck her with a hatpin.

"Oh, my goodness, yes, I am!" she replied. Viv had written several letters to Charley Floyd care of his mother's address in Akins and had gotten no reply. One of her ambitions as a reporter was to do an interview with Pretty Boy Floyd. She had actually gone to Akins and Sallisaw and spoken to folks who had known him since he was a boy—they didn't believe he was the killer the police magazines made him out to be. She had kept up with every story written about him so far, and it was her view that a lot of them contained big fat lies. So, Vivian decided she wanted to give Charley Floyd a chance to tell his side of the story and get it heard.

But lately, getting no response from Charley or his family to any of her efforts had made her feel hopeless about the situation: Charley Floyd would never let her interview him. She had gone back to writing short stories for *Redbook*; the story she was working on at the moment was about a girl reporter who falls in love with a bronc rider while doing a story on the big rodeo over in Oklahoma City.

"Do you know the Floyds, ma'am?" Viv asked. "I would love to meet any one of them, anytime, anyplace."

"Hop in, then," Bob said, opening the passenger-side door. "Charley's waitin', and guess who else?"

Viv could tell the blunt, skinny woman had a sense of humor.

"J. Edgar Hoover," she said, trying to respond in kind.

"That hound-dog lookin' rascal?" Bob said. "Not on your life. The fella waitin' with Charley is the handsomest bandit in the U.S. of A.!"

"George Birdwell!" Viv said. "Did I guess it?"

"You guessed it, honey—hop on in the car."

Since she was on her way home from work, Viv had her

282

reporter's notebook under her arm. She hadn't had time to freshen up, though—it was windy, always windy—and she hadn't even had an opportunity to run a comb through her curly brown hair. When she sat down in the passenger seat of the flivver, she thought she might ask the woman driving to borrow her comb. But when she got a closer look at Bob, whose mop was arranged like it belonged to a crazy thing, she resigned herself to looking merely windblown.

"Are you some relation to Mr. Birdwell?" she asked, as the woman gunned the flivver out of Muskogee.

"No, but I'm married to him," Bob said, and broke out in giggles. Before they had gone a mile, Viv was giggling, too. Bob told Viv the story of how she had met George, and from then on, everything Bob said struck her as funny.

"I can't believe this," Viv said, several times. "I'm so lucky, I can't believe I'm gonna interview Charley Floyd and George Birdwell!"

After twenty minutes of driving, they turned off the highway. At a narrow, dusty, dirt crossroads, Bob grabbed a big bandana from the back seat.

"Turn your head, I got to blindfold you for this next little stretch. The boys don't want you to be able to give away their location," Bob informed her.

"Why, I'd never do that," Viv said.

"Can't take the chance," Bob said. "Besides, it ain't you they're worried about. Alfalfa Bill might take it into his head to send some ornery bulls over to Muskogee to beat it out of you."

"Alfalfa Bill" Murray was the governor of Oklahoma. He had stern views about justice, and had just launched a campaign to reinstate flogging in the state prisons.

"There's freedom of the press in this country," Vivian said. "He can't do a thing to me."

Bob looked at her, and shook her head.

"Honey, you're just a girl—he's the governor," Bob reminded her. "Now turn your head around, I won't pull it too tight."

When the car finally reached its destination, and Bob Birdwell removed the blindfold, Viv was completely turned around. It was a cloudy day, and they were parked between two fields of corn stubble. A green car was parked just in front of them, almost nose to nose. Two men stood beside it, both of them very spiffily dressed: Charley Floyd had on a grey suit and vest; he wore a necktie with a stickpin, and he had on fine black leather gloves. He was even more handsome than Viv thought he'd be. George Birdwell looked just as he did in all his pictures —he was dressed like a cowboy movie star, in a white suit and a beautiful Stetson hat.

Charley Floyd himself stepped forward, and politely opened the car door for her. Viv was so nervous she almost tripped getting out.

"Miss Brown, I'm Charles Arthur Floyd," he said, taking off his hat. "This cowboy here is Mr. George Birdwell. I guess you done met his better half."

"I sure have," Viv said. "She's a snappy driver."

George Birdwell tipped his hat, and smiled his most charming smile.

"Why, you're pretty enough to court, ma'am," he said. "If my better half runs off with some scoundrel, I'll move to Muskogee just to serenade you."

"Mind your tongue, George," Bob said. "I could live six lifetimes and not meet a worse scoundrel than you."

Then, before anyone could move, she drove off, leaving a cloud of dust in her wake.

"Well . . ." George said, slightly embarrassed as he watched his wife drive off. "It ain't the first time she's left me eatin' dust."

"Can't you behave for five minutes, George?" Charley said, shaking his head at his partner.

"Do you think she'll come back?" he added.

"Maybe, maybe not," George replied. "A fortune teller couldn't predict what Bob's gonna do next."

"But how does she expect us to get Miss Brown back home?" Charley asked, a deep crease forming between his eyes. The chaotic nature of the Birdwell marriage weighed on him heavily at times. It had been his idea to speak to the young woman reporter; now, it looked like he and Bird would end up with the task of taking her home, to a town whose bank they had robbed not six weeks earlier.

"I feel so lucky," Viv said, again. Getting home was the last thing on her mind. "Of all the reporters in these parts, how come you picked me?"

"We like the way you write up the ball games, ma'am," George said. "I play a pretty good game of ball myself, and I'm often unhappy with the reporting. We watched two games you wrote up—maybe you saw us. You done an accurate job, so here we are."

"Do I get to ask questions, or how will this work?" she asked, opening her reporter's notebook.

"You can ask anything you want, only we won't comment on specific jobs," Charley said. "We're tired of being blamed for every crime in the country, it just plain ain't fair. The papers got us robbing banks from Chi Town to Florida."

"But you do rob banks, don't you?" Viv asked. "How's anybody gonna know which ones you rob and which ones you don't?"

"Why, we know," Bird said. "We could give you a list, and it wouldn't be no sixty banks, or anywhere near it."

"We can't give her no list, Bird," Charley said. "That's one of the rules—no lists."

"Okay, scratch that question," Vivian said. "Could you tell me how you got started in the criminal life?"

"We'd prefer to be called outlaws, or bandits," George put in. "Callin' us criminals don't do us justice, to my mind.

"You see, there's outlaws, and then there's criminals," he added. "Me and Charley, we're outlaws."

"We're like the James boys," Charley said, with a grin. "Or the Daltons."

"Okay, then," Viv said. "Outlaws it is. First question: How come you to start the outlaw life? Did you try something else first?"

"Plowin'," Charley said, still grinning. "I just plain got tired of sand in my socks, day and night."

"What about you, Mr. Birdwell?" she asked.

"Horse bucked me and broke my neck, down in Vernon, Texas," Birdwell informed her. "I couldn't cowboy the rodeos for six months. I got so tired of that dern cast, I went berserk and robbed a bank—can't tell you which one."

"You went berserk?" Vivian said, writing furiously.

"Aw, don't believe him, miss," Charley said, rolling his eyes. "He's just tryin' to outdo me. I'll be straight with you."

He put his foot up on the front bumper of his flivver.

"I was just like any other kid growin' up in Oklahoma. Then I got in that trouble at Akins about the post office, and I thought I better tear out of the country and get me some work. I landed up in St. Louis, and pulled that job, and of course they got me and took me back to serve my time up in Jeff City."

Charley paused, looking off into the field of corn stubble.

"I was just a green country kid that got caught on a job that I didn't know much about, but I guess that was the job that put its mark on me and I could never shake it off. I tried, though."

"If we'd done both these interviews separate like I wanted, we could lie as much as we wanted to," Birdwell interjected.

"Me, lie—after that one you told about your broken neck?" Charley asked. "Your damn neck ain't never been broke."

"A neck can heal, like any other limb," George informed them.

"I don't think the neck is a limb, Mr. Birdwell," Vivian corrected.

"The way George is always stickin' *his* out, might classify it as a limb," Charley remarked.

"Don't you ever feel guilty, robbing some little bank that's barely making it as it is?" Vivian asked.

"Ma'am, all the money we take is bonded money," Charley informed her. "It don't hurt nobody's pocketbook except the big boys, and they can stand a little hurt."

"You've been accused of more than sixty bank robberies and ten killings," Viv said. "Have you done all you've been accused of?"

Charley shook his head. "We'd have to be eighty years old to have done everything we've been accused of," he said. "And we ain't killed no ten men."

"We've done more robberies than any other bandits, though," Birdwell said. "Charley's too modest to count his victories, but I ain't."

"The worst part of runnin' with George is the braggin'," Char-

286

ley said. "I was raised to tell the truth. If George was raised that way, it didn't take."

"Hide not thy light under a bushel," Birdwell said, unfazed.

"I have to ask about the killings," Vivian said.

Birdwell gazed off at a covey of quail that had been flushed from a thicket by some varmint. Charley, suddenly pensive, stood up straight, and took a deep breath.

"We ain't cold-blooded killers, ma'am," Charley said solemnly, after a moment. "I never killed except to survive. It was shoot or be shot."

"Any regrets?" Viv asked.

"I ain't educated, and my folks didn't have much, but I was raised to be decent, Miss Brown," Charley said. "I have plenty of regrets. Bushels, as George might say."

A hawk soared over, high, riding the wind. To Vivian's and Charley's surprise, George Birdwell pulled out his pearl-handled revolver and fired several shots at the hawk. The hawk flew on to the west.

"What would make you think you could hit a flyin' hawk?" Charley asked.

"I was trying to get revenge for all Bob's chickens they've et," Birdwell said, carefully taking the empty shells out of his pistol.

"Mr. Floyd, I know you've torn up mortgages and given away money—folks all over these parts think of you as a hero because of that. Your name will live in the history of these country folks for generations. Do you consider yourself a Robin Hood?"

"Nope," Charley said. "I've helped folks who've helped me. I've always tried to treat folks square. We've helped a few others who were needy because of the hard times."

"He has—I ain't in it for charity," George said.

"He ain't as hard-hearted as he acts, Miss Brown," Charley said.

"Mr. Floyd, the Justice Department's Bureau of Investigation has you on the Public Enemies list now," Viv said. "How do you feel about that?"

"I hate it," Charley said bluntly. "I ain't nobody's enemy. Folks that know me can tell you I ain't a danger to nobody who ain't shootin' at me."

"What's the worst thing about life as an outlaw?" Viv asked. The light was beginning to fade.

Charley looked at Birdwell, who was inscrutable, for once.

"Is it the danger?" she asked. "Gettin' shot at?"

"It's not bein' able to go home, Miss Brown," Charley said, finally. "I got a wife and son. I miss 'em bad. Not bein' able to see my wife and boy—that's the worst thing."

Charley's mood quickly sank; Vivian knew then that the interview was over. The stars came out, but Bob Birdwell didn't reappear. Finally, Charley and George drove the young woman back to Muskogee themselves.

"Now, why would Bob do that, just run off?" Charley kept asking, as they headed toward town.

"Maybe she had an appointment," Vivian said, in an effort to keep things even.

"An appointment to drive her husband crazy—that's the only appointment that gal had," Birdwell said. "She has one of them appointments ever' two or three days. It's what made me a rambler."

"I doubt that, bud," Charley said. "You were born ramblin'."

"So were you, Robin Hood," Birdwell replied.

Vivian thanked them both profusely when they let her out at her house.

"Our pleasure, ma'am," both men said.

Then they drove off, like phantoms, into the night.

20

J. Edgar Hoover chewed up three quarters of a cigar as he read Vivian Brown's interview with Pretty Boy Floyd. Agent Melvin Purvis watched his boss chew the cigar with a good deal of apprehension. The Director of the Bureau of Investigation was not one to slobber up a good Cuban stogie; he only chewed cigars when his temper was rising. Agent Purvis wished he'd had the good sense to throw the Muskogee paper in the wastebasket. But if he had taken that sensible tack, some eager-beaver G-man would have yanked it out and taken it to Hoover anyway. Trying to hide something from the Director was usually the wrong thing to do; it was that *not* hiding it wasn't exactly the *right* thing to do, either. On certain days, there was no right thing, where the Director was concerned.

"I'm beginning to think all Okies are criminals," Hoover said.

Agent Purvis held his peace.

"Who let this girl talk to Floyd, anyway?" Hoover asked, grinding what was left of the stogie between his teeth. "Where's our nearest office?"

"We've got a man in Fort Worth," Purvis replied. "Maybe we got two."

"Get 'em up there, today!" Hoover said. "Tell them to have the editor of this goddamn paper fire that girl at once. I'll want a retraction, too—front page, soon as possible."

"What if he won't?" Purvis asked.

"Why wouldn't he?" Hoover asked. "This is the Bureau, Purvis. When we demand a retraction, we get one."

"I've known people from Oklahoma to be a little stubborn, sir," Purvis remarked. "They're apt to act independent, down in Oklahoma."

"The hell they will," Hoover said, picking up the telephone. "I'll phone and have that girl fired myself. In fact, I'm going to blister her ear a little, first."

When Sam Raines, editor of the *Muskogee Blade*, picked up

the phone in his inky little newsroom and was told he was talking to none other than J. Edgar Hoover himself, he thought it was one of Viv's boyfriends, playing a joke.

"I think it's Rickie," Sam told Viv. "He's pretendin' he's J. Edgar Hoover."

Viv was trying to finish her report on yesterday's Rotary Club social, and she was in no mood to tolerate any fiddle-faddle from Rickie Burnett when she was trying to get an assignment in shape for print.

"Hello, what do you want?" she asked, annoyed, tucking the phone against her neck so she could keep typing.

"Are you Miss Brown of the *Muskogee Blade?*" Hoover asked, not pleased by the temerity of the young lady's tone.

"Yes, who is this?" Viv asked, glancing at Sam Raines. Whoever it was, it definitely wasn't one of her boyfriends.

"I'm J. Edgar Hoover, weren't you told?" the Director spat. "You've done a grave disservice to your country by printing those lies about two dangerous criminals. I'm sure you know who I mean."

Despite her youth, Vivian Brown was not to be bullied, as Rickie Burnett and a number of other men, young and not so young, had discovered, to their collective dismay.

"I beg your pardon, sir," Viv said. "I'm an honest reporter. I don't print lies. What I wrote about Mr. Floyd and Mr. Birdwell was the truth."

The Director was not used to being talked back to, by brash girls from Oklahoma—or from anywhere, for that matter. He took the Cuban stogie out of his mouth for a second, and glared at Agent Purvis, as if the whole affair were entirely his fault.

"You're out of your depth, young lady," Hoover said. "Not only that, you're out of a job. I won't tolerate front-page stories that glorify public enemies. Pretty Boy Floyd is a killer, wanted in several states. You've let him use you and your newspaper to help win public sympathy."

"He already has public sympathy in these parts!" Vivian snapped back. "Bankers are no friends of the tenant farmers in Oklahoma, and folks down here look up to Charley Floyd and George Birdwell—they'll remember things they've done

290

for years and years, and their children will remember them, too!"

"Miss Brown, you're clearly hysterical," the Director replied. "Give me your editor. Perhaps he has more respect for law and order. You should have contacted the authorities at once!"

"What I did was give two men a chance to tell their side of the story," Vivian informed him. "They've been accused of everything under the sun. I don't think it's fair."

"Who told you to think?" Hoover asked. "These are serious matters, beyond your grasp. You should stick to writing up socials and leave serious reporting to men. Give me your editor, now!"

Viv shrugged, and handed the phone to Sam Raines, who was squinting at a page of proof. Sam had ink on his forehead, a not uncommon occurrence.

"Sam Raines, *Muskogee Blade*," Sam said. "What can I do for you?"

"You can fire that impertinent girl, and print a retraction on your front page tomorrow," Hoover said. "That's an order."

"Print a what?" Sam asked.

"Retraction—retraction!" Hoover ordered. "The public should know there wasn't a word of truth in that story you printed today."

"Why, there were words of truth in it if Viv wrote it," Sam said. "Viv's our best reporter . . . in fact, she's our *only* reporter. I wouldn't fire her if the sky was to fall."

"I'm the Director of the Bureau of Investigation," Hoover informed him. "I won't have this kind of palaver."

"And I'm an American citizen. We got freedom of the press in this country, don't we?"

"Yes, and you're abusing it," Hoover said. "You're aiding and abetting public enemies—killers, robbers, disturbers of the peace. If you want to help your country, do what I tell you— fire that girl, and retract that story."

"No, sir," Sam Raines said. "You got your nerve, calling up a newspaper in the United States of America and trying to tell an editor what to print."

He hung up the phone, and went back to squinting at a page of proof.

"Thanks, Sam . . . thanks for backing me up," Vivian said.

"Honey, are you sure this basketball score's right?" Sam asked. "Seemed like Chickasha beat us by more than six points."

"It's right, Sam," Vivian said. "You left and got drunk, and missed the best part of the game. They got way ahead, but we nearly caught up."

"Oh," Sam replied. "That was the night before the morning I had that hangover."

Sam Raines looked reflective.

"You oughtn't to drink so much, Sammy," Vivian said. "Couldn't you slow down a little?"

Sam Raines looked out the window. The wind was whipping dust across the street, no different than any other Muskogee afternoon.

"Maybe when the weather gets better," he sighed. "These long winter nights get to me."

21

Charley was home just long enough to bake three pies. Ruby thought she was dreaming when she saw him walk in the back door. She was peeling spuds, and cut herself with the knife when Charley grabbed her and kissed her. Then he swooped upstairs, and in a minute, swooped back down, with Dempsey in his arms.

"What are you doin' here?" Ruby asked. "They watch this house twenty-four hours a day, hoping you'll show up."

"Hi, Daddy," Dempsey said. He kept saying it, as if he couldn't believe his daddy was really home.

"Hi, Daddy," he said, over and over.

"Hi, bud," Charley said, smiling and rolling up his sleeves. It always felt so right being with his family. He had come in with a big sack of groceries which he promptly began to unpack, while Ruby and Dempsey sat at the table and watched.

"Have you found me a pony yet, Daddy?" Dempsey asked. Every morning since the saddle came, he'd jumped out of bed and looked out the window, to see if there might be a pony in the back yard.

"No, because I'm lookin' for the best pony in the world, for my boy," Charley said. "Honey, I thought we had a rolling pin."

"I'm sorry, I'm so nervous I ain't thinking," Ruby said. "The rolling pin's in that cabinet by the stove."

Charley turned, and flashed her a grin.

"If you're worried about them bulls up at the corner, forget it," he said. "They're drinkin' hootch. I seen 'em pass the bottle when I snuck into the alley. They wouldn't notice me if I sat on the front hood of their flivver."

"I sure hope not," Ruby said, not entirely convinced.

Charley came back to the table, and gave her a big kiss and a squeeze.

"I ain't made pies since we were in Fort Smith," he said. "I been gettin' a strong urge to make pies. You sit back and relax —leave the meal to me."

The kitchen was warm and comfy. Charley liked to sprinkle cinnamon on his piecrusts. Soon, the kitchen was filled with good smells. Dempsey kept staring at Charley, as if he wanted to be sure his daddy was really there.

"Can we have spaghetti, too, Daddy?" Dempsey asked, as Charley was rolling the piecrusts.

"Yep, spaghetti and pie, that's the menu," Charley said.

Dempsey ate three helpings of spaghetti, and a whopping piece of cherry pie. He had an appetite like his father's. Ruby held Charley's hand under the table while they ate. She didn't eat much; food wasn't what she wanted. She knew it would be impossible to get Dempsey to bed, so the three of them sat at the table—Charley and Ruby drinking coffee—until Dempsey started to yawn. His eyes grew heavier and heavier. Finally, he put his head on the oilcloth, and went to sleep.

Ruby wanted to carry him upstairs, undress him, and put him

to bed, but Charley had other plans. Ruby was the one who got undressed.

"Every time I'm about to give up, you come and do this," Ruby said, lying in his arms. "I wish you could stay, Charley . . . I wish so much that you could stay."

Charley went back downstairs, and carried Dempsey up to his room.

"He's like a rag doll," Charley said, when he slipped back under the covers beside Ruby. "I thought I'd never get him into them pajamas."

The smell of the three pies came up the stairs. In the night, it started snowing; then the snow turned to sleet. Ruby heard it peck against the windowpanes. With Charley warm beside her, she didn't care if it snowed or sleeted. She clung to him all night, but when she dozed a little and woke up, he was putting on his overcoat. It was still dark, and sleet was still pecking at the windowpanes.

"If they don't know you're here, couldn't you stay just today?" Ruby asked. "I'll let Dempsey stay home from school, if you like."

"Honey, I can't," Charley said. He sat on the bed for a minute, and put both his warm hands on her face.

"Why? They don't know you're here."

"George waited in the car all night, he's probably froze by now," Charley said. "I better sneak out before the bulls bring in the day shift. Them old boys I saw last night are probably pretty hung over."

Ruby was thinking of how much she'd be wanting to touch him, in the nights ahead. She'd be wanting to touch him so bad that she'd have to sit up reading movie magazines half the night before she could trust herself to try and sleep.

Two mornings later, when Dempsey looked out the window, a black-and-white spotted pony was tied to the back yard fence. It was cold; the pony's breath made big puffs of smoke.

"Mama, Mama, my pony!" Dempsey yelled, as he ran out the back door. He was so excited he forgot to put on his coat; Ruby chided him, but he was too happy to notice.

Ruby had to go out in her bathrobe and houseshoes to saddle

the pony, so Dempsey could ride around the back yard before he went to school.

22

When Willie the Turnip, as he had come to be known, was captured, Charley wanted to go north, way north—but Birdwell got stubborn, and wouldn't budge.

"Willie ain't gonna rat—we don't need to panic," Bird said. They had slipped over to Arkansas for a few days, to think matters over. A little hotel in Clarksville was their home away from home. For a whole day, they drank hootch, and debated their next move.

"It ain't a matter of Willie ratting," Charley said. "It ain't that he'd rat, it's just that he's dumb. He's the dumbest person I've worked with since Billy Miller. A dumb person is apt to say things that would give us away—you know, clues."

"What clues? We don't hardly have a clue ourselves where we are, or what we're gonna do next," Birdwell informed him. "Willie even confuses me, sometimes. Why wouldn't he confuse the cops?"

Willie had been arrested in Lawton, for pocketing a can of snuff. He had meant to buy the snuff, but he had left his coin purse in the car. The car was parked two blocks away, and Willie was lazy. He didn't want to walk to the car and walk back, so he pocketed the snuff. The old lady who ran the general store saw him do it, and promptly pointed a .44 revolver at him.

"If you don't think I can shoot, ask the last thief I plugged," the old lady told him.

Before Willie knew it, he had been identified as a member of the Floyd/Birdwell gang. It made him quite a celebrity in the Lawton jail, which was filled mostly with Indians who had been arrested for going on toots. While Willie was being led into the jail, Charley and Bird drove by in the car. They didn't look at him, and they didn't wave. Willie knew it wouldn't have been wise for them to look at him, or wave, but the fact they didn't made him blue anyway. They passed within twenty feet, and the deputy sheriff didn't even notice.

"We ain't prosperous enough to go north," Birdwell argued. "What we need to do is rob one of them nigger banks—*then* we can go north in style!"

Oklahoma was full of towns that were all Negro. There were about thirty of them. The Negroes were descendants of slaves freed by the Cherokees, Choctaws, and Creeks. Birdwell had it in his head that one of the black townships in particular, a little community called Boley, would be ripe for the plucking.

"George, we're white, and they're colored," Charley argued. "If we drive in there and jump out at the bank, we're gonna stand out like whores at a church picnic."

"That's the whole idea," Birdwell said. "Ain't you ever heard of the element of surprise? They won't think we've come to rob no bank, they'll think we've come to *buy* it."

"Who's gonna drive?" Charley asked. "Who's gonna watch the street? The girls are in K.C., and Turnip won't be out for at least a couple of years."

"I know a nigger burglar," Birdwell said. "Pete Glass. Maybe he'd drive—folks in Boley will think he's our chauffeur."

"What makes you so optimistic about this particular bank, Bird?" Charley asked. "You're all smiles. Here we are, in a fleabag in Arkansas. We can't see our wives but once a month, if we're lucky, and our girlfriends ain't even handy."

"How would you know how handy my girlfriends are, bud?" Birdwell asked. "I might have more girlfriends than you suspect."

"If you've got a couple here in Arkansas, why are we sittin' in this fleabag, playin' rummy?" Charley asked, disgusted. "You could loan me one, and we could go somewhere and cut a rug."

"Very few of my girlfriends like to consider themselves available for loan," Birdwell said, smirking.

"Hell, I'm as famous as you are," Charley said. "I can go out and look for my own girlfriend, if you're gonna be so damn stingy."

Birdwell suddenly looked solemn.

"Did you ever do business with Red?" he asked, much to Charley's surprise. Charley was so surprised, in fact, that he decided to pretend he'd heard the question wrong.

"Business with who?" he asked.

"Red. Whizbang Red," Birdwell replied. "The whore that's in love with me."

"Oh," Charley said. "I did do a little business with her, Bird. In Seminole, when I was roughnecking. She was working out of a tent.

"That was a while back," he added, wondering if George was going to take offense.

"She's dyin', Charley," Bird said.

"Whizbang's dyin'—why didn't you spill it sooner? My God, George," Charley said, shocked.

George Birdwell put down his cards, and looked out the window.

"Where is she?" Charley asked. "What is it she's dyin' of?"

"Dyin' of a tumor, down in . . . her parts," George said, grave. "Red's a right good gal."

"I'll second that," Charley said. "I like Red a lot. Where is she?"

"In a hospital up in Salina, Kansas," Birdwell said. "Her ma lives there. It ain't too far from Boley."

"What's Boley got to do with the fact that Red's drawn a bad hand?" Charley asked.

"I thought if we pulled the job, we could go up and see her," George explained. "I been meaning to go—Red's been worried about the funeral—her ma don't have a cent. I'm low myself, but if we was to pull a good job, I'd give Red money enough that her ma could afford to bury her nice."

"Why does it have to be a nigger bank?" Charley asked. "Why can't we just pull some job, and take Red the money?"

"Well, we could, but Boley's right on the way," George said. "We could pull the job and head straight for the hospital. Nobody would ever look for us in a hospital."

"I used to think you was a sane fellow, but the longer I know you, the less sure I am about that," Charley said. "You want to rob a nigger bank, to pay for the funeral of a redheaded whore."

"Red's been real good to me, Charley," Bird said. "I'm gonna miss her. It's only right that I do somethin' for her."

"You know what?" Charley said, after a while.

"What?"

"I'm gonna miss her, too," Charley said.

23

The first thing Charley noticed when they drove into Boley, Oklahoma, was that every colored man on the street seemed to be carrying a shotgun. In fact, except for an old lady here and there, no one was on the streets of Boley at all, except colored men carrying shotguns.

"Say, Pete—do the men in this town always carry shotguns?" Charley asked, looking out the window of the flivver.

"Just on the first day of bird season," Pete Glass replied. He was the Negro burglar Birdwell had recruited to guide them to the bank and then out of town, once the job was done.

The driver, Adam Richetti, a greasy little hood they had picked up in Little Rock, took a dim view of working with Pete Glass. He didn't bother to conceal the fact that he didn't like Pete.

"I didn't know niggers was allowed to hunt birds," Richetti said, in as sarcastic a tone as he could manage.

298

"Anybody can hunt birds, Eddie," Birdwell said.

"My name ain't Eddie, it's Adam," Richetti reminded him.

"No, but if I call you Eddie, your first name rhymes with your last name," Birdwell said, winking at Charley. Neither of them had taken a shine to Adam Richetti, but they needed a driver and hadn't time to be choosy. The news was that Whizbang Red had only a few days to live. Birdwell wanted to get to work, and take her some funeral money.

"This is sharp plannin'," Charley said, caustically. "Three white fellas decide to rob a bank in a town full of niggers on the first day of *bird* season, Bird—when everyone's in town buyin' shells. It takes a real genius to come up with a plan this idiotic!"

"Those are shotguns, not deer rifles," Bird reminded him. "If you're so damn cautious, you better just stay in the car."

"Yeah, what are you, soft?" Richetti said. "We'll eat this bank like it was cherry pie."

Charley looked at Birdwell, who looked uncomfortable after Richetti's tactless remark.

"How'd you like your goddamn brains squeezed out your ears, chum?" Charley said, leaning close enough to Richetti so that the driver could feel Charley's breath on his neck.

"There's the bank," Richetti said, quickly.

"Pull around back. We'll park in the alley," Charley instructed.

"Why? The front door's only two steps from the curb," Richetti pointed out.

"The front door's across the street from the hardware store, too," Charley said. "Or you could call it the shooting gallery— and we're the wooden ducks. Pull around to the back into the alley, like I told you."

"Charley, are you testy today?" Bird asked.

"What do you think?" Charley asked. "Why *this* bank, on *this* day, if all we want to do is grab enough money for Red's funeral?"

"I doubt anybody's ever robbed a nigger bank before," Birdwell said. "It'll make a good story for the newspapers."

"I hope we're alive to read it," Charley said. "Park there, and keep the motor running," he said to Richetti, pointing near the back door of the bank. "You lead the way, Pete."

It was early. Only one of the three tellers, Mrs. Forbes, had arrived, and Mrs. Forbes was notoriously nearsighted. She hadn't even noticed the first customers. She was over in the corner, trying to clean her specs.

Jericho Carter, the bank manager, knew the two white men and the one colored man walking in the back door meant trouble the minute he laid eyes on them. Jericho himself was unarmed, but the bookkeeper, Rawls Yardley, had just gone into the vault, where there was a shotgun and two rifles.

"I'll watch the door," Charley said. "You and Pete get the cash, George. I don't want no crowd pourin' in from the street."

When George Birdwell pointed his pistol at Jericho Carter, who also wore specs, the bank manager looked at him calmly.

"You ain't robbin' us, mister," he said to George. "You better uncock that hogleg and just mosey on home."

"Why, you tar-faced fool," Birdwell said. "I'll take that stack of hundreds there, and then I'll think about goin' home."

Charley got the immediate feeling that something was off—a bank manager who talked as bold as this one wouldn't have a stack of hundreds in easy reach, unless the stack was rigged to an alarm.

"Leave the hundreds!" he yelled, but it was too late—Birdwell had already reached into the cage and picked them up.

The second Bird grabbed the bills, a siren sounded. It was a loud siren, the kind small towns used to warn neighbors of tornadoes, or grass fires. Charley glanced across the street, and saw that all the hunters were looking at the bank.

Rawls Yardley, in the vault, heard the siren, instantly grabbed one of the .30/.30's, and peeked out. He saw a tall white man in a cowboy hat holding a pistol, standing at the teller's window. Rawls let go with a shot, but he was not much of a marksman; his shot missed, and broke out a window.

Startled, Birdwell looked toward the vault and saw Rawls, but couldn't get a clear shot himself because of the teller's bars.

When Birdwell looked toward Rawls, Jericho Carter took the one step to his desk and grabbed for a pistol. Just as he turned to fire, Birdwell cut him down—Jericho Carter was dead before his head hit the top of his desk.

Charley quickly opened the front door and fired a blast from

300

the Tommy gun, aiming for the sign over the hardware store. He thought a little song from the Tommy gun might slow down the hunters, and he was right—they ran for cover, though enough of them threw shots at the bank for pellets to rattle on the windows like sleet.

"Let's scram, George—this is a bust!" Charley said, heading for the back door.

George turned away from the bank manager's desk, and started for the back door after Charley. But before Birdwell could take two steps, Rawls Yardley, crouched behind the door to the vault, opened fire again with the .30/.30—two slugs took George in the back. He fired as he went down, but the bullet zinged off the heavy door to the vault.

Charley threw a blast from the Tommy gun in the same direction, hoping to cow the rifleman long enough for them to get out the back door. George was down, and blood oozed from the wounds in his back; Pete Glass seemed to be momentarily paralyzed.

Charley went around the counter and stooped down, trying to lift George.

"Help me, Pete," he said. "We'll have to carry him—you take his feet."

Pete did as he was told, grabbing George's legs. The two of them carried him out the back door. They set George down on the ground, and Charley fired one more blast into the bank—a bullet hit the water cooler, which exploded. Water even sprayed over Mrs. Forbes, who was still in the corner. In the excitement, she had dropped her specs and was afraid if she moved, she'd step on them.

Charley waved for Richetti, who gunned the car toward them. Just as it arrived, two old colored ladies shuffled down the sidewalk past the alley. Both had grocery baskets over their arms.

Pete helped Charley stuff Birdwell into the back seat of the car, and then Charley hurried over to the ladies, tipping his hat as he went.

"Ladies, I need to borrow you for about two minutes," he said. "I need somebody respectable to ride on my running boards."

Just as he said it, there was a rifle shot, and Pete Glass went staggering down the alley behind the car—Charley couldn't see where the shot came from. He had no time to study the situation.

"Hurry, ladies, please," he said.

"But I got to make my deposit, mister," one of the old ladies said.

"You can make it a little later, ma'am," Charley said, raising his Tommy gun so they could both get a good look at it. "There's confusion in the bank right now, I don't think they're quite ready for business yet."

"We better listen to this young man, Georgette," the other old lady said, as she grabbed her companion's elbow and scooted over to the getaway car.

The rifle cracked twice more. Whoever was shooting at Pete hit him with both shots as he lay on the ground. Charley started over to him, but the rifle cracked again, hitting dust right at his own feet. There was a pool of blood under Pete Glass, and he wasn't moving. Charley ducked back to the car, and put one of the old ladies on each running board.

"Let's go," he said, to Richetti. "Take it slow. If we bounce our hostages off the running boards, we'll be pickin' birdshot out of each other's behinds for the next year."

"I ain't worried about the shotguns—who's got that rifle?" Richetti asked, turning out of the alley and onto the street.

Birdwell was sprawled in the back seat. Charley got in back with him, and reached out each window and held his hostages in place by grabbing an arm.

"Just a few blocks, ladies—hold on tight, and don't get upset," he said. They were cruising past about three dozen hunters with loaded shotguns; but no one fired.

Two blocks from the edge of town, Charley told Richetti to stop. A few hunters were running toward them, but they were far out of shotgun range. He got out and helped each lady off the running boards, handing them each a fifty-dollar bill.

"Sorry for the inconvenience, ladies," Charley said, tipping his hat again.

"Why, we're out here by Cousin Ella's, Georgette," the old lady said to her companion, as if surprised.

302

Charley jumped back into the car, and Richetti gunned it to the limit.

"George is bad wounded," Charley said. "We need to find a town with a good doc. Maybe Ponca City."

The floorboards of the back seat were puddled with blood from George Birdwell's wounds. Birdwell's eyes were closed, but he was still breathing.

Richetti glanced back over the seat a few times as he drove.

"No doc's gonna help him," he said. "The man'll be dead before we get ten miles."

"You were hired to drive, keep your eyes on the damn road," Charley said. "George Birdwell's tough—he'll pull through."

But Charley had his doubts—Bird was losing a lot of blood, and there was a red froth on his lips. Charley used his handkerchief to wipe it away, but it soon bubbled up again. Both Charley's shoes were covered with blood from the puddles on the floorboard.

As they were crossing an old, rickety bridge on the Arkansas River, just south of Ponca City, Birdwell suddenly opened his eyes. They had a wild look in them, a look far different from any Charley had ever seen.

"Where's Bob, I gotta have a word with her about the tykes," Birdwell said.

"George, she's not here," Charley said. "You need to keep quiet and rest till we get to the doc's."

"I fear the big water," George said, struggling up so he could look out the window. "If we're over the big water, I'm a goner."

"It ain't that big, George," Charley said, trying to reassure him. "It's just the old Arkansas. You and me've crossed her many a time."

"I'm afeared of the big water," George said, getting frantic. "You better let me out, Charley . . . I'll steal a horse and lope off home to Bob, she'll be waitin' for me."

"Settle down, now, Bird, just rest," Charley said, trying to make the delirious man lie back down in the seat.

But Birdwell was possessed of a wild strength—he wouldn't lie back down. He kept his eyes fixed on the river below. Though it took only a minute to cross the old bridge, it seemed to Charley like an hour.

"Charley, you gotta let me out," Birdwell insisted. "I need to find me a horse . . . I'm afeared to cross the big water . . ."

"We're nearly to Ponca City, I don't think you can find a horse this close to town, George," Charley said—he was so distraught, he ran a bloody hand through his hair, before he realized it was bloody.

"You're talkin' to a dead man," Richetti said, as they drove off the other side of the bridge. "Birdwell's gone."

Charley looked, and saw that it was true: George Birdwell was gone, one hand hanging off the seat in a puddle of his own blood.

"Oh, God, George!" Charley moaned. "What am I gonna tell Bob, and Red?" He began to cry, then to sob. Richetti kept driving—he didn't make a sound.

By the time they had traveled another ten miles, Charley had stopped sobbing and was staring out the window, a blank look on his face.

"There was an armed man in the vault," he said, finally. "He had a .30/.30. That's what finished George."

"Whatever it was, he's finished, and the nigger burglar along with him," Richetti said. "We need to find a place to dump him."

"What?" Charley asked, not connecting the remark with Birdwell at first.

"Dump George—he's dead," Richetti said firmly, as if Charley were dense. "We can't be drivin' around with a corpse in the car."

"What kind of a skunk are you?" Charley asked. "This is George Birdwell—we're not gonna dump him!"

Richetti decided Charley Floyd must be a little crazy. Only a crazy person would want to drive around with a dead man in the car.

"That blood's gonna be smellin' pretty bad by mornin'," he said.

Charley knew the man was right: George was dead. They had to do something with him, and just driving up to a funeral home didn't seem to be an option.

Right outside of Ponca City, they saw a little shack of a gro-

304

cery store, with a porch on the front, and several hounds under the porch. Smoke was coming out of the chimney.

"Pull over there," Charley said. "Maybe these folks will take him."

Richetti stopped in front of the porch. The hounds bayed, but Charley paid no attention to them. He eased Birdwell's body out of the back seat, and carried him up onto the porch. As he did, an old lady with a cob pipe in her mouth opened the door. She didn't seem particularly surprised to see a man carrying another man up her front steps.

Once Charley laid Birdwell down, he went back and got his Stetson. It was a little bloody, but it still had a perfect crease. Charley placed it gently over his friend's face, and then looked at the old woman.

"Ma'am, my friend's met his death," he said, reaching in his pocket and pulling out five one-hundred-dollar bills.

"I'd appreciate it if you'd call a funeral home, and arrange for him to have the best of care," Charley said, handing her the money. "A hundred dollars of this is for your trouble—the rest is for his funeral."

"Who shot him, son?" the old lady asked, taking the cob pipe out of her mouth.

"A man over in Boley, Oklahoma," Charley replied. "I didn't get his name."

"I reckon Dad can run into Ponca City and roust out the undertaker," the old lady said. "Does your friend have a name?"

"Yes, a famous one," Charley said. "This man is George Birdwell. I suppose you've heard of him?"

The old lady shook her head. "No, can't say as I have," she said, puffing slowly on her cob. "One of my second cousins was married to a Birdwell, but that was in Kentucky, and his name wasn't George."

Richetti, impatient, tapped the steering wheel. Charley ignored him.

"Ma'am, would you have a pencil and a tablet?" he asked. "I'd like to leave a little note, for the authorities."

"I'll get the tablet," the old woman said, shuffling back toward the door. "There ain't too many authorities around here, though."

When she came back with the tablet, a toothless old man in a greasy hat came with her. He peered down at Birdwell.

"Admire his hat," he said. "That's a 30X beaver Stetson. I've hoped all my life for a hat like that."

"Yeah, and you can hope all your next life, too," the old lady informed him. "That hat's beyond you, Dad."

Charley sat on the steps to write his note:

To Whom It May Concern
This is George Birdwell, great bandit of the prairies. He was a true friend and loyal companion. Never deserted a comrade. Treat him with respect and bury him nice, we will all miss him.

Chas Arthur Floyd

He tucked the note into Birdwell's shirt pocket, and started down the steps. The old couple stood where they were.

"Much obliged," Charley said, as the hounds milled around his legs.

"Just kick them dogs, if they're in your way, son," the old lady said. Charley managed to make it to the car without having to kick any of the dogs.

He climbed in the passenger seat and Richetti pulled off, leaving behind them a cloud of red dust, and the body of George Birdwell.

24

Charley folded the newspaper carefully and put it in his pocket, as he walked into the little hospital in Salina, Kansas. It was a chilly day, and there was frost on the dried stems of grass on the hospital lawn. Thin sunlight glinted on the frost, but it didn't improve Charley's mood any.

George Birdwell had been buried the day before. The newspaper estimated that ten thousand people came to his funeral. The photo on the front page of the Oklahoma City paper showed the fields around the cemetery, filled with people. Every time he looked at the picture, Charley wept. He had not been able to get the thought of Bob Birdwell out of his mind. He had driven all night to tell her the sad news—she had been so shocked, she walked straight out the door, barefoot and in her nightgown, to feed her hens.

Charley only stayed thirty minutes—he was afraid the cops would stake out the house. Bob was sitting at the kitchen table, all three children in her lap, dripping tears into her coffee cup, when Charley had to leave. Richetti was nervous—he kept honking every five minutes. Charley knew he should leave, but the honking still annoyed him.

"I'll be back, Bob," he said. "Can I bring you anything?"

"Yeah, bring me a new husband," Bob said, absently rubbing one of the little girls' heads.

"You need to lay off that honkin'," Charley said, when he got back to the car. "That woman's grief-stricken. She don't need to hear a lot of honkin'."

"I gotta live, too," Richetti said. "The heat will be on us like ants on sugar, if we don't keep moving."

"I don't care, I would've liked more time with Bob," Charley said.

Richetti also resented the fact that Charley wanted to stop and break the news to Whizbang Red.

"We could spend the rest of our lives lookin' up George's girlfriends just to tell them he's dead," he complained.

"Shut up and drive," Charley said. "You wasn't hired to make the plans."

"If I'da been makin' the plans, we wouldn't have tried to rob no nigger bank," Richetti whined.

"We're runnin' low on hootch, too," he added.

"We can get more hootch—just keep the car on the road," Charley said. He himself had a blinding headache. What he would have liked to do was turn back to Tulsa and curl up in bed with Ruby for a few days, but he knew that was a hopeless dream.

"Don't be honkin'," he warned Richetti, when he got out at the hospital in Salina. "This is a hospital. There's sick folks to think of."

"We'll be sick folks, too, if the law corners us," Richetti said. "This jalopy is barely running. We need to steal a car, when you can spare the time from comfortin' the bereaved," he added sarcastically.

Charley went on in the hospital. The thought that Whizbang was dying, so soon after George, weighed heavily on him. He found her in a ward with a little boy and two old people. The little boy had a leg cut off by a harrow; the old people had the vacant looks that dogs sometimes got, when they were waiting for the end.

Whizbang was in the last bed. Charley knew right away that he didn't have to break the news, because a copy of the Oklahoma City newspaper was on her lap. She had gone to sleep. Charley pulled up a little straight-backed chair, and when the chair scraped across the floor, Whizbang opened her eyes. Charley was shocked at how thin she was. She'd always had chubby cheeks, but they were chubby no more. Her hand was so fragile, Charley was almost afraid to touch it—it looked as if her fingers might just break off if he lifted them.

"Hello, Red," Charley said. "I see the bad news beat me here."

Whizbang nodded. "I didn't get to go to his funeral, and now he won't get to come to mine," she said weakly. "It don't seem right. If there was anybody I would have liked to pay my respects to, it was George Birdwell."

"Red, you need to get well and get out of here," Charley told her. "Once you get on your feet, I'll take you down and we'll visit the grave."

He knew it was a lie: Whizbang Red wasn't going to get well, and neither of them would be likely to visit George Birdwell's grave. He didn't know why he said it; the words just sort of popped out.

"Aw, stop kiddin', honey," Red said. "They can't fix what I've got.

"Even if they could, I wouldn't let 'em, now that George is gone," she added. "He was the light of my life—did you know that?"

"Sure, I knew it," Charley said. "He sent me here. We were on our way to see you when the trouble happened."

"To see me?" Red asked. "George was comin' to see me?" She smiled a ghost of a smile, and her eyes stopped being quite so dull.

"He heard you was doin' poorly, and he wanted to bring you some cash to help with the doctor bills."

"He was always talkin' about robbin' that nigger bank," she said. "Once he took a notion, you couldn't talk him out of it, no matter how foolish the notion was. Did he tell you about the time him and me set off for Canada?"

"No, I guess I ain't heard that one," Charley admitted.

"There's a big rodeo up in Calgary, which is way north of here," Whizbang said. "George set his heart on winnin' the bronc ridin' at the Calgary rodeo. He told me if he won it, he'd marry me. This was before he ever set eyes on Bob."

At that point, her strength seemed to give out. She stopped talking, and stared out the window. The weak sunlight made dust motes in the little room.

Charley waited a bit. Whizbang's eyes closed for a minute; he thought she'd fallen back to sleep. He took some bills out of his pocket. He knew he couldn't afford to stay much longer. He meant to slip the bills into her hand and leave, if she stayed asleep.

A nurse walked into the ward, and looked at Charley a moment too long. He knew she recognized him. He was about to leave the money and slip out, when Whizbang opened her eyes.

"Where was I, Charley?" she asked.

"About to leave for Canada," Charley said.

"We broke down in South Dakota," Whizbang said. "George had to give up on Calgary, but we made it to Cheyenne instead. He didn't win the bronc riding, though. The first horse he rode pitched him over the fence into the third row of the stands.

"So that was the end of that," she said, after a bit.

"I suppose it was fun, at least," Charley said.

"You're right about that," Whizbang said. "If George Birdwell was around, you could bet there'd be some fun."

Charley gave her the money.

"This is the money he sent for the doctor bills," Charley said.

"For the funeral, you mean," Red said, looking at him with tired eyes.

Charley couldn't answer. He started to; but then too much sadness came up.

He gave her a quick kiss, and a long hug, and left.

25

About sunup, four miles from Bolivar, Missouri, the flivver gave out. Charley was asleep at the time; it was a little before dawn. He felt the car lurch three or four times, and then tip to the right. When he opened his eyes, smoke was coming out from under the hood. Richetti had been drinking most of the night, and was bleary-eyed.

"Why are we in the ditch?" Charley asked, rubbing his eyes.

"We ain't in the ditch, we're on the shoulder," Richetti corrected. "Four more miles, and we'd have made it to Joe's garage. Goddamn the luck."

Richetti had a one-legged brother who worked in a garage in Bolivar. They had lurched across Kansas most of the night, and then on into Missouri, eating slices off a ham Charley had bought at a country store outside of Salina. He had also bought a half-gallon of moonshine, very little of which was left in the jug.

Charley'd had bad dreams about Ruby and Dempsey during his brief moments of sleep.

"At least we ain't in Oklahoma," he said. "I'd rather be in the ditch than be in Oklahoma. I expect they've raised the reward. There may even be a reward for you, for all I know," he said to Richetti.

"I wish Joe would drive by, but he won't," Richetti said.

"Why not?" Charley asked. "Ain't it about time for him to be headin' for work?"

"Yeah, but he won't be headin' up this road," Richetti said, smoke still billowing out from under the hood. "He lives on the other side of town."

A farmer in a rusty pickup drove by, stopped, then backed up. As the old pickup approached, they began to hear a squealing, so sharp and piercing that Richetti had to cover his ears.

"What's that?" he asked.

"You ain't seen much country life, have you, bud?" Charley said. "That's pigs. This old pioneer's probably takin' his shoats to market."

The farmer didn't back up too accurately; Charley and Richetti both flinched when he missed clipping their left fender by only an inch. Sure enough, five squealing shoats were hog-tied in the back of the pickup. The old man was dipping snuff and sneezing. By turning his head, he could direct his snot out the window, as cleanly as if he were spitting. The sight didn't improve Adam Richetti's humor any.

"I never cared for Missouri," he remarked.

The old farmer in the pickup finished cleaning his passages, and squinted at the two of them through dirty specs.

"You young fellas broke down?" he asked.

"We ain't sittin' in this ditch for our health," Richetti said, in his customary surly tone.

"Here now, be polite," Charley said.

He got out and went around to discuss the matter with the farmer, who was busy dipping more snuff.

"Would we be holdin' you up if we asked you to tow us into town?" he asked the old man.

The old man squinted at the car.

"That's a pretty big car, and I'm totin' five shoats already," he said. "Five shoats is dern near a load. Have you got a chain?"

"Damn it, no," Charley said.

"I ain't neither, but I've got a rope—keep it handy in case these shoats get loose," the old man said. "It's in the back there, may have a little shit on it by now. But you're welcome to hitch me onto your bumper. If the rope don't break, I can haul you right on in."

The rope was far too short. By the time Charley got it hitched, there was only about a yard of space between the front bumper of the flivver and the rear bumper of the pickup. Richetti proved useless when it came to tying knots.

"That old fool is apt to wreck us worse than we're already wrecked," Richetti said, nervously.

"Stop your complainin', or I'll thump you on the noggin with the nearest rock," Charley said, exasperated by the man's sour temperament.

The Bitzer Garage, where Richetti's one-legged brother worked, was a run-down affair whose roof sagged like a sow's belly, despite which a small-town crowd of over half a dozen people were already lined up, waiting to get their vehicles serviced. Joe Richetti was under a car when the old pickup towed them up to the lot. The shoats were still squealing. Two of the ladies waiting in line for service were forced to cover their ears.

"Damn, it's barely sunup, and this place is already jampacked," Charley observed.

"My brother's a helluva good mechanic," Richetti said.

"I believe it—look at this crowd," Charley said. "I probably should have hired your able brother, and left you to rot in Arkansas. He's probably better company, too."

Once they had removed the tow rope and thanked the farmer, Richetti leaned on the horn, to let his brother know of their arrival. Charley got out of the car, and straightened his tie. He had a change of clothes in his suitcase, and was hoping to change in the rest room, if there was one.

Joe Richetti rolled himself out from under the vehicle he was working on. He looked oily, in the way of a mechanic, and seemed to have his brother's lack of humor. When he saw Charley straightening his tie, he was a little taken aback.

"Who's this swank you brought with you?" he asked, dispensing with familial greetings.

312

"Never mind, get to work on this flivver," Adam Richetti said.

Joe Richetti looked down the line of waiting customers.

"These folks are all ahead of you," he pointed out. "I can't just stiff 'em because you're my brother."

"Well, you better, or I'll shoot your other leg off," Adam threatened.

Charley couldn't remember when he had met any two men as uncooperative as the Richetti brothers. He opened the trunk and removed his Tommy gun, which he was careful to point straight up in the air. Despite this precaution, the crowd immediately took note.

"Here, now," Charley said, slamming the trunk closed. "Let's not have any scufflin' between brothers."

He casually strolled over to the line of customers.

"Folks, I'm sorry to crowd in ahead of you," he said. "I know it ain't polite. But I've got an emergency at home, and I can't wait. I'll have to ask you to all take a seat, just for a little while," he added, motioning his Tommy gun toward the bench along the wall.

An old-timer with a blue ear looked at him quizzically.

"You're Pretty Boy, ain't you?" he asked.

Charley decided the blue ear must be a birthmark.

"I'm Charley Floyd," he said, patiently.

An old lady with dead rosebuds on her hat didn't accept the situation in silence.

"What air you, crooks?" she asked, with no sign of fright.

"You could call us bandits, I guess," Charley said.

"In other words, we're hostages," another lady said. She looked, if anything, more impatient than the first lady.

"Well, just till we get this car fixed, ma'am," Charley told her. "I regret the inconvenience as much as you do."

"The devil you do," the old lady said. "What about my appointment at the beauty parlor? I was gonna get one of them new permanents."

"Well, maybe you won't have to put it off but about an hour," Charley said, turning to Richetti.

"Eddie, why don't you run out and get a big bag of doughnuts for these nice folks?" he asked. "No need for 'em to be uncomfortable."

Richetti was chewing a match.

"Why don't you go shit in your hat?" he said. "I ain't providin' doughnuts for no garage full of hicks."

One of the old-timers bridled at being called a hick.

"Where's this fool think he's from?" the old-timer said. "Paris, France?"

"Just ignore him, sir, he's ignorant," Charley told him.

"Has he always been this rude?" he added, to Joe Richetti.

"Adam's mean enough to bite, always has been," Joe replied. He had been looking at the flivver with a practiced eye.

"If you're in such a hurry, why don't we trade cars," he suggested. "I'll even let you keep them new tires—won't take half the time to switch tires as it would to take this carburetor apart."

"Let's have a look first," Charley said, skeptical—he wondered if a criminal mind ran in the family.

One of the old-timers went over to a bench, and turned on the radio. Jimmie Rodgers was singing "I'm in the Jailhouse Now." Adam Richetti looked at the radio as if he wanted to shoot it, but he restrained himself.

Just then, over the sounds of the old Blue Yodeler, they heard a loud clanking from the street.

"You got a good little business here, Joe," Charley said. "I hear another customer comin'."

Joe looked out the garage door, and was visibly shaken by what he saw coming.

"Aw, jeez—it's the sheriff," he said. "What the deuce am I gonna do now?"

"Nothin', I'll just shoot him," Adam Richetti said. He reached in his pocket, and drew his pistol.

"Hey, now!" Charley said. "If you don't stop this wild talk, I'm gonna have to whack you with the biggest wrench I can find on your brother's workbench."

"What's the sheriff's name?" he asked Joe.

"His name is Killingsworth—Jack Killingsworth," Joe Richetti informed him.

"We may have to detain Sheriff Killingsworth for a few minutes while we work out this auto trade," Charley said. "Go ask him what's wrong with his car, and I'll do the rest."

Sheriff Jack Killingsworth was a big, strapping man, as good-

314

natured as anyone in Bolivar, Missouri. Joe hobbled out, as quick as he could, trying to keep him from driving the car any farther and damaging it more.

The sheriff got out of the car, and grinned at Joe.

"My horse is winded," he said. "If I was to have to chase any desperadoes today, I doubt I'd catch 'em."

"Uh, come on in, Sheriff," Joe said. "I'll get to you as soon as I can."

The sheriff gave the waiting customers a big wave and a holler, and walked into the garage. The second he did, Charley covered him with the Tommy gun. He smiled when he did it; he wanted to keep things as amiable as possible.

"Uh-oh," the sheriff said.

"There'll be no trouble, sir, if you'll just relax," Charley said, quickly lifting Killingsworth's revolver.

The old lady with the appointment at the beauty parlor didn't take the amiable view of things.

"It's about time you showed up, Jack," she said. "These bandits have been holdin' us hostage for nearly an hour. I've done missed my appointment at the beauty parlor."

"Joe, I'll make the trade," Charley said. "Would you switch them tires? I don't want to keep this lady from her appointment any longer than I have to."

"Aw, tell her to shut up about her damn appointment, Charley," one of the old men said. "She wouldn't look no better if she spent a week in that beauty parlor."

Sheriff Killingsworth, assessing the situation and realizing he was caught, tried to follow instructions and relax.

"I think I know you from pictures," he said, to Charley. "You're Pretty Boy Floyd, ain't you?"

"Charles Arthur Floyd," Charley corrected. "You can just take a seat with these other folks, if you will. As soon as Joe switches them tires, we'll be moseyin' on out of here."

Joe Richetti got his jack, and immediately started to work.

"Somebody should've made a picnic," the sheriff observed, dryly.

"You can make all the picnics you want, Sheriff, after the next election," the old lady said. "I ain't votin' for you, and I doubt anybody else will either. Not after this disgrace."

315

The sheriff gave Charley a see-what-you-got-me-into look.

"Your ordeal is about over, ma'am," Charley said patiently. Then he looked over at Killingsworth, and shrugged—Charley couldn't remember seeing a friendlier or more jolly fellow since he'd met George Birdwell robbing the bank in Earlsboro, long ago.

"Maybe they can still work you in at the beauty parlor," he said, trying to get the old lady to look on the bright side.

"I doubt it," the woman said. "They're tight on Fridays."

Charley had begun to feel that it would not be wise to drive off and allow Sheriff Killingsworth the opportunity to pursue them—he looked like an able man.

"Sheriff, I'm gonna have to inconvenience you a little more," Charley said. "The safest approach to this situation is for you to ride along with us for a while. That would be the best way to keep the peace."

"Hell, a safer way would be to shoot him," Richetti said. "I ain't gonna like drivin' around with no law in the car."

Charley was just about at the end of his rope with Richetti.

"Don't worry about my partner, Sheriff," Charley assured Killingsworth, while glaring at Richetti. "He's nothin' but a trigger-happy torpedo—he's the only one around here that's gotta worry about gettin' shot."

Nonetheless, Sheriff Killingsworth wasn't enthusiastic about traveling with a hothead like Adam Richetti.

"Why do you wanna take me?" he asked, hoping Charley would change his mind.

"You know the roads, Sheriff—the dirt roads, I mean," Charley told him. "And if you're with us, you can't be chasin' us."

"I guess you got a point," Sheriff Killingsworth admitted.

"Even if I ain't, I got the drop," Charley replied.

When the tires were switched, Charley insisted that Richetti drive. He put the sheriff in the front seat, and sat directly behind him. Killingsworth was pretty nervous at first, but he gave clear directions when asked.

"Switch on that radio, Eddie," Charley said. "I'm tired of ridin' along listening to the tires turn."

"I've told you, my name ain't Eddie," Richetti said.

"Well, it can be your nickname, then," Charley said. "Turn on the damn radio."

Richetti did, and this time, Jimmie Rodgers was singing "Waitin' for a Train."

"I guess old Jimmie owns the airwaves," the sheriff commented.

Then, with no warning, an announcer broke in to announce a bank robbery in a place called Mexico, Missouri—two lawmen had been killed.

"Scores of lawmen and volunteers are searching for the killers," the announcer said. "Authorities believe Pretty Boy Floyd and his gang are the most likely suspects."

"What gang?" Charley asked. "And where the hell's Mexico, Missouri, anyway? I never even heard of the place."

"It's a helluva ways from here, Mr. Floyd," the sheriff informed him. "I believe it's up past Hannibal somewhere. It's north—way north—I know that much."

"Well, here I am, Sheriff," Charley said. "I ain't in no Mexico, Missouri. It's gettin' so if anybody anywhere gets robbed or shot, if they can't pin it on Dillinger, they pin it on me."

"You don't have to worry about this one," the sheriff said. "You got me for a witness, this time."

"That's what happens when you get a reputation," Richetti pointed out.

"I oughta make a list," Charley said, annoyed.

"What kinda list?" Richetti asked.

"A list of towns I never heard of, much less visited, where I'm supposed to have pulled all these jobs," Charley said. "This is gettin' goddamn irritating. I'm bein' blamed for everything except the kidnapping of the Lindbergh baby!"

"You're mighty prominent in your profession, Mr. Floyd," Killingsworth said. "Now that they've finished Bonnie and Clyde, there's just Dillinger, Baby Face Nelson, and you."

Charley felt a gloom take him, a mood lower than the floorboards.

"Ain't but one way it can end, Sheriff," he said.

"How's that?" Killingsworth asked.

"Lead—and lots of it," Charley said. "I'll go down full of lead, just like Bonnie and Clyde—and George Birdwell."

"He had a big funeral, I hear," the sheriff said.

Charley didn't answer—he found himself wondering if Whizbang Red was still alive.

26

"Look on the bright side, Jack," Charley said, to Sheriff Killingsworth. "Crackers and cheese is better than nothin'."

They were stopped by the side of a narrow Missouri back road, with two flats on Joe Richetti's car, and the winter day was fading fast. The tire switch Joe had pulled in Bolivar turned out to be a tire switch entirely in his favor.

"Crime runs in the family—I should've kept a closer eye on your one-legged brother," Charley said to Richetti, when the spare blew. Fortunately, they had stopped at a little grocery store a few miles back, so at least they had the cheese and crackers, and a couple of jugs of cider.

"I'm usually home eatin' supper this time of day," Sheriff Killingsworth remarked. He had gotten unusually silent after the second tire blew. "I guess I miss my boy," he added.

"Well, you're eatin' supper, you just ain't eatin' at home," Charley said.

The sheriff's remark brought Dempsey to mind; and Ruby, of course. Charley knew all too well how the big sheriff felt.

"You oughtn't to kick about one day, Jack," he added. During the afternoon, he and Sheriff Jack Killingsworth had worked their way up to a first-name basis. Charley liked the good-natured lawman—even though he was a sheriff, talking to him reminded Charley of how lacking in conversational skills Richetti was, and just how much he missed his old partner,

318

Birdwell. The two men talked about farming, fishing, baseball, and they even talked of how they had gotten into opposite lines of work. They joked about married life, and they exchanged stories about their sons. Charley thought it was interesting, how much they had in common—him, an outlaw; and Killingsworth, a lawman.

Charley's mood started downhill again like a runaway wagon, passing Killingsworth's melancholy at breakneck speed.

"As soon as we get to Kansas City, we'll let you go," Charley told him. "You'll be home tomorrow, and you can have your boy with you every day. You can play ball, or go fishing with him, or just sit and look at him, whenever you want."

"I guess you're right, Charley," Jack Killingsworth said, noticing that the young man's dark mood had returned.

"I'm hunted day and night now," Charley said. "Don't you think I'd like to see my boy? I'da damn sight rather be holdin' him across my knee, instead of this Tommy gun. I only get to see him once in a while—all I could manage to do last time I saw him was drive by the schoolyard at recess, and look at him for a minute—I couldn't even get out of the car."

"That would be hard," the sheriff said. He had come to like the young bandit himself—Charley Floyd sure didn't seem like the cold-blooded killer J. Edgar Hoover and the newspapers made him out to be.

"It is—harder than you'll ever know," Charley said. "Eat your cheese and crackers, and don't be kickin' about one day."

The road they were stopped on went northwest, up toward the plains. A pair of hawks soared over, hunting quail, but otherwise, there was not a living thing in sight.

"If you went up this road and just kept goin', you'd come to the North Pole, eventually," Jack Killingsworth said.

"Drop me off in Iowa somewhere, if you're thinkin' of makin' the trip," Richetti said. "I was in Amarillo once, in the wintertime—that's close enough to the North Pole for me."

Just then, they saw a speck in the far distance.

"I think that's a car," Charley said. "If it is, I want you to put your sheriff's hat on, and use your authority to flag it down. We won't do nobody no harm, we just need a lift."

Richetti, skeptical, took the dim view.

"Nobody but desperate fools would travel on a road this empty," he said.

In fact, though, it was a car—a spanking new blue Pontiac, driven by a shoe salesman named Griffiths. He was a small, bald man with specs, wearing a black suit that would have looked better on an undertaker, in Charley's opinion. Sheriff Killingsworth had no trouble flagging him down.

"Sir, we've got an emergency," the sheriff said. "We need a lift bad."

"Oh, uh . . . where to, sir?" the little shoe salesman asked.

"Kansas City," the sheriff said.

"Kansas City? My wife will divorce me, if I run off to Kansas City," Mr. Griffiths said. "She's probably starting supper right now, expecting me home."

"We can offer crackers and cheese," Charley said. "I doubt it'll compare with your wife's cooking, but it beats going hungry. Could you scoot over, please?"

"Scoot over where?" Mr. Griffiths asked, looking alarmed.

"To the passenger side—I know a quick route and would prefer to drive," Charley said.

"Why, sir, I know nothing about your abilities, and this is a brand-new car," Mr. Griffiths said. "If I let a total stranger drive it and you was to wreck, my wife would divorce me."

"I can't help it if you've got a shaky marriage," Charley said, impatient. "Scoot over."

"I can vouch for my friend's driving," the sheriff said, thinking fast. "Mr. Charles is an expert."

Charley hated to put Killingsworth in the back seat with Richetti, given that the latter was dumb and trigger-happy, but he decided to try it. Richetti was not a steady driver. He was always letting up on the gas, a habit Charley could barely tolerate. Also, he was lax on curves, and had swerved nearly into the ditch several times. Besides, the Pontiac was brand-new, and he had always liked driving sharp new cars. Even in the predicament he was in, it felt good to speed down the road in a new vehicle.

Emil Griffiths had been a traveling salesman all his adult life. He had traveled the plains from North Texas up through the

320

Dakotas. He considered himself a sober man, experienced, and generally able and willing to take life as it came. But now, life had taken a completely unexpected turn. Just as he was beginning to think about the excellent supper he would soon be eating, he found himself in the passenger seat of his own car, with three total strangers. Besides that, they were headed in the opposite direction from his excellent supper, and heading that way fast—far too fast for his peace of mind.

"Sir, would you please slow down?" he asked. "This car is not broken in yet. You're not supposed to drive it this fast until the engine's settled a little."

Charley ignored the comment. The road was gravel, and they were leaving a long column of dust behind them.

"Besides that, you're kicking up the gravel," Mr. Griffiths said. "You might scar the paint. If I come home with this paint job all scratched up, my wife will divorce me."

"Sounds like you're henpecked as it is," Charley said. "Maybe a divorce would be the best thing. There's always greener pastures."

"Why don't you let me shoot this wimpy little weasel?" Richetti asked. "He's gettin' on my nerves."

"Shoot me?" Mr. Griffiths asked.

"Just a joke," Killingsworth said. "Why don't you lean back and enjoy the ride? Let Mr. Charles here drive as he sees fit."

"But it's my new car!" Mr. Griffiths protested. "Why can't he drive as *I* see fit?"

Nobody bothered to answer the question.

The next thing to disturb Mr. Griffiths was that Charley drove right across the nice, paved road that would have led straight to Kansas City, and kept plowing along through the gravel at a reckless pace.

"Say, that was the road to Kansas City," Mr. Griffiths pointed out. "It runs straight into town. What was wrong with it?"

Charley was amused. He knew the man must feel that life had suddenly twisted off in a crazy direction; he himself often felt the same way.

"Them paved roads are slick when it snows," he replied.

"But it ain't snowing," Mr. Griffiths said.

"No, but it could start any minute," Charley said. "That's the prediction."

By the time they saw the lights of Kansas City, Mr. Emil Griffiths was in such a state of nerves that he had produced a bottle of hootch from under the seat. After taking a long, warming swig himself, he relaxed a little and passed the bottle around. No one declined it.

When they saw the lights, Charley pulled off on a little knoll and killed the motor.

"Why are we stopping here, Mr. Charles?" Griffiths asked. "That's Kansas City, dead ahead. I thought this was an emergency."

"Oh, it is," Charley said. "It's just the kind of emergency that requires us to roll into town around midnight, or maybe one o'clock in the morning."

"I never heard of that kind of emergency," Mr. Griffiths said.

"Well, you have now, you yappin' magpie," Richetti barked.

"I still wanna shoot him," he added.

Charley ignored the remark. Then he noticed that the sheriff was looking nervous again. Probably, he did expect to be killed —after all, he was a law.

"Everybody relax, Eddie's just piss and wind," Charley said. "There'll be no gunplay tonight, and you'll both be on your way home by breakfast time."

"You ain't gonna let this copper go, are you?" Richetti asked, taking his pistol out of his pocket when he said it. "That don't even make sense."

"Put the cannon away, bud," Charley said.

"My wife's never gonna believe this," Mr. Griffiths said. "She'll think I got a sweetie somewhere."

"Sounds to me like you lead a dog's life when you're home— it might not be a bad idea to get one," Charley recommended.

It got later, and more chill. Richetti, too dumb to put his hands in his pockets, kept blowing on them. When it was a few minutes past midnight, Charley drove on into Kansas City and stopped two blocks from the streetcar line.

"End of the line, folks," Charley said. "You're free to hop the streetcar."

322

"What about my new car?" Mr. Griffiths asked. "You ain't aiming to steal it, are you?"

"Nope, it'll be parked at the corner of Sixth and Main, in about an hour," Charley said. "If you care to hike that far, you can pick it up and give the sheriff a ride home. The keys will be under the front seat."

During the wait on the knoll, Mr. Griffiths had produced a second bottle of whiskey. Jack Killingsworth had drunk more than was his habit—despite himself, he felt sad for Charley Floyd.

"Why don't you give it up, Charley?" he asked. "I mean it—give it up. Except for your record, you seem decent. Give it up, and take your chances in the courts."

"Go home to your wife and boy, Jack," Charley said—he didn't smile.

"But why not?" the sheriff asked. "Ain't it better than bein' shot down?"

"I say we kill the copper, and the drummer, too," Richetti said. "They're both gonna crow like roosters."

"Aw, button your lip," Charley snapped. "Let 'em crow."

"I sure wish you'd think about it," Jack Killingsworth said.

Charley just shook his head.

"I'm like an old wolf, Jack," Charley said. "I'm like an old wolf who's been hunted too long. There's not much left now but the hunt—not for me. Once upon a time, I might have made a good hound. But that time's gone . . . now, it's just the wolf against the hounds."

"Charley, there's too many hounds," Killingsworth said. "You can't outrun them all."

Charley straightened up.

"It takes quite a few hounds to bring down a wolf, Jack," he said.

"There's a nice set of golf clubs in that car with the two flats, Sheriff—if you're back that way, take 'em, to remember me by," he added.

"I don't think I'll be needin' anything to remember you by, Charley," the sheriff replied. "I'll be tellin' my grandkids this story, someday. And I'll tell you something else—for the business you're in, you've been a real gentleman."

323

"You'll notice I didn't scratch the paint, Mr. Griffiths," Charley said. "Thanks for sharing the hootch. Streetcar line's that way," he said, pointing.

Griffiths and Killingsworth got out, and started up the cold, dark street.

Charley put the car in gear, and drove up beside them for a moment.

"Say, if you get hungry on the way home, there's a swell cafe in Lee's Summit," he told them. "Good flapjacks."

The wind picked up as soon as the moon rose in the night sky. The two men hunched their necks down into their coat collars, and started walking again, toward the lights of downtown Kansas City.

"Was that Pretty Boy Floyd?" Mr. Griffiths asked, when all they could see of the Pontiac was two tiny red taillights.

"Charles Arthur Floyd," Jack Killingsworth said. "That's the way he prefers to be addressed."

Book Four

1933-1934

1

Beulah Baird had just stepped out of the corner grocery store, when a paperboy held up the newspaper and she saw the headline: "MASSACRE AT UNION STATION—FIVE DEAD!"

She started to buy the paper, then realized she didn't have but three cents in her coin purse. She had run out to buy spicy sausage for Charley's breakfast, and bought some fudge on impulse. Now, she was broke.

"Would you just hold that paper steady for a minute?" she asked the newsboy. "I wanna read about the massacre."

"Lady, can't you buy it?" the newsboy asked. "What if everybody wanted free reads?"

"You'd starve, so what?" Beulah barked.

"So what yourself!" the newsboy said, annoyed. Beulah was forced to be a little nicer before he'd let her read past the headlines. Finally, she was nice enough that he gave her the paper. She promised to bring him the nickel for the paper the next day.

On the way up the stairs to her rooms in the boarding house, she saw a line that upset her so much she dropped the sausage, and the fudge, too: "J. Edgar Hoover claims the massacre was headed by Pretty Boy Floyd. A reliable witness, Hoover said, placed Floyd at the scene."

Beulah was so unnerved, she left the sausage and fudge on the stairs, and raced into the room. Charley was still under the covers, dressed in nothing but his undershirt. He had slept hard —even now, Beulah could see that he hardly had his eyes open.

"Look at this!" she said, throwing him the paper. "You gotta get out of here."

"Why? I just got here," Charley said, before he focused on the headlines.

"Oh, they got Jelly Nash, he was nothin' but a snitch," he said. Then he saw the line about Pretty Boy Floyd.

"This is a lie, I was nowhere near Union Station," he said. "I was right here with you."

"I know that, but Hoover don't," Beulah said. "He's gonna try to pin this on you for sure."

It was the first time since George Birdwell's death that Charley had slept soundly. He didn't even dream—a rare thing in itself. Waking up had been like pulling himself out of quicksand. He barely remembered he was in Kansas City with Beulah. In fact, until she shoved the newspaper in his face, he thought he might be back in Oklahoma; he almost expected to roll over and see Ruby next to him. Now, life itself was beginning to resemble a nightmare, one from which he might never wake up. Charley felt dazed. He kept reading the same sentence of the newspaper story over and over again, trying to grasp the facts. Two federal agents were bringing the notorious outlaw Jelly Nash up from the McAlester pen in Oklahoma, which was not far from Sallisaw. Several other agents met them at Union Station and helped them get Jelly into a car. Nash was due to testify at a big trial involving the rackets. No sooner was he in the car than several men rushed up, and let go with Tommy guns. Jelly and four G-men were killed. One G-man, sitting right next to Jelly, didn't suffer so much as a scratch.

328

"They *can't* pin this on me!" Charley insisted. "I'm just a bank robber. I don't even know Jelly Nash.

"I ain't involved in the rackets in K.C., why would I wanna kill him?" he added.

"Charley, we gotta get out of here," Beulah said. "Every cop in Kansas City knows I'm your girlfriend. It won't be no time before they'll be swarming all over this place."

"I don't even have a car," Charley said. "Richetti was going to try and steal one, but that was before this happened. We won't get far in a stolen car. You'll have to go buy one."

"Me? I don't know nothin' about cars," Beulah said. "All I know how to do is ride in one."

"Go cook the sausage," Charley said, getting out from under the covers. "I got to think this over."

He jumped up and got dressed. His head throbbed from drinking too much the night before. The fact that he had let Sheriff Killingsworth and Mr. Griffiths go only a few hours before the massacre wasn't going to look good: it placed him in K.C. just in time to be part of what happened at Union Station.

While Beulah was frying eggs and making sausage, Charley grabbed a tablet and hastily penned a note:

Dear Sirs,
I Charles Floyd want it made known that I did not participate in the massacre of officers at Kansas City, Missouri.
                              Charles Arthur Floyd

He and Beulah had no sooner sat down at the table than they heard a car drive up. Beulah looked out the window, and saw a police car. Charley had just taken his first sip of coffee.

"I told you we should have left," Beulah said. "Now it's too late. They're headed up the sidewalk."

Charley took a quick look out the window.

"It's just three goons," he said. "Stick my plate in the kitchen and keep drinking your coffee."

"But Charley, what'll I say?" Beulah asked. "They'll be here in a minute."

"Flirt, if you get the chance," Charley said. He got down on his hands and knees and crawled under the breakfast table, taking the Tommy gun with him. Fortunately, it had a long table-cloth covering the top of it.

"Flirt? I ain't good at flirtin' this early in the day," Beulah said. "I ain't even had my coffee yet."

"Just do it, Beulah," Charley said, exasperated.

"What if they want to come in?" Beulah asked.

"Of course they'll want to come in," Charley whispered. "If they get pushy, it'll be their lookout.

"Turn up the radio," he ordered. "Turn it up, and keep it turned up."

Beulah did as she was told. "Shuffle Off to Buffalo" blared through the room, just as the policemen knocked on the door.

"Say, who is it? I'm in my robe," Beulah said loudly.

"Open the door, lady," one agent said. "It's the law."

"Maybe you are and maybe you ain't—I need to see a badge before I open up," Beulah said.

"You can't see a badge through a door, lady," the man said. "We're G-men—let us in."

"Couldn't you slip a badge under the door?" Beulah asked, stalling. "I'm a single girl, I have to be careful."

"The badge won't fit under the door—quit stalling," a second agent said.

"Will you be gentlemen if I open up?" Beulah inquired. "I don't tolerate rude behavior, I'll tell you that right now."

"Open this door or watch us bust it down!" the first agent snarled.

Beulah turned the lock, the door burst open, and the agents lunged into the room—all three G-men had their pistols drawn.

"All right, where is he?" the first agent asked.

"Don't come bargin' into my home askin' questions!" Beulah said, indignant. "You could at least take off your hats."

All three kept their pistols ready. None of them removed their hats.

"I said, where is he?" the first G-man repeated, through clenched teeth.

"How long ago did Floyd leave?" the second agent asked. "We know he was here."

330

"I ain't answering questions from no rude men!" Beulah snapped—her ire was up. "And stay out of my kitchen!" she added, when the third agent went in to look around. He popped right back out.

"He's been here," he said. "There's a plate on the sink, the sausage is still hot."

Charley was trying to watch feet—he wanted the men to be as close together as possible before he made a move.

"Oh, blow your nose, that was my pa left that plate in the sink," Beulah said.

"Yeah, and I'm Ty Cobb," the third agent said. "Let's go downtown, sister. We got a lot to talk about . . ."

Charley put one palm on the underside of the tabletop and grabbed the table edge with his other hand—lifted it—and charged the agents. Glassware and plates flew everywhere, but he slammed the agents so hard with the table that all three went down. Before they could recover and collect their wits, Charley had them covered with the Tommy gun.

"Let's have the pistols, boys," he said. The agents didn't put up a fight—they were all too scared to move.

Charley reached in his shirt pocket for the note he had scribbled.

"Mr. J. Edgar Hoover's your boss, ain't he?" he asked them.

"Yeah, he's the director," the first G-man answered.

"Beulah, give him this note," he said, handing it to her. She handed it to the first agent.

"I want you to read it, and then I want you to make sure it gets to your boss," he added, speaking to the first G-man.

The agent took the note from Beulah and hastily read it.

"It's the truth," Charley said. "I had nothing to do with it. I just got into town late last night. I've got two witnesses to prove it. I never laid eyes on Jelly Nash, and had no reason to kill him."

"We don't expect you to admit it, bud," the second agent said.

"If I went in for Tommy-gunnin' folks, all three of you goons would already be dead," Charley informed them. "I would have plugged all of you while you were out there on the sidewalk."

The agents said nothing.

331

"You ain't no jury," Charley told them. "I don't care if you believe me. Just give that note to Hoover.

"If the law wants to cut me a fair deal, I'm ready to talk," he added. "Be sure Mr. Hoover knows that."

Beulah was nervously trying to gather up the spilled glassware, forks, spoons, and the butter.

"If the landlady sees this rug, I'm in trouble," she said.

"Get packed, we're leavin'," Charley said. "Don't take a ton of clothes, either. I'm not interested in movin' your private department store."

"What about these mugs?" Beulah asked. "Are we gonna just leave 'em sitting here?"

"Sure we are," Charley said. "If they get hungry, they can lick up the butter. Then the landlady won't be so mad at you."

He covered the agents, while Beulah tore up a sheet. Then she covered them with one of their own pistols while Charley tied their hands and ankles and made three crude gags. He was good with knots. The agents could eventually wiggle out, but it would take them at least an hour.

"I meant what I said," Charley told them. "If I'm offered a fair deal, I'll come in."

Beulah went down the hall to the phone and called a taxi. Then she lugged her two suitcases, one by one, down to the street and waited for the taxi to show up. When the taxi finally arrived, the elderly driver was smoking a stogie the size of a pipe.

"That's a noble smoke you got there," Charley told the driver. "How much to take us to Mexico?"

"Mexico, Missouri?" the man inquired.

"No, not Mexico, Missouri," Charley said. "Mexico . . . the country!"

"I was born in Mexico, Missouri," the old man said. "That's the only reason I asked. Pretty Boy Floyd just gunned down six lawmen there."

"Applesauce," Charley said. "It was only two, and Charley Floyd was several hundred miles away at the time."

"That ain't what the radio said. How'd you get to be such an expert?" the driver asked, turning to look at him.

332

"I'm J. Edgar Hoover," Charley said. "My G-men are hot on his tracks, but he didn't pull the Mexico, Missouri, job."

"Can't we just buy a car?" Beulah asked. "I don't want to ride all the way to Mexico in this smelly old taxi."

"That stogie's so big it's liable to last all the way to Mexico," Charley said. "He ain't named his price yet, though—Mexico might be beyond my means."

"We got to go get Rose first," Beulah reminded him.

When they got to Rose's place, Adam Richetti was in bed with her, a fact that didn't sit well with Beulah. Rose answered the door in her gown; they could hear Richetti snoring before they even got in the room. Charley had sent him to Rose's to hide out, but he hadn't anticipated any romantic developments. He didn't care himself, but Beulah was clearly annoyed.

"Who told you to sleep with that little jerk?" she asked her sister. "What was wrong with the couch?"

Rose didn't answer. The truth was, since leaving Bradley, she had been sleeping with more and more men—it covered the hurt for a little while, at least. She didn't talk about it with Beulah. Beulah had hated being on the farm and didn't understand how much Rose loved Bradley, or how much it hurt her to leave him. Richetti was just a fellow she could hold onto at night; it didn't mean any more than that.

Richetti sat up in bed, a smirk on his face.

"What's for breakfast?" he asked.

Beulah could barely keep herself from cracking him.

"A knuckle sandwich," she told him. "It's what you'll get, too, if you don't treat my sister nice."

When Adam Richetti learned that he, too, was implicated in the Kansas City Massacre—the paper had named him as one of Charley's gunmen—he stopped smirking, and went pale.

"We need to scram," he said. "It wasn't my idea to come to K.C., anyway."

"If you've had an idea since we met, other than to plug somebody, I don't recollect what it might have been," Charley said. "Maybe you ought to rest your brain for a few years—let me do the thinking."

"What's your idea?" Richetti asked.

"My idea is that we split up," Charley said. "You take the girls and head north. Try Cleveland, or maybe Buffalo."

"But what about you? Where'll you be?" Beulah asked.

"Memphis—I'll be down the river, eating hot biscuits and redeye gravy," Charley said. "If I don't like the feel of Memphis, I might try Atlanta. They won't be expectin' me to go south."

"Why can't I come with you?" Beulah asked. "You just got here."

"I wouldn't be here if I'd known somebody was gonna mow down Jelly Nash and blame it on me," Charley informed her. "You go with Eddie and Rose—I need to move quick and sly, and I can't be dragging you and your department store around. They'll be looking for me on the highways— I'm gonna ride the rails until I get someplace safe."

It was a lie—he had no intention of going to either Memphis or Atlanta. But he saw no reason to put Richetti or the Baird girls in possession of any information that might get him *or* them in trouble, in case they got nabbed. And, in his view, it was more than likely they would get nabbed.

Beulah had a fit, and then cried. Then she had another fit, and cried some more. She punched Charley twice in the arm, she was so disappointed that he wouldn't take her with him. But Charley held his temper, took the taxi down to a used car lot on West Kansas Street, and came back with a four-hundred-dollar flivver.

"You'll have to wrap up good, it don't have a heater," he told the gloomy threesome. "It gets chilly up toward Cleveland."

Beulah kissed him seven or eight times, as passionately as possible, trying to get him to change his mind and take her with him. But Charley was firm.

"I can't, honey," he said. "It's drafty in them boxcars. Delicate as you are, you'd catch pneumonia, and I'd have to leave you in a hospital in some town where you don't know a soul."

"But when will you come, Charley?" Beulah asked. "How will you know where to find us?"

"Send Bob Birdwell a letter, once you get settled," Charley said. "George is dead—I doubt they'll be watchin' Bob's mail."

Beulah's eyes were wet when the threesome drove away. She

334

hated leaving Charley after such a brief visit. Also, she didn't like it that Rose had a boyfriend available for the trip, and she didn't. Her fellow would be down in Memphis or somewhere. It didn't seem fair. Charley hadn't even been in Kansas City long enough to take her shopping. Beulah knew that was mostly Mr. Hoover's fault, but it still didn't seem fair.

That night, in Belleville, Illinois, Adam Richetti suggested that it would be more economical if they all three slept in the same bed. The only hotel in town charged two bucks apiece for rooms, and Adam balked.

"It's high," he said, after inspecting the room, "but the bed's big enough for three."

"That's what you think, buster," Beulah informed him. "The biggest bed in the world wouldn't be big enough for you and me to sleep in."

"I was just thinkin' of the money," Richetti claimed, making a futile attempt to appear innocent of anything more than concern about their finances.

"Like fun you were, you heel," Beulah replied.

She threw him a pillow, and Adam Richetti slept on the floor.

2

As soon as Richetti and the Baird sisters drove off, Charley made a phone call to Lulu Ash. When she answered, her voice had a rasp to it that Charley had never heard before.

"Have you got the croup?" he asked.

"Come in the back door," Lulu said. "Half the bulls in town have been here looking for you already."

When Charley saw her, he was shocked. Her face looked like

her name—it was the color of ash. Her hand shook when she unlatched the back screen, and her eyes were blurry and unfocused. She had the look of a dying woman. Just seeing her made Charley weak in the knees, for despite all, Charley looked to Lulu as a last resort. She knew a lot more than he did about getting around the law. Her greed in the bedroom was just sauce; it was her brain he had come to rely on, as he had relied on no one else—not even George Birdwell.

"What is it?" he asked. "What's hit you?"

"Cancer," Lulu said. "It's in my jaw and the roof of my mouth."

"Can't they operate?" Charley asked. Again, he thought about Red, and wondered if she had passed away.

"I won't let 'em," Lulu said. "I ain't gonna have no docs cutting on me."

Her voice had an awful rasp. It reminded him of a blacksmith's rasp scraping a horse's hoof. Charley didn't know what to say. The boarding house had an empty feel. He opened a few cupboards but saw nothing to eat, though there was a coffeepot on the stove.

"What do the boarders do, starve?" Charley asked. "I don't see any grub in the kitchen."

"I got rid of the boarders," Lulu said.

"Why?" Charley asked.

"Got tired of listening to a roomful of men belch," Lulu said. "I'm tired of cooking and tired of eating."

"But you got to eat," Charley reminded her. "It's eat or die, Lulu, you know that."

Lulu Ash gave him a flat look. Since the first morning in the hallway of her boarding house in St. Louis, when she had walked up and unbuttoned his trousers, Charley half expected her to unbutton his trousers every time they met. Not only did he half expect it, he half wanted it—maybe a little more than half.

But this time, Lulu made no move toward his pants.

"I eat enough," Lulu said. "It ain't tasty, I'm taking too much dope to taste much. But I ain't likely to starve. My own ma lived on coffee for the last ten years of her life. I can, too, if I have to."

336

Charley felt awkward. He had rushed to Lulu, as he had several times before, seeking her advice and her help. Now he was in the worst situation of his life, with the local police and the Bureau of Investigation looking to haul him in and hang him for a crime he didn't commit. But here was Lulu Ash, in a worse situation still: cancer of the jaw. He might, with luck, elude the G-men and the state police; but Lulu's cancer was inside her. How could she escape?

Lulu came a little closer to him, with a little smile on her lips, and punched him lightly in the stomach.

"Don't give me no advice, Charley," she said. "You ain't half smart enough to advise me. And don't be giving me no sympathy, either. I'm sick, but I'll still outlive you, unless you're mighty lucky."

"Then you give me some advice, if that's how you feel," Charley said. "I didn't have nothin' to do with what happened to Jelly Nash, but how am I gonna make Hoover and the other laws believe that?"

"You ain't—you'll swing if they catch you," Lulu said. "They've got enough against you to hang you two or three times over, even without Jelly."

"Did you know Jelly?" Charley asked. It wasn't so much that he was curious about Jelly Nash as that he was curious about Lulu's own past.

"I hated his slimy guts," Lulu informed him. "Nothing's lower than a snitch. I would have gone to the station and killed him myself if I'da had any idea they were bringing him to town. I've always suspected he was the mug who had my boys shot."

Wally and William Ash had been found dead about six months earlier, in a car parked at the edge of a cornfield, outside Kansas City. Both had been shot in the back of the head with a small-caliber revolver.

"Folks thought I done that, too, out of jealousy," Charley said.

"My boys wasn't no ladies' men," Lulu said. "If they'd found you dead, I would have suspected Wally, though. He hated you ever since you took Beulah away."

"I didn't take her away," Charley said. "She just sort of followed me off."

Lulu gave him a hard look. "If we get to talkin' about that situation, I'll end up slapping you," she said. "If she followed you off, it was because you laid down plenty of scent."

"I need to get out of here, but I ain't got a vehicle," Charley reminded her. "You think I'd be safe to hop a train?"

"There's no safety left for you, hon," Lulu said, softening a little.

She said it quietly, but the words still made the hair stand up on the back of Charley's neck. She made it sound so final, as if he already had an execution date.

"What should I do, then?" Charley asked. "You think I should just give up, and fight in the court?"

Lulu snorted. "Are you drunk?" she asked.

"I drank some last night, but I ain't drunk now," Charley told her.

Lulu suddenly cracked—a flood of tears poured out of her, and she stumbled into Charley's arms. She had been living alone with the knowledge that she was dying for too long. Now Charley was in mortal peril, too. The depth of her love for him had always been hard to live with, but the thought that they were both going to die—probably not even while they were together—upset her so much that she couldn't hold back her feelings.

"I wish they would just leave us alone," Lulu said. "I never went out of my way to hurt a soul. Why can't they just leave a person alone?"

Charley was no doctor. He knew he couldn't help Lulu, and he was bothered by the feeling that the three goons who had showed up that morning at Beulah's would have wiggled loose by now and could be arriving at Lulu's anytime. Only this time, they'd come with reinforcements, and he wouldn't be able to hide under a long tablecloth. He had a sense that he needed to move, and move soon—maybe as soon as Lulu Ash stopped crying.

"Why'd you ask me if I was drunk?" he asked.

"Because you asked about the courts," Lulu said, attempting to regain control of herself. "The courts ain't for people like us —we're bottom feeders. Hoover would never let you set foot in a courthouse—you'd be too apt to fool the jury. He'd set up a

338

prison break a few days before the trial, and you'd fall for it. Then forty or fifty G-men would shoot you down, just like they slaughtered Bonnie and Clyde."

Charley turned white at the comparison. Pictures of the bullet-riddled car Bonnie and Clyde had been riding in at the time of their ambush were in all the newspapers. Just looking at the car and imagining the bullets and the blood was enough to make him queasy. It was worse than what happened in Boley—many times worse.

"If that happens, they'll have to ambush me, too," Charley said. "Have you got a car?"

"That car you brought down from Ohio's still in the garage, four blocks from here," Lulu said. "I expect the battery's down, but it's your car."

"No sir, that's a death car," Charley said. "Billy Miller had just stepped out of that car when they killed him. Beulah got shot in the head, too—it's a miracle she lived."

"Beggars can't be choosers," Lulu said. "It's the only automobile available. The police kept Wally's car—for evidence, they said."

"I won't ride in no death car—not me," Charley said. "I still remember how Billy looked, lying in the street in a puddle of blood."

"He's luckier than I'll be," Lulu said. "He died quick. About all that helps me now is the dope. I wish I smoked. I don't care to eat, or screw—there's no pleasure left."

Charley was beginning to wish he had hopped a train instead of coming to Lulu's. He had put on his last fresh shirt; now it was covered with Lulu's tears. He suddenly had a terrible longing to be home, to be with Ruby, to hear Dempsey laugh helplessly as he did when he was really amused. When he walked up to Lulu's back door, he had been thinking about her unbuttoning his pants; at least it would have taken his mind off his fear for a few minutes. But Lulu was grey as a plank with the paint worn off —she was past that, as she had plainly said. It made him want to be home, whatever the risk. It seemed to him that a night with Ruby and Dempsey would be worth hanging for. If, as Lulu said, there was no safety anyway, why not have one more night with his family?

When Charley told Lulu he thought he had better go, she broke down again, and clutched at him.

"Stay the night, Charley," she said. "You don't have to do nothin'. Just stay the night."

Lulu slept in his arms, but Charley lay awake all night. The next morning, as he was slipping out, she gave him two hundred dollars, and managed a little smile.

"It ain't often a whore pays a stiff for not screwin' her, is it?" she remarked.

Charley started to say that she had it all wrong, that she wasn't a whore, that the money was a loan. But when he opened his mouth, he choked up and couldn't say a word.

He blinked at Lulu, and left.

3

"I'm surprised you wasted good money on that trash," the Director said, from behind Agent Purvis's chair.

Agent Purvis jumped about a foot—no mean feat, considering that he was sitting down. He could easily imagine many catastrophes—being shot by a madman, for example—but one catastrophe that had never seemed likely to occur was that the Director would pop into his office while he was wasting time reading *Police Gazette*. The Director never popped into any office. He was rarely seen, even in the halls. If there was one rule that seemed to hold true in the Bureau, it was that you went to see the Director: the Director didn't come to see you.

But now, he had come to see Agent Purvis. He was chomping on his Cuban stogie, and glaring at the issue of *Police Gazette*.

"But boss—you're on the cover," Agent Purvis hastily pointed out, in his defense.

"Didn't like the story," Hoover informed him.

"Well, but the picture's nice," Purvis said. He hoped not to have to admit to the Director that he had not yet read the story on Hoover and the Public Enemies list.

"A picture of me won't get us a penny more out of Congress," Hoover told him. "The Public Enemies list will, if the public can only be made to see what a menace these criminals are to society.

"You don't understand how these things work, Purvis," he added. "And you never will, if you waste your time reading trash."

IIe snatched thc magazine out of Purvis's hands, and threw it in the wastebasket.

"We need to get Dillinger," he said. "That's priority number one. And we need to get Pretty Boy Floyd. I'm moving him up to Number Two."

Agent Purvis was a little surprised. Pretty Boy Floyd was currently Number Eight, nearly at the bottom of the list. That didn't seem unfair, in Agent Purvis's view. After all, Floyd was just a hick bank robber. He had killed one lawman and a bounty hunter, and had caused the insurance rates on bank money in Oklahoma to go sky-high. Floyd needed to be taken off the streets; probably, he even needed to be hung. But, as mcnaccs go, he wasn't in the same league as a mean weasel like Dillinger, or crazy old Ma Barker and her boys, or the vicious and sadistic Baby Face Nelson.

"Charley Floyd? Number Two?" Purvis asked, in surprise. "What's he done to pull rank on the six above him?"

"The Kansas City Massacre, that's what!" Hoover snapped, chomping his cigar. "There are four dead agents, and one dead informant. Would you agree that's enough?"

Agent Purvis knew he had to be careful in his remarks, or he would end up in more hot water than he was already. None of the young G-men at the Bureau thought Charley Floyd had anything to do with the K.C. Massacre. Floyd was a bank robber. Gunning people down on railway station platforms didn't even come close to any job the Oklahoma outlaw had ever pulled before. The Director had announced immediately that Floyd had done it, but the Director was always quick to name a perpetrator when some big crime was committed. He wanted the public to think the Bureau knew everything. But the young G-men knew better. So far, they didn't have a clue about the Kansas City Massacre—it had been a clean job. Going public with a name before the blood was even dry on the street was just the Director's way. When the real culprits were identified and captured, their names would get front-page play. Probably, by then, the public would have forgotten that Charley Floyd had even been accused.

"Oh, have we got new evidence?" Purvis asked.

"We have several reliable witnesses who place Floyd at the scene," the Director said. "Unfortunately, they're all coloreds—I'm not sure we want to put them on the stand. What time you can spare from Dillinger I want you to put on Floyd," Hoover said. "If the man shows any fight at all, eliminate him. It will save taxpayers the cost of a trial."

"I thought I read in some paper about a sheriff in Missouri who claimed Floyd didn't do it. He said he was with Floyd the night before it happened."

"That sheriff was drunk," Hoover said. "I hope he loses the next election—in fact, I'm sure he will. Here's a note from Floyd. Every word in it is a lie."

He handed Purvis the note Charley had given the agents in Kansas City.

"It's a short note, sir," Purvis observed. "How'd we come by it?"

"Floyd himself handed it to three of our men," Hoover said.

"Handed it to them?" Purvis asked, shocked. "If he handed it to them, why didn't they arrest him?"

"Because they were incompetents," Hoover said. "Of course he denies his involvement."

"It sounds like the work of the mob, to me," Purvis ventured. He himself didn't smoke, and he resented the fact that the Director was letting cigar ash fall on his well-swept floor. Now it would have to be well swept all over again.

"Charley Floyd's just a bandit," he said. "I doubt he's got the brains to plan a job like that."

342

"You don't know much about police work, I see," Hoover said.

Purvis had been tempted to speak when he knew he should have kept his mouth shut. Now he was in hot water, and anything he said would only make the water hotter. He decided to keep his mouth shut.

"Let me worry about who planned the job," Hoover said. "Pretty Boy Floyd pulled it, that's all you need to know."

"Where is he now, sir?" Purvis asked.

"He was seen leaving the house of a whore, in Kansas City," Hoover said. "That was yesterday. We think he headed north."

"I wouldn't, if I was him," Purvis said. "It's the middle of winter."

"Why would Floyd care? He's a cold-blooded killer," Hoover said, throwing his cigar in the wastebasket as he turned to leave.

4

By the time the train got to Wichita, Charley was having sneezing fits. The floor of the boxcar he ended up in was covered with oats, and the fine chaff blew everywhere while the train was moving. It got in Charley's nose, eyes, ears, up his pants legs, and in his sleeves. He was traveling in a kind of whirlwind of oat chaff. Besides that, he was freezing. Sleet was blowing when he jumped the freight in Kansas City, and it was still blowing when they sighted Wichita. The plains were grey with sleet, as far as he could see.

An old hobo was in the boxcar with him, wrapped up in a

uniform of sacks. The old man's long, tangled hair was so full of chaff and straw that he looked like a scarecrow. His face was yellow, as if he had jaundice; his grey eyes were as pale as the sleet.

"I hate these damn oats," Charley declared. He decided he was too old to be riding in boxcars, but he couldn't say so with the ancient hobo sitting there. The old man looked to be seventy at least, and he seemed perfectly content to rock along with oat chaff blowing up his nose.

They hit the Wichita yards at night. The hobo stayed put, but Charley slipped out, and found a fleabag hotel a few blocks from the station. He had hoped for a bath, but the shower only yielded a cold drip. He gritted his teeth and stood under it anyway, until most of the oat chaff was sluiced out of his hair and off his body. There were three empty whiskey bottles on the floor of his room, and sleet had iced over the windowpanes. All night, he could think of nothing but Ruby and Dempsey. Christmas was three weeks away. If he kept to the boxcars the rest of the way home, there was a good chance he'd freeze to death. When he did finally sleep, he dreamed of all the presents he'd take to Ruby and Dempsey. But he had left K.C. with only the two hundred dollars Lulu Ash had given him—he'd have to come up with more than that, if he wanted to have enough left over for a few months' rent and some decent groceries for them as well.

The next morning, he brushed the chaff off his overcoat and walked to a haberdashery, where he spent three dollars on a fine new tie. Choosing the tie took a while. It had stopped sleeting by the time he left the store, but the wind was icy, and the sidewalks were pocked with patches of frozen sleet. The nearest bank, a small one, was only three blocks from the haberdashery. Charley had hoped to be the first one in the door. He thought the ice storm and the freezing wind might discourage most of the locals from doing their banking that day. He hoped to lift a few hundred dollars without causing much of a stir, but his hopes were immediately dashed by a cop who had just cashed his paycheck at one of the teller's windows.

Charley mistook the man for a streetcar conductor, and drew his pistol before he realized his mistake. The cop saw the pistol, and turned white as a sheet. There was a young woman at the other window with twin boys, chubby as piglets and maybe three years old. The young woman spotted the drawn pistol at the same moment as the cop did, and she grabbed her twins. Both kids began to scream at once, probably because their mother had frightened them by her sudden move.

Charley was annoyed with himself for pulling the gun so quickly. He had left his nice buckskin gloves in the hotel room, and had his hands in his overcoat pockets to keep them warm. The gun was in his right pocket, and he pulled it without thinking.

"Now, folks, don't get excited," Charley said. "This is just a friendly holdup. Officer, sit down on that bench—let me have your sap first. Cold as it is, if you was to hit me with it, you might break off one of my ears."

The pale cop handed over his blackjack and did as he was told.

"Oh, Lord, and it's nearly Christmas, too," he said, but he could barely be heard over the screaming little boys. Their mother began to get hysterical, though Charley had not done anything directly to her or her children.

Charley didn't even have to point the gun at the tellers, both tiny old ladies who looked as if they might be sisters. They began methodically piling bills on the counter. Charley had only planned on taking about a thousand; he could stuff that much in his pockets. But the old ladies worked so quick that he was forced to request a sack.

"And two suckers, please, if you have suckers," he said, glancing at the little boys.

"What flavor?" one elderly teller asked. "We got lemon, grape, and cherry."

"Florence, don't be offerin' him suckers," the other teller said. "He's a bank robber. What would he need with candy?"

"He asked for them—you heard him," Florence replied.

"The suckers are for our young customers, sir," she added. "We've got instructions not to waste 'em."

Charley put a dollar on the counter.

"That's to replace the suckers," he said.

Then he walked over to the two wailing twins, and offered

them each a sucker. Both boys grabbed the suckers in their fat little fists; one twin popped the sucker in his mouth without even taking off the paper wrapper.

"Oops, you gotta take the paper off," Charley advised. "It'll taste a good bit better, if you do."

The first twin kept the sucker in his mouth, paper and all; the other twin was laboriously peeling his. The young mother stared at Charley with her mouth open, still terrified.

"Ma'am, you can set your boys down," Charley said. "I'm a daddy myself. I'm sorry I gave them such a fright."

Charley tried to pull the sucker with the paper on it out of the plump little boy's mouth, but the child set his teeth and wouldn't let go.

"Say, can you tell your brother that suckers taste better with the wrapper off?" he asked the other boy.

The boy just stared at him. Sticky red juice from the cherry sucker was already dripping down his chin.

"They're not so messy if you leave the wrapper on, I guess," Charley said, smiling at the mother. The smile didn't have any effect—the young woman still looked paralyzed with fear.

Charley tucked the sack of bills under his overcoat, and handed the cop back his sap. The cop looked as if he might be about to lose his breakfast.

"Don't hit nobody in the ear with that—not today," Charley said, as he went out the door.

5

The promoter from the road show was named Louie Raczkowski. Ruby would never have been able to spell the last name if Mr. Raczkowski hadn't given her a card. *CARDINAL ENTERTAINMENT*, it read. *Louie Raczkowski, Owner.* Ruby studied the card carefully, hoping it would yield some clue as to what she ought to do, but it didn't.

Mr. Raczkowski was very tall, and so stooped that when seen in profile, his figure resembled a very large capital S. A cigarette drooped from the very corner of his mouth, and hung almost straight down. If it had fallen out of his mouth, it would have landed in his shirt pocket.

"What would we do?—Dempsey's in school," Ruby said. "It wouldn't hurt to let him miss a few days now and then, but if it was gonna be much more than that, I don't know."

Mr. Raczkowski tilted the cigarette up briefly, puffed on it, and then let it drop again, as two streams of smoke drifted out of his nostrils.

"Our idea was to call the show 'Crime Doesn't Pay,'" Mr. Raczkowski said. "You're Cherokee, ain't you? It's mainly Cherokees around here, ain't it?"

"Well, I've got Cherokee blood," Ruby said. "Some Cherokee blood. Mostly, I'm white, though."

"We'll get you a squaw dress and some squaw moccasins to wear, and we'll get the little boy one of them toy Tommy guns. You could stand up and talk a little about how hard it is to be married to a famous robber. Maybe sing 'Red River Valley' at the end, and have the folks sing along with you."

"I sang in the church choir a few times," Ruby said. "Folks said I had a nice voice. I guess I could learn the music, if it wasn't too hard."

"Can I shoot the Tommy gun? I could pretend to be Daddy," Dempsey chimed in. He liked the idea of being in the show already. It sounded like it would mean missing at least a little school, and he also liked the idea of a toy Tommy gun.

"Will there be pretend G-men I could shoot at?" he asked.

"Son, we ain't laid out the whole program," Mr. Raczkowski said. "We might get volunteer G-men from the audience—lots of times payin' customers enjoy an opportunity to get up on stage themselves.

"It's twenty dollars a show and expenses," he added. "We'd try to schedule you on Friday and Saturday nights, so the tyke wouldn't miss too much school."

"I don't mind," Dempsey said. "I wouldn't mind it even if I missed a lot of school.

"Even if I didn't have to go to school at all," he added. He wanted the tall, stooped man to know that he, Dempsey Floyd, was ready to join the show at once.

Ruby had her doubts. For one thing, she was shy. She had never much liked to get up before the public; even singing in the church choir had been hard because of her shyness. She couldn't get near as strong a tone in her voice singing in the choir as she did when she was just warbling around the house. Of course, she never sang hymns at the house; singing hymns always made her feel a little bit guilty. Even being in church reminded her of what a sinner she had been. Many times, she and Charley had slicked up and set off for a camp meeting, only to stop someplace and make love half the night rather than go hear the preaching.

"We'd try for a show on Friday night, and maybe two shows on Saturday—one in the afternoon to draw the kids," Mr. Raczkowski said.

"Would it mainly be in Oklahoma?" Ruby asked. "I lived up in Coffeyville, Kansas, for a while, but other than that I've never been an inch out of Oklahoma." She didn't think she should mention Arkansas, where she and Dempsey had lived with Charley, or Jeff City, either.

"We might try to dip a few miles down into Texas, and maybe hit a corner of Arkansas," the man said. "Mostly, though, we'd just work the Okie belt."

Ruby didn't really want to do it. She would never have thought of herself as a show business sort of person—or as any special sort of person, for that matter. Her biggest ambition had been to be Charley Floyd's wife. But now, Charley was who-knows-where. He was hunted, and always would be. If luck went against them, she would never even see him again—a thought she didn't let her mind approach—not if she could keep her mind from it, anyway. It had been a while since Charley had gotten any money to her, and she didn't like to think about how bleak Dempsey's Christmas would be if some money didn't turn up soon. The only thing she could do that anyone would pay for was washing laundry. It paid, but it didn't pay much. She needed a warm winter coat badly, and Dempsey's shoes would need resoling in another month. It was hard to see how she could turn down an offer that paid twenty dollars a show.

"You did say plus expenses, didn't you?" she asked.

"Plus expenses—of course," the man said.

Ruby didn't want to leave her house, but it was money. Her ma and pa didn't have a cent to spare, and times were getting worse and worse. More than half the folks that lived around the Hardgraveses had long since lost their farms to the bank—Ruby didn't want to have to end up living on the road, like so many other families had wound up doing. Even her aunt and uncle and their six kids had given up on Oklahoma and headed out west to California, where folks said it was always warm, and there was lots of food, and plenty of work. But Ruby didn't think she could stand being that far away from home, no matter how hard the times got.

Bradley and Bessie Floyd might take them in, but Ruby didn't want to impose on them, and wouldn't unless she was desperate. In her heart was the wish that Charley would one day open the front door and step back into their lives, so she wouldn't have to say yes to the tall man with the dandruffy hair, who kept blowing smoke out of his nose. To be fair, though, it wasn't Mr. Raczkowski's dandruff, or his smoking, that made her hesitate—it was the fear of having to get up before an audience of total strangers and talk about her and Charley's life together.

"Of course, we'd advance you a little—it's just about Christmas," Louie Raczkowski said. He could see that the little lady was wavering; with a bit more encouragement, she might say yes. She was a beautiful young woman, and the wife of Public Enemy Number Two. Louie thought she might prove a big draw in little towns in the red hill country where no performers of any consequence ever showed up. Mrs. Floyd and her boy might prove a smash.

"What would you say to twenty-five dollars, payable now?" Louie said, sucking on his cigarette again. "You think about it over Christmas, and if you decide to try it, we'll start the shows around the first of the year."

"I'll try it—I guess," Ruby said. Dempsey was pining for boxing gloves for Christmas, and if he didn't get them he was going to be mighty disappointed. Almost anything would be better than disappointing her son on Christmas Day.

"I hope I do good. I'd hate to disappoint you," she added.

"Oh, you won't disappoint me, Mrs. Floyd," Louie said. "We'll try to book the first show around Sallisaw, or somewhere close by. I expect we'll pack the house."

Louie Raczkowski sat down at her kitchen table, unscrewed the top from a leaky old fountain pen, and carefully wrote Ruby a check for twenty-five dollars.

"Could you give me your dress size, please?" he asked. "And maybe your shoe size. I'll drop by right after Christmas with some of the squaw costumes, so you can try them on."

When Louie Raczkowski left, Dempsey was out in the front yard mowing down pretend G-men with a pretend machine gun made from part of a crutch he and his little buddies had found in the dump.

"Did my mama say yes?" Dempsey asked, running over.

"You bet she did," Louie said. "You and her will be up on that stage real soon."

He gave Dempsey two peppermint jawbreakers as he left.

350

6

Dempsey had managed to stay awake two hours later than usual on Christmas Eve, hoping to see Santa Claus, but fatigue finally overcame him, and he fell asleep on the floor in front of the little tree. Ruby carried him back to his room, and put him to bed. Dempsey wasn't as easy to pick up as he used to be. Once or twice, lifting him when he was in a dead sleep, Ruby put a catch in her back.

She was wrapping the boxing gloves, when there was a knock on the door. She thought it was probably her sister, Pauline— she had said she'd drop by with a little present for Dempsey.

"Ho, ho, ho," Charley said, when Ruby opened the door. He had on a big white beard, and a red Santa Claus hat. "Is Dempsey still up?"

Ruby felt the shock she always felt when she opened the door and saw Charley. Her blood stopped for a moment, and then started racing so fast through her veins that she thought she might faint. She wasn't moving, but she knew if she did, she would stumble over her own feet.

"Did anybody follow you?" she asked, feeling suddenly afraid.

"Just Donder and Blitzen," Charley said, before he kissed her. His cheeks were cold, but Ruby didn't care. She held onto him tight, feeling light-headed.

After he had warmed himself and kissed Ruby a bunch of times, he went back out to his car, and started carrying in presents. He wouldn't let Ruby help, either. The whole car appeared to be full of gifts. When Charley finally got them all in the house, they seemed to fill the entire room where the little tree was set up. Charley went in and looked at the sleeping Dempsey. It was all Ruby could do to prevail upon him not to wake him.

"But I want him to see my Santa Claus outfit," Charley protested.

351

"He can see it in the morning, early," Ruby promised. "It's like a miracle that you came home for Christmas."

"I rode the rails from K.C. to Wichita," Charley said. "I been here more than two weeks. I've been keepin' an eye on the house, making sure the law didn't come by and pay you a visit."

Then they heard footsteps, and Dempsey appeared. "I thought I heard Daddy," he said when he saw the Santa Claus beard on the face of a man who otherwise looked just like his daddy.

"Ho, ho, ho, little boy," Charley said. "Have you been good all year?"

Dempsey was sleepy, and confused—he began to cry a little from the confusion. He remembered wetting the bed once or twice; he didn't know whether that counted as being bad or not. Also, he felt uncertain about the man with the beard. He wanted him to be Santa Claus, but even more, he wanted him to be his daddy.

When Charley saw Dempsey crying, he immediately took off the beard and hugged his son. Dempsey sobbed for a minute; then he noticed the huge heap of presents piled in the room.

"Where'd all those presents come from?" he asked.

"Well, Daddy brought them," Ruby said. "Maybe he's been up at the North Pole all this time, visiting Santa Claus."

"The North Pole?" Dempsey said, his eyes widening. "Did you see the elves?"

"You bet, and I rode a reindeer," Charley said. "Its horns were as wide as I am tall. An Eskimo caught it for me. It was a flying reindeer, too. I followed old Santa right down through the sky."

Dempsey thought his father might be pulling his leg. But the packages piled up in the room looked real. The packages interested him more than anything happening at the North Pole.

"Can I open these packages now?" he asked.

"It's more fitting to open them in the morning," Ruby said. "In the morning is Christmas."

"Can't I open just one?" Dempsey asked.

"Aw, let him, honey," Charley said. "Nobody's gonna care if he opens one."

After some deliberation, Dempsey chose a long, skinny package. He tore into it wildly and came out with a .410 shotgun, a small double-barrel. Dempsey was so excited he could scarcely keep his feet on the floor. He began to race around the house, pointing the gun at everything—Charley had to take it away from him and explain that it was a real gun, not a toy gun; he was never supposed to load it inside a house, or point it at anything he didn't intend to shoot.

Ruby was shocked when she saw the gun—it took some of the lift off her mood. Charley noticed, and tried to get her back in the right humor by making her open one or two of her presents. The first one was a wonderful warm coat with a fur collar, the kind of coat Ruby had given up on ever being able to afford. Charley had brought a bottle of champagne, too. When Dempsey finally settled down and fell asleep, his shotgun in the bed beside him, Ruby helped Charley drink the bottle and forgot her little pique about the shotgun. She would just have to make strict rules about the .410.

"Hey, you didn't notice any shells for it, did you?" Charley said, when Ruby chided him mildly for giving Dempsey a dangerous weapon.

"No, but what good's a shotgun without shells?" she asked.

"No good—that's the point, honey," Charley told her. "He'll get the shells when he learns how to handle it safe."

"Okay," Ruby said. If there was one thing she didn't want to do, it was quarrel with Charley on Christmas Eve. She had been making up scenes in her mind for days, scenes in which Charley showed up and brought Dempsey wonderful presents. She imagined they had a nice Christmas dinner together and enjoyed the holiday, just like a normal family. She knew they weren't a normal family, but she kept hoping anyway. She wished Dempsey could have just one Christmas like other kids —with a tree, and presents, and his father and mother both at home. She had wanted that for Dempsey so bad, she could taste it. And now it was more than just a pipe dream.

When it was all still just weary hopes, Ruby had gone to the jewelry store and had the old jeweler order her a cameo ring with her likeness and Dempsey's on it. She spent twelve dollars on the ring, nearly half her advance money from the road show.

She meant to give it to Charley the next time she saw him. Even if it wasn't at Christmas, it could still be her Christmas present to her husband, late or not.

Ruby decided to wait till morning to give Charley the ring. She was a little drunk and so anxious to be with him in bed that she didn't want any more hesitating over presents. Part of her couldn't quite accept that Charley was actually there. She had hoped so much for it that it seemed impossible that hopes so deep could come true. Ruby didn't know if she would come to really believe it until they were in bed together and she was holding Charley in her arms. Sleeping in his arms, being able to hold him all night, listening to him breathing—that was all she needed for Christmas.

Ruby woke up early Christmas morning. In the night, she had become anxious about the cameo ring—what if it didn't fit? She wanted their Christmas to be perfect. She slipped downstairs in her gown, got the ring, crept back up the stairs, and slipped back into bed beside Charley, who was sound asleep and snoring lightly. Ruby pulled his hand out from under the covers, and carefully slipped the ring onto his ring finger. It went on without much pushing, but she was still worried. She turned on the bed light to check it. To her relief, it fit just fine—their Christmas *would* be perfect. She switched off the bed light.

There was just the faintest grey in the window, and a tint of red in the east. Ruby lay with her head on Charley's shoulder, watching his face while he slept. In his sleep, he looked so much like Dempsey—or Dempsey so much like him—that it brought a catch to her throat. A lock of his hair hung over his forehead, just as Dempsey's forelock hung over his small forehead. Charley's breath smelled of tobacco. He had smoked a cigar last night while they were having drinks. Charley had a very small wen on one of his eyelids, and as soon as the light improved, Ruby bent close and checked it carefully, to assure herself that it wasn't getting larger. His whiskers grew quick; he had stubble on his chin. Ruby rubbed it with a finger—it felt like sandpaper.

"You could give me a shave as a Christmas present," Charley suggested, his voice still heavy with sleep. He managed to open one eye.

354

"I ain't a barber, what if I cut you?" Ruby asked. "Besides, I already got you a present. It's on your hand."

Charley had to blink a few times and rub sleep out of his eyes before he could get a good look at the cameo ring.

"Turn on the bed light," he said, holding up his hand in surprise. "I got to have a good look at this. I never expected a present this good."

"Do you like it?" Ruby asked, nervous. Charley had such good taste, and was so finicky about every detail of his suits and his shirts, that she didn't know if the ring would be up to his standards.

"Aw, honey . . ." Charley said softly, taking the ring off and turning it over carefully. "How'd you ever afford to get me a ring this nice?"

"Do you like it, Charley?" she asked. "I wanted you to have something to help you remember me and Dempsey, when you can't be with us."

Charley's face looked grave. "I could never forget you and Dempsey, honey," he said, in a low voice. "Lots of times, you and Dempsey are pretty much all I remember. Sometimes I think about you two all day, and most of the night, too."

"I guess this is the best Christmas ever, then," Ruby said, settling into the crook of his shoulder. "It's the best for me, I get to have both my men at home."

Charley still had the serious expression, though. He was looking past her, out the window. Ruby hadn't asked him when he had to leave. Maybe he couldn't even stay through Christmas Day. Maybe she wouldn't get to have both her men at home—at least not for all day.

"I wonder if it's gonna snow?" he asked, after a little while. "If it snows, I might take Dempsey rabbit hunting with his new shotgun."

Ruby relaxed a little then—maybe he would stay the day. While she was watching him look out the window, Charley turned and slipped a hand under her gown, onto her warm breast. He cocked an eye at the door that led to Dempsey's room.

"I wonder how long before that punkin'll be up?" Charley asked. "Do you think we got the time, honey?"

Ruby turned toward him, and put her hand on his cheek. "It's Christmas morning, Charley—let's take the time," she said.

7

The first time Dempsey fired the .410 shotgun, the stock whacked him in the shoulder, causing him to fall back a step.

"I told you to hold it tight," Charley said. "You didn't hold it tight enough—that's why you got kicked."

Dempsey had fired at an empty beer bottle, which his father set on top of a post. There it was, still on the post. They were walking down a snowy country road, looking for rabbits. But no rabbits appeared, and Dempsey wanted to shoot his new gun so badly that his father finally gave in.

"I missed," Dempsey said, keenly disappointed. He had not expected to miss; in the movies, people almost never missed.

"You still got the second barrel," Charley told him. "Step a little closer to the post, and lower your head a little more. Look right down the barrel."

Dempsey edged closer, until he was only about five feet from the post.

"That's close enough," Charley said. "If you hit it from any closer, you might get glass in your eye."

He was beginning to question the wisdom of buying the boy a shotgun. A lot of things could go wrong with a shotgun, even a little .410. But it was too late to backtrack—Dempsey was as proud of the gun as could be. He got plenty of other Christmas presents: boxing gloves, a punching bag, a sled, a toy train, and a new bridle for Chuck, his pony. But those things were just normal presents. The shotgun was magic. Dempsey would hardly stop holding it long enough to play with his other toys, or to eat his Christmas dinner, either.

At five feet, Dempsey blasted the beer bottle. Glass flew everywhere, but none went in his eyes.

"I hit it!" Dempsey said. In his excitement, he didn't notice that the shotgun had whacked him solidly in the shoulder again.

"You sure did, bud," Charley said. "You got the makings of a dead shot. The cottontails and jackrabbits had better watch out now."

The fields of corn stubble where they hunted had a thin coverlet of snow. Dempsey shot several times at cottontails, and once at a racing jackrabbit, but the pellets merely kicked up snow. A hawk soared and dipped over the cornfield, a dark spot against the gloomy sky. Dempsey's ears got numb, and his feet were like icy stumps, but he kept plodding along, his shotgun at the ready, with the safety on—just as his father had instructed.

As the two of them were walking back to the car, Charley spotted a small covey of quail under a red haw bush. The birds were bunched under the skinny bush, and they were well within range.

"Here's your chance, son," Charley whispered, pointing at the covey. "Just slip the safety off, and let 'em have it."

"But Daddy, there's so many—which one do I shoot?" Dempsey asked.

"Shoot right into the middle of them—this is pot hunting we're doing," Charley said. "I'd love a couple of fat quail for breakfast."

Dempsey squinted down the barrel and tried to pull the trigger, but the trigger wouldn't pull.

"You forgot to take the safety off," his daddy said.

Dempsey unfastened the safety. The quail began to walk through the corn stubble, more or less in a line.

"Daddy, they're getting away . . . what do I do?" Dempsey asked.

"If I was you, I'd shoot," Charley said.

Dempsey pointed the shotgun at the line of small birds, and pulled the trigger. Most of the birds flew away, filling the air with their loud buzz. But two birds lay on the snow. One kicked a little; the other lay still.

"You got 'em!" Charley said. "Good shot, son!"

The dead quail had soft, brown feathers, with grey and white at their breasts. One had a tiny bead of deep red blood by its eyelid. The quail that had been kicking slowly stopped kicking; it lay on its back, its thin feet in the air. Dempsey approached them hesitantly.

"Pick 'em up, son," Charley said. "They're your birds. Wait'll Mama sees them."

Dempsey wasn't sure he wanted to pick up the two birds. He wasn't sure he wanted his mother to see them, either. Their eyelids hid their eyes; the little bead of blood by the eyelid of the one bird made Dempsey wish he hadn't done it.

"They were walking in the snow with their friends," he said. "It makes me sad that they're dead.

"I want to go home," he added, after a moment.

Charley picked up the quail. To Dempsey's horror, he pulled their heads off, then pitched the heads out into the snow.

"No, I don't want to take them—put their heads back on, Daddy!" Dempsey said, his voice shaking.

Charley put his hand on the boy's shoulder.

"We didn't just kill them to kill them, son," he said. "We killed them to eat. They'll keep better with their heads off."

"I don't want to eat them," Dempsey insisted. "I don't want to take them home."

"Nope, we're gonna eat them—that's the point of hunting," Charley explained. "When you eat a chicken, somebody's had to kill it first. When you eat a beefsteak, somebody had to kill a cow."

"I still don't want to," Dempsey said, looking down at the ground.

"Let me carry the gun till we get to the road," Charley said, taking the shotgun from Dempsey. "You got one for you, and one for Mama. Maybe I can get one for me."

A minute later, he did. There was a sudden whirr of brown wings. A quail was just curving over the fence, when his father shot it. The whirr stopped; the quail fell like a softball. After helping Dempsey over the fence, and reminding him how important it was to unload the shotgun before crossing a fence with it, Charley found the third quail and popped its head off.

358

That night, Dempsey didn't sleep with his shotgun, as he had on Christmas Eve.

He asked his mother to put it in the closet.

8

"I'd rather you brought us a side of beef, or a shoat we could butcher," Bob Birdwell said, looking at the pile of Christmas presents Charley had brought for her and the three kids.

"We might get through the winter, if we had a side of beef," she added. Her face was thinner since the last time Charley had seen her.

The kids didn't feel that way. They were ripping into the packages like little coons, scattering wrapping paper all over the kitchen floor, their eyes bright as buttons. But their mother's eyes were dull and sad.

"Good Lord, I had no idea you was so low on cash," Charley said. There was nothing at all to eat in the Birdwell house, except a sack of dried beans and a little cornmeal. There wasn't even any coffee.

"Where would I get cash?" Bob asked. "George gave me fifteen dollars when he left on his last trip. Fifteen dollars don't last forever."

All the kids had coughs and snotty noses. Bob was shivering in a threadbare robe; the house was ice-cold.

"Is the stove broke?" Charley asked. "I've been in icehouses that wasn't this chilly."

"The stove works, but the axe broke," Bob informed him. "All I got left to chop firewood with is the hatchet. I get tired of choppin' wood with a hatchet."

Charley went outside and chopped an armful of firewood with the old hatchet. When he got the stove going and the kitchen warm, he drove eight miles to a general store in Lawton, bought a new axe, and filled the back seat of the car with foodstuffs. The old man who owned the store did some butchering, and so Charley arranged for a side of beef and a fat shoat to be delivered to the Birdwell smokehouse as soon as possible.

He unloaded the groceries, sharpened the new axe, and chopped two weeks' worth of firewood, while Bob sat in her kitchen drinking a bourbon toddy Charley had fixed for her. The toddy had lots of molasses in it; he had always heard that molasses and bourbon were good for coughs—and Bob had a nasty cough. The children were fighting over the toys Charley had brought. Bob drank toddy until she was drunk, but her spirits didn't improve much that Charley could tell.

"You got to snap out of it," Charley told her. "You got three tykes to look after, Bob—you need to do a better job of lookin' after yourself."

"Shove off, bud," Bob said. Two red spots showed in her thin cheeks. "Don't sit there in your pretty suit tellin' me what I need to do."

"Why, it was just a suggestion," Charley said—he was taken aback by Bob's sudden belligerence.

"No it wasn't, it was a goddamn lecture," Bob said. "I won't tolerate bein' lectured, Charley—I lost my man—if I had my way, I would've died when George died."

"I tried to talk him out of robbin' that nigger bank," Charley said. "I knew the minute we got to town that it was a mistake."

"I wasn't talkin' about that," Bob informed him. "Listen to what I'm sayin', or get out: I don't need your damn charity. I'd rather die, but I can't. And my kids are doin' fair—they got snotty noses, but they ain't starved, and they ain't homeless. Sometimes fair's just the best a person can do."

Bob took a long swig from her toddy.

"I lost my man—don't ask me to get over it overnight," she added.

Charley knew Bob loved George, but he hadn't expected her to be quite so affected. She had seemed to have her own life, to pay only minimal attention to George in his frequent comings and goings—but now Charley realized that he'd been mistaken.

"How do you think Ruby's gonna feel when they finally shoot you down?" Bob asked Charley, the red anger spots still on her cheeks. "You don't think about her no more than George thought about me."

"That's not true, Bob," Charley said. "I think about Ruby a lot."

But Bob Birdwell wouldn't relent.

"Maybe you're better than George was about leavin' grocery money, I don't know," she said. "George had a tight streak. He was only loose with money if he was spendin' it on himself."

Charley didn't know what to say. When he had arrived home on Christmas Eve, Ruby hadn't had much more food in her cabinet than he'd found at the Birdwell house. She had coffee, and she'd bought some little cupcakes with reindeer on them for Christmas, but Ruby could have used a side of beef and a fat shoat, too.

"You probably think about how nice it would be to come home and screw her," Bob told him. "George liked to show up when he knew I'd be at my wit's end, so I'd be more interested in screwin' than naggin'—he never gave a thought to how I'd feel the day they brought him home dead."

"I expect I better mosey on," Charley said, standing up.

"Yeah—mosey on," Bob said. "George didn't like hearin' the truth, and neither do you. I never cared about no man except George. I doubt Ruby's ever cared about any man except you. When they shoot you down, it'll be over for her—just like it's over for me."

"Hey, now," Charley said—he was starting to feel awkward. "Ruby divorced me and married a baker while I was in the pen —if I was to die, I expect she'd just go marry him again."

Bob shrugged a bony shoulder.

"She can marry till she's blue in the face," Bob said. "I expect I'll bed down with somebody sooner or later myself. But I could bed down with every stiff in this county, and not miss George one bit less."

Then she swigged down the last of her bourbon toddy, got

up, and fixed herself another. Charley put on his overcoat while she stirred in the molasses.

"I ordered you a side of beef and some pork," he said, as he put on his hat. "The butcher will be out with it next week."

"You bandits ought to leave nice women alone—it'd be kinder if you'd just run with your whores," Bob said bitterly, as Charley headed out the door.

9

Charley couldn't get Bob Birdwell's bitter words out of his mind. He knew he should leave Oklahoma and go north, as far and as fast as he could. Sooner or later he'd be spotted, if he hadn't been already. Bob had given him a letter from Beulah when he'd arrived at the Birdwell house; Beulah, Rose, and Richetti were holed up in Cincinnati, Ohio, waiting for him to join them.

Yet Charley kept lingering, allowing himself just one more night in which to make a spaghetti supper, or cook a couple of vinegar pies for Dempsey. His nights with Ruby were ardent —and sometimes his afternoons, as well. The knowledge that Dempsey would be showing up from school at any moment seemed to inflame them.

Ruby was just as torn. She knew Charley should go, but she didn't want him to. Every time he had left before, she'd had to work harder and harder to persuade herself that she and Dempsey would ever see him again alive. In the night, fear would come on her so strong sometimes that all she could do was cling to him, sleepless and hopeless, listening to him snore.

Another problem was money. After seeing what a pass Bob

Birdwell had come to, and realizing that Ruby had not been much better off, Charley felt uneasy about going away. The job in Wichita had yielded almost fifteen hundred, but he had spent almost a thousand of it on a car and on Christmas. He knew when he finally left that he wouldn't be seeing Ruby and Dempsey again for a while. They would need cash to help them live; he would need cash to stay on the run.

"What?" Ruby asked one night, realizing that Charley was awake.

"Nothing—go back to sleep," Charley said.

"You're as wide awake as I am," Ruby said.

Charley didn't deny it.

"Charley? Are you getting ready to leave?" she asked. That fear was in her mind every night now: in the morning, Charley would leave.

"I'm too broke to leave," Charley told her.

Neither one of them spoke after that.

"Folks think that bank robbery is the road to riches, but it ain't," he added, after a time.

"But Charley . . . you can't stay much longer," Ruby said. She felt a moment of panic—Charley had told her that he'd hang if they caught him. He had tried twice already to make a deal with the Bureau, but J. Edgar Hoover hadn't responded. Ruby didn't hate hardly anybody, but she hated Mr. Hoover— it made her furious that Charley was Number Two on the Public Enemies list. Charley wasn't the public's enemy; he wasn't anybody's enemy.

"I know I can't stay," Charley said. "I got to pull one more job before I leave, though."

Ruby didn't say anything, but her heart started beating so fast, she was afraid Charley would feel it and know how scared she was. All the banks had armed guards in them now, even little small-town banks. What if they shot Charley down? What if he died in a pool of his own blood, as George Birdwell had? What would it do to Dempsey? What would it do to her?

"I want to go with you, Charley," Ruby said, suddenly.

"Go with me where?" he asked.

"To pull the job," Ruby said. "I want to be some help, if I can."

Charley was so startled, he sat straight up in bed.

"Don't you even think it, Ruby!" he said. "You think for a minute I'd let you walk into a bank and take the chance of gettin' killed? Who'd raise Dempsey if that happened?"

"They wouldn't shoot a woman," Ruby ventured.

Charley lay back down, but the thought of Ruby pulling a bank job disturbed him so, he knew he would be a long time getting to sleep.

"They shot Bonnie Parker," he reminded her. "Bonnie was a woman . . .

"Don't you be talking like that. Not to me!" he demanded, a little later. "Suppose they caught you and stuck you in the pen? You got Dempsey to think of. Just don't be talking like that, Ruby—not to me."

Ruby didn't answer. Charley's tone was so harsh that she had to stifle a sob. She knew it was wrong to say what she'd said; she knew she had to think about Dempsey. But she wanted so badly to be with Charley a little longer that the words got away from her. She even had moments when she felt so scared that it almost seemed better if they were all dead—maybe they could be together, with Jesus, in heaven. It seemed to her a better prospect than just month after month of her and Dempsey being alone, worrying every night that Charley might be in trouble, or hurt, or even dying. She didn't know if she could take many more months of worrying; she didn't know what she might do.

Charley would be thirty years old in less than a month. Ruby herself would soon be twenty-seven; she wondered if life might get less complicated as they got older. She had her doubts, though. It seemed to Ruby that life had only gotten harder and harder as the years passed. It had begun to feel as if she and Charley were on a runaway train—a train traveling so fast that they might never be able to stop it and get off. If she thought about it too long, her stomach would start to hurt. She needed to stop thinking, even if it was only for a little while.

She touched Charley, and tried to get him to touch her. But he wouldn't—he was silent, and remote.

Ruby finally rolled away from him, and went to sleep on her side of the bed.

10

Bob Birdwell kept flinging gasoline on the Plymouth, trying to get it to burn. Ruby and Bessie stood by in the ditch, feeling helpless. The snow in the stubbly ditch froze their feet.

"Goddamn this piss-ant car!" Bob snapped. "Why won't it burn?"

"Don't throw no more gasoline on it," Bessie cautioned. "You might catch fire yourself."

"I'm mad enough to catch fire without a match," Bob said. "Why'd he go off and leave us the job of burnin' his car? It's his car—if he was so sure he wanted it burnt, why didn't he burn it himself?"

"Charley was afraid the law would show up," Ruby said. Bob's willingness to criticize Charley annoyed her. She didn't like to hear anybody criticize her family. Even though she and Charley were divorced, she still considered him her family.

"The law will show up, all right," Bob agreed. "They'll come and find three women from Oklahoma standing in the snow like idiots, tryin' to burn up an automobile and makin' a poor job of it, too.

"It's the kind of dumb plan George would come up with," she added. "George would always be drunk, at least that's an excuse. I don't know what excuse Charley Floyd thinks he could make for himself."

To make matters worse, it was drizzling and freezing. The narrow road back up to Oklahoma would be slick as glass. Ruby was beginning to be sorry she had come on the job and that she had persuaded Bessie Floyd to come, too. Of course, Bessie only did it out of boredom; anything to escape her kids for a few hours seemed good to Bessie, even bank robbery in Texas. Not that Charley had let them get anywhere near the bank, or even the town, the name of which was Crum. He made Bob Birdwell drop him off at the Crum Grocery and hurry on back to the crossroads where they were attempting to burn the car.

"Why the grocery store?" Bessie asked. She had never been on a criminal adventure before, and was curious about the whys and wherefores.

"Because it's cold," Charley said. "The easiest place to steal a vehicle is outside a grocery store on a cold day. Most folks in these small towns don't bother to turn off the motor—they'd rather the car stayed warm."

He must have had his technique down pat, because Bob had barely got back to the crossroads when Charley came speeding up behind her, having already robbed the bank and made his getaway. Ruby and Bessie had been left to huddle in a little shack the locals had built as shelter for kids who had to stand in the weather and wait for the school bus. There was no stove in the shack. Ruby was half frozen, and would have been altogether frozen if she hadn't been so mad at Charley for taking Bob Birdwell to town with him, instead of taking her.

Charley had explained that it was because Bob was the most reliable driver, an explanation which did nothing to dilute Ruby's anger. How did he know whether Bob was a reliable driver or not? Ruby was jealous—she couldn't help it.

Charley only stopped for a minute to exchange the stolen getaway car for the automobile he had bought in Wichita. He had driven it to the crossroads himself. Bob and Bessie had come down in the Birdwell flivver.

"Burn this car, that's why we brought the extra gasoline," he instructed. Then he gave Ruby the name of a hotel in Lawton where she was to meet him the next night.

"Hey, where's our money?" Bob asked, as Charley started to drive away.

"I can't leave this money with you—it's too fresh," Charley said. "If the law was to come along and find you, you'd all end up in the slammer."

"Yeah, and if the law comes and catches us burnin' this jalopy, we'll all be in the stir without a cent," Bob retorted.

Charley gave them thirty dollars and drove off, throwing up a spume of snow in his wake.

He was barely out of sight before a black car came speeding up from the direction of Texas. The low bluffs of the Red River were visible to the south, only three miles away.

"I bet that's the Texas Rangers," Bob Birdwell said. She threw the empty gasoline tin into the back seat of the stolen Plymouth. The seats were smoldering and smoking, but most of the car was scarcely singed. A tiny flame licked out from under the hood.

"It can't be Texas Rangers because this ain't Texas," Bessie said. "Texas Rangers got no right to be in Oklahoma, unless they're visitin' relatives or somethin'."

"Let's throw snowballs at the Plymouth," Ruby suggested. "Let's pretend we're trying to put the fire out, instead of trying to start it."

"You and Bessie can, I ain't," Bob informed them. "I wasted a lot of gasoline tryin' to burn it, why would I want to put it out?"

"To fool the laws from Texas," Bessie reminded her.

"If Charley had left us the Tommy gun, we wouldn't have to fool 'em," Bob said, crossing her arms on her chest in anger. "We could just mow 'em down."

A little man in a blue suit and bow tie jumped out of the police car before it even stopped—he promptly ran right in front of the car, which skidded on the slick road and almost teetered into the ditch, trying to miss the little man in the bow tie. Then the little man lost his footing, and landed hard on his back. He had a frantic look about him. While still on his back, he began to yell at two lanky Texas Rangers who got out of the police car.

"That's it, that's the getaway car!" he yelled. "Hurry up and get the money out of it before it burns!"

Ruby and Bessie had managed to scoop a certain amount of snow onto the Plymouth, but the little flame still licked out from under the hood, and the back seat was still smoldering, making curls of smoke which streamed out of the back window and on up into the grey, drizzly sky.

The little man in the bow tie turned out to be the manager of the bank Charley had just robbed—the First State Bank of Crum, Texas. The two Rangers gingerly searched the smoking car and found nothing, except a box of candy the owner of the car had purchased to give to his wife on their anniversary. Charley had taken the keys to the stolen Plymouth with him; the Rangers were forced to use a tire iron to pry the trunk open.

The trunk contained a spare tire, a pair of wire cutters, and two five-gallon jugs of moonshine. It did not contain even a nickel in cash, a fact which sent the bank manager spiraling into panic.

"Keep looking, men—it's got to be there," the bank manager said. "He took over two thousand dollars, the bastard."

Ruby wanted to smack him for calling Charley a bastard, but she kept heaping snow on the smoldering car, to impress the Texas Rangers. They were both hunching their shoulders against the cold drizzle. They had been having coffee when the alarm sounded; both were in their shirtsleeves.

"Keep looking!" the bank manager insisted, when the two Rangers stopped searching.

"Aw, can it!" the taller of the Rangers said. "We looked—it ain't in the car."

"Then where is it?" the manager asked. "It's got to be some-where."

"It was a man robbed your bank, is that right, sir?" the second Ranger asked.

"Of course it was a man who robbed my bank," the manager retorted.

"Well, do you see him in this crowd?" the first Ranger inquired, winking at Bessie.

"No, I don't see him here, there's only women here," the bank manager said. "I'd like to know where they came from."

"Hey, Sam, be a little more polite," Bob Birdwell said. "We didn't come from nowhere—we *live* here. What I wanna know is, what business do you got bringin' these Texas laws onto Oklahoma soil? Governor Murray won't appreciate it."

"Shut up, lady, this is serious," the bank manager said. "We're trying to get back two thousand dollars that was taken from our bank today—it was in that car right there."

"It was, but it ain't at the moment," the taller Ranger said. "My guess is, the bank robber took it with him, which would only be smart. Why go to the trouble of robbin' a bank, if all you intend is to burn up the money? Why not just set the bank on fire and burn up *all* the money?"

"Ask them," the manager said, pointing at the women. "They're here, they must have seen which way he went."

"He went that way," Bessie said immediately, pointing down the road toward Texas.

Ruby was shocked that her sister-in-law could lie so easily. Of course, Charley had gone in the opposite direction.

"Then why didn't we pass him on the way up?" the bank manager inquired.

"That's 'cause he went through the pasture and turned west," Bessie assured them. "There must be a feed road down south a ways. We seen him open a gate and go west."

"Oops, damn," the second Ranger said. "We did pass a gate, Lem."

"If he's south of here in a pasture, I expect we got him," Lemuel, the taller of the Rangers, said. "Most of them little feed roads just peter out somewheres in a pasture. He'll have to come back out the way he went in, most likely, unless he decides to sit out there and freeze."

"Why, this hussy's lying," the little man with the bow tie said. "I don't believe he went in any pasture. She's probably his girlfriend."

Again, Ruby wanted to smack the nervous little man. The thought that Charley would have his own sister-in-law for a girlfriend was an insult. Ruby realized the bank manager didn't know Bessie was Charley's sister-in-law; he didn't even know that it was Charley who robbed his bank. But the mention of Charley and girlfriends was infuriating to her anyway, particularly with Bob Birdwell standing there—it was all Ruby could do to keep her hand from flying up and popping the little man with the red face and the bow tie.

The Texas Rangers looked up the long, slick road where Charley had gone. The bank manager in the bow tie was slipping and sliding on the icy road, trying to peek into the burning car.

"You sure my money ain't under the seat?" he asked.

"No, but you're welcome to look for yourself. You might get your eyebrows singed, though," the younger Ranger said.

"You laws from Texas need to scat back down across that river," Bob Birdwell reminded them. "This ain't Texas. Governor Murray's a personal friend of mine, and he's gonna raise the roof when he hears you two invaded Oklahoma territory."

369

"We didn't exactly invade it," Lem corrected. "We just kinda skidded this far on a slick road."

"Alfalfa Bill might not see it that way," Bob said, giving them a steely look.

"She's got a point, Lem," the other Ranger said. "We was in hot pursuit, which is one thing—the pursuit's kinda cooled off, due to this drizzle."

"No it's not, he's still got my money. We have to keep after him," the bank manager insisted. "It's two thousand dollars—I'll lose my job!"

"This here's interstate crime," Lem said. "I expect this lady's right. Governor Murray wouldn't appreciate us driftin' around up here. It's Mr. Hoover's job. The Bureau and the G-men will get him."

"Yeah, but he'll spend my money before they can get it back," the bank manager said.

"Are you guys gonna stand there jawin', or are you gonna leave our state?" Bob demanded.

"Arrest her, she's a moll! They're all molls!" the little man demanded, but the Texas Rangers made no attempts to comply. They even tipped their hats to the three women before they drove back down the road to Texas.

On the way home, Ruby hardly said a word. Despite herself, she couldn't stop thinking about Charley and Bob Birdwell. She tried her best, when Charley was gone, never to imagine him with other women. When it was night and she was lonely in bed, wondering where Charley was, she tried to walk her mind way around the thought that he might be in another bed somewhere, with another woman. Sometimes she was successful; sometimes she wasn't. Now, she could hardly look at Bob's short, frizzy hair without having bad thoughts. Bob had skinny legs, too, and Charley had always been keen on women with skinny legs. When he and Ruby first dated, she was so young and skinny that he said her legs were like a roadrunner's. In those days, whenever he grabbed her, he'd exclaim, "Ha, I caught a roadrunner!"

The road grew slicker as the day faded and the drizzle began to freeze. Ruby thought they would never get back to Bessie's

370

house. Bob and Bessie chattered, but Ruby didn't join in the conversation.

Despite herself, she couldn't stop thinking about Charley, and how much he liked women with skinny legs.

11

The old bus bumped into Lawton about eleven o'clock at night. There were only six passengers on it: two cowboys, three Indians, and Ruby. She was the only woman, which made her nervous. She was not used to traveling at night; that also made her nervous. It was still bitter cold, and she didn't really know where Charley would be. She just knew she was supposed to look for him in a cheap hotel near the bus station. He would be registered as Arthur Charles. Ruby had always heard that Lawton was rough—an oil town where the cops were hard on Indians.

The bus station was just one room, painted yellow. The floor was covered with spit and cigarette butts. Ruby needed to use the rest room, but when she got into the ladies' room, the smell nearly knocked her out. The toilet was broken, and turds floated in it like dead fish. Bad as she needed to go, Ruby couldn't bring herself to use it. Two roughnecks, drinking in a corner, looked at her when she came out.

"You're a good-lookin' squaw, come on over here and sit with us," one of the men said, with an insolent grin.

Ruby pulled the fur collar on her coat tight around her throat, and went out into the chilling wind. An Indian was lying drunk on the sidewalk, just a few feet from the door of the bus station.

He was an old man. Ruby thought she should probably drag him inside, so he wouldn't freeze, though the thought of going back into the room where the roughnecks sat drinking didn't please her. But when she tried to lift the old man, he suddenly pushed her away, struggled to his feet, and lurched off into the street.

There was a sign that said "Rooms" on a brick building only a block from the bus station, but it was one of the longest blocks Ruby had ever walked. The sidewalk was icy, and she was afraid she would fall. She was also afraid that Charley wouldn't be in the hotel; if he wasn't, the roughnecks might follow her and catch her. She was freezing, and she was worried about Dempsey, who had been running a fever when she left him with her sister. Much as she wanted to see Charley, she wanted even more to be back with Dempsey in their home. They didn't have much, but it was better than being on the street in Lawton, in the middle of the night, looking for a man that most of the cops in the country were looking for, too. It almost seemed to Ruby that there were two Charleys—the sweet one, who liked to come home and cook spaghetti and bake pies; and the restless one, who drove around robbing banks, being shot at, and hiding in cheap rooming houses. Ruby wished there could be some way for the second Charley to just sort of melt into the first Charley. But she knew there wasn't.

As she was about to turn into the rooming house, she looked up and glimpsed somebody peeking at her from behind a cracked window shade. She knew it must be Charley, and it was.

The hotel smelled musty; it was just a thirty-five-cent room. Charley looked scared when he let her in. Usually he took a devil-may-care attitude toward his predicament. But he had lost his reckless look, and now he seemed just plain scared.

"There's no heat—this radiator could make ice," Charley told her.

"I'm worn out, let's just get into bed," Ruby said. "I'll get you warm, honey."

The blanket on the bed was thin. They had to pile their coats on top of it to keep warm. When they made love, the coats slid off, and their feet stuck out from under the covers, freezing.

Ruby tried to be passionate for Charley, but it seemed like the chill had settled inside her. She did all she could, but her feet were freezing, and her fear wouldn't go away. Charley was upset. He was used to driving her just about crazy when they made love; if he didn't succeed, he was apt to be moody for hours.

"How come they don't give you no blankets in this hotel?" Ruby asked, rearranging the coats. "I'm sorry, my feet are freezing."

"I guess there's not much in this world you can really count on," he replied, with his pouty look.

"Oh, shut up, I said I was sorry. You got plenty to count on," Ruby said. His pitiful attitude made her want to slug him.

"Wives oughtn't to talk that way to their husbands," Charley said.

"Charley, don't be like this," Ruby said, impatient. "I come a long way, at night, just to see you."

"I know it's a poor bed," Charley admitted. "I was afraid to stay in any of the better places."

"Dempsey wanted to come, hon," Ruby told him. Talking about their child usually put him in a better humor. If she could raise his mood so they could feel happy for a moment—happy with the love they had—it would be worth all the effort it had taken her to get there.

"You did right not to bring him," Charley said. "A gang of G-men could bust in here any minute. I don't want Dempsey in the middle of a gunfight."

"Have you got any whiskey?" Ruby asked. "I can't seem to warm up on the outside. Maybe if we drank some, I could at least get warm on the inside."

Charley pulled a bottle out of the drawer in the bedside table. It was a full bottle, but it didn't stay full for long. Ruby raised up on an elbow and drank several long swallows. Then Charley drank some, and Ruby glugged some more.

A little later, the radiator began to sputter, and heat finally started coming out. Before long, the room had gone from being too cold to being too hot. It kept getting hotter and hotter, until it felt like they were in an oven. They kicked the coats off the bed, and then the covers, too.

"I guess you don't get perfection for thirty-five cents," Charley said.

"I gotta go north—it'll be even colder, up north," he added, after a minute.

"I wish there was another country we could go to and live," Ruby said. "I wish there was a country where we could live like a family, and be happy."

Charley didn't have an answer for that.

Now that she was warm, Ruby wanted to make love, but Charley showed no interest. When she touched him, he rolled away. Ruby felt rebuffed, and didn't try again. They lay beside one another all night, not touching, not talking, sleeping little.

In the morning, Charley gave Ruby half the money he had taken from the bank in Crum, Texas.

"I want you to give a hundred to Bessie, and a hundred to Bob," he told her. "You keep the rest, and be careful with it. If I don't get back, it'll get you through summer."

"Through summer?" Ruby asked, horrified. "That's six months, Charley!" Since he had come to get her and Dempsey in Coffeyville, the longest Charley had been away from them was two whole months. Now, he was talking about being gone for six months, or even more. A lot could happen in six months. Ruby didn't want to think about it.

"I got to go way north this time, Ruby. Just about every law in the country is after me now. I'll get back when I can, but it may not be for a while."

"You take the money to Bob," Ruby said. "Why are you giving her money, anyway?"

Charley looked at her solemnly. "George was my friend," he said. "Bob don't have a cent, and she helped burn the car."

"Then you take it to her—why should I have to do it?" Ruby asked.

"I ain't goin' that way . . . what's got into you?" Charley asked, a frown wrinkling his brow. "Just do as I say, and take the hundred to Bob."

"Maybe I will, and maybe I won't," Ruby said—she was remembering Bob's skinny legs.

"Hey, now. Behave yourself," Charley said, glaring. "Bob's got it coming—you give it to her, first chance you get."

374

Ruby didn't answer. She looked out the window at the cold, ugly street. The old man she had tried to save the night before was still lurching around, slipping now and then on patches of ice.

"Don't you like Bob . . . or what?" he asked.

"I don't know Bob," Ruby said. "She's your friend. I'll take the money to her, if that's what you want."

"It's what I want," he repeated.

She turned to him, and her expression made Charley's face sag.

"Ruby, let's don't fight," Charley said, fearful. "I didn't mean to get into no fight with you, honey."

It had been only a day and a night since she'd last seen him, but to Ruby, Charley looked as if he'd aged ten years.

"I don't feel like we're fightin', Charley." Ruby felt as cold inside as she had the night before. "I feel like we're dyin'."

Charley drove her to the bus station in silence. They exchanged a brief hug and a kiss.

Then Ruby caught the same bumpy old bus back to Sallisaw.

12

"You mean they stayed here—both of 'em?!" Ruby asked. For a second, she felt cold with shock; then she flushed with rage.

Bessie Floyd knew immediately that she had let slip information she should have kept to herself. It had never occurred to her that Ruby didn't know about Beulah and Rose staying at the farm while Beulah recovered from her head wound. She started out to complain that Brad was still in love with Rose Baird. But then she realized, from the look of puzzlement on Ruby's face, that she had never even heard of the Baird sisters.

"Ruby, I'm sorry," Bessie said. "I don't know what to say. I guess it never occurred to me that you didn't know about Beulah and Rose.

"Anyway, it's *my* husband that's in love with one of them," she added, hastily. "*Your* husband is in love with *you*."

When Bessie referred to Charley as Ruby's husband, it usually gave Ruby a good feeling—she liked the idea that even though they were divorced, folks still thought of them as married—as a family. But all of a sudden, it didn't feel good anymore to think of herself as Charley's wife—not when he had a girlfriend, and everyone knew it but her. She felt furious, jealous, embarrassed, all at once.

"That's mush, Bessie!" Ruby said. "He brings his whore here, and leaves her with his family for six months! I'll kill him myself the next time I see him, and save Mr. Hoover the trouble."

"Don't talk like that, Ruby," Bessie said, horrified. "It's bad luck."

But Ruby's rage was up; if she had been in her own kitchen, she would have broken everything in it. Her anxieties about Bob Birdwell and Charley were nothing—he had another woman that he thought enough of to board with his family for six whole months, long enough for Bradley Floyd to fall in love with the woman's little sister. It made Ruby fighting mad: her rage was so intense it made her feverish. It raced through her body, and made her face beet-red. But she had no way to express it. Charley wasn't there; she had no one to attack.

"Honey, it was when you was still with Lenny," Bessie reminded her. "Charley hadn't been out of the pen very long. He felt low as a dog. Then Beulah got shot in the head, in that job they pulled up in Ohio. She was wobbly on her feet for quite a while, so Charley sent her down to us, and Rose came along to take care of her."

"Yeah, and she ended up taking care of Brad!" Ruby snapped. "What are they, sluts? I don't see how you stood it, Bessie."

Bessie felt on the spot. Ruby was staring at her, her dark eyes blazing.

376

"No, but they were city girls, they were used to different ways," she said. "I think Rose took to Brad just because she was bored."

"I would have whacked her with a two-by-four," Ruby said. "I'll whack Charley with one, the next time I see him. I suppose he showed up here every few days, for a little visit."

"No, honey—he was just here twice," Bessie said.

"You were married to another man, remember?" she said again, hoping Ruby would cool off and take account of the circumstances.

"Whose fault was that?" Ruby said. "I had to live. I had to feed my child. I didn't ask Charley to leave me, I didn't tell him to start pulling bank jobs. When they sent him to the pen, I did my best. I just lost hope, finally. I would have gone back with Charley anytime. But he didn't hurry to my door, and now I know why."

"I bet Lenny still misses you," Bessie said. "He seemed like such a nice fella."

Ruby wanted her to shut up about Lenny. Nice fellow or not, Lenny was something she couldn't do anything about. It didn't alter the fact that she belonged with Charley Floyd. That Charley'd had a woman in his life for years named Beulah Baird might not affect that fact in the long run, if there was a long run, either. But it *would* affect the reception Charley got the next time he showed up at her door with a few presents, and a big grin on his face.

"I'll knock that grin right off his kisser!" she said, thinking out loud.

"I'm sorry, honey—I thought you knew," Bessie said, again. She knew that whatever she said would probably make matters worse, but she didn't know what else to do.

"If I'd have known, I'da come right down here, and run her off," Ruby said—she was imagining herself chasing Beulah Baird and her sister down the dirt lane that led from Bessie and Brad's, all the way to the highway.

"Wobbly on her feet or not," she added.

Later, though, when her feelings had settled down, she realized that her anger was selfish. Bessie was the one whose marriage had been harmed by the Baird sisters. Bessie's husband had fallen in love with one of them; probably, that explained why Bessie'd had such a lost look in her eyes the last few years.

"You could leave him. Let him go find the whore and see how long it lasts," Ruby suggested.

Bessie shook her head.

"Leave him, and live on what?" she asked. "I got kids I can barely keep fed as it is.

"He ain't a bad man," she added, thinking of her husband, who also had a lost look in his eyes, despite which he had continued to work hard and be a good father to their children.

"He's just susceptible to city girls. They got more stylish ways—at least, I reckon that's it."

Ruby got up to leave. She had to take Bob Birdwell the hundred dollars Charley had wanted her to have. She'd already given Bessie the money he had given her for Brad's family.

"I ought to keep my big mouth shut," Bessie said, as Ruby was getting into the flivver. "There's some things a person's better off not knowing."

"Speak for yourself. I want the truth," Ruby said. "I might not know what to do with it when I get it—but I want it."

"I hate to see you get so mad at Charley. He's just a man," Bessie said.

"He needs a better excuse than that," Ruby said. She felt annoyed with Bessie for not being more of a fighter. She tried to imagine what she would do to Charley if he had the gall to keep a woman he was in love with under *her* roof.

If the news Ruby had just received hadn't taken most of the sting out of any resentment she felt toward Bob Birdwell, the sight of the Birdwell farmhouse would have removed the sting anyway. There wasn't a blade of grass in the Birdwell yard—just dirt. Water came from a pump by the smokehouse. Bob was out pumping on it when Ruby drove up, but no water was running into the bucket.

"Needs new leathers, not to mention new sucker rods," Bob said, when she saw Ruby. Her hair had hay in it, and she had on muddy trousers. In fact, her trousers were mud-coated all the way to the knees.

378

"The sow tried to eat her babies, I had to wade into the slop and rescue 'em," Bob explained.

Just then, a trickle of water leaked out of the pump.

"I can piss faster than this well runs," Bob said. "Go on in the house and stand by the stove, it's chilly out here.

"The kids won't bite, but they may yell a little," she added.

The kids didn't yell at all. They stood timidly in a group, and stared at Ruby. They were all dressed in clothes that were just rags. Compared to these children, Dempsey dressed like a rich city boy.

"Hi, what's your names?" Ruby asked. The wood stove kept the kitchen warm, but the rest of the house was like ice. Three piglets slept in a basket by the stove.

"Speak up, she asked you a question," Bob said, coming in with the water bucket.

The children remained silent. They all had Bob's eyes, Ruby thought. She felt a little embarrassed by her own resentment. It was clear after even a few minutes in the bare, cold house that Bob Birdwell had enough to deal with—she obviously had little energy to spare for cavorting with other women's husbands.

In an attempt to break the ice with the Birdwell children, Ruby got out a little picture she carried of Dempsey on his pony, Chuck. She thought the children all looked skinny as rails. Dempsey was a butterball by comparison. It was the right move —all three children immediately crowded around, and pretty soon the two little girls were sitting on her lap.

"I rode a calf once," the little boy said. "We don't have no pony."

"You rode it two steps," his mother reminded him.

"No, Ma—five steps!" the boy insisted. His voice reminded Ruby of George Birdwell. She started to say as much to Bob, but caught herself at the last second. She didn't know if it was wise to mention George.

"You're welcome to stay for supper if you like mush," Bob said. "We're mostly a mush family, these days."

"You don't have to be tonight," Ruby said. "Charley gave me some money to leave with you. It's for helping with the last job."

"How much?" Bob asked.

"Two hundred," Ruby said, though Charley had only asked her to give them one hundred. Her resentment had disappeared completely. She took the bills out of her purse and handed them over. Bob counted the money quickly, and then stuck it in the pocket of her muddy trousers.

"At least he ain't tight, like George," Bob said. "Course, George wasn't tight with everybody."

"No, he wasn't," Ruby agreed. "He paid my hospital bill when I had pneumonia."

"Yeah, and left us eatin' mush," Bob said. "Charley Floyd left me money once before. He bought me a side of beef, too—if the butcher ever delivers it, we'll be fryin' steak every night."

Then she looked Ruby in the eye, a direct look that took Ruby slightly aback.

"Ol' Charley leads you a merry chase, don't he?" Bob said.

Ruby didn't know what to say, so she just shrugged.

"George had a whore, too," Bob informed her. "Had her for years. I think she died a week or two after George did."

"Did you hate her?" Ruby asked.

Bob shook her head. "Whores gotta live, too," she said. "I hated George, even though I loved him. He could have all the pussy he could handle, anytime he cared to come home— what'd he need a whore for?"

"Did you ever ask him?" Ruby asked.

"Sure, I asked him," Bob said. "The first time I asked, he lied. The second time I asked, he told me to mind my own business. I told him where he put his pecker *was* my business, and he popped me. After that, I kept my trap shut. I didn't have much choice."

"Charley said George talked about you all the time," Ruby told her. "Charley said he talked about you so much, he got tired of listening."

"I don't doubt it—talk's cheap," Bob said. "Any hard dick can make a baby, but hard dick sure can't raise one. George was a rover—I expect Charley is, too."

"He's got no choice but to rove," Ruby said. "Not now."

"If he's much like George, he'd rove anyway," Bob told her. "When I married George, I was young and foolish. I thought he'd stay home and help me put in a garden, and maybe raise a

380

few kids. We planted one garden, and George was off rodeoin' before the tomatoes got ripe.

"I never forgave him," she added. "I meant for us to pick those tomatoes together. Maybe that's why he took up with that whore. She was from town, I heard . . . she probably didn't care about growin' tomatoes together."

The look of disappointment on Bob Birdwell's face was so sharp, it scared Ruby—it made her want to leave, as fast as she could. But she couldn't bring herself to drive off and leave the lonely woman and the three ragged children in the cold, bare house. Every time she looked at Bob's kids, she felt that she and Dempsey were lucky in some ways. She needed a little relief, though. Maybe Bob's mood would pick up if she left for a while. So she did what Charley had done: drove to the little grocery store and bought groceries, including peppermint sticks for the children. The butcher, looking embarrassed, insisted on sticking the side of beef he owed the Birdwells in Ruby's trunk. It was huge; the trunk wouldn't close. It took all of Bob's and Ruby's strength to carry the meat into the smokehouse when she got it back to Bob's.

"There was supposed to be a pig, too, according to Charley," Bob said. "I ain't complainin', but if he bought it, I want the pig, too."

"The butcher said his truck was broke," Ruby told her. "He said he'd bring the pig soon as he got it fixed."

There was a bottle of gin in Ruby's car that Charley had overlooked when he left.

"I hope you don't mind gin," she told Bob, while they were frying some meat. "Charley drove off without it."

"Do you regret not going with him?" Bob asked her.

"Going with Charley? He wouldn't have taken me," Ruby said. "Charley's on the run. He's Public Enemy Number Two now."

"I regret not goin' with George. I should've insisted," Bob said. "If I'd been in Boley, at least I might have shot the son-of-a-bitch that killed my man."

The Birdwell kids ate their peppermint sticks before supper. Bob was finishing off the bottle of gin, when Ruby left to drive home to Dempsey.

13

"Go with me, Ma," Charley said. "We'll just stay a minute."

"I don't want to go to the graveyard with you, Charley," Mamie said. She was making him chicken and dumplings, and cutting salt pork into a pot of red beans. Charley sat at his mother's kitchen table, drinking his coffee out of a saucer.

"You go pay your respects if you want to, son," Mamie told him. "I paid my respects to your pa while he was alive. I'm not one for standing around graveyards."

"I got to be skedaddling north," Charley told her. "I came here against my better judgment."

"Why did you, son?" Mamie asked. He was neatly shaven, and wearing a suit and tie. Mamie could not quite get used to seeing him look so fancy. He had grown up in overalls, just like his brother Brad. So far as she knew, Bradley Floyd didn't even own a suit. They were very different men, Bradley and Charley; and yet, they'd had her for a mother and Walter Floyd for a father. Bradley was fair, plain, hardworking, and sad; Charley was dark, handsome, wild, and sad. Mamie could remember when both her boys had happy eyes.

"I just wanted to come home," Charley said. "Every once in a while I feel like comin' home. It's nice to sit in this kitchen and watch you cook. Nobody's cooking ever smells as good as yours, Ma, or tastes as good once it's done.

"I don't know when I'll get this pleasure again," he added. "It'll probably be a while before I can get back to see Ruby and Dempsey, either."

To Charley's surprise, Mamie had taken up pipe smoking in her old age. Lots of old mountain women in the Cookson Hills smoked corncob pipes, but Charley had never supposed his mother would acquire the habit.

"When'd you give in to tobacco?" he asked, as he was eating his chicken and dumplings, and soaking up red bean juice with several biscuits.

382

"It's somethin' to do while I'm worrying," Mamie informed him. "If I didn't have my chickens and my pipe, it'd get mighty lonesome around here. I been thinking of gettin' turkeys, and maybe a few guinea hens. If Bessie quits Bradley, her and me might go into the turkey business."

"Why would Bessie quit Brad?" Charley asked.

"Why is water wet, and dirt dry?" Mamie asked. "I don't know the answers to riddles of the human species. But if she does quit him, her and me might just do it—it'd be something to occupy us."

Charley lingered in the kitchen till dark fell. Mamie had nothing on hand to make a pie with, but she had some clabber and she sprinkled a little cinnamon on it for her son's dessert.

"You look wild as a bobcat, Charley," she said, when it was full dark. "Why don't you go out to the Rocky Mountains, or somewhere you ain't well known. You need a rest from all this runnin'."

"I'm well known everywhere, Ma—thanks to Mr. Hoover," Charley said. "I'll be better going north, where there's more people. I went out to the Rockies a few years back, and got arrested before I could walk three blocks to a hotel.

"Strangers stick out more there," he added. "I'll do better up in Cleveland or Chicago—somewhere that's full of people."

"Did you leave Ruby any money?" Mamie asked. "Times are so hard now, folks ain't sending out their laundry much. That's about the only work Ruby knows."

"I left her some cash," Charley said. "There's some people from Oklahoma City who've been after her to do a show. It might pay pretty good, if it works out."

"A show?" Mamie asked, surprised. "What could Ruby do in a show? She can barely sing a lick, as I recall."

"I don't think she'd have to do much singin'," Charley said. "They're thinkin' of calling it 'Crime Doesn't Pay.' All she'd have to do is talk about how hard it is to be the wife of a bandit like me."

"Why, they ought to have hired me," Mamie said. "I could tell 'em how hard it is to be the mother of a bandit like you."

Mamie Floyd looked at her boy, in his pretty suit with his wild eyes. It was easy to be angry about how he lived his life while he was off living it, but it wasn't easy to stay angry once he showed up at her door. Charley had a look about him, an innocence, that tugged at her heart every time she looked at his face. It must be just as hard for Ruby, she thought.

"I bet I could lecture them proper on how hard it is," she added.

Charley had tears in his eyes when he gave her a hug and a kiss.

"You're still the best cook, Ma," he said. "Them dumplings was first-rate."

"There's half a dozen biscuits left," Mamie told him. "If you're going to be drivin' all night, you oughta take 'em with you. I worry about your eatin' habits, when I don't see you for months at a time."

She wrapped the biscuits for him, and made him two egg sandwiches for the road. Charley had always had a big appetite for egg sandwiches.

When he finally drove off, Mamie let a couple of her favorite hens into the kitchen and listened to them cackle, while she smoked her pipe.

14

Knowing Beulah would expect a bauble, Charley stopped in a little jewelry store in Cincinnati and bought her a gold watch with rhinestones around the face. When he finally found the rooming house where they were staying, Adam Richetti was sitting in the car, smoking and sulking.

When Charley parked behind him and walked up to shake

hands, Richetti stuck a paw out the window, but his general demeanor didn't improve.

"Hi, bud," Charley said. "Long time no see."

"Hi," Richetti mumbled.

"It's nice you're so glad to see me," Charley remarked. "Are you livin' in the car now, Eddie?"

"I slapped Rose—she sassed me one time too many," Richetti informed him.

"Rose sassed you?" Charley asked. "Rose never sasses anybody. You sure it wasn't Beulah? Sass is her middle name."

"Aw, it was Rose all right," Richetti said. "She called me a pud—she must think I'm soft, but I showed her different."

"Called you a what?" Charley asked.

"A pud," Richetti said.

"What's a pud?" Charley asked. "I ain't familiar with the term."

"I ain't either, but I won't tolerate insults," Richetti said. "Rose deserved a shiner, and she got one."

"If you don't know what a pud is, how do you know it's an insult?" Charley asked. "Maybe she meant it as a compliment."

"I doubt it," Richetti said, taking the dim view. "Even if it was, I don't appreciate it."

At that point, Beulah stuck her head out a second-story window, her hair in pin curls. She looked excited.

"Charley, get up here!" Beulah yelled. "Quit talkin' to that skunk, he just gave Rose a nosebleed."

Several people walking along the street looked up when Beulah yelled his name.

"Why don't you rent an airplane and write my name on a sheet and pull it all over town?" Charley said, when he got upstairs. "That way, Hoover don't have to even look for me."

"Shut up, you lug," Beulah said, jumping into his arms. "I been waitin' months for a kiss, and all you want to do is pick on me."

Charley gave her the kiss, and then a few more.

"Where's Rose? I wanna see her shiner," he asked, when they stopped kissing for a moment.

"She locked herself in the closet," Beulah said. "She's crying, I 'spect. It was a nosebleed, not a shiner."

"It ain't safe to leave Eddie in the car," Charley pointed out. "He'll either steal it, or start shooting pedestrians. Rose just needs to keep her head tilted back for a few minutes, that'll stop the bleedin'."

"Got anything for me, cutie?" Beulah asked, her eyes dancing.

"Here, since you're so bold as to ask," Charley said, giving her the watch with the rhinestones around the face.

"Aw, are them diamonds?" Beulah asked, throwing her arms around his neck.

"What else would they be?" Charley lied. "Do we have our own bedroom in this joint, or do we have to bunk on the couch?"

Hearing Charley's voice, Rose Baird came out of the closet.

"How's Bradley?" she asked, before Charley could give her a hug. He couldn't tell that she had either a shiner or a nosebleed.

"Bradley's lonesome for you—Ma thinks Bessie might leave him, if he don't improve," Charley said. He himself didn't expect Bessie to leave Bradley, but he didn't see much harm in telling Rose what she wanted to hear, especially since she had been putting up with the likes of Adam Richetti for several months.

"I wish I could see Brad," Rose said simply.

"You can't, but you can see my new watch with diamonds on it," Beulah said, handing the watch to Rose. Charley wished she hadn't—Beulah was too nearsighted to tell a rhinestone from a diamond, and much too vain to wear specs—but Rose had excellent vision. Charley tried to look at her, to indicate that she should go along with his little deception, but Rose was thinking of Bradley, and didn't see his look.

"Aw, who're you kiddin'?" she asked her sister. "Them's rhinestones."

"Hey, girls, let's go eat," Charley said quickly. "My stomach's empty as Eddie's head."

"What makes you think you can tell a diamond if you see one?" Beulah asked—she was annoyed with her sister.

" 'Cause I worked in the five-and-dime, and I can tell rhinestones when I see 'em," Rose said calmly.

386

"Why'd you call Eddie a pud?" Charley asked—he was anxious to change the subject.

"A pud? What's a pud?" Rose asked.

"It's what he said you called him," Charley told her.

"I never heard of a pud," Rose said. "I called him a dud, and I could have said worse."

"I don't blame you," Charley said. "I've called him worse, myself."

Beulah peered at the watch—the stones that sparkled in her blurred vision seemed diamondlike to her. Even if they weren't, she wasn't interested in having her mood dampened, not just then. After all, Charley was back, and full of energy.

"It ain't Charley's fault you got a dumb Sam for a boyfriend," Beulah said. "Go fix your face, and let's get some eats."

Richetti was still sitting in the car when the three of them came out. Charley got in the front seat with Richetti, and the Baird sisters slipped in the back.

"She didn't call you a pud—it ain't a word," Charley informed Richetti.

"Mind your own business, you wasn't even there," Richetti said. "I know what I heard."

"You don't know that, or anything else, either," Beulah informed him testily. "Start the car and drive, Charley's starving."

"I won't put up with but so much," Richetti said, trying to stand his ground.

"Aw, applesauce," Charley said. "I been back half an hour, and I ain't heard a pleasant word yet. Let's have some of this famous Cincinnati chili, maybe it'll cool you two off."

While they were eating bowls of the famous chili, the man in the next booth got up to leave. He put down a nickel tip for the waitress, but neglected to take the newspaper he had been reading. He went on out the door, chewing a toothpick, and Richetti promptly reached back and grabbed the paper.

"Let me have the funnies," Charley said.

"Why can't I read 'em first?" Richetti asked.

"I been traveling the back roads," Charley said. "What papers I've seen didn't have much in the way of funnies."

"Let's see if any good movies are playin'," Rose said. "I'd like to see a movie—maybe there's something with Jean Harlow in it."

"I've been told I look a lot like Jean Harlow, myself," Beulah said, pouring a little more ketchup on her chili.

Richetti gave Charley the funnies, and kept the business page. He liked to think he understood the stock market. Beulah and Rose huddled over the movie ads.

"They don't put Jean Harlow in enough movies," Rose said, disappointed that her idol wasn't in any of the movies playing in Cincinnati at the time.

When Charley finished the funnies, he turned to the front page, to see if any wars had broken out. His eyes immediately spotted a big headline:

DILLINGER KILLED IN CHICAGO!
PUBLIC ENEMY NUMBER ONE NABBED BY G-MEN

"Oh, no," he groaned—he felt like all the breath had been knocked out of him. He looked out the window for a moment, and then back at the headline. A skinny waitress walked over and handed him their check. Charley took it without looking at it, and started to read the story under the headline.

"What's the matter, honey?" Beulah asked. She noticed that Charley suddenly looked peaked. "Don't the Cincinnati chili agree with you?"

"They got Dillinger," Charley said, handing her the paper.

"Who did?" Richetti asked, startled out of his dream of Wall Street riches.

"The Bureau," Charley said. "Agent Melvin Purvis led the hunt."

"Hell, a whore betrayed him," Richetti said, scanning the story.

"You might know," he added, glaring at the Baird sisters.

"Say, who're you lookin' at, buster?" Beulah asked, incensed. "We ain't betrayed nobody."

"They gunned him down like a varmint, sounds like," Richetti said. "First Bonnie and Clyde, and now Johnny Dillinger."

With effort, Charley forced himself to look at the check. Then he put a bill and the ticket under an ashtray.

"Finish eating. I wanna be moving," he said, grim.

"Moving?" Beulah asked. "You just got here this morning."

"Moving where?" Richetti asked. "What's wrong with Cincinnati?"

"I don't care for the food," Charley said. "I don't care for no more conversation, either. Get some toothpicks, Eddie. We need to get on up the road."

15

Ruby's voice gave out on her just as she began to sing "Red River Valley." She opened her mouth to sing, and nothing came out but a whisper. Dempsey was doing fine, though. He loved the singing part of the show, and put all he had into the rendition of "Red River Valley." Dempsey could have been heard even in the back rows of the high school auditorium, if there had been anyone in the back rows to hear him. But there were only a dozen customers, mostly older people, and they were huddled down near the front.

Ruby had to fight back tears of discouragement. She tried to keep a smile on her face, though about all she could do was mouth the words to the song.

"All you mothers remember, now," she said, when the song was finally finished. "Take your boys to Sunday school and try your best to keep them out of trouble."

There were only three women in the crowd, but all three clapped politely. A few of the men clapped, too.

Louie Raczkowski was waiting to lower the curtain, his cigarette dangling straight down out of the corner of his mouth, as usual. He barely got it down before Ruby began to cry. It was the third time in two weeks that her voice had gone out on her.

Dempsey, fully satisfied with his own performance, couldn't understand why his mother was upset.

"Mama, they clapped," he said. "I think they liked us."

Ruby was too upset to answer. She went back to the cold, bare dressing room and took off her squaw outfit. Her ma had made the outfit for her. Mr. Raczkowski had brought several Indian maiden outfits for her to try on, but they were all too big —Ruby was still skinny, even after her pregnancy with Dempsey. The white moccasins and the little headband fit, though. Her ma had worked hard on the squaw outfit, but it still didn't make Ruby feel like an Indian.

Dempsey wore a white suit and a bow tie, and was equipped with a cap pistol, which he whipped out and popped at the audience from time to time.

"I swear, I thought we'd do better in Tishomingo," Louie said, when Ruby finally composed herself enough to come out of the dressing room.

"Charley robbed two or three banks right around here—I thought it would bring the folks out," he added.

"I'm sorry, I just can't trust my voice," Ruby said. "I don't know what happened . . . I guess I'm not a singer."

"Well, you give her a good try. So did the boy," Louie said. "I should've took out a bigger ad."

"But they liked us," Dempsey insisted. "They jumped when I shot my pistol."

"I know, honey. You're a little trouper," Ruby said to her son.

"Mrs. Floyd, I believe it's time we give it up," Louie said, finally. "I thought this would work, but I've been wrong before.

"Show biz ain't predictable," he added.

"I guess that means we're fired," Ruby said. In a way she was glad, but in a way she wasn't. She felt she had let Mr. Raczkowski down. He was a kind man, and had paid her faithfully; he even bought Dempsey hot dogs on some of the long drives between shows.

"It just means it ain't workin' anymore, ma'am," Louie said.

"We only had a dozen payin' customers tonight—that won't even cover the light bill."

"Maybe we oughta try some more of the bigger towns," Ruby said. "We done real good in Tulsa, didn't we?"

"Oh, we did good in Tulsa, and in Oklahoma City, too—but the rent's higher in the bigger places," Louie informed her. "I expect our big mistake was in not getting an actor to play your husband—after all, he's kinda the star of this show. If we'd had an actor act out some of the big robberies, we might've done a whole lot better."

"You don't even wanna try Kansas City?" Ruby asked. "Charley's well known up there."

"I believe it'd be too big a gamble, Mrs. Floyd," Louie confessed. "A place like K.C., they want them swing bands, or big-time singers. We'd be wise just to throw in the towel right here and now."

Ruby was discouraged—any way she looked at it, it was another failure. Dempsey, though, didn't see it that way at all. The important thing in his view was that, all told, he had missed a whole month of school, and got to shoot his cap pistol every time they did a show.

Louie Raczkowski not only took them to the bus station, he waited until the midnight bus showed up. He bought them both a ticket, and pressed a twenty-dollar bill into Ruby's hand as she got ready to board the bus.

"Aw, you don't owe me this," Ruby said. "All I done is croak out on you."

"No, you earned the money," Louie said. "You're a fine woman, Mrs. Floyd. You and your little boy take care."

"I ain't little—I'm nine," Dempsey said, as they boarded the bus.

16

Richetti looked out the window. It was snowing hard, as it had been for a week solid. All it did in Buffalo was snow. The summer had been mild, but winter had hit hard, and early. Besides that, he held a poor hand. Charley was looking at his cards with a grin on his face. He didn't waste time being poker-faced when he held a good hand.

"Why can't we go hole up in Florida?" Richetti asked. "At least it's warm there. I never seen so much goddamn snow in my life."

"Shut up and bet," Charley said.

"I ain't gone insane, I'm not gonna bet on this hand," Richetti said, folding his cards. "I still wanna know why we can't hole up in Florida."

"We could, but Buffalo's safer," Charley said, shuffling the cards and handing them to Richetti. "Your deal."

"You're Public Enemy Number One, not me," Richetti reminded him. "I can go where I please—and I'm thinking of going someplace where I don't need snowshoes to go out and buy smokes."

"Deal the cards," Charley said again, ignoring him. "The girls will be back soon."

"They will if they don't get buried in a snowdrift," Richetti said. "They better not forget the booze, or I'll have to send them right back out."

A few minutes later, Beulah and Rose walked in. Fluffy snow-flakes melted on their coats and hats, and in their hair. They had the booze, and Beulah had a wicked little gleam in her eye as well. She pitched a copy of *True Crime* magazine in Charley's lap.

"Hello, Charley boy," she said. "Have I got a surprise for you —look what your old lady's been up to, while I been up here keepin' you in smokes and hootch!"

The first story in the magazine had a half-page photograph of Ruby and Dempsey, taken in Tulsa. The story was about the "Crime Doesn't Pay" show, but Charley wasn't interested in the story—he couldn't take his eyes off the picture. Ruby had on a squaw dress, and Dempsey had on a white suit with a nice bow tie.

"Say, don't Dempsey look swell!" Charley exclaimed.

Then he got tears in his eyes—just seeing a picture of his wife and son made him realize how badly he missed them.

"Aw, I told you not to bring it home. Now Charley's upset," Rose said to her sister.

Richetti peeked at the magazine for a minute.

"Ruby's wrong, anyway," he said. "Crime does pay, for you two—our crime. All you do is shop."

"Can it, Eddie, who turned on your faucet?" Beulah asked. She saw the tears in Charley's eyes, and she knew what they meant. It made her so jealous she wanted to break something, preferably over his head.

"So what if he's upset?" she asked. "Ruby oughtn't to be going 'round the countryside stirring up folks against Charley."

"That's enough, Beulah—I told her to take the job," Charley said, glaring at her. "It's the Depression, ain't you heard? Ruby's gotta do what she can to make a living—she's got our child, remember?"

"Strange way to make a living, rattlin' on about what a crook your husband is," Beulah said, her temper rising. "You're nothin' but a sucker, Charley. You'd take up for Ruby no matter what she did."

Charley just shrugged, and looked at his cards. He knew Beulah wanted a fight; she'd been primed to start one for a week. He didn't want to fight, but he was tired of Beulah and her guff. She picked the wrong thing to jump on him about, too.

"I may do more than take up for her," he told Beulah. "I may just go home and see her—they might be on the street by now, for all I know."

"Oh, yeah?!" Beulah retorted. "You leave me sitting in Cincinnati for three months, biting my nails, but all it takes is a silly picture in a magazine to send you home to Ruby."

"Are you crazy, bud?" Richetti asked, shocked. "You can't go to Oklahoma—every hick sheriff in this country is just itchin' to plug Public Enemy Number One!"

"You were the one complainin' about the snow, Eddie," Charley said. "If I can make it to the Cookson Hills, I'll be all right. Folks know me in the hills—I got lots of friends there—they'll hide me out."

"You're nuts!" Beulah said. Charley was still staring at the picture in the magazine. She realized she'd been a fool to show it to him. She thought it would make him mad at Ruby, but instead, it had made him miss her even more. It seemed to Beulah that no matter what she did, Ruby was always there.

Beulah grabbed the ashtray off the table and threw it at the wall, ashes and all. Then she burst into tears and ran into her bedroom, slamming the door so hard it shook the whole rooming house.

"I bet that startles the neighbors," Charley said. "They'll think it's an avalanche."

"Did you really tell Ruby to do that show?" Richetti asked.

"Sure," Charley said. "I ain't been able to get a dime to her since last spring. Ruby's gotta eat, and she's got to provide for Dempsey.

"Anyway—it's just a show," he added.

"Beulah's mad as hops!" Rose informed him.

"Rose, that's like tellin' me it's snowing," Charley said, impatient. "I can *see* that it's snowing, and believe it or not, this ain't the first time since I've known her that Beulah's been mad as hops.

"I doubt it'll be the last, either," he added. "Beulah's got one of them hair-trigger tempers. You breathe wrong, and it's bam-bam-bam."

Richetti cracked the seal on one of the whiskey bottles, and promptly glugged down three or four swallows.

"I can't concentrate on cards with all this arguin'," he said, disgusted.

"You couldn't concentrate on blowin' your nose if you was drownin' in snot, Eddie," Charley said, laying his cards on the

394

table. "I guess I better go try to make up with Beulah before she kicks the house down."

He let himself into the bedroom, expecting to have to duck another ashtray. But Beulah lay flat on her back on the bed, tears streaking down both cheeks. She didn't look mad anymore; she just looked sad.

Charley eased down cautiously on the bed beside her.

"Are you gonna stay mad at me, just because I miss Ruby and Dempsey?" he asked.

"Looks like after all this time, you could tell the difference between when I'm mad and when I'm sad," Beulah said. "If you can't, then we ain't gettin' nowhere."

"You looked mad when you threw the ashtray," Charley ventured.

"That was a while ago," Beulah said. "Now, I'm sad."

"You got as many moods as a cat has lives, honey," Charley said. "Sometimes I can't switch shirts fast enough."

"I wish we'd had a baby, Charley," Beulah said. "I been thinking about babies, more and more. Maybe if we had a baby, you'd love me as much as you love Ruby."

"I love you pretty much, honey," Charley said. He took off his shoes, and swung his legs up on the bed.

"Not as much as you love Ruby, though," Beulah said.

Charley looked as if he was about to speak.

"Don't tell me it ain't true, because it is—and don't try to explain, neither," she said, putting her finger against his lips.

"I'm too tired to explain, even if I knew what there was to explain," Charley said. He took out his handkerchief, and wiped her cheeks dry.

"Too tired . . . and too worried, about too many things," he added.

Beulah took his hand, slipped it under her blouse and placed it on her breast. She held it there, but she didn't look at him.

"I love you to pieces, Charley," Beulah said. "I've always loved you. But Ruby found you first, and there's nothing I can do to get around that."

She pressed his hand more tightly to her breast, and managed a wry smile.

"It's like she's stuck in your heart, and you're stuck in mine," she said. "You know how something will get stuck in your teeth, and you gotta use a toothpick to get it out?"

"I think I know what a toothpick's for, honey," Charley said.

"Well, there ain't a toothpick sharp enough to get Ruby out of your heart," Beulah said. "I try to be hopeful, and I try to be perky, and I try to be sexy, and do things the way you like 'em. But Ruby's still stuck right there in your heart." She poked him in the chest with her finger.

"Like right now," Beulah said, looking at him. "I'm here in bed with you, and she ain't, but that look on your face makes me feel like she's here, and I ain't."

Charley tried to kiss her, but Beulah turned her head.

"You *are* here with me, though," Charley said. "It ain't some accident that we're together, and that we've been together all this time. We're together because I want you with me."

He started to remove his hand from her breast, but Beulah caught his wrist and held it where it was.

"You mean that? You want me here with you?" Beulah asked.

"You know I do, Beulah," Charley said. "We've been through hell and back together—like when Billy Miller was killed, and when you was shot in the head.

"I'm sorry you're blue, honey," he added.

"I ain't quite as blue as I was," Beulah said, smiling at him.

"It's never been a secret that I love Ruby," Charley said. "But I wouldn't have made it this far without you. You stuck by me, Beulah. And if I live, I'll always stick by you—not every single day, maybe . . . but I'll stick by you as best I can."

"What do you mean, if you live, Charley?" Beulah asked, sitting up.

"I just mean, if I live," Charley said.

Beulah threw herself on him, and began to smother him with kisses.

"Don't you be talkin' that way, Charley Floyd!" she said, between kisses. "You have to live. I wouldn't have a thing to hope for, if you died. I wouldn't be worth the powder on my nose without you."

"Aw, Beulah, sure you would," Charley said. "You'd still be your wild self, whether I was around or not."

396

"You got that wrong," Beulah said. "When I'm with you, I feel like it'll be forever. I get my hopes up that we'll have a baby someday, and live like normal folks do."

"Aw, applesauce," Charley said, slipping his hand under her skirt. "We're normal folks, honey—we just ain't as bored."

"I ain't bored at all, Charley," Beulah said, moving closer to him. "I ain't never been bored when you're bein' sweet to me."

"You mean sweet—like this?" Charley asked, as Beulah scooted closer to him.

"That's one name for it," she answered, as she kissed him.

17

The phone seemed to ring louder when it was the Director calling. It rang so loud, Melvin Purvis jumped in his chair.

"Yes, sir," he said, into the phone.

"Floyd's in Ohio, get up here!" Hoover said.

"Yes, sir," Purvis said, grabbing his hat.

Before he could get out of his office, the phone rang again, just as loud.

"Yes, sir!" Purvis said, running back to grab it.

"Sir who?" his wife asked.

"Oh . . . I thought you were the Director calling back," Agent Purvis said.

"Nothing that grand," his wife said. "Could you pick up a chicken on the way home? The butcher's holding it for you."

"I will, if I get to come home. There's an emergency in Ohio," Purvis said.

"What kind of emergency?"

"A Pretty Boy Floyd emergency," Purvis said. "I got to run, honey, the Director's waiting."

"Bye—if you're not back by Christmas, send us a card," his wife said, as she hung up.

"Where were you, you move like glue," Hoover said, when Purvis dashed into his office.

Agent Purvis decided not to mention that his wife had called. Wives were one of the many elements of life the Director didn't approve of.

"I got slowed down in the hall," he said.

"I don't see why, we have excellent halls in this building," Hoover informed him. "Floyd and Richetti robbed a bank in eastern Ohio. My guess is he's headed home."

"I doubt he's that crazy," Purvis commented.

"I didn't ask your opinion," Hoover said. "I want you on a plane to Ohio in half an hour. Take three agents with you. When you get there, organize the locals. I want sharpshooters."

"I expect we better locate him first," Purvis said. "It's deer season. Half the men in Ohio will be out shooting at each other with deer rifles, anyway."

"Deer season doesn't concern me, and it shouldn't concern you," Hoover said. "All you need to think about is that Public Enemy Number One is terrorizing Ohio. Your job is to eliminate him."

"Uh . . . eliminate him?" Purvis asked.

"The Dillinger solution was the right one," the Director said. "I'm holding you personally responsible for this operation, Purvis. I don't want Floyd to leave Ohio alive—is that clear?"

"Local sharpshooters would be better, sir, they'll know the terrain," Purvis said. G-men had only recently been given permission by Congress to carry guns, and in Purvis's view, the Director was lax with this newly acquired status.

"What if Floyd surrenders?" he added, worried about over-zealous citizens shooting first and asking questions later.

"He won't," Hoover assured him. "The car's waiting to take you to the airplane. I want reports on the hour."

"Who said it was Floyd?" Purvis asked.

"The bank manager, that's who," Hoover said. "Get going."

"I hope the bank manager had his specs on," Purvis said. "Otherwise, some small-time hoodlum will have most of the deer hunters in Ohio shooting at him."

"I told you, get going—we don't need any Hamlets in this bureau!" Hoover barked.

Agent Melvin Purvis had no idea what the Director meant by the remark, but he knew he'd asked enough questions.

The plane had to come back to the airport twice because the door kept blowing open. The second time it blew open, it sucked off Agent Purvis's hat.

"Somebody wire that damn door shut when we get down," Purvis said. Somewhere far below, his hat was fluttering toward the Anacostia River.

"I hope I don't get my picture taken before I get the chance to buy a new fedora," he remarked.

"Why, are you going bald on top?" the pilot asked.

"No, but the Director doesn't like to see pictures of G-men without their hats," Purvis said.

18

Charley was lighting a stogie when the cows ambled into the road.

"Watch where you're goin', Charley!" Beulah yelled.

It was drizzling rain, and the road was slick. Charley braked and swerved, just enough to miss the cows, but the car went into a skid and bounced across the ditch. Before he could stop, it whacked into a fence post. Beulah, Rose, and Richetti all hit their heads on the roof of the car when it bounced across the ditch.

"Charley, I smashed my chapeau!" Beulah said, looking at her mashed hat. It was a pink hat, acquired in Buffalo, where they robbed a bank of enough traveling money to buy the car they had just wrecked.

Charley was disgusted with himself for not paying better attention to his driving. When he got out and saw the crumpled fender, he was even more disgusted.

"See!" Beulah said. "I said you was driving too fast."

"I wasn't driving too fast," Charley said—he hated to have his driving criticized.

"Then why are we in the ditch?" Beulah asked.

"Because the cows was walking too slow," Charley informed her.

The cows, meanwhile, were back across the road, looking at the car and the passengers. One of them mooed; Richetti immediately opened the trunk of the car and yanked out the Tommy gun, promptly taking aim at the cows.

"What the hell are you doin', Eddie?" Charley asked, looking at Richetti as if he had suddenly lost his senses. "Those are *milk* cows."

"So what? I don't drink milk," Richetti said. "They look dangerous to me."

"Put the heater away, bud," Charley said, waving his hand at Richetti.

"I'm a city gal—they look dangerous to me, too," Beulah said.

"Jeez—I never met grown people in my whole life who were afraid of milk cows!" Charley said, shaking his head in exasperation.

Beulah's hair-trigger temper was about to go off again.

"Yeah, well, what about you? You were in such a hurry to get home to your tattletale wife that you had to go and have a car wreck."

"Aw, lay off him, Beulah," Rose said. "He can't help it if the road was slick."

Charley looked down and noticed water leaking out of the radiator, which didn't improve his spirits any.

"Aw, let her rattle," he said. "Who cares?"

400

"Not you, you stiff!" Beulah said. "All you can think about is Oklahoma."

"That radiator's gotta get fixed, or we won't make it out of Ohio," Charley said. "Damn the luck—I ain't worried about the fender, but the radiator's serious."

He looked over at Beulah, who was busy trying to straighten out her pink hat.

"You think you can find your way back to that last little town?" he asked.

"Sure, and if you give me a couple of hundred-dollar bills, I can find my way to Chicago, or maybe Philadelphia, too," Beulah said. She hated having her clothes messed up, and the newer the clothes, the more she hated it.

"With a little cash, I can always find my way to someplace lively," she added.

Charley took several bills out of his wallet, and handed them to her.

"Forget the lively, or I'll lively you," he told her. "Just get the radiator fixed and hurry back. If they want to hammer the fender out, that's all right, too. Give 'em a big tip and tell them to hurry."

"Ain't you coming?" Beulah asked.

"No, I seen two laws when we was driving through," Charley said. "Me and Eddie can't risk it."

"What'll you do in the meantime?" Beulah asked. "I hate to leave you out here in the wet."

"I might teach Eddie how to milk a cow," Charley said, grinning at Richetti. "Once we get that out of the way, we'll count squirrels."

"Aw, come with us, honey," Beulah said. "I'm sorry I lost my temper."

"Nope," Charley said. "There's too many nosey folks in these small towns. Some sheriff might spot us and try to make his reputation by catching a notorious public enemy, like Eddie here."

"I ain't notorious," Richetti said—he thought he'd been insulted.

"Charley, I don't like leavin' you here," Beulah insisted.

"Rose don't like it, either. Can't you just sit in a cafe with your hat pulled down or something, while we get the car worked on?"

"It's too risky," Charley said. "You and Rose go buy yourselves ice cream sodas while you're in town—there's nothin' better on a rainy day than a root beer float."

"Yeah, there is—and you know what I'm talkin' about, too," Beulah said, winking at him as she climbed behind the wheel of the car.

With Charley and Richetti pushing, she managed to get the car back across the muddy ditch.

"What's to keep 'em from stealing the car, once they get it fixed?" Richetti asked, after the girls had disappeared around a curve in the road.

Charley turned, and winked at Richetti.

"Why, our handsome faces, bud," Charley replied, hunching his shoulders down into his overcoat.

19

Agent Melvin Purvis went straight from the little landing field to the bank in Salem, Ohio, that had been robbed the day before.

The manager, Mr. McNair, was eager to tell his tale. In Purvis's experience, all bank managers were talkative after a robbery; what they weren't apt to be was accurate in their accounts of their big adventure.

"You are sure it was Charley Floyd?" Agent Purvis asked.

"Sure as sure can be," Mr. McNair said. "It was Pretty Boy, all right. I've had his picture right here in my desk for several months. I happened to look up, and there he stood, pointing a gun at Clayton here."

Clayton, the clerk who had handed over the money, lacked his boss's air of certitude.

"Only problem is, Pretty Boy's hair is dark," Clayton said. "The fella who robbed us had blond hair."

Mr. McNair was annoyed with his clerk—no one had asked him to volunteer his opinion.

"Well, naturally, he dyed his hair," Mr. McNair said. "Wouldn't you dye your hair, if you were about to rob a bank?"

"Floyd's never dyed his hair that we know of," Agent Purvis said.

"Well, he dyed it this time," Mr. McNair insisted. "I guess I know a man whose picture's been in my desk for six months.

"His hair wasn't so much blond as it was light," he added.

"What did his accomplice look like?" Purvis asked.

"His which?" Mr. McNair asked.

"The second man," Purvis said. "The one with the Tommy gun."

"It wasn't no Tommy gun, it was a sawed-off shotgun," Clayton volunteered.

"Clayton, you need your specs changed!" Mr. McNair said, irritably. "It was a Tommy gun—I should know, he pointed it right at me."

Agent Purvis felt tired. He hadn't had time yet to purchase a new fedora, a fact which made him feel undressed. Even after the door of the little plane was wired shut, an unpleasant draft had whistled through the cabin during the whole flight. One of his ears seemed to have closed up, perhaps in response to the draft. Then the sheriff in Salem had informed him that four banks had been robbed the day before, within a fifty-mile radius of Salem. Agent Purvis concluded that he was either in the wrong bank, or the wrong town, or both. The Director had failed to inform him of at least two of the other Ohio bank jobs.

"The accomplice was tall," Clayton put in. "He nearly bumped his head on the door when he come in with that shotgun."

"It wasn't Richetti, then," Purvis concluded. "Adam Richetti's a runt. And if it wasn't Richetti, I doubt it was Charley Floyd.

They robbed a bank in Buffalo together four days ago. Our suspicion is that they're traveling together."

Mr. McNair was reluctant to abandon his conviction that he had been robbed by Pretty Boy Floyd. Being robbed by Public Enemy Number One would be something to tell his grandkids, the first of which had arrived the week before. Being robbed by a lesser criminal would spoil the story.

"It sure looked like Pretty Boy to me," he repeated.

"Thank you for your time," Agent Purvis said. "Where might the nearest store be, so that I could purchase a hat?"

"Right across the street," Clayton suggested.

"Next time we get the Bureau in here, you better mind your own business, Clayton!" Mr. McNair said emphatically, once the G-man was gone. "Who do you think manages this bank, anyway?"

Clayton knew perfectly well who managed the bank, but he chose to dodge the question.

"Well, the man needed a hat," he said, looking out the window.

"If Pretty Boy didn't rob this bank, I'd like to know who did," Mr. McNair said, to no one in particular.

"A blond fella, and a tall man with a sawed-off shotgun," Clayton replied.

20

"Can't we build a fire?" Richetti asked, shivering. "I'm freezing."

Charley sat on a stump about a hundred yards from the road,

smoking. Richetti was walking around in circles, trying to keep warm. He was getting more peeved by the minute.

"Sure, build a fire," Charley said. "Then the first hayseed that drives past will report us to the nearest fire department.

"Go on, build one," he said, again. "Order me a ham sandwich, while you're at it, too . . . I wonder why the girls ain't back?"

"If there's a store in that town, they done been trapped," Richetti said. "They're shoppin'."

"I doubt there's much in East Liverpool that's up to Beulah's shopping standards," Charley observed. "I could be wrong about that, though."

Just then, a farmer with half a haystack piled in the back of his truck came purring along the road. He turned his face toward Charley and Richetti, and slowed down for a moment. After he'd had a good hard look, he sped up and was soon out of sight around the bend.

"Two bits says that old sucker calls the sheriff," Charley said. He was beginning to feel nervous; he had probably been wrong to send the girls into town alone.

"Maybe we should've gone on into town ourselves and stole a car," Charley said. "I don't like this part of Ohio, there's a town every mile or two. It's too easy to locate a sheriff, if a sheriff's what you want. Down on the plains, it's thirty miles at least between towns."

"I say we go to Florida," Richetti said. "It don't ever get this cold in Florida."

"Shut up about Florida, Eddie," Charley snapped. "I got more on my mind than palm trees . . . I could kick myself for letting those girls go off alone."

"So what if that old clodhopper finds a sheriff?" Richetti asked. "It ain't a crime to sit on a hill and freeze, is it?"

"You got a short memory, bud," Charley said. "We pulled two jobs in the last week—remember?"

"They wasn't big jobs," Richetti ventured.

"No, but they were bank jobs," Charley said. "Every sheriff in eastern Ohio's probably heard about them by now. It might look suspicious, two fellas in overcoats sittin' on a hill, enjoying the drizzle."

Before another quarter hour had passed, they saw a police car come speeding around the same bend the old man had disappeared beyond. The car stopped not far from where they had wrecked the car. A short sheriff and a fat deputy got out.

"I knew it—here comes trouble," Charley said.

"Now what do we do?" Richetti asked.

"It's their move," Charley said. "Don't pull your cannon yet, maybe we can bluff 'em."

The sheriff snagged his pants leg getting over the fence, almost losing his balance. Charley and Richetti sat and watched as the fat deputy tried to get him unstuck. The sheriff cursed a few times, but finally got free without too much loss to his dignity. The two men came slowly up the hill.

"Howdy," the sheriff said, when he was in hearing distance. "What are you fellas doin' here?"

"Getting wet, mainly," Charley replied. "We're waiting for a surveyor, I'm lookin' to buy some property around here."

"Well, you won't be buyin' this property," the sheriff told him. "This property belongs to Earl Lowder, and Earl would cut off both legs and probably an ear before he'd part with an acre of land."

"I thought this was where the surveyor told us to wait," Charley said. "We could be lost, I guess—we ain't from here."

"Earl don't like trespassers," the sheriff told them. "He's the one turned you in."

"You mean it's a crime to sit on a hill?" Charley asked.

"It is, if it ain't your hill," the sheriff said.

Two more cars came blazing along the road, screeching to a stop when they passed the sheriff's vehicle. One of them skidded, and almost went into the ditch not far from where Charley'd had the wreck. The men who jumped out of the two cars were all armed.

"The Marines just arrived, looks like," Charley said, bringing his pistol out of his pocket. "I'll take your weapons, officers— give 'em over, and nobody will get hurt."

"Son, we're just talking about trespassin'—it's only a misdemeanor," the sheriff said, startled.

"Maybe, but them Marines are all carryin' rifles," Charley observed. "I didn't know you shoot folks for trespassin', in Ohio.

406

"Give over the weapons, quick," he added.

The sheriff and the deputy handed over their pistols at once. Charley gave one to Richetti, and stuck the other under his belt.

Down on the road, the riflemen were watching.

"Damn, there's eight of 'em," Richetti said. "What do we do now, bud?"

"Run for the trees," Charley said. "Crawlin' might be safer, but we won't be able to crawl fast enough."

Charley ducked as low as he could; the line of trees was less than fifty yards away. Before he had gone ten steps, bullets began to zing into the weeds, none of them very close. The sheriff and the deputy stood as if paralyzed, directly between Charley and the riflemen. He took as much advantage of their position as he could. He felt confident he could reach the trees before any of the riflemen got far enough down the road to be sure of missing the lawmen.

Adam Richetti slipped on a slick patch of grass and fell. He leapt up at once, but in his panic, he veered away from the trees a bit. Charley yelled—but just as he did, a bullet hit Eddie in the leg, taking him down again. He struggled up, but dropped his pistol. Bullets began to hit all around him, and Richetti raised his hands.

"Charley, I'm hit!" he yelled, but Charley didn't look back. He ran for all he was worth. Most of the bullets were missing by wide margins, but one rifleman seemed to be an above-average shot. One bullet nearly clipped Charley's heel, and another ricocheted off a rock, practically at his elbow.

By the time he hit the trees, he was a bit winded, but he kept running. He jumped a little creek, and skirted some thick underbrush. When he knew he was finally out of range, he slowed to a trot. East Liverpool, the town where he had sent Beulah and Rose, was no more than two miles away. If he could sneak in and locate the girls, there still might be a chance he could get away.

Behind him, the firing had stopped.

Suddenly, wings were everywhere, followed by a wild gobbling sound that scared Charley more than the peck of bullets in the grass. A wild turkey nearly flew into him as it took off: he had run into a flock of at least twenty turkeys, feeding on acorns. Charley almost fired his pistol at the thundering noise before he realized it was just turkeys, struggling up through the foliage.

He had never been that close to a wild turkey in his life. He stopped running, and stood and looked. Soon the gobbling faded, and only a few falling leaves marked the turkeys' passage. For a time, the only sound in the forest was Charley's own ragged breathing. Once he caught his breath, though, he could hear the sound of cars on the nearby highway, and the sound of the lawmen, calling to one another from the edge of the forest. Not since the night he had jumped off the train taking him to the Ohio pen had he felt so much like a hunted animal. He had been pursued in towns and cities and along country roads. But then, he had been in a house, or in a car, and with companions, usually—in towns, he at least felt like a man among men.

But now, he was in the forest, where the deer lived, and the bear, and foxes and bobcats and turkeys; he was alone, as a hunted animal is alone. Beulah and Rose were probably less than two miles from where he stood, but they were in a store, or a garage, with people around them, and a cafe close by. They were in the realm of people—he was in the place of animals. He could run and be free—or he could go back to where the people were, and be a captive. Richetti was already in custody. It wouldn't be long before Mr. Hoover's boys figured out who he was, if they hadn't already.

Hearing the voices of the men, Charley had a longing to go back—the lonely, gloomy woods did not entice him.

But he remembered Jeff City; he remembered Big Carl, the night before his death. Jeff City had brought its own loneliness, and its own heavy gloom.

Charley put the pistol back in his pocket and walked on into the woods, kicking himself for not having the foresight to take a shot or two at the turkeys. He might've got lucky; a turkey would have kept him in grub for several days. He resolved to keep his eyes open as he walked—he might be lucky twice, and end up with a fat gobbler for supper.

21

Agent Purvis felt fortunate. The dry goods store in Salem had a nice fedora, and it was last year's model, which meant it was cheap. As he was paying for it, one of the young agents from the Cleveland office came running in to tell him that two suspects had been captured near East Liverpool.

"East Liverpool?" Purvis said. "I thought Liverpool was in England."

"Don't know about that, sir," the young agent said. "*East* Liverpool is in Ohio—it's just down the road."

But before they got to the car, the message was amended by even more recent information from another one of the Cleveland agents: one suspect was in custody, not two. The East Liverpool sheriff was of the opinion that the captured man was Adam Richetti, though the prisoner denied it.

"Richetti's just a small fry," Purvis said. "What about Floyd?"

"One of them made it to the trees," the young agent said. "They ain't been able to flush him out yet."

"If the Director heard you use the word 'ain't,' you'd soon be back to shining shoes in the railroad station," Purvis said. "The Director insists on good grammar."

The young agent blushed. He was too overcome with embarrassment to venture another opinion during the fast ride to East Liverpool.

"That's the trouble with local law," Purvis said, as they sped along the narrow road. "They always catch the small fish, and let the big fish swim away."

"I expect they've surrounded Pretty Boy by now, if it's him," the driver said.

"I doubt it," Purvis said. "Not unless they've managed to surround the entire state of Ohio."

As they were passing through East Liverpool, headed for the scene of the conflict, Purvis happened to notice two stylishly dressed, attractive young women standing outside a garage. One wore a pink hat. A mechanic was hosing water into the radiator of a late-model Ford.

"Hold on a minute," Purvis said, looking back over his shoulder at the young women.

"I thought you were married," the agent driving said, looking at Purvis with a smirk.

"Just slow it down," Purvis said. "Those girls don't look like they're from here."

"How would you know, we only been in town thirty seconds ourselves," the young agent said.

"Hey, bud," Purvis said sharply. "Why don't you try using your foot, and not your brain. Put your big foot down on the brake pedal, and leave it there—if you do, I think the car will stop."

"Then what?" the driver said, annoyed by Purvis's tone.

"Then turn around, and take me back to that garage," Purvis said. "And cut the wisecracks—they might be Charley Floyd's molls."

When the G-men drove up to the garage, the mechanic was screwing the cap back on the radiator. Beulah had the money Charley had given her in her hand. Rose was already in the car, waiting.

"Hurry up, Beulah," she said. "The boys are gonna be frozen."

Melvin Purvis jumped out of the car, just as Beulah handed the mechanic the money.

"Hello, ma'am," he said, to Beulah. "Could I ask you a few questions?"

"What are you, a masher?" Beulah asked, impatient. "Can't you see I'm in a hurry?"

"In a hurry to go where?" Purvis asked.

"In a hurry not to be looking at your ugly puss, for one thing!" Beulah said, indignant. "Who are you, anyway?"

"Agent Melvin Purvis, Bureau of Investigation," Purvis said, holding up his badge. "And if I'm not mistaken, you're Beulah Baird—and that's your sister, Rose, sitting there in the jalopy," he added, pointing at Rose.

"Mister, you're barking up the wrong tree," Beulah said, her indignation rising. "How dare you come around here bothering me when I'm in a hurry?!"

"It's my job, ma'am," Purvis said, calmly. "You *are* Beulah Baird, aren't you?"

Beulah gave him her iciest look. "Mister, if you must know, I'm Jean Harlow," she said. "And my friend over there in the car is Mary Pickford."

"Sure, and I'm Herbert Hoover," Purvis said. "I think we better go down to the sheriff's office and have a little chat."

"What's going on?" Rose asked, sticking her head out the window.

"This bozo acts like he's arresting us," Beulah said. "He's been plenty rude to me already."

Three more agents had stepped out of the car. One agent reached in the Ford, flipped off the ignition switch, and took the car keys. The fact that she was outnumbered only made Beulah angrier.

"Hey, you jerk, who asked you to kill my motor?" she said.

"Want me to cuff these molls, boss?" the agent asked.

"Why, no," Purvis said, adjusting his new hat a little. "I wouldn't think of handcuffing Mary Pickford and Jean Harlow. You bring Miss Pickford, and I'll bring Miss Harlow, and we'll all go along politely to the sheriff's office."

"I'll make you think politely when my lawyer hears about this," Beulah said, digging in her heels.

She got out her compact and made them wait several minutes, while she combed her hair and powdered her nose.

22

In the night he heard dogs, but the dogs never got very close. Charley figured that was because the men handling them didn't want to take a chance of getting plugged by Public Enemy Number One.

As soon as it was light, though, he began to hear the airplane, buzzing not more than fifty feet over the trees. Dogs and an airplane meant an all-out search. Once or twice, he sneaked within sight of the road, hoping to dash across it, but every time he got within dashing distance, two or three police cars went by. He had no way of knowing what Richetti had told them, or whether the girls had been picked up, though he assumed they had. Local sheriffs couldn't commandeer an airplane to buzz the treetops. The fact of the airplane meant that Mr. Hoover must be involved. And if Mr. Hoover was involved, he was going to have to keep well down into the woods and walk a long way before he could hope to cross the road, much less sneak into a town and steal a car.

Charley had made it through the night without a fire—a fire would surely have brought the dogs. He wrapped up in his overcoat, and slept for a few hours with his back against a tree. Every time he nodded off, he dreamed about turkeys. Once he dreamed about pigs. He was getting pretty hungry. The thought of three or four pork chops or a turkey drumstick with gravy and stuffing popped in and out of his daydreams. He could imagine exactly what a bite of stuffing or a nice, greasy pork chop would taste like.

Charley knew, though, that daydreaming about tasty meals wasn't going to save him. He figured that a twenty-five-mile walk north, through the thickest woods he could find, would put him beyond the cordon of G-men and local deputies with deer rifles. He knew better than to let himself panic, too. He wasn't caught; they could fly the spotter plane until it ran out of gas and not spot him, if he kept to the deep woods. As long as he was free and kept disciplined and on the move, he felt he had an even chance. It was chilly, and he was hungry, but it wasn't cold enough yet to freeze him. His one regret on that score was that he had left his warm gloves in the car. He wasn't going to starve, either, not for a few days. He could eat acorns, the same as turkeys, and he did nibble a few. They were too mealy to taste very good, but they were edible. By good luck, he walked by a wild pecan tree and picked up a few little hard-shell pecans that the squirrels had missed. The little creeks ran with clear water, so he wasn't thirsty. He knew he could get through the day and another night without weakening; maybe even two days and two nights. Twenty-five miles in thick underbrush was a fair walk, but it beat the alternative. He remembered something Big Carl had told him, one night while he was in Big Carl's cell, watching him down a steak.

"Don't get the big head—don't get to thinking you're smarter than the laws," Big Carl said. "Some of them lawmen have been to school, and schooling's an advantage, sometimes. There's plenty of dumb cops, but the high-up ones usually ain't the dumb ones. Once in a while you can outsmart them, but you can bet that once in a while they're gonna outsmart you."

"What happens then?" Charley asked.

Big Carl shrugged. "You tough it out," he said. "When you can't be smarter, the next best thing is to be tougher."

Charley figured the time had come to be tougher. If he could elude pursuit for a day or two, a lot of the locals would lose interest, and begin to miss pork chops and turkey dressing as much as he did. The soft ones would slack off, and go on back to their families. The G-men would have no choice except to stick to the chase, but the G-men couldn't cover every patch of road in eastern Ohio. If he could keep hidden till he wore them down, he might make it. If he could just get a car and get down to Brad's, Brad would drive him deep into the Cookson Hills and find him a hideout—the Feds could bring a hundred dogs, and still not find him there.

Later in the day, moving north in the heavy brush, he had another piece of luck. He stumbled onto a deer hunters' camp. The hunters hadn't been gone many hours, and they had been careless with their garbage. Two coons were investigating it when Charley walked up. The coons gave ground reluctantly, but they gave ground. Charley scavenged half a can of baked beans, some bread scraps, a boiled egg that somebody had eaten only one bite out of, and a molasses cookie. It wasn't hot, but it was food. There was also a whiskey bottle with a swallow or two in it, and a blanket that somebody had puked on and abandoned. Charley took it to wrap around his feet, in case he had to spend another night on the ground, which was highly likely. He figured three days at most, and the locals would begin to give up. The weather didn't seem to be getting colder, which was a lucky thing, too.

Charley's worst problem turned out to be the Little Beaver River, which he knew he had to cross if he was to get far enough north to be safe. The first time he struck it, he walked a few miles along its bank, hoping it would bend in the direction he wanted to go.

But the river refused to bend northward. There was a skim of ice along the edges of the water, from an earlier cold snap. Every time Charley thought about wading it, he felt his teeth begin to chatter. He knew he couldn't afford to get his clothes wet; he was susceptible to sore throats and didn't look forward to one, when he couldn't even allow himself a fire.

Charley kept walking along the riverbank, scaring up quail now and then, but no more turkeys. The Little Beaver was only ten yards wide—he kept hoping for a fallen tree, or an old bridge, or a low spot where he could just roll his pants legs up and wade. But no bridges, fallen trees, or low spots appeared. Finally, hoping for a little afternoon warmth to work with, Charley took off every stitch of clothes, put them in a bundle on top of his head, and waded the Little Beaver River. The water was so cold it numbed him—it was all he could do to keep moving. At its deepest, it was up to his armpits. The mud on his shins when he waded out was like an ice pack. But he scraped it off with a little stick, dried himself with the puked-on blanket, and got dressed. The airplane hadn't been buzzing for a while, and for an hour or two before sundown, Charley's spirits lifted. He had crossed the river, and he felt good. He was still free, and the G-men weren't getting any closer. Another day of walking north, and he might be able to get a car. With a vehicle to make

414

time in, it would be a long while before any lawman caught sight of Charley Floyd.

That night, he slept in a deep hollow, under some sumac bushes. He had a warm dream about Ruby in her nightgown.

But the next morning, the first sound he heard was the buzz of the spotter plane.

23

"It's Mr. Hoover," the sheriff said, offering Agent Purvis the receiver.

Agent Purvis's one consolation was that he'd had on his new fedora in the photograph that had appeared in many of the nation's newspapers that very morning.

The headline above the picture could not be said to be a consolation, though: "PRETTY BOY FLOYD ESCAPES HOOVER'S DRAGNET!" was the headline.

"It's Mr. Hoover, sir!" the sheriff said again, still holding out the receiver.

Melvin Purvis took it, with reluctance.

"Yes, sir?" he said, trying to force himself to at least sound brisk, though he had barely slept a wink for two days and two nights, and definitely wasn't feeling brisk.

"I thought I told you I wanted reports on the hour," the Director said. "It's been three hours since we talked—what's your excuse?"

"I've been interrogating Richetti, sir," Agent Purvis said. "Also, I had to run out to the roadblock south of here. They picked up a bum that had just hopped off a freight—some of the locals thought it might be Floyd."

"But it wasn't, I take it?" Hoover asked.

"No, sir—it wasn't," Purvis admitted.

"I don't like the sound of this, Purvis," Hoover said. "If a bum can hop off a freight, our Public Enemy Number One could hop *on* one—have you considered that possibility?"

"Oh, yes, sir—we're watching the railroads closely," Purvis said. "Very closely."

"At night, too?" the Director asked. "Do you have men with decent flashlights?"

"Oh, big flashlights. He won't get on a train without us spotting him," Purvis said.

"Nonetheless, he's gotten *somewhere* without you spotting him!" Hoover said. "Every hour you allow that killer to remain on the loose, the Bureau's losing ground with Congress—they consider it an outrage, and so do I."

"I'm doing everything I can, sir," Purvis said. "We've got the highways blocked, and the dirt roads, too. We're keeping an airplane in the sky eight hours a day. We're watching the railroads. He's alone, and he's cold and hungry. I don't expect him to hold out much longer."

"Your expectations don't concern me, Purvis," Hoover informed him. "What I need are results. Don't you realize that every newspaper in the U.S. is holding its evening edition, hoping for word that we've got Floyd? If we don't get him soon, there will be more headlines glorifying his escape. People will start calling him Robin Hood again. Do you know how much damage this will do to the cause of law and order in our country?"

"I think I do, sir," Purvis said. Besides other troubles, he had a toothache, the result of biting down on a piece of venison sausage that happened to have buckshot in it.

"Do you realize how much damage it's doing to *me*?!" Hoover said. "This criminal's already more popular than Dillinger. He's more popular than the Barkers. If we don't eliminate him now, he'll be more popular than *me*!"

"Oh, that'll never happen, sir—you're the head G-man," Agent Purvis said.

"And he's Public Enemy Number One. He's supposed to fall!"

416

the Director shouted into the phone. "He's not supposed to keep getting away, time after time."

"He won't get away, sir," Purvis said, but he was talking to an empty phone—the Director had hung up.

"I wouldn't be too sure he won't get away," the sheriff said. "Ol' Pretty Boy's slippery."

"I'm not too sure he won't get away, either," Agent Purvis said. "I just don't want to think about what'll happen if he does."

24

Ellen Conkle was in the process of attacking her smokehouse when she saw the young man walk up to her back door and knock. She had been putting off cleaning it out for almost a week now, and was not pleased at the prospect of being interrupted. By some standards her smokehouse looked fine: the corn and beets, the stewed apples, tomatoes, and snap peas that were her winter provender were stacked neatly, each on a separate shelf. Hams, beef, and sausages dangled from hooks fixed solidly into the roof beams.

But, like it or not, smokehouses got dusty. Mouse nests showed up in the corners, and dust settled on the rows of jars. Ellen could never figure out where the dust came from, but it was her enemy. Once a month, she removed every jar, dusted it, wiped the shelves, swept out the mouse nests and an occasional snakeskin, and got the smokehouse looking proper.

She had been at her cleaning almost an hour, long enough to get dusty and bedraggled, when she heard the young man's knock. Ellen gave him an irritable once-over before announcing her presence. He was a solid-built, good-looking young fellow, wearing a suit that looked as if it had been slept in for a night or two. It was a blue, three-piece suit, with a red tie stuck in the coat pocket. There were stickers all over his pants leg, and a few days' beard on his face. He had a thick, dark head of hair.

Her visitor was a little thin in the cheeks—he looked hungry. Anxious as Ellen Conkle was to get on with her work, she decided she might as well take a break and deal with the fellow. There was a depression on, and it was not uncommon for a hungry man to show up on her doorstep.

"Yes, sir, can I help you?" Ellen asked, stepping out of her smokehouse.

The sky had cleared in the afternoon; it was going to be a beautiful fall evening, with a full harvest moon expected. Just looking across the golden fields was a pleasure to Ellen Conkle; she was a farm woman, through and through.

"Beg your pardon, ma'am—I'm lost, and I'm hungry," Charley said. "Would you have a little food?"

He had been two nights and the better part of three days in the woods now, and had had nothing substantial to eat except the few scraps he had scavenged from the deer hunters' camp. The farmhouse sat all by itself in a clearing near some fields; the paved road where the G-men and local posses patrolled was a mile and a half away. Charley had passed up several other farmhouses because they were situated too close to the highway. He knew he was going to have to gamble soon and get some grub, or else begin to weaken.

"Mister, I live on a farm," Ellen said. "I've got food. The point is, I ain't got no food that's fixed. Food don't just jump on the table and plop itself on a plate, you know."

"I know that, ma'am," Charley said, smiling. "I'll be glad to pay."

Ellen strode briskly past him, up the steps and into her house. One thing Ellen Conkle had never been accused of was a shortage of energy. Even the menfolks admitted that she could outwork the average farmhand.

"Payin' ain't the point," she said to Charley. "I ain't runnin' a restaurant, and I don't want you to pay."

She held the back door open for him, a little impatient.

418

"I'm Ellen Conkle—come in and get washed up," she said. "You look like you slept in a ditch."

Charley grinned at her, sheepish. It was the grin of an over-grown boy. Ellen had three boys of her own, two of them in the overgrown category. She was familiar with the grin, and still susceptible to it.

"It wasn't a ditch, but it wasn't no feather bed, neither," Charley admitted. "My brother and me went squirrel huntin', and I guess we got lost."

Ellen turned, and gave him a what-kind-of-fool-do-you-take-me-for look.

"I reckon you was huntin', all right," she said, "but I doubt it was squirrels you was after, not in that suit. That suit needs a good pressing, but I ain't a laundry, no more than I'm a restaurant. I'd bet you got fresh with your girlfriend, and she put you out on the road, which is exactly what she should've done. She must still be mad, 'cause she ain't come back looking for you, has she?"

"No, ma'am, she sure ain't," Charley said, with a tired smile. He felt he had made the right choice—this woman was going to feed him.

"You're a good-looking young fella," Ellen said, leading him into the kitchen. "Maybe she'll overlook it. I wouldn't, but then that's me. I can make you pork chops—you like 'em with apple-sauce?"

"Yes, ma'am—I like 'em with applesauce," Charley said.

Ellen directed him to the bathroom, and had the pork chops and applesauce almost ready by the time he had made himself more presentable. While he ate, Ellen peeled apples expertly, each apple yielding one long, unbroken strand of peel.

The sun had begun to settle, and a warm light shone through the kitchen window. The young man looked gaunt to her, and tired—as soon as he got his belly full, he'd be wanting to go to sleep.

"You must be a banker," Ellen said, as she briskly sliced the apples she had just peeled. "You got a mighty nice suit to go courtin' in.

"Bankers are apt to get fresh, too," she added. "I've even had bankers get fresh with me, old as I am."

Charley had been drinking buttermilk—he was on his third glass. Ellen Conkle, though nearing fifty, was an appealing woman. He grinned at her shyly.

"Ma'am, you ain't so old," he said. "And I ain't a banker— but I *was* a farmer, once."

"Oh yeah? What part of the country?" Ellen asked.

"Oklahoma," Charley said. He put his hand in his pants pocket and pulled out a ten-dollar bill, laying it on the table.

"Keep your money, I told you I wasn't running no restaurant," Ellen said. "I guess you ain't a banker after all—no banker would offer ten dollars for two pork chops . . . and you didn't even eat your rice pudding."

"I would, but I've got to get going and try to catch a ride home," Charley said. He finished the third glass of buttermilk, and stood up.

From the back porch, Ellen could see across the fields. She spotted her sister and brother-in-law walking slowly out of a cornfield down by the creek.

"That's my sister and her husband," she said to Charley. "If you hurry, I expect they'd give you a ride into Clarkson, or partway, if that's the direction you're headed."

"I'd surely appreciate it," Charley replied.

"They live about a mile from town," Ellen informed him. "If Stewart Dyke is too cranky to haul you all the way in, you could hoof it the last mile and call your girl—she might be in a better humor by now."

"I thank you from the heart for that food, ma'am," Charley said.

He let himself out the screen door, and started down the back steps. Ellen was right behind him, eager to finish up the smokehouse before she lost the light. But before the young man turned and started to walk away, Ellen looked at his face and felt a disquiet—a mother's disquiet, really. She saw that the young man was very tired, weaving on his feet. But more than the unsteadiness was a weariness in his eyes, a melancholy that was troubling. She had seen it in the eyes of her own boys when they were low. It was as if one of life's many problems had suddenly brought them to the brink of desperation.

420

"Are you okay, son?" she asked the young man. "You don't look right."

Charley turned to her and smiled a little smile.

"I'm just fine, ma'am," he said.

Charley turned back, and looked off toward the fields. "If I could choose a heaven, I reckon it would be to sit in your kitchen and eat your cookin', till I couldn't hold no more," he said.

Then he started on down the dirt road that would lead him to the Dykes. But Ellen Conkle, still troubled by the look in his eyes, decided to make one more try.

"Son?" she asked.

Charley stopped walking, and again he turned.

"You look like a nice young man," Ellen said. "If you'll just calm down with the courtin', I expect your girlfriend would take you back. Get on home, and have a good rest—things will look better when you're rested."

"Thank you, ma'am," Charley said "Your husband's lucky, to be married to a good cook like you."

"My husband dropped dead five years ago," Ellen confessed. "But I've still got our three boys."

Charley looked down at the cameo ring Ruby had given him last Christmas. For a moment, thinking of Ruby and Dempsey, his eyes filled. He twisted the ring a little on his finger. Then he wiped his eyes, looked up, waved to Ellen once more, and went on down the road, in the golden light of the late afternoon, toward a black jalopy parked at the edge of a cornfield.

Ellen Conkle lingered on her back steps for a moment, watching the young man go.

She was troubled, and not sure why.

25

Stewart Dyke was surprised to see a young man in a suit approaching his car from the direction of his sister-in-law's house. His wife, Martha, a few steps behind him, carrying a little sack of corn, hadn't spotted the visitor yet.

"Howdy, folks," Charley said. "Mrs. Conkle thought maybe you'd allow me to bum a ride to Clarkson."

"We don't live in Clarkson, son—we're out of town a ways," Stewart said. "Ellen's always coming up with chores for other folks to do."

"Why is it a chore?" Martha asked. She had arrived in time to hear the conversation. "We're going that way, ain't we?"

"Part-way, yeah," Stewart admitted. He wore a torn straw hat and could not quite conceal his annoyance that both his sister-in-law and his wife had chosen to butt into his affairs.

"Well, then, what's the matter with us taking him into town? It's only a mile," Martha said. "My time ain't so valuable but that I could give a boy a lift. If yours is, then maybe I'll walk, too."

"Who said anything about time? It's gasoline I was thinkin' about," Stewart said. "Automobiles don't run on air, you know."

Charley was hoping the Dykes would finish their argument. He was uncomfortably aware that he was standing in full view of the highway; he would have liked to slide into the jalopy, out of sight, but he knew he couldn't afford to be acting pushy. It was plain that Mr. Dyke would use any excuse to leave him hoofing it—and he was about hoofed out.

"Stewart, it's one mile," Martha reminded her husband.

"Two," Stewart said. "We'd have to take him in, and then we'd have to come back, unless you're plannin' to move to Clarkson tonight."

"I might, if you keep on bein' this ornery," Martha said. "If I'd known you were so tight with your time that you'd begrudge a young man a mile in your flivver, I doubt I'da married you."

Stewart saw that Martha had her back up—she would stand there and argue from sundown to sunup, unless he yielded. That was the way it was with Martha and with her sister Ellen, too, a prime busybody if there ever was one.

"Get in, mister," he said, with not much grace. "I'll carry you as far as our road—from there in, you'll have to hoof it."

"No he won't, I'll drive him myself!" Martha said.

"You'll drive him?" Stewart said, startled. "Who will cook supper, if you drive him?"

"You can skip supper tonight," Martha said. "I ain't in a mood to cook for a tightwad who won't help out a young fella in need."

"That ain't the only consideration," Stewart reminded her. "You can't drive."

"I can drive a mile and back," Martha said. "It'd be a good chance to learn."

"No, it would be a good chance to wreck my car," Stewart said. "Get in, young fella—what are you waitin' on?"

The invitation came a moment too late. Two black cars, traveling almost bumper to bumper, came speeding around a curve on the nearby highway. The second they came into sight, both hit their brakes and skidded to a stop.

Charley knew at once that he'd been spotted. He patted the two guns he had in his belt, to reassure himself that they were still there.

"Pardon me, folks, I know it'll inconvenience you, but I have to borrow your car," he told the surprised old couple. "I'll take good care of it."

He jumped in, switched on the ignition, and took off toward the highway, hoping to make the road before the cops cut him off.

The Dykes were too surprised to say a word as they watched their car race away. Stewart was the first to recover his powers of speech.

"Now see what your sister's nose trouble's got us into," he said, resignation in his voice.

26

Agent Purvis was in the lead car, with the sheriff and two deputies. The two deputies were said to be the best shots east of Cincinnati. Both had rifles with scope sights.

"Hit the brakes, that's him!" Purvis yelled, the instant he saw the man in the dark blue suit and the two people standing at the edge of a cornfield, next to a black jalopy.

"Anybody know those two?" Purvis asked.

"Why, that's Stewart and Martha Dyke, and that's their flivver," the sheriff said.

Just then, Charley jumped into the car and headed toward the road.

"He must of snuck up on 'em," the sheriff added, as the jalopy picked up speed.

"We're lucky," Purvis said, excited. "Ten more seconds, and he would have gotten away."

The approaching car veered south, across the corner of an open field. Evidently, Charley meant to smash through the wire fence, jump a ditch, and try to make it to the highway.

"Turn him, turn him—jump out and start shooting!" Purvis yelled.

Both deputies piled out, dropping to their knees. In a second, the deer rifles began to spit bullets at the car as it bounced across the field. One bullet flattened a front tire, and the car spun and nearly tipped over.

"Keep shooting," Purvis said. "You've turned him."

The deputies kept pouring bullets into the car, which spun and headed back the way it had come.

"Where's that road stop, can he get away in that direction?"

"It stops at the Dykes' corncrib," the sheriff said. "He can't get away on that road, unless he flies."

Deputies, most of them local and very recently deputized, poured out of the second police car and began to pump lead in the direction of the flivver, to the sheriff's intense annoyance.

424

"Hold your fire, you goddamn idiots!" he yelled. "You're shooting at the Dykes!"

Stewart Dyke was not unaware of the danger. The highway wasn't that far away. Bullets began to kick up dirt a few yards in front of them; meanwhile, the car was coming back, which would surely mean more bullets. The only cover handy was a wheelbarrow he had been using to tote fertilizer into the corn patch. He quickly turned it over, and yanked Martha down behind it. His anger at his sister-in-law's inconsiderate behavior was rising sharply.

"Get us kilt, that's what your nosey sister's about done!" he snapped.

Martha Dyke had listened to her husband gripe about her sister for the better part of thirty years. She had long since learned to turn a deaf ear.

"You'll be complainin' about Ellen when we're in heaven, I guess," she said.

"If you don't stay down, you'll soon get the chance to find out," Stewart said, hunkering as low as he could.

"No I won't, because if we're kilt, you won't be in heaven, you'll be goin' to the other place," Martha informed him.

Stewart Dyke was taken aback by his wife's opinion—his firm intention had always been to go to heaven.

"What makes you think that, I'd like to know?" he asked, as the bullets whistled closer.

"Bein' married to you, that's what," Martha informed him.

27

When the rifle bullet blew out the front tire, Charley realized he had lost his chance for a breakaway race down the highway. The chance wasn't much of a loss, since the gas gauge on the Dykes' flivver was sitting on empty. The car might have taken him a few miles, but then again, it might not have taken him any miles. It was just his luck to have stolen a car from a man who was tight with gas. He thought his best chance might be to get in among the tall cornstalks; maybe he could make it back into the woods. At least his belly was full. If it didn't turn cold, he would be good for a few more days, and so far, the G-men had exhibited no appetite for following him into the forest.

As he bounced past the wheelbarrow, he noticed the Dykes crouched behind it. They seemed to be discussing something, which momentarily amused him: talky folks just kept on talking, even with .30/.30 bullets whizzing past.

There was a heavy wooden corncrib right at the edge of the field. Charley whipped around behind it, and jumped out of the car. At least he would have the crib and the car for cover when he ran for the cornfield. A glance toward the highway was discouraging, though; several more cars had piled off the road, all of them filled with riflemen.

Charley knew better than to waste time. He ducked as low as he could, and ran into the corn.

"Circle him!" he heard someone yell, but he didn't look around, or slow his pace. The cornstalks were seven feet high. Once among the cornstalks, the deputies could shoot till their rifle barrels melted and have no chance of hitting him, if he kept low. The fact that there was an army of deputies after him, as there had been for days, buoyed him a bit: He was still free; his luck had held even to the point of finding an excellent cook to fix him pork chops and applesauce. All he needed to do was make it into the deep woods again, and take himself twenty or

426

thirty miles north. Sooner or later, there'd be a car he could steal, a car that would take him home to Ruby and Dempsey. Maybe they could get into Mexico and go on down to South America—that had been Jesse James's plan, before he got killed by the coward Robert Ford.

Once in the deep, tall corn, Charley slowed down a little. He didn't want to wind himself; some of the local deputies were probably coon hunters, as his father had been. They could run after hounds a long way, if their blood was up. He didn't want to have a shoot-out with some Ohio hound dog man if he could avoid it.

No sooner had he got into the corn than the shooting stopped. Apparently, the local deputies had some smart G-man directing them, someone as opposed to wasting ammunition as Stewart Dyke was to wasting gas. Charley had two full revolvers, but no spare cartridges. He had no intention of wasting ammunition, or of shooting at all, unless it came down to sheer survival.

When he trotted through to the west end of the cornfield, Charley got a shock: there was a good quarter mile of open ground, running uphill, between the cornfields and the woods. Sneaking right out of a corn row into some thick underbrush was just one more vain hope.

Charley knew he couldn't hesitate. In ten minutes, the deputies would have the cornfield surrounded, and then it would be a matter of time before the dogs flushed him out. He vaulted the fence and went for the trees, running as hard as he could— running as he hadn't run since he was a boy, in footraces with his brother Brad.

He was at the crest of the slope and less than forty yards from the trees, when suddenly his run turned into a spin. He spun around as if he were dancing. It was vexing—all he'd had to do was keep up his speed for a few more seconds, then he would be into the trees, and safe.

He had been running so hard he didn't hear the riflemen or the shots. Only as he came out of the spin and tried to move toward the trees again did he spot them. They knelt at the foot of the slope, not a hundred yards away. A G-man in a brown hat stood behind them, pointing. Charley drew one of his guns, but popping at the deputies at that distance would be as futile as shooting at turtles in a tank.

"Shoot—don't let him get to the trees!" he heard the G-man shout.

Charley knew he had to run, but his feet were heavy, as if caked with pounds and pounds of Red River mud. He began to move toward the trees again, but so slowly that he wondered if he could be in one of those dreams where he never quite reached the place he was headed for. But it couldn't be a dream; just minutes ago, he had stolen a flivver and run through a cornfield. He was awake and moving, but too slow. He dropped the pistol, but didn't stop to pick it up. He was thirty yards from the woods now. Out of the corner of his eye, he could still see the kneeling riflemen. There was not a weed or a sapling between him and the deputies—just open hill. If you can't hit me now, you're piss-poor shots, Charley thought.

Then he fell. Something had gone wrong with his balance. Of all the times for his sense of balance to fail him, when he was almost safe!

"Don't let him get up!" the G-man shouted. Before the next bullet hit him, Charley realized what had happened to his speed and his balance. He had been running too hard to hear the guns, or feel the bullets. But the bullets had found him. He looked up, and saw that the welcoming trees were still thirty yards away.

Charley heard feet behind him; he heard the click of a rifle bolt. He pulled out his other pistol, and threw it as far as he could. No sense inviting assassination, not while he was still breathing. He saw a line of men coming up the slope toward him, all with rifles or revolvers drawn.

"Hold off!" the G-man said. The rifle whose bolt had clicked behind him didn't fire.

"He's down—you got him, Bob!" another voice said.

"He's hit in the lights, he's done for, if it's him," a third voice said.

Charley knew he must be wounded and wounded bad, but he had felt nothing, and didn't know where the slugs had hit him. His feet were growing numb, which was worrisome.

"He had two pistols—wonder why he didn't shoot?" a young voice asked.

"Son, we were way out of range," the sheriff said. "He's stayed on the loose all these years, he's no fool. He wouldn't waste ammunition."

"I would've wasted some, if I was him," the boy said. "I'd figure maybe I'd get lucky."

Charley lay back on the grass. He was caught; the running was over, though the numbness in his feet still troubled him. Pretty soon, he was surrounded by legs, some of them in leather boots. A few of the men's feet were as muddy as his own feet had felt when they got heavy, right after his curious spin.

The skinny G-man in the brown hat knelt beside him. The hat was a bad fit, in Charley's view.

"That hat don't fit," Charley remarked. "You must've been in a hurry when you bought it."

Purvis ignored the remark. "You're Pretty Boy Floyd, aren't you?" he asked.

"That's your guess, mister," Charley said. "I ain't tellin' you sons-of-bitches nothin' . . ."

The truth was, he could summon little interest in the legs massed around him, or the feet, or the dangling rifle barrels, some of which were still pointed at him. He felt like taking a nap; he wanted to drowse, while he digested the good pork chops.

The thought nagged at him, suddenly, that he might have forgotten to pay the woman for the meal. After all, she had interrupted her work to feed him. He thought he had offered her money, but he couldn't remember. He had a bill in his coat pocket, and managed to get it out. He couldn't see it very well; he thought the bill was a ten, but he couldn't be sure.

"Mister, give this to Mrs. Conkle," Charley said. "She's a first-rate cook . . . I meant to pay her, but I may have forgot."

"Floyd, you're losing blood," Purvis snapped. "Just own up to it . . . you're Pretty Boy, aren't you?"

Charley lay still for a moment on the soft grass. He had never been much for sleeping on the ground, but the slope he lay on was as comfortable as a bed. The last of the day's sunlight shone on the legs of the deputies, and on their rifle barrels.

"Say, didn't you get Dillinger?" Charley asked. He had a vague recollection of seeing the skinny G-man's picture in a newspaper, though the hat he'd worn then had a better fit.

"I was there, yes . . ." Purvis said, impatient. The man's eyelids were half closed—Purvis saw that he was dying.

"Are you Pretty Boy Floyd?" he asked, once more.

Charley thought about it for a second; he remembered the night Beulah Baird, pretty as the sunrise, had bounced into Lulu's dining room in St. Louis. She had started off their acquaintance by calling him Pretty Boy, and the nickname had stuck, though he himself had never liked it. It rankled him that a skinny little G-man, with an ill-fitting fedora, would be barking it at him now, when all he wanted to do was take a long nap.

"Get this," Charley said, raising up on one elbow. "That ain't my moniker . . . the papers started that . . . I'm Charles . . . Arthur . . . Floyd."

"It's him, all right," an old man said. "It's Pretty Boy."

"Yep, it's him," another voice said.

"That's him . . . that's Pretty Boy Floyd," the young man said.

"Damn right it is, that's Pretty Boy," Bob, the rifleman, said.

"Did you take part in the Kansas City Massacre?" Purvis asked.

"You Hoover boys ask too many damn questions . . ." he replied wearily.

Charley lay back on the grass of the easy slope, and stared at the golden evening sky for a moment.

Then he closed his eyes.

EPILOGUE

ELLEN CONKLE

When he finished his buttermilk, I got the feeling that he really didn't want to leave. It wasn't nothing he said. I asked him if anything was wrong, and he said no. I didn't believe him, but men are like that—young men, particularly. They'll look you in the eye, and deny what anybody with a lick of sense can see. Charley Floyd complimented me on my cooking, stared at that ring on his finger, and went on down the road. He had a look in his eyes that I'll never forget—I figure he knew then that his time had run out.

Stewart Dyke was so mad about Charley running off with his car that he didn't speak to me for a year. He decided it was all my fault. Martha couldn't do a thing with him. If you want to know why she married a cranky fellow like Stewart, you'll have to ask her.

Once the word got out that Pretty Boy Floyd had eaten his last meal at my house, visitors came in droves. Some of them I liked; others, I didn't care for.

I kept the plate that I served him on, and the knife and fork, and the glass he drank the buttermilk from, for over a year. I didn't let nobody else use any of it. Then a man came along, offered me a hundred dollars for the whole kit and caboodle, and I sold it to him.

A hundred dollars was a lot of money, in the Depression.

AGENT MELVIN PURVIS

We'd run a long way, most of it uphill. After I realized that Floyd was dead, it took me a few seconds to catch my breath. The sheriff came up beside me, and put his hand on my shoulder.

"It's a big day for you, Purvis," he said. "I reckon this will get you a promotion."

"You don't know the Director," I told him. "What'll happen is, it'll get me fired."

The sheriff looked at me like I was crazy, but like I said, he didn't know the Director. It was Mr. Hoover's Bureau; he wanted the headlines. If a G-man got too many headlines, that was usually the beginning of the end.

I got two big headlines in a row—Dillinger, and then Pretty Boy Floyd.

The next thing I knew, Mr. Hoover went down to Louisiana and made it look like he caught Alvin Karpis all by himself—that's when the Bureau came to be known as the Federal Bureau of Investigation.

Ten months after we shot Pretty Boy down, on a hillside in Ohio, I left the FBI.

SHERIFF JACK KILLINGSWORTH

When I got out of the car in Kansas City that night, I took a look at Charley, and I thought right then that he was a man who didn't have long. The hounds was nipping at the wolf's heels, and the wolf knew it.

It ain't like me to take a shine to an outlaw, but I took a pretty good liking to Charley Floyd. We got to be plumb good friends. His sidekick, Richetti, would have shot me in an instant, but Charley wouldn't allow it. For a man in his profession, he was a decent fellow.

I changed my mind about the golf clubs Charley offered me, and went back to get them. But I was too late—there was nothing in the car but an empty whiskey bottle. I guess some traveler with a bent for golf seen them clubs, and took them home.

Nowadays, when I think about Charley, I regret I didn't go back a little sooner and get them clubs.

VIVIAN BROWN

Sam Raines took the news off the ticker. He must have known it would upset me, because he kind of hemmed and hawed before he told me. Sam didn't like to be around crying women, which was why I tried to do most of my crying at home.

When he finally told me about Charley Floyd, I couldn't help but cry—I burst right out, and cried for twenty minutes.

Later in the day, I calmed down enough to write the story for the paper. But it wasn't the end of my sorrow. For years, I got sad every time I thought of Charley Floyd. I know he did bad things, but life isn't all cherry pie. Some good men do bad things. Charley was good to the folks that were good to him. The country people around Sallisaw thought Charley was a decent man, and I take my cue from the folks who knew him best.

His deeds, good and bad, will be remembered forever around Oklahoma territory.

BOB BIRDWELL

I don't think Charley Floyd had any notion of what it was to be honest. George Birdwell was the same way. Either one of them would say something and mean it, but if you expected whatever they said to hold true for more than five minutes, you'd be a fool. George would tell me he loved me fifteen times an hour when we were in bed. Then he'd get out of bed, put his boots on, kiss me goodbye, and be gone for three months.

Charley Floyd was the same. All he talked about was how much he wanted to settle down with his family, and be normal. But nobody could've kept him in the same place for a year if he had twenty anvils tied to his legs.

He was crazy about Ruby, and plenty fond of Beulah Baird, too. But it didn't stop him, any more than it stopped George.

Now, me and Ruby are paying the price—Beulah, too.

BESSIE FLOYD

The train carrying Charley's coffin came into Sallisaw at night. There were five hundred folks waiting at the station. It was two in the morning when they finally unloaded him into the hearse. We all followed the hearse through the streets. Nobody was saying much.

Thousands of people came to Akins to the funeral. Beulah and Rose showed up; at least they had the good sense not to come near Ruby.

Once or twice, I thought Ruby was going to collapse. But she got through it all, somehow.

I grabbed a photographer by the leg and yanked him out of a sycamore tree. I just got plain tired of him firing off his flash, while the preacher was trying to say a few words over Charley. He claimed later that I crippled him for life—popped his knee or something. I hope I did, too. He had no business being up in that tree in the first place.

They say the crowd was the largest seen in seven states.

Only two hundred people came to Governor Murray's funeral.

Twenty thousand came to Charley Floyd's.

LULU ASH

I was in the hospital, and I thought the only way I was going to be leaving there was in a box. I heard a nurse say they got Charley. I'd never meant to outlive him; I just didn't want to.

But we don't always have a choice, in matters like that; I outlived my own boys, and that was real hard.

Why did I have to outlive Charley Floyd? He was my last good sweetie . . . the ones after him were just bums.

Half the reason I'm dying is because I'm tired of bums.

BRADLEY FLOYD

My best memories of Charley are of us going off beer drinking.

There was a local brew called Choctaw—Choctaw beer. Charley drank so much of it, we nicknamed him Choc for a while. We'd find us a good fishing spot, and Charley would drink ten bottles of it before I could much more than bait my hook. Then we'd use the bottles for target practice. He was a dead shot with a rifle, but he couldn't hit a wall with a pistol.

They say Charley killed several men. I guess when he was cornered, his aim got better.

After my brother was dead, they handcuffed him anyway, and tied his legs with a rope. I guess they were afraid the Phantom of the Ozarks might try to make one more escape.

His like won't be seen again in Sequoyah County—not in my lifetime.

MAMIE FLOYD

When the news come, I didn't believe it—I told everybody around home that it wasn't so.

Later on, when I had to accept it, I sent a telegram to the U.S. Department of Justice. I forbade any pictures of him; I didn't want no pictures of my boy laying on a cold slab. I told them to take him to a reliable undertaker, and then send him home to me.

They took the pictures anyway; I despise them for it.

It was way in the night when the train pulled into Sallisaw. Hundreds of folks were waiting outside the station—waiting to walk Charley home.

I wish he'd never left. It ain't right for a mother to have to bury her own beloved child.

BEULAH BAIRD

"I doubt you'll ever have anybody buy you nice presents like Charley bought you," Rose said, when we heard he was dead. Those were the first words out of my sister's mouth.

I slapped her face, and she cried and cried.

I never laid eyes on Ruby, until the funeral. She glared at me every time she looked my way. None of us had enough time with Charley; his wife shouldn't begrudge me the little bit of time I had with him.

I kept him fairly happy when there was no way he could have been with Ruby. I had to work at it, too—Charley had them low moods. But when he smiled, it warmed me like the sunlight.

Later, Rose apologized for her remark. She knew it was more than presents that made me stick by Charley Floyd.

"You're loyal, Beulah," he told me once. "That's the best thing a person can be—loyal."

I wish I had Charley back, to be loyal to again.

RUBY FLOYD

After they killed Charley, I read about a Mrs. Ellen Conkle, who fed him his last meal. She didn't have a bad word to say about him, not in any paper that I ever saw.

When some time passed, I wrote Mrs. Conkle a letter offering her my thanks for feeding Charley his last meal. I told her Charley was one of the nicest men she could ever meet; I told her that if he had lived, he would have repaid her a thousand times. The thing that made it especially nice, though, was that Charley was a man who really liked to eat.

What it means to have a broken heart is that my heart ain't whole no more. It works just enough to get me through life—it's like a car that will run in low gear, but not in high. And the sadness—it feels like a great big overcoat that I wear all the time and never take off, even when I go to bed at night.

That's me, now; that's the way it will be until the day I die. I don't have a whole heart to live my life with anymore, or to offer anyone else. A lot of my heart died with Charley. And if it wasn't for Dempsey, I would have followed him already.

But you can't be that selfish—not when you have a child to raise.

DEMPSEY FLOYD

My folks were the best-looking parents any child ever had. My dad was big and handsome, and my mother was tall and beautiful.

I used to get out of bed early in the morning sometimes, when we all lived together as a family. I'd tiptoe down to my parents' bedroom and peek inside. I can still see them, sleeping in their bed. My father would have his arms around my mother, and their heads would be together, like the sweethearts they were to one another. Their faces were so young and innocent. I dream about them still.

When they were in bed together, they looked just like sleeping kids.

THE END